THE
SHOOTING

PRAISE FOR JAMES BOICE

THE SHOOTING

a novel

James Boice

The Unnamed Press
Los Angeles, CA

The Unnamed Press
P.O. Box 411272
Los Angeles, CA 90041

Published in North America by The Unnamed Press.

1 3 5 7 9 10 8 6 4 2

ISBN: 978-1-939419-74-3

Library of Congress Control Number: 2016949289

This book is distributed by Publishers Group West

Cover design & typeset by Jaya Nicely

To Rasika,
for her faith, her trust, her fearlessness

THE
SHOOTING

SEE-YOU-NEXT-TUESDAY

Cunt is a terrible thing to call a person. But to many, there is no person more terrible than this one here wandering through Terminal A of Kentucky's Blue Grass Airport. She is a slender, designer-dress-wearing woman of vague olive-toned ethnicity and indeterminate age—she could be black, she could be white; she could be thirty, she could be fifty—with clacking heels and rich thick hair dyed to conceal strands of white, pulling her wheeled suitcase behind her with one hand while she flicks through her phone with the other hand, earbud in her ear, punching in the dial-in code to join the conference call she is late for—and she, her enemies believe, will bring about the end of America. Compared with this woman, Hillary Clinton is the gang bang queen of the GOP. She likes that they refer to her as simply the Cunt—*My mononym,* she jokes. *Like Beyoncé.* The extreme Republicans—the Tea Party buzz-cutted, divorced, red-faced, racist Internet types—call her *cunt* straight out, while the rest of the party, those publicly moderate types pretending for voters to be embarrassed by their open-carrying John Birch/NRA cousins but in fact are counting on them and winking to them through the lens of C-SPAN at every floor speech, prefer calling her See-You-Next-Tuesday. You know—in case of a hot mic or undercover operative with a phone and its video camera open and the red light on. *Cunt.* On cue, whenever they see mention of it, her staffers and supporters and members—90 percent female—get twisted up about *cunt,* they get mean and indignant, stomping around, losing themselves in sputtering monologues and in hammering out op-ed rants; these young diverse women, with educations and abilities, who drool seeing such a big, fat, disgusting, denigrating dismissal thrown down the middle of the plate by these smug, white, aging, entitled men.

But See-You-Next-Tuesday likes it, she loves it—they don't call you *cunt* unless you're *good,* she reminds them, unless you're *scary*— and she is great at what she does, she is fucking scary. She loves *cunt*—*cunt* has balls. You need those if you have been called to do what she has been called to do, which is start the next American Civil War. Though she prefers calling it the next *American Revolution* or the first American *Age of Enlightenment.* She considers herself a Gandhi or MLK Jr.—hell, even a Jesus (*though if I were to walk into a church,* she jokes, *I'd probably catch on fire*). America needs someone to usher it into the future and she is tired of waiting—she is that someone. The disappointment of Obama was the straw that broke See-You-Next-Tuesday's back, in that regard. There are no people in the history of the world who hate enlightenment and progress more than the American people, as far as she's concerned, so if *cunt* is the worst she gets and not nails through the hands or a bullet through the head or any of the other ways this country likes to repay its saints, then she will take *cunt* all day long. Not that she is afraid of the nails or of the bullet. Not that she is concerned about dying for the cause.

Cunt. It's a beautiful thing to be called by your enemies. She likes her nickname so much she uses it herself. Had a nameplate printed up for her desk: THE CUNT. Is always ready to drop it into her speeches at fund-raising events and political rallies. The word is like a firearm, appropriately enough, in that if you try to use it without knowing how, if you use it coming from a place of arrogance and hubris, you will probably get yourself killed. You have to know how to use *cunt.* She knows how to use it. How to use it is this: first of all you have to be a woman or you have to be British, preferably both. See-You-Next-Tuesday is the former and her father is the latter, therefore she meets the criteria. So she can say *cunt* and say *cunt* and say *cunt* so as to remind folks what it is her enemies call her, what kind of people her enemies in fact are, the small minority of white men who are responsible for America still being an insane culture of constant unchecked gun violence even after all these massacres—*Still Crazy after All These Massacres,* as her theme song says—and if that's how they see her, an unmarried, educated, independent, self-supporting, professional, successful woman and accidental activist enlisted to the Cause when it came kicking down her door and stole her baby girl, Michelle, then how do they see *you* women? *These are what we talk about when we talk about Real America: these people. These are the people whose quote-unquote values and principles we accommodate over the lives of our children, with regard to gun violence, these are the people we still allow to stand in the way of progress, of moving America forward into a time of gun-free sanity when our children can go to school and swing on the monkey bars and go to church and shop at the mall without the risk of bullets fired from an assault weapon ripping their little bodies apart.*

She says *cunt* up and down the East Coast, back and forth throughout the Midwest, through the South, to the blackest-tie-est bluest-blood-est billionaire fund-raiser crowds in Washington, to the humblest churches of the Adirondacks, and her message *resonates,* town by town, state by state, year by year, vote by vote, because she is great at what she does and because her enemies prefer to be the kind of bullying man-children to not only call successful, effective women cunts but to also carry semiautomatic rifles into fast-food restaurants during lunchtime, and you can feel when someone is right and *the country feels that about her.* And in every town, night after night, as she is leaving the stage, they are pulling handfuls of cash to stuff into her coffers, they are going home and voting in their local and national elections how she demands, booting out this NRA puppet in favor of this gun-sense hero. Her work is visibly altering the landscape of Congress and state legislatures and the culture.

Anti-American, freedom-hating, gun-grabbing CUNT. Yeah, baby, say it—say my name. If they want to clear rooms, including the one that matters most and is hardest to find—the room of popular mainstream public opinion—she is not going to stop them. Because where else will the crowds go but to her? And they are always welcome. *I'll receive you with open arms,* she says. *One arm might not open very wide*—she laughs—*but it's open.*

Her arm. As what will happen in America to a *strident* woman of color, a shrill, emasculating harridan, a nagging, shrieking harpy threatening to pry from big, strong white men the gruesome things they feel entitled to only because no one has had the guts to try to take them away before, they have fired at her on four occasions. Four shootings, twenty-seven shots in total, hitting her just once—in Tucson, in the shoulder. She was in town to appear with Gabby Giffords in victory outside the local franchise of the national sporting goods chain she and Gabby had convinced under threat of boycott to stop selling ammunition. The hollow-point .380 fired from a white male's semiautomatic pistol as See-You-Next-Tuesday shook hands in the parking lot shattered the bones of her shoulder and shredded the cartilage, giving her a permanent John McCain–like limited mobility to her arm that works in her favor the same way it did for him—by reminding everyone that she is heroic and a leader and has lost and survived more than they and therefore should be listened to, should be followed. Yet still she travels with no security detail. Never has. Just her aides—women all—and attorneys, with a little gaggle of disciples trotting after to keep up. She does not even wear a Kevlar vest. They shoot at her because she is the man they swore would never come, a brilliant, cutthroat, Machiavellian anti-gun political force of nature capable of using fear to motivate her followers into hysterical action the same way the NRA's Wayne LaPierre, a man she studies and idolizes, does to motivate his.

For forty years the NRA has kicked anti-gun ass all over Washington and maintained the status quo of senseless gun violence. How? Money. Yes NRA members show up at rallies at the drop of a hat when asked, yes they vote as instructed in large enough numbers to influence party platforms, but most important they send in cashola when LaPierre shrieks for it. In America, your vote is not your vote—your money is your vote. And NRA members pay up. Because they care more than the other side does.

Or did, until the turning point: the aftermath of the massacre at Sandy Hook Elementary was the first wave of a cultural change, but the tsunami was the elementary school massacre in Ohio that killed sixty-three children, including her Michelle, as the nation watched—the killer, as you will never forget, live-streaming the carnage from his wearable camera. Screaming, dying children being executed in their pink sweatpants and Velcro shoes—this is what we had become, this was our country. The footage of that was the Pearl Harbor moment. There was no more hiding from it—this is what guns meant. They were no longer a symbol of liberty and self-sufficiency and had not been for a long, long time—this is what our beloved guns do to human beings, in real life. This is what they do to the bodies of children, in real life. You could not pretend that firearms, in real life—especially our new, modern, War on Terror–inspired weapons, once removed from movies and video games— represented anything but dismemberment, ripped-off skull chunks, little boy and girl brains, jawbones left dangling, gaping holes in eye sockets of six-year-olds. Through it all, LaPierre stayed on point. *This is the fault*, he said, *of laws preventing teachers from carrying firearms in the classroom. We are funding a program to give all teachers training in use of firearms. The only thing that stops a bad guy with a gun*, he said, *is a good guy with a gun.*

Before the massacre, See-You-Next-Tuesday had been a constitutional law professor at Ohio State and an appeals court judge. She had never been active in politics, taking pride in her neutrality on the bench. But when she watched LaPierre's press conference (she watched it online, did not see it live as she was busy at the time at the cemetery burying Michelle), she realized that nobody else was going to do anything about gun violence in this country and reluctantly entered the arena. She was not yet another mourning mother toting her dead kid's picture around the halls of the state house and Congress, begging for someone to do something. She was not interested in cooperating with the etiquette of the system or *reaching across the aisle*. These had resulted in nothing after Newtown, she remembered, but more heartbreak and insult and humiliating defeat—no meaningful change. She was not there to work with the other side, or to compromise, or to bow down to the Second Amendment. She was there for war. Revenge. To destroy LaPierre, castrate the NRA, and win the war. Quickly she emerged as a reluctant spokesperson for a new kind of anti-gun movement. She said, *The NRA is right—we do have too many gun laws that do not work, so let's not make any more of those. No, let's cut the crap, pry their guns from their cold dead hands once and for all, and say enough is enough with the deadly Second Amendment that is getting our children slaughtered on a mass scale!* ("Cut the crap" became her "You betcha"—a rallying cry for one side, something to mock and sneer at for the other.) *It took a war to free their slaves,* she began saying at rallies and speeches, *and it will take a war to get their guns. Are you ready for it? Because I am! But I can't do it alone.*

And America finally was ready for it—or beginning to be.

How she saw we could take their guns: money. Turn bullets into money. Tax the ammo. Tax the shit out of it. And when you're done taxing the shit out of it? Tax it again! Let them have as many guns as they want—and we have no choice at this point, do we, with more than 300 million guns out there—but if they want anything for their guns to fire, they have to pay for the damage they cause everybody else. It's social responsibility—if they're going to fuck us, at least buy us dinner, and if they're going to shoot us, at least foot the hospital bill. She frames it thus: *Listen, what do we need more: bullets and death and incompetent fat white guys armed to the teeth with military weapons they do not know how to use right—or do we want money for schools and health care and jobs and all the other things our states never have money for? Which do we need more?* That was effective, that bullets vs. schools campaign, which took off from those old Mac vs. PC ads. The donations poured in; she used them to establish her organization, Repeal the Second Amendment. The RSA.

The Brady Campaign was too pussyfooted, broken down and depressed, so traumatized after the NRA abusing it for thirty years that it considered the most minor, loophole-fucked, symbolic legislation to be a historic victory, signaling change that never came. Everytown for Gun Safety, in her view, was NYC billionaire Michael Bloomberg's smug, unintentionally hilarious self-humiliation vehicle that resulted in nothing because it came from the same place as his Mayors Against Illegal Guns, which was a place of total, astounding ignorance about the things it sought to control, which voters sensed and therefore tuned out off the bat. Because America *wants* guns. That is what the others have missed. They do not need guns explained to them. They know about them and they know they are dangerous and they want them, they feel safe with them, even if they do get more of them killed than any war, any terror group. See-You-Next-Tuesday, however, being smarter than Bloomberg and the others, takes firearms very seriously, gives them the utmost respect. She has become an expert on them, can talk circles around the most technical gun nut you could find. Outshoot him too.

The first big victory came when pro-RSA single-issue voter turnout was credited with dumping three members of the Ohio state legislature based on their pro-NRA voting records. The second big victory came when they got a version of the ammo tax on the ballot and came within a percentage point of passing it. Wayne LaPierre shat himself, See-You-Next-Tuesday heard. Rush Limbaugh exploded all over his studio like a microwaved metal bowl of grease and pills. That's about the time they started calling her what they call her. When asked about the C-word on *Meet the Press*, she slaughtered it: *Finally,* she said, *the NRA's base is being honest about how they see women.* And that's about the time they took their first shot at her, outside Houston. Missed. As a result money flowed in to the RSA, membership jumped by 11 percent. So they took another shot at her, in Florida, as she was leaving a meeting with a shooting victim. More money, more members.

RSA membership has since passed 1 million (she's just getting started—the NRA boasts 4.5 million). They have hired a full-time lobbying operation to camp out on the Hill. The board has increased her salary to $500,000 a year. The NRA's board, she's heard, pays LaPierre more than double that. So she wants double *that.* It's not greed—that kind of salary means you're winning the war, that you're the best. RSA has built a new state-of-the-art headquarters on I-66 in Fairfax, Virginia, right across the street from the NRA's. Know about the NRA's National Firearms Museum—Pilgrim guns, colonist guns, Civil War guns, presidential guns, cowboy guns, War on Terror guns—all the dusty, teary-eyed symbols of the American Myth? Well, the RSA built its own National Firearms Museum, containing not symbols but reality: graphic, bloody, heart-wrenching exhibits of JFK, RFK, Martin Luther King Jr., Medgar Evers, John Lennon, Kurt Cobain, Biggie, Tupac, Trayvon Martin. Of Columbine; Pearl, Mississippi; Jonesboro, Arkansas; Aurora; Newtown. Of the Beltway Sniper, Virginia Tech, DC Navy Yard, Fort Hood, Chiraq, San Bernadino, etc., etc., etc., and the rest of the dozens of mass shootings a year, plus an exhibit for all the women killed each year by a man with a gun (women in the United States are eleven times more likely to be murdered with a gun than in any other first world country), or raped by a man with a gun, or otherwise intimidated and abused by a man with a gun, not to mention (and no one else does!) the thousands and thousands of black and Latino children routinely and unremarkably slaughtered or permanently maimed by gunfire every year in Chicago; New York City; Los Angeles; Washington, DC; New Orleans; etc., etc., etc. It's a beautiful museum—for every war- and frontier- and horseshit-celebrating exhibit at the NRA's museum, there is an exhibit of reality at the RSA's: unspeakable heartbreak and ruined lives and death, death, death. *Mine eyes have seen the glory... !*

Women like her. Part of why women like her is because she likes women. Few others seem to. The NRA certainly does not seem to. In the hallway outside her hotel room in Utah someone once left her a female mannequin that had been stripped naked and riddled with bullets. It had been shot so many times with such high-caliber rounds that it looked like it'd been hacked at with a dull hatchet. Not the worst thing they have left for her outside a hotel room. The worst was on this past Mother's Day, when they got *inside* her hotel room in Tennessee while she was out and wrote on the picture of her Michelle that she travels with and always hangs on her hotel room wall: *If only my teacher had had a gun!* She made sure to tweet the pictures of these, to send out press releases to the American and international media to ensure maximum humiliating exposure for the NRA by proxy.

She's cool about these things—once you've been through what she has, dolls and graffiti do not bother you as much—and cool in general, naturally beautiful, dynamic, throws *Scandal* references into conversations as often as possible, cries in public when she feels like crying, laughs at herself but can eviscerate dunderheaded conservative male Republican nemeses with an offhand joke that has women re-clicking and retweeting for days after, but she's authoritative, can and does quote Supreme Court precedents and constitutional texts and firearms statistics from memory, uses a teleprompter as often as she wears bulletproof vests, and could give and has given a barn-burning speech on the side of I-84 in the rain, has just enough intimidating alpha-female mean-girl energy wafting off her to make women trust her without feeling like she does not like them. She's Sheryl Sandberg meets Shonda Rhimes meets Judge Judy. She's a girl version of 2008 Obama.

It is vital that women like her. As every rock band knows, you get the girls to your show and the boys will follow. That is what will be the downfall of the NRA, she knows: no women. No love for half the population. Soon all those old white men will die. So will their "values" and "traditions." Which, when you look closely enough at them, are nothing but fear. And when they die, women and people of color will remain, eager for the future, not scared of it. Men versus women. As in every other arena, the women and people of color may not be winning (yet), but they sure have the momentum. Perfect. It is happening like it was meant to be. This was the meaning of Michelle's death, she has realized: To do this great thing for future little girls and boys. To do what the Founding Fathers intended for America, which was to change the Constitution, to change *ourselves* as needed, to protect our rights to life, liberty, and the pursuit of happiness.

She is in Kentucky—small town in the mountains called Brownmore. A three-year-old girl played with the little shotgun-for-kids left leaning like a broom in the corner of her trailer while her mom cooked dinner and, wouldn't you know it, the little girl shot herself, took off half her little head, and the reaction from folks around here was *Well, it's a tragedy, but guns are our tradition, you see, so whatcha gonna do?* So See-You-Next-Tuesday goes there to raise hell and exacerbate the media coverage to highlight the casual horror of gun culture, to try to convince the mom to do an ad spot supporting the ammo tax in Kentucky, and to maybe even, if all goes well, get herself shot at again. That is the Triple Crown—viral news coverage, ad spot, shot at—whatever it takes to fortify the story so it does not rinse out in the one-hour news cycle, so *something* meaningful comes out of such a meaningless, *stupid* tragedy, be it money or membership or media or all three of what she calls the three M's—and when her work seems to be done in Brownmore, she hears about a new shooting, this one in New York City. A teenage boy knocked on his neighbor's door and his neighbor emptied his gun through the door, killing the boy. Was the boy black? Duh. Was the shooter white? Double duh. Was the shooter rich? Triple duh. Was the black boy poor? Sold! And is the ammo tax on the ballot in New York this fall? I said, *Sold! Sold, sold, sold!* The Brownmore mom seems like she's going to be amenable to the ad spot and no one seems to be planning to take a shot at See-You-Next-Tuesday and the media is all over this, two of the three goals met, so she entrusts Kentucky to her deputies and heads to the airport.

As she waits at her gate a man walks up to her. He is tall and thin and dark-eyed and serious and white, wearing a Carhartt jacket and an old worn baseball cap. He says, —Ain't you... ?

Before she can deny it, he lunges toward her and she screams and puts her hands to her face and—

THE GUN

A screeching gaggle of children comes roving through the park—
dozens of them, big red faces cleaved by open-mouthed grins, all their
breaths bursting out in gobs of fog, and their short arms pumping
and swinging, fists balled to bone in their mittens, as the gaggle
careens in their winter coats, scarves flapping behind them. The
herd of little boys and little girls—brown, white, tanned, pale, black,
yellow—all strangers to one another, none knowing another's name
or who they are, knowing nothing about each other but that they too
have been brought here and plopped down, and that they too saw the
puppy scampering free off its leash through the playground where
the children swing. Their nannies and mommies first laughing and
following slowly, then, their calls unheeded, jogging and crying out,
demanding the children return—but the puppy must be chased, the
puppy is fast and little and they are gaining no ground, but they are
not tiring, especially not the largest boy ambling after the rear, his
nanny calling his name with dwindling amusement and increasing
concern as the gaggle roves on into the distant trees in the horizon:
—Lee! Lee Fisher! It's time to go home.

A house on a mountain. The house is grand and new and still smells
like sawdust and paint. It is cavernous, mostly empty except for
expensive things he may not touch or sit on. His footsteps echo

off its high naked walls. His voice calls out and comes back to him alone. And like the house, the mountain is grand and it is new— though he wonders at how a mountain could ever be called new. And the mountain smells too, but not like the house, and only when it rains—an almost imperceptible stink sitting on the wet wind that no one but he can smell, because every time it comes and he asks them, *There, don't you smell it?* they always say no. It is his mother he asks, or the staff. To see anyone else on the mountain is a special occasion, and to see a stranger is nearly unheard of. But to be sure, he can look out his bedroom window and watch for anyone making their approach on the one road leading to the house. Which he does every morning. Maybe someone will come, and maybe it will be his father.

All fathers are myths and so is Lee Fisher's. All fathers are myths and all mothers are actresses. Lee's mother is an actress—a onetime actress who since she met Lee Fisher Sr. does little but stay alive and wait for her husband's return. She assures little Lee his father is real and will return. He has a lot of money, a lot of responsibility: it is the family's money, but people tried to take it and his father had to do certain things to keep it from them; he had to go away because of those things they made him do, and it is a lot of money, and God forgives, and he kept it safe, and one day it will be Lee's. *Your inheritance,* she calls it. *One day it will be up to you to keep it safe for your children too.*

Lee is on the floor cross-legged playing with his soldiers. *A gift, babu! From him!* Five years old. His mother's Elvis records play over and over on his bedroom's record player. He has become deeply infatuated with Elvis Presley after seeing him on television. Violet and all the other staff have, to an individual, rounded a corner or exited a bedroom they have just finished cleaning or barged in through the service entrance of the home with crates of groceries to find the young master enthusiastically, if weirdly, shaking and convulsing for them—something approaching dancing—having waited sometimes hours to surprise them like this, alone in a dark hallway, breathless and giggling with swelling impatient anticipation. He knows many fascinating things about Elvis Presley and he will visit Elvis in Memphis, Tennessee—he has asked his mother if they could, she said yes (he had to wait to ask until she was off the phone with his father and did not have the meanness in her mouth anymore, the same meanness that is her mouth when she sits in a rocking chair at night alone in the dark staring out the window murmuring, *He's coming back, he's coming back*).

She sweeps into his room, glowing, singing. She looks young and dangerous, her white perfect teeth flashing from behind her lips that are covered in bright paint, her hair a different color and shorter now, wearing clothes he has never seen her wear, and her body sweet-smelling and fruit-smelling but strange and foreign.

—Babu, she sings. —There is someone downstairs for you!

He smells him before he sees him. He smells like the mountain. The house is now filled with the stink, dispelling the sweet scent and fruit scent of his mother. *There it is,* he thinks. The first time he sees him he is taking down one of their pictures from the wall—a framed photograph of his mother holding an infant Lee in New York City— and hanging a new one in its place: a scene of dusty war and Indians and white men killing the Indians in the war and fire and blood and cannons and guns and dead horses. Lee stands there halfway down the stairs watching him, scared of the new picture, hating it. His father wears jeans and a plaid shirt with the sleeves rolled up, cigarettes in the breast pocket, his jaw grinding as he chews his tongue and straightens the new picture and stands back to admire first before turning to Lee and saying, —Well, howdy.

Lee does not answer, turns to look up at his mother on the stair above him. —Why does he say howdy?

His father says, —Just the way us cowboys talk, I reckon.

Lee silently mouths the words: *Cowboys... reckon...*

—Why did you take our picture down?

—Ah, well, because this is a better picture. Look at these guys. These are men. There were just twenty-three of them against four hundred Indians. They and their families faced imminent death against the enemy but did that stop them? Hell no. They kept fighting and they *won*. These guys are heroes. Don't you like it?

Lee says, —No.

His mother hisses through her teeth, —*Lee*.

—He's not a real cowboy.

—*Lee Fisher*.

His father silences her with a wave of the hand and comes over. He climbs up the stairs until he's eye level with Lee. —Pardner, one thing about me? he says. —I'm as real as they get.

A party for him, to welcome him back. The house on the mountain is now stuffed with people. Among these intellectuals from the city with their jewelry and suits and hair and cigarettes and wine, Lee's father looks very alone. He is polite but quiet, listening to them talking about President Nixon; he stands beside his wife in her pretty dress kissing men and women, so many she cannot keep up, talking as fast as she can, it has been so long since she has seen them, there is so much to tell about her life and to hear about theirs. At the bar Lee overhears a bald man say to another man as they pour more wine into their glasses, —Good God, when did he turn into a *Klansman*?

Lee's mother is so proud of his father, Lee can tell, the way she clings to his arm. She says to him, —We need to take you shopping. Will somebody please take him *shopping*? Look at what he's wearing now! *Look* at this! She tugs at the flannel shirt. —It's filthy! It has *sweat* stains!

She and the people they stand with laugh, bending over with their drinks, Lee's father smiling with his lips tight and watching them.

—I like my shirt, he says, no one hearing but Lee.

—You have to try acupuncture, someone is now shouting, apropos of nothing.

—Oh, it's *amazing*, the bald man from the bar says, joining them. —It's Japa*nese*.

—Chi*nese*, Lee's mother corrects him. She turns to Lee's father. —You have to *try* it.

He shakes his head. —Not for me.

—How do you *know*? You haven't *tried* it.

—Believe me, I know.

—Well, how do you relax then? the bald man says to him. —How do you clear your head and get *centered*?

—Masturbation, someone mutters.

—He hunts, someone else suggests. They all groan and roll their eyes.

—Never! Lee's mother cries, her glass sloshing, Lee's father catching her at the elbow to steady her. —I wouldn't allow it.

Lee's father shrugs and smiles blandly.

—So what's with all the guns then? the bald man says. He turns to the man next to him. —Downstairs? In the basement? He has *all these guns*.

Lee's mother is trying to silence him but he does not see her. Lee's father says to him, serious, —When did you see my guns? Who let you down there?

She says, —Oh, I did, darling. They're *interesting*. They're *dangerous*. She turns to the bald man. —Weren't they *interesting* and *dangerous*?

Maybe Lee alone is the only one who can see the darkness in his father's face, how clearly furious he is with his mother though he is not looking at her. But the bald man, not answering Lee's mother, is asking Lee's father, —Well, if not animals, then what do you shoot? People?

—No, Lee's father answers, trying to appear patient but, Lee can tell, bristling, —only targets. You know, for marksmanship.

One of the others, clearly oblivious, says, —So are you carrying one right now?

—Carrying what?

—You know, a heater! A Saturday night special!

The bald man says, —Can we see it?

Another one says, —Whip it out already!

Lee's father smiles in silence and his mother looks at him, touches his face, searching for something in it, then stands up for him. —You're being mean. Don't make fun of him.

Somebody changes the record to the Beatles and they talk about that as Lee's father breaks off from the circle and goes outside, Lee following, and stands on the back porch watching the stars and listening to the wolves out in the trees and their human counterparts inside.

—Did your mother bring anybody around here when I was gone? Any new friends? Any new uncles? They are in the basement, his father bent over the worktable, his guns splayed naked and incapacitated before him, rubbing their holes and tubes with oil that smells like bananas. —Were there ever people here like there were people here last night?

—No, Lee says.

—Sure there were. Of course she brought them around. How many?

—None.

—You should know that your mother's a reckless person, Lee. She is selfish. And irresponsible. And she lies. Most of the things that come out of her mouth are a lie. She can't even help it. And it's dangerous. And people get hurt. She lies to you, you know. Do you know why I came back? I came back to protect you from her. His father falls silent then as he puts down the oil rag and lifts from the table the rifle he has cleaned and puts it against his shoulder, peers down the sights at the wall as though the rifle lets him see through the wall into another realm. He looks up at Lee, one eye still squinted, tanned flesh crinkling at the corners of it. —Now tell me the truth.

The truth. There were nights, late—there were the sounds of tires on the gravel drive starting at the bottom of their hill and climbing, climbing louder and louder still until they were so loud beneath Lee's bedroom window that he sat up in bed and turned to the window over his headboard and pulled the curtains aside to look down at a strange car, rattling idle with its headlights on, and there would be the doors opening on both sides and music spilling out— Bob Dylan, Gladys Knight—and on one side would emerge the bare white leg of his mother, its toes pointed out, no shoe on. And on the other side a man's leg would emerge, trousers on and a beautiful slim brown shoe. Then there would be laughing, then shushing. The headlights would turn off. Then the sound of the doors closing. Then more laughing. Even though the lights were off and it was all night, Lee on his knees in his bed with face smooshed against the window could still see. And Lee would see the man, or some other man— skinny men, long-haired men, black men, even women sometimes who only looked like men; men who were men nothing like Lee's father was a man—Lee would then see this man waiting at the front of the car for Lee's mother, giggling and barefoot and stumbling against the car, drink in one hand, shoes in her other hand. *Sssssssh*, she would whisper, laughing, the man holding out his arm to put around her waist and walk with her inside and out of Lee's view.

Lee's father looks at Lee now with the rifle against his shoulder and the oil that smells like bananas. He looks like he can see through Lee's eyes to see what Lee sees—the cars, the bare feet, the men. His father just nods, puts down the rifle, picks up another gun, a handgun, an old revolver like cowboys have. He sighs, pours oil onto the rag, rubs it inside the gun's empty chamber. —She's ashamed of me. Embarrassed. After all I've done for her. Well, don't worry, you and I are going to spend more time together once she's gone.

—Where is she going?

—Doesn't matter.

—Why is she leaving?

—Because she has to.

—I don't want her to.

—She has to. She has problems. One day you'll understand. You're not safe with her here. All I want is you to be safe. Don't you want to be safe?

—Yes.

—I know it's hard, it makes your daddy very sad too. Your daddy's heart is broken, he's been crying. He'd like nothing more for us to be a family out here. It's all he ever wanted. But men like us know that sometimes the right thing is the hardest thing to do. Those men your momma brought around here ever teach you that? How to do what's right even if it's hard?

Lee says no.

—I didn't think so. He looks at Lee again, grinning. —Hey, you like this gun? I've noticed you looking at it. Of course you have been, it's beautiful. It's a very special gun. If you're a good boy, maybe one day soon I'll teach you to shoot it. And then maybe one day maybe I'll give it to you. Like your granddaddy gave it to me. And his dad gave it to him. This is your inheritance, son. Your *real* one, I mean. Your momma's boyfriends ever teach you how to handle a firearm? How to protect yourself and your family?

Lee shakes his head no.

—Of course not. Well, don't worry. Daddy's home now.

They come up the driveway and they get out of the car wearing suits. He follows her through the house, out to the driveway where they wait. She is furious, weeping, the stomping of her heels and the jingling of her bracelets echoing, staff carrying her suitcases. —*He's the liar!* she is saying. —He's paranoid! Insane! She is dressed in a bright orange dress and her lips are painted red and her eyes blue and her hair is different again.

—Don't go, Lee says.

—The lawyers say I don't have a choice.

—It's not fair.

—No, it's not, of course it's not, but it's the way it is, so for now we just have to do what he says and not make it worse by antagonizing him, and we'll, I don't know, figure it out. She stops being furious and becomes sad; she bends down to him, hugs him, and cries. Then she stops being sad and becomes very happy, and it is like she was only pretending to be furious and then only pretending to be sad, or maybe it is like she is only pretending to be very happy.

—Hey, she says, —you know what? Maybe this will turn out to be okay. Maybe whether I like it or not, a boy does need his father and you haven't had him. A father teaches a boy how to be a man. Momma can't teach you that. You want to learn to be a man, don't you?

—No! he cries.

She laughs at him, a high, loud song of a laugh: *Oh, ha ha ha!* —It will be good, she says, and kisses him again. —Anyway, at least this will give me the chance to work again and be *me* again. And then I'll be happy, and Momma hasn't been happy for some time, she should never have let him convince me to come here. I need a *break*. I'll take a break and figure it out, and when I do you can come see me and even be with me. And everything will be good. I promise.

He passes the living room where his father sits reading the newspaper in the big chair he brought in. His things are everywhere; the house is filled with old, massive American things pregnant with the ghosts of a sacred other world: war uniforms and badges for heroism, tools and instruments, fifes, drums, tricornered hats, funny black shoes, black hats with buckles. There are Thomas Jefferson and George Mason and Patrick Henry, shelves lined with American poets of individualism. Only his father's pictures hang on the walls now, scenes of war and homesteads, portraits of humble bearded generals praying before battle, of the proud, righteous, bullet-frayed underdog star-spangled banner in the dawn above water, of lone cowboys, of free frontier families singing hymns at the hearth, shotgun above it. His father calls to him, tells him to come here. He puts down the newspaper and stands over Lee. He puts his arm out and makes a muscle. —Feel that, he tells Lee, and Lee does. —Hang from it, he says, and Lee does.

They wrestle on the floor. He gives Lee sips of beer in a teeny, tiny mug, a micro version of his own, even says ALASKA on it like his does. He brings Lee down with him to the shooting range he has resurrected at the foot of the property near the trees—a pile of sand for a backstop and some tree stumps on which to set bottles and cans and watermelons and the pictures his mother left—string art, nude people at Woodstock, John Lennon, Martin Luther King Jr., hairy Vietnam War protestors—and blast them with noise so loud Lee must stuff his fingers into his ears as he watches from behind him. His father uses the gun. The special one. The one that will be Lee's. Lee watches it twitch and spit in his father's hand, a gorgeous miracle perfectly crafted as if all in one single piece, not an inch of waste, not a single flaw. You can trust it. And it trusts you. It is simple and honest: —Just like us, his father says. The gun, Lee understands, is who he is. He lies in bed at night dreaming of the gun and his mother. He carries a toy gun and pretends it's the gun. Aims it at the trees and the bad guys his daddy says will come sneaking out of them. And it is who he is and who the Fisher men are and who his countrymen once were, and Lee, for a time, feels safe.

His mother calls from New York and she says she misses him and does he want to come see her, and he says yes and says when, and she says soon. She asks how he is and he says okay; she says she loves him and he says, —I love you too, and he says, —I miss you, and starts to cry, and she does too, and he begs her to come back but she says she cannot, and now she is crying harder, and she says but soon he will come see her in New York, soon he will.

His father digs in the ground and drags pieces of wood from his rusted pickup truck and saws them and hammers them and curses and spits brown juice from his lips and wipes his lips with the back of his hand and hammers more, curses more, Lee there with him in little Levi's rolled up at the cuffs and a boy's flannel shirt, with his own wood to saw, with his own dull children's saw from his own children's tool kit, toy gun stuffed down the side of the Levi's to be like his father who carries the special gun in a holster on his hip as he works. They are building a garden. —So we can provide our own vegetables and things, his father says. There is a high mound of mulch packed in bags from the store in town. They are building fences for animals, little houses for them to live in. They are going to have pets: pigs, cows, chickens. —So we can provide our own meat.

Lee cries when he says that. His father says, —What the hell you crying about?

—I don't want to kill them.

—Relax, we don't even have them yet, we have to build their barn and fences first. Anyway, where do you think meat comes from? Meat is animals that someone has to kill, Lee. It's nature. It's life.

—Then I don't like life.

—Life doesn't care if you like it or not. Life is life. Anyway, it's better we do it ourselves than some corporation doing it for us. You think the Founding Fathers went to Safeway? Hell no. They provided for themselves. They were men of the field and the plow. They were peaceful and happy. Much happier than people are now. They were happy because they were self-determining. Self-determination is the name of the game.

—What game?

—I don't know what game, it's a figure of speech, Lee. Though you could say it's all one big goddamn game. A rigged one.

—Do you think children are in the new house?

—What new house?

—The one they're building.

—Where are they building houses at?

—Down the mountain. I see it from my window. Lee has been watching for his mother from his bedroom window all summer, and there is a spot farther down the mountain where one by one the canopies of the trees went away and were replaced with the gray roof of a brand-new house, the first one to have ever been built anywhere near their mountain.

His father stops digging and looks at him like Lee has done something bad. —Shit, he finally says, shaking the sweat from his head like a wet dog and stomping the edge of his shovel into the earth with his steel-toed boot. —Didn't know that land was for sale or I would've bought it just to keep anyone from building on it.

—Shit, Lee says.

—Watch your mouth. How close by is this house?

Lee shrugs. And then he says, —So do you?

—Do I what?

—Think there are children there?

—Well, yessir, I reckon children probably do live there. You'll want to play with them sometime, I guess, huh? He says it with his face pained, like he's getting a shot. Lee nods. —Okay, well, once we find out what kind of people they are and what they're all about, maybe I'll take you down there.

He keeps working, sweat steaming his glasses, which are secured to his face by a piece of thin rope he cut off the curtains inside and proudly rigged to go around the back of his head and tie to both ends of the glasses.

Lee asks him, —Where do you come from?

—Where do you think I come from?

—New York.

—Is that what she told you? No, New York is where I was *born*, but that's not where I *come* from. Do you understand the difference? Just because you're born somewhere doesn't mean anything. It doesn't mean that's who you are. You *choose* where you come from. No one else gets to decide that for you.

Lee stares at the wood he has sawed, the bright fresh teeth marks he has made in it, the thin curls of wood that have been shaved away and gather at the edge of the teeth marks. —Then where are you from?

His father dumps a shovelful of rocky dirt atop the mound he has made to the side of the garden site and wipes his face with the sleeve of his plaid shirt, drinks from one of the beers he has brought out in a blue plastic cooler. —The West. The frontier. That's where I'm from. And that's where I've been. And that's where I am. And that's where I'll be. He shakes the empty can, drops it in the cooler, opens a fresh one before he has even finished swallowing. —You know what? We should build ourselves a little brewery up here too. Provide our own beer. George Washington used to do that, you know. All those guys did. He becomes excited, animated. He is almost yelling now. —Yessir, once we get all this up and running, we'll have everything we'll ever need, Lee. We'll never leave. We'll never have to!

His mother calls from New York and he is working on the farm and does not want to talk, but when she calls from New York he has to talk to her, so he goes inside and holds the phone up to his ear and listens to her talk and says yes when she asks if he is okay and if he misses her and if he loves her. She asks if he loves her even if she's not an actress anymore, and he does not understand so he says yes, and she says, —Will you always love me no matter what? and he says yes and she says, —No matter what? and he says, —No matter what. And she says, —The attorneys have been talking and they say you can come visit me in New York any time, even next week, what do you think, do you want to come next week? And he says, —But I don't want to, and she says, —You'll love New York, I'll take you to the Central Park Zoo and see the animals, and he says, —We're building a farm, we'll have our own animals. And when it is time to be done talking to her on the phone he can hear her start to cry as she hangs up.

They are working again on the farm and on the house for the animals. The mulch is laid, bright brown and sweet-smelling. A good deal of the fence is up, the barns are coming along. Lee says, —Can you take me to the new house now?

—Help me with this some.

—You promised.

—All right, don't cry about it.

—You'll take me?

—I can't take you, son, I'm working. Violet will take you.

Lee goes inside, finds her standing at the window watching his father and shaking her head.

—Will you take me to the new house to see if any children live there?

—Of course, I'll get the car keys.

—Can I go by myself?

—I don't know, can you?

—*May* I go by myself?

—No, you absolutely may not. It's too far.

—No, it ain't, his father says from behind them. He has come inside to refill his cooler and he stands in the doorway. He is tanned and cheerful and sweating, beer can in one hand, the other in his back pocket, gun on his hip. —At least let the boy's balls drop first before you go loppin' 'em off, Violet.

—You said to me to keep him *away* from those woods at all costs. You said we don't know who could be in there, there could be anyone in there. You said that—

—It doesn't matter what I said, it's what I'm *saying now*: a boy should be free to run in the woods, learn about nature and himself, see what he's made of, free from women always criticizing him and trying to break his spirit. It builds character. Look at Huck Finn.

—Huck Finn is a fictional character, Mr. Fisher.

—Thoreau then. Ain't nothing made up about Henry David Thoreau. Anyway, it's not exactly the great untamed wilderness, there's a damned paved road.

—A major highway.

—Major highway. Good God. It's just a daggone road and there ain't never hardly anyone on it but us. Ain't that right, Lee?

—That's right, says Lee.

—Mr. Fisher, Lee is a very sensitive boy. If something should bite him, or if he runs through poison ivy, or—

—My son ain't gonna live his life afraid of the daggone world.

Violet is gripping the edges of the table she stands beside, her arms quivering and knuckles white. Lee's father laughs at her.

—Thank God a man is finally around, right, Lee?

—Thank God, says Lee.

Violet says, —I'm only doing as instructed by Mrs. Fisher.

—Well, do you see Mrs. Fisher anywhere around here? And her picture in your gossip magazines doesn't count.

Lee says, —So can I go?

—Of course you can, his father says.

Lee emerges from the woods with briars in his hair and pricklers on his shirt, mud caked on his butt from having lost his footing along a little gulch. Runs through the house's backyard and up the porch, knocks. A woman answers the door.

—Do any children live here? he asks.

—Where on earth did you come from?

—Up there.

—All the way up there, you must be exhausted.

—No, he says. —So do they?

—I'm afraid not, no.

A car pulls into the driveway and it is Violet, she has come down after him. —Come on, Lee, she says from the open window.

Lee whines, —But he said I could.

—Hello, the lady calls to Violet, —I'm sorry, he just knocked on my door, I was going to—

—No, no, Violet interrupts her, smiling but not really smiling. —
Come on, Lee.

Inside the car as they drive back up the mountain Violet says, —
He changed his mind. Please don't ask me to try to explain that man.

He wakes up and his right eye is sticky and he cannot move his jaw.
To swallow saliva is to swallow a golf ball. He looks at himself in
his bedroom mirror—an opaque red-gray sore stares back at him.
Sobbing, he goes to his father's bedroom; he's asleep on his stomach,
face buried in his pillow. The room smells of sweat and beer. It takes
several shoves to wake him up. He grunts and groans, lifts his head.

—What? he says. He looks very sick.

—Look, Lee says.

—God Almighty.

—What's happening to me?

His father sits up, peers in close, forehead furrowed in concern.
—Does it hurt?

Lee feels like he should say no, so he says no.

—Good boy. Just a little irritation. Allergy or something. You can
see out of it okay, can't you?

Everything Lee sees with it is blurry. —I can see out of it okay.

—Well, if it doesn't hurt and you can see out of it, let's just keep an
eye on it and see if it goes away, all right? Getting in to town to the
doctor's is such a pain in the ass, we'll be there all day, and we have so
much work to do today on the farm. And the medical establishment
is a machine, it crushes people, I don't want you entering into it if
you don't have to. Look, you can tough it out, right?

—I can tough it out.

—Good man. You're a good tough little guy. Nothing gets to you,
does it? A little minor irritation doesn't get to you, does it?

—It doesn't get to me.

He hugs Lee, kisses him. —Daddy loves you.

His mother calls from New York and she sounds very sleepy, and
he wants to tell her about his eye but before he can she says she just

called to say good-bye, and he says, —Where are you going? and she says, —I am dying. He says, —What do you mean? Are you sick? What happened? and she says, —No, I mean I am going to die very soon, I am going to kill myself, because you won't come to New York and see me, you don't love me, no one loves me, they have taken everything from me and I do not want to live, so good-bye, I love you, and he yells, —No, stop! But the line goes *click* and he screams for his father, who comes, and he tells him, —She's died, she's dead, and his father just rolls his eyes and mutters, —Dead drunk, and leaves, not caring. For days Lee wonders if his mother is dead. Then one day she calls and says, —Hello, babu, and she sounds bright and happy, as if nothing ever happened, and asks if he misses her and if he loves her and if he will come see her in New York. He says yes but only because he does not want to say no, the truth is he does not want to be anywhere near her.

Things are already beginning to grow in the garden: little hard potatoes, tiny sprouts of greens. —Enough food to feed a city, his father says, standing proudly with his hands on his hips, gun in its holster, observing his dominion. Lee watches him lovingly water the poo-smelling dirt, pointing out to Lee where the tomatoes will soon be coming in, the broccoli, the carrots, the beans. —*Fertile* here, he says happily. —This land *wants* to grow food, it *wants* to feed us, don't it?

It's only Lee and his father in the house now, no staff, his father has fired them, Violet too, who raised Lee from infancy. —We don't need things done for us anymore, his father explains to Lee. He leaves early in the morning with one of his rifles to hunt but returns later in the afternoon with frozen meat in grocery store packaging. They cook the potatoes and the greens and the meat outside over an open flame, and his father seems happy and says things are going even better than expected.

His father refuses to use the phone. Whenever it rings he cries out as though in great pain, —Go away! He does not bathe, spends his days digging and cutting and measuring and hoisting and planting and preparing the farm and his nights in his easy chair reading the newspapers, keeps red pens nearby to annotate them and argues with the lies they tell him. He carefully cuts out articles and gives them to Lee to read even though Lee is too young to understand. Lee holds the articles before his face pretending to read; his father watches Lee's face, needing something from Lee that Lee cannot give. —Scary as hell, ain't it? his father says. —It's very bad. Very bad. It didn't used to be like this, Lee.

Day after day he goes out to hunt but returns only with frozen meat.

The eye pulsates hot day and night. Lee puts a hand over it and it scalds, has its own heartbeat. He cannot feel his face; in the mirror his face is shiny and fat, but if he could not see it in the mirror he would believe it is not there. A rare sip of air sneaking down his strangled throat and into his lungs is a great pleasure. Wakes in the mornings with little silver bugs in his eye feeding off the thick pink-green discharge. He is sweaty, feverish. —Let me see, his father says, taking Lee's chin in his and tilting up his grotesque little face toward his own. —Look at that! Getting better!

In the mornings before school, Lee traipses around the kitchen and living room in the darkness of dawn, bending down to pick up his father's empty bottles with cigarettes in them and bring them to the trash. When his father appears on the stairs with his rifle and camouflage heading out to hunt, he makes fun of Lee. —Uh-oh, it's the cops. Do you have a warrant officer?

One night Lee wakes up in bed smelling smoke. Calls out for his father but he does not answer. He goes through the smoke to his father's room and sees his father in his bed, asleep. He calls to him but he does not wake up. Goes into the kitchen, it is on fire. His father left a burner on. Lee stamps out the flames with the lid of a pan, and when his father wakes up hours later—having slept too late to hunt—he asks Lee why it smells like smoke, but Lee shrugs and never tells him how he saved both their lives.

He and his father are at Safeway a day or two later for more meat. Lee's eye is dripping slime. His father has given him a straw to stick between his lips so he can breathe. People are staring. His father is red-faced, muttering to Lee that they all need to mind their own damned business.

—Poor little boy, a woman says.

His father smiles falsely and says, —He's okay, just a little infection, it'll clear itself right up.

—I don't know, she says, —it looks horrible.

—Looks worse than it is. He ain't in pain, and he can see out of it just fine. Still grinning he turns, the smile vanishing. Lee keeps lagging behind. —Come on, now, Lee, *walk*. You have to get the blood circulating otherwise your system won't fight off the infection. Christ, you must think you're the first buckaroo ever to get himself a little pinkeye. Come on, we're successful homesteaders, let's start acting like it. If this were the range, we'd have put you in the stockade for being so damned difficult. We'll get some sunlight today when we're working on the farm, that'll help. Sunlight is the best disinfectant—ain't you ever heard that before?

They go straight to the meats and fill the basket with beef. Every trip to Safeway is mechanized, because his father hates Safeway and believes maybe, if he is mechanized, Safeway will somehow know that he hates it. In and out in ten minutes flat is the goal. No cart—a hand basket provides greater maneuverability for darting around the old ladies standing about clogging the aisles, nothing to do with their lives, he says, but peruse a daggone grocery store, picking things up and putting them down and fussing and fretting over every trivial little thing and getting in men's daggone *way*. — These people are cattle, they're sheep. They're *sheeple*, is what they are, he says. The word sticks in Lee's brain and never leaves. His father carries the gun on his hip. The sheeple glance at it, give him space and respect, think he must be a police officer, which he likes. At the checkout he is sweating. He smiles through his sweat at the teenage cashier.

—Howdy, li'l darlin', he says. He seems to forget Lee is there. — My you're pretty. Though you'd be a lot prettier if you smiled a little bit.

She acts like she has not heard him. She is looking at Lee, his eye.

—Whoa, she says, —what happened?

Before Lee can answer his father says, —Just a lil' bug bite, darlin'. Comes with working the land like we do. It'll clear right on up on its own. Pay it no mind. Now the polite thing to do when someone pays you a compliment like I just did is say thank you and smile.

She smiles halfheartedly, mutters thanks. His father wipes the sweat off his forehead with his hand, takes the bags, handing the one with only bread in it to Lee to carry. In the parking lot, crossing to their car, his father is saying, —Come on, Lee, we gotta get home, we gotta work, there's a lot to be done yet today. He's way ahead of Lee, who's trying to go fast and keep up. A pickup truck backs out of a space as Lee is passing by. The driver pulls up hard but hits him, the high bumper striking the side of Lee's head, on the side of his bad eye. Driver jumps out, a young man, high school.

—I'm so sorry!

His father comes hustling back for Lee, smiling, waving the young man off. —He's fine.

Lee is on the ground, dizzy, face in the pavement. —He almost killed me, he says as he climbs to his feet.

—Hell he did.

—I'm so sorry, the driver says again.

—Nothing to worry about, Lee's father says to him.

—I hit him, is he okay?

—You missed him, it's fine.

—He didn't miss me, Lee cries.

—He missed you. You fell, you tripped over your own feet. Anyway you should have been paying better attention to your surroundings. His father turns to the high school boy. —Does it all the time. He's as reckless as hell and one day he's going to get himself killed. I've been telling him but he ain't listened. Maybe now he will.

Lee is staring at his hellish mangled reflection in the silver bumper of the truck, an inch from his head at eye level.

—Doesn't he need a doctor for that eye? the young man says.

His father snorts. —No, he's fine. All right, Lee. Apologize to the man.

—He doesn't have to apologize to me, the driver insists.

—Don't tell my son what to do, please. He nudges Lee. —Lee. Apologize.

—You don't have to, the driver says.

—I'm sorry, Lee says.

The young man sighs and throws up his hands, then turns to get back into his truck, looks at Lee once more. —You didn't have to do that, he says, and closes the door.

They walk off and get into his father's truck. It is quiet. His father keeps looking at him. After a long time, his father says, in a voice that sounds different, even more like a cowboy than usual, —Hey pardner, did I ever tell you about the time your daddy got himself bit by a rattler out in Oklahoma? Hoooo, doggy! You think you're bad, you should have seen your daddy. His foot was as big as your entire body, God's honest truth. They gave your daddy last rites. The carpenter was fixing him up the coffin. They were out there diggin' the grave. Know what your daddy did? I'll be damned if he didn't get himself up off that plank they had him on, limp over to where they were diggin' the grave, grab him a shovel, and pitch in! Dug twice as much as any healthy man there too! Put them all to shame, your daddy did. Sweated that poison right out. That's where you get your toughness, son. You're a tough son of a bitch, Lee. Tougher than any boy I know. I was the same way at your age. That's the kinda people we are. You're just like me. I see a lot of myself in you. It's eerie sometimes, I have to say. Downright eerie how much I see myself in you.

He pulls out, drives home, telling Lee all about it, forgetting again about Lee, who sits with his face pressed against the glass of the window as the box he is locked inside zooms past the sunshine world outside.

The fences are up, the barn is raised, the troughs are in—but the food is dying. The little hard potatoes still grow, but the tomatoes never appear on their vines and nothing ever comes up through the places in the dirt where things were supposed to come up. And some of the greens turn yellow then brown, became brittle and now tumble away in that foul wind. Lee watches his father squatting to examine the dead leaves and wilted buds, picking up the dirt in his hands and watching it run through his fingers. He squints up at the sky, the sun, as though appealing to the gods. —Must be dry this year, he says. Lee starts to ask what they will do but he cuts him off: —I don't know. Dammit, I don't know what we'll do, stop asking me what we'll do, you're always asking questions, so many goddamn questions, go find something to do, go fix us some supper.

—We don't have any meat.

—Well, mash up some potatoes or something then.

—We don't have any potatoes, we don't have anything.

—Well then, dammit, order us a pizza I guess then, I don't know. He kicks the dirt and walks away and Lee goes inside to order a pizza. Then he calls his mother in New York, but a man who answers says she is not home and he doesn't know where she is or when she will be back. The man says she will call him but she never does.

Lee likes to go inside the new barn, which is still empty, and climb around, hide out. He likes the fresh smell of the wood, the way the light of midday comes in through the little windows and seems to bake the wood, seasoning it with the dust motes moving down through the light beams. Soon there will be pets here. He will name them and ride them and be nuzzled by them and talk to them. They will be his friends. There will be a pig. He will name it Porky. Soon the men will come with Porky and the cows and the chickens. He will name them all. —When? he keeps asking his father. —When are they coming?

—Soon, soon. Next week maybe. Depends on the guy.

—When is next week?

—I don't know. Five days maybe. Five sleeps.

Five sleeps. In five sleeps Lee will have Porky. That was yesterday, he thinks now, in the barn. So four sleeps now. Four. He cannot bear to wait four sleeps.

A force shuts the door and the windows too and Lee is suddenly alone in hot blackness. He pushes against the door but it does not open. He pushes harder and the door seems to push back against him. He can see nothing. It is very hot, he cannot breathe, he is a pig, dying. —Help! he cries, pushing and pulling on the door, the door rattling and pushing back.

A voice on the other side mocks him with oinks and snorts and high whining echoes of his own crying. —Where that piggy at? That piggy in there? Knock, knock, little piggy! Little pig, little pig, let me in! *Heeee! Heeee! You gon' squeal, piggy! You gon' squeal! Heeeeeee! Heeeeeeee! HEEEEEEEEE! HEEEEEEEE!*

—Let me out! Lee begs.

—You ain't never gettin' out, little piggy!

Then there is relentless knocking, pounding from the outside, and Lee backs away against the wall to get away from it. It gets louder and louder, the banging now on the inside walls of his skull.

—Leave me alone!

—*You ain't never getting outta here, boy! You ain't never getting out!*

—Please!

—*Pwea-he-he-hease! Heeeee! HEEEEEE!*

The knocking grows more violent and the squeals and snorts more savage and deranged. Lee slides to the floor, shouting, —*Go away!* He reaches for his hip, pulls from the waistband of his Levi's his cork gun. He points it at the door. —Go away! he cries. —I'm warning you!

—*HEEEEEEEEEEE!*

He pulls the trigger. The pounding stops. The squealing and the torment stop. The death goes away. And he is alone and peaceful in the dark. When he tries the door again it opens. The sunlight floods in and he inhales it like oxygen itself. Lee steps outside, silent, face wet and even puffier than it already was, lower lip trembling. The trees in the distance sway in the breeze. The trees, the breeze, the *distance* itself, he understands, are terror. All is death.

Over in the garden stands his father, his back to Lee, still chuckling to himself as he twists a can of pesticide to the nozzle of the hose.

At last his mother calls and says she hears he has not been doing well at school. He says he hates school, he's not good at it, he does not want school he wants the animals, and his eye hurts, and he's hungry, and when she sounds very angry at what he is saying he feels angry too and tells her things are not good here anymore, why did she leave him here, he wants to come see her in New York, he wants to come now, but she says he can't, that she's not in New York anymore, now she is in Africa, for work, and he does not know where Africa is but he is not allowed to go there, *the custody agreement* she says, but as soon as she gets back to the States *the custody agreement* will allow it and things will be good again. He asks when that will be and she says she doesn't know, it's hard to say right now, but she says, —Will you try to do better in school? and he says he will and she says, —Will you think of being with me in New York every day and dream of being with me in New York every night? And he says he will, and he does. But months go by, and years, and she never gets back to the States, and he never stops dreaming of being with his mother in New York.

Lee listens to his father on the phone with the school, yelling about Lee. —Is your nurse a doctor? Did she go to medical school and become a doctor? Answer me: Is she a doctor?

He listens to his father on the phone with his mother, yelling about Lee. —He's fine, it's clearing up, he's doing completely fine, he's a good healthy boy, he's just impatient about the livestock getting here, it's all he's been talking about, you know how he is when he gets his mind set on something, he needs to learn patience. Anyway, you left the damn country so you get zero say in this, thank you very much. He listens and says, —Go right ahead and call them then. I dare you. They can go right ahead and try coming up here onto my property. Go right ahead and try.

When he hangs up his face is red and he is shaking. He tells Lee to come here. He holds Lee's face in his sweaty hands and looks at Lee's eye and says they are crazy, it's fine, it's clearing up, says school is a machine. Then he takes Lee to town for more guns and ammunition to keep themselves safe.

His father has put on tight jeans and snakeskin boots, a cowboy hat and a bright red western shirt; has tobacco in the pouch of his lip, carries a cup to spit in; has the gun on his hip in its holster. The men in the store stare at him as he enters, looking him up and down. —Howdy, he grunts at them. They nod back. He asks the salesman to see one of these new semiautomatic polymer pistols from Austria. Lee stands on tiptoes to see over the counter as the bearded salesman, speaking in intimate quiet tones like a doctor, explains to Lee's father about the lightweight body, the safety trigger, the brilliant engineering that avoids jams and minimizes kick, the unique grip required and the high level of accuracy that results from it.

—Get a load of this thing, Lee, it looks like a daggone space gun, don't it? I think I'll stick to my granddaddy's gun, thank you very much. He gestures to it on his hip. —Tried and true. Battle-tested.

Says the salesman, —Cops and military have been switching over from those to these. This is what they're all carrying nowadays. Much more reliable. Fires twice as many rounds without having to reload— He sees Lee's eye and cuts himself off. He is large, his face emotionless, but it breaks into quiet horror. —Good Lord, he whispers.

Lee's father glares at the salesman as though daring him to say another word about the eye. —Cops and military, huh? How much they going for?

—Three-fifty and tax.

—Gimme four of 'em.

—Four?

—Four. What caliber are they? You got hollow points for 'em?

—Nine millimeter, and yes, sir, we do.

—Okay, gimme a shitload of hollow points. Turns to Lee. —What about you, buckaroo? You want one? You do, don't you? He turns back to the salesman. —Give me one more, for my son.

—Five, then?

—Excellent math. Hell, better yet? Make it ten.

The man has now forgotten all about the eye. A buoyancy has entered his hefty frame now as he says, —That's my entire stock.

—Is that a problem?

—No, sir, not at all. He hurries into the back to fetch them. Comes out with the guns in their big bombproof-seeming cases stacked in his arms over his face, places them on the counter. Returns to the back for the bullets. —Hundred boxes is all I got. Hundred okay?

—I reckon that'll do, says Lee's father. —For now. He winks at Lee. Fills out the forms, pays. —You ever make a sale this big before? —No, sir, no, I have not.

Lee's father winks at Lee again and drums his knuckles happily on the glass countertop.

The man hands them their new weapons and ammunition and hurries around from behind the counter to get the door for them, grinning so broadly and strangely now that Lee thinks he will hug his father. —Y'all come back any time now, any time at all.

They drive off, passing a hospital, Lee peering out at it through his good eye. They go home, go directly to the range to shoot the brand-new space guns. The space guns are supposed to hit the bull's-eye without your even aiming them, they are supposed to fire without your even feeling it or hearing it—isn't that what the salesman said? But neither turns out to be true, and Lee's father cannot hit anything with the first one he shoots, says it feels like a daggone block in his hand; he does not like how it smells or even how deep black it is, too industrial and inhuman. Tries a second one and it's no better. Lee has his empty one, pointing it downrange.

—What do you think, buckaroo? We don't like this, do we? It don't feel like a gun. It feels like a toy. We miss *our* gun, don't we?

Lee nods. His father puts the space guns back into their big, heavy safe-like carrying cases and unholsters the special gun. Glances down at Lee. He is a big shadow between Lee and the sun. The shadow says, —Wanna learn to shoot it today, son?

The day the pets come in, Lee stands at a safe distance from the fence beholding these large, smelly things that are not as cute or as nice as they should be. Flies crawl all over the cows' eyeballs as they stare at Lee. The chickens shit as they walk and make angry squawks. The pigs are scary and mean and filthy and stinky. He will not ride these terrible things, he will not nuzzle them or talk to them or even go near them. He watches the animals feeding and groveling in the mud, stepping over each other, and wishes the man who brought them would come take them back. His father leans on the fence, one boot up on the lowest slat, happily observing his stock. —Yessir, he keeps saying. —Yessir. You're happy now, ain't you, now that your animals are here. He laughs and ruffles Lee's head and says, —Yessir, yessir. You're happy.

In the morning all the pigs are lying on the ground, their bellies and throats open and their flesh white and fly-covered, guts hardening in the dirt. He wakes his father up and his father looks out the window and says, —*Shit, shit, shit, shit.* He runs outside, climbs over his fence, and squats at the first pig, wanting to touch something with his hand but not knowing what. —*Shit!* he yells. Someone has let the cows out and they stand in the pigpen with blood on their hooves. —Where are the chickens? his father says. The coop is open and they are nowhere to be seen, it is like they were never here. Through his diseased eye Lee watches his father run around looking for them. —What the fuck? he says. —What the fuck? He is covered in sweat, reeks of yesterday's whiskey. Lee begins to cry. —Stop crying, his father shouts.

The man who sold them the animals comes from town in a pickup truck just like Lee's father's but bigger, newer, and made not by Chevrolet but Toyota. He gets out and walks through the gravel dust settling around him.

—He was born and raised here, Lee's father tells Lee, voice somber with respect. —His family's been grazing livestock 'round these parts since 1850. He's one of us.

The man wears a cowboy hat like Lee's father, a flannel shirt, boots, jeans—just like Lee and Lee's father. A new plastic European space gun is holstered on his hip. He shakes Lee's father's hand, shakes Lee's. Looks in silent amusement at the dead animals, at Lee's father who around this man is very talkative and moves around a lot. The man says nothing, just nods and grunts as Lee's father explains how last night they were fine.

—Think it's wolves? his father says.

The man says, —That ain't animals. That's a knife did that. That's slaughtering.

—Slaughtering? his father says, looking around as though whoever it was might still be seen.

—Probably oughta call the police.

His father shakes his head at the idea. When the man leaves, Lee's father's face is red and he does not look at Lee or at anything. —I know who it was, he says. Lee says, —Who? but his father won't say, and he takes the gun out of its holster, stomps off fifty feet out toward the trees, and points it and, screaming, fires once and fires again and keeps firing until it's empty. Comes back, gestures over his shoulder.

—Pick 'em up.

—Huh?

—The bullets. It ain't good for the land for them to be out there, they'll poison our soil. Go out there and fetch 'em and bring 'em back. All of 'em. And don't come back until you do.

—Why?

Warm pain splatters across the back of his head and his hat falls off.

—We obey our daddies where we come from.

His father goes back inside and shuts the door, and Lee wanders toward the trees, crying, face hurting. He goes as slowly as he can. When he gets too close, when he cannot bear to go any farther, he turns and runs off to the guest house on the far side of the property, one of four, his hiding place. When he returns to the house four hours later, stopping at the gun range to dig six crushed bullets from the sand mound there, his father is in his chair in front of the TV, watching *Happy Days*. He does not look at Lee and he is drunk, and Lee thinks he looks like a little boy. Lee drops the bullets on the coffee table but his father does not look at them or acknowledge him.

Over the ensuing week the garden stops growing altogether. Soon it is just wood and dirt, and soon fall comes and chills it, then winter comes and finally kills it off completely. They buy their groceries from Safeway, overpriced and infused with chemicals and hormones, in cartons and plastic packaging, meat killed by other men, crops grown on other men's land. The bullets his father fired into the trees remain out there.

His father disappears with no explanation. Lee wanders around the arsenal in the basement, picking up guns, feeling his father in them;

he puts the special gun in a holster on his hip and admires himself in the mirror, wanders around the house like that. Steps outside and feels the breeze blowing over his skin, watches the green tops of the trees. He finds himself walking down the long driveway to the street, stands there for a moment, then continues. At the hospital they know who he is, the nurse takes him by the hand without asking him any questions, as though she has been waiting for him. People waiting in chairs holding wads of bandages to bleeding bodies call out in protest but she ignores them, leads him back through a winding hallway. On the way Lee looks over a doorway and his own name is there: THE LEE FISHER WING. They give him medicine and a man wearing a tie drives him home. It is night and he is in bed when he hears his father come home. He listens to him going through drawers in the kitchen, pulling things out, putting things away. Glasses clink. He is talking to someone. Lee thinks he hears another voice, a man's. He holds his breath and listens very intently but does not hear the other voice again. Lee gets out of bed, stands against his closed door, listening, his heart beating very hard, lungs burning from holding his breath. Then it is quiet. Lee slips out of his bedroom, goes down the long hall, squats at the top of the stairs. A dim orange light Lee has never seen emanates from down there. His father's long shadow is cast upon the wall. Lee hears the other voice again.

His father appears at the foot of the stairs, looking up at him as though suspecting he would find him there. —What are you doing, Lee?

—Nothing.

—Go to bed.

—Who's here?

—No one.

—I heard someone.

—No one's here.

—I heard a man.

—There's no man. Go to bed.

Lee does as he is told. In the morning his face is almost back to its normal size and he sucks in gob after gob of air. Two days after that, as he keeps taking the medicine in secret, hiding it from his father under his mattress, the infection clears.

—Look at that, his father says. —Just like I told you it would.

Lee finds him in his bedroom pulling everything from the closets. A pile of clothing rises in the center of the room, all his cowboy hats and fringe vests and leather chaps and boots and dungarees and Levi's. He tosses another armload of clothing atop the mound and mops a swath of sweat from his face with his palm. He is not a cowboy anymore. Now he is a soldier.

Soldiers train. They join with others to form armies. They drill on the new course built where the farm was by a former drill sergeant who was responsible for the training courses on Parris Island, where they trained US Marines for battle in Vietnam.

Soldiers go to church. They bring along their son, to be a good example to him. They manage their son's activities and diet. As virtue is measured in indirect proportion to hair length, they shave their head, they shave their son's head.

Strange new men are around now, each with a rank. They wear camouflage. They shoot. After days of wearing camouflage and shooting, they sit around bonfires drinking beer in the shadows.

—These are the most dangerous times in our history, the man called the General says. —Nothing less than the future of our country, the lives of our people, nothing less than our very *freedom* is at stake. Never in any time since our Founding Fathers waged war for this great free nation have our fundamental rights been under attack like they are now, at this very moment. We are living in crucial times, men. Our families, our beloved nation, the futures of our children and grandchildren are depending on *you*. Only *you* stand between freedom and tyranny. Wicked elements are at work in America today. Jackbooted government thugs are kicking down our doors *as we speak*. They will seize our homes, our arms, make off with our women, our children. All governments are bent toward tyranny. Ours is no exception. The ones you must be most wary of are the ones who come to you under the guise of democracy. Do not be fooled—they want to take our country from us.

Lee feels despair and hatred for these people, the ones who want to take his home and his country from him.

—There is no gray area, the Second Amendment of the Constitution of the United States has no fine print. *Shall not infringe.* Yet every day powerful moneyed people are *infringing with impunity* on our rights. A regulation here, an ordinance there. They call it gun *control* but they are *disarming us. Eradicating our freedoms.* They are termites. Termites do not stop when they have had one bite, they do not stop after two bites, they do not stop after they've had their fill, no, they go until the whole house topples in on itself. They want to tell us what to do and how to be, and they want to take away our means of liberty, make us reliant on them, the government. In which case we are no longer citizens but subjects.

Lee looks at his father, who is listening very closely to the General, a trim, tall man with a long gray beard, eyes deep with brave acts of war and unblinking against the spitting rain. He sits on a log, the rest of the soldiers at his feet. Across his lap is a military-issue fully automatic M16 carbine rifle. The other soldiers nod and shake their heads in indignation and mutter vows to uphold their duty and defend what is sacred. The General looks at Lee.

—I fear for your generation, little private. I pray to God your fellow boys and girls see what you see, which is the truth, and have what you have in you, which is *fight*, but I have to admit I feel very grim when I think about it. Your generation's parents are not doing their part. They are failing you. With the exception of Lieutenant Fisher, your generation's parents are not instilling the right values in you. Your generation is not going to appreciate their freedom the way mine does. Because mine died for it. And killed for it. I look at boys your age and I am not convinced they have been raised the way Lieutenant Fisher has raised you. I can't say I am convinced they are willing to die and kill for freedom and liberty, and that saddens me. It frightens me. It is not their fault—it is *our* fault. We have to do more, don't we?

The others nod solemnly.

—Lieutenant Fisher has done his part. Let's take an example from him, bringing his boy out here like this today.

Lee's father's face burns with pride, he looks near tears.

—Yes, this will all one day end if we don't do something about it. But not this day.

—*Hoo-ah!* the soldiers all bark in unison.

—You are doing sacred work. You are heroes. True patriots. If General Washington himself were here he would be real proud of you. Real proud. *This is what I watched so many men die for,* he would say. Unappreciated thankless work—but sacred work. The most sacred. The only payment is one more hour of freedom. Remember that when they mock you, when they taunt you and talk down to you. Later when catastrophe strikes they will not be laughing. They'll be begging men like you to save them. Maybe you will. Maybe you won't. The choice will be yours. The power will be yours. As it is now. They don't know that. So let them laugh. Let them laugh all the way to the grave.

NRA material and memorabilia are scattered around the house: pamphlets, fund-raising letters, publications from the executive vice president. That Christmas they decorate the tree in ornaments bearing the NRA logo on the front and the text of the Second Amendment on the back. Lee's father takes him to the convention in Cincinnati. There is something exciting trembling beneath the gaudy maroon carpet of the hotel conference rooms. His father says a coup is under way. Lee doesn't know what that means.

—It means the organization is run by pussy-ass sycophants who want to acquiesce every chance they get to the tyrannical, gun-hating, freedom-hating, anti-American bureaucrats of the United States government. But the good guys are here, the good guys are kicking them out and taking it over. That man there? He points to a squat bald man whose face quivers with intensity as he spits into a walkie-talkie. —That's Harlon Carter. A great man. When he was sixteen he shot a man to death in self-defense. He's a true Second Amendment warrior. He's our hero, he's going to lead the revolution. At least he better or I'm getting my money back.

Lee does not know what that means either, but he likes his father explaining things to him and he is looking forward to seeing a war.

—He's coordinating right now. It's going to be a sneak attack. I'm the guy behind Harlon, I'm the money, the strategist. The sycophants have no idea what me and Harlon are about to pull. They want to keep it a benign little squirrel-shooting club and stay out of politics and *cooperate*. They want to move the NRA from Washington, DC, to fucking Colorado and let them just go ahead and trample our rights. So me and Harlon are gonna take it. We're gonna take the NRA. And save the country. Tonight. Come on, I'll introduce you.

His father brings Lee up to the bald man, Harlon Carter, who is talking to someone else. They stand there for a moment, waiting for Harlon Carter to finish, but before Harlon can turn to them his father says, —Know what? Let's not hog all his attention. I'll introduce you later. Come on.

—Why are you sweating, Dad?

—I'm not sweating.

—Yes, you are.

—I don't know why. I gave a lot of money, is all. I funded the whole damned thing. I bought those fucking walkie-talkies. And he waves me off. He waves me off.

—He didn't wave you off.

—Don't tell me he didn't wave me off. He waved me off. Come on.

They wander around looking at the display tables. Lee collects stickers and pins and pamphlets and books. He is drawn to the table with the guns—army guns and cop guns and big guns and little guns and so many guns. Everyone has a handgun on their hip or a rifle slung across their back. The General is there, the soldiers from the house. Lee stands there as his father shakes their hands, pretends to pass on sensitive information obtained from being an insider with Harlon Carter.

—How is Carter, Lieutenant? the General says.

—Harlon's good, General, Lee's father says. —He's feeling strong, he's feeling good. We're in prime position and everything's on schedule, Harlon tells me we're in great shape, outstanding shape.

The General and the soldiers nod, glowing from the proximity to power.

—What's he like? the General says. —Good guy?

—Great guy, Lee's father says. —Great guy.

The convention consists mostly of people talking and clapping and sitting and eating, with their guns. For some speakers his father leans over and whispers to Lee, —This guy's a hero, and he claps hard, even whistles, and Lee does the same, clapping hard and whistling for the hero. For other speakers his father says, —This guy's a sack of shit, and he and Lee boo. Most of the conventioneers are somber men with white hair and clothes that Lee imagines being found in an attic of an abandoned farmhouse. The few women resemble the men. It is boring. Lee wants to go in the pool. He saw some boys his age in there earlier; he wants to meet them, play with them. He asks his father if he may. —Later, his father says, —I want you to experience this, this is important.

At midnight they are still there, in their folding chairs in that conference room, cheering for heroes and booing sacks of shit. God, how he would love to go running on the deck of the pool and take off from the edge and fly in the air above the blue water, pulling his knees to his chest, and splash. How he would love to race those boys from end to end. He is trying to keep his eyes open. —Wake up, his father says, nudging him, —you're missing it.

Lee looks at what he is missing and he is missing more speeches and they are the same speeches, and he is missing men in orange hats standing around the edge of the crowd with walkie-talkies, and he is missing other men, these in suits, walking quickly from group to group and talking and nodding and pointing at the men in orange hats and talking.

—Can I have a Coke? Lee says.

—No, the machines are all empty. The bad guys did it on purpose to try and weaken us with dehydration.

Lee is crying.

—What the hell's the matter?

—I'm tired.

—Christ Almighty.

Lee knows he is disappointed in him, even disgusted, but he must sleep, his face burns with exhaustion. Gets up, walks out past all the energetic men in orange hats and frazzled, confused men in suits, carrying all his stickers and pins he has collected—his favorite sticker bears an image of a skeleton clutching a wood-and-iron rifle and the words *You can have my gun... when you pry it from my cold dead hands*. It is proud and manly and heroic. He passes the pool. There are no kids playing in it now, it is dark and empty and the water is still and the door to it is locked. Goes to the penthouse, there are two suites; he and his father have both, each his own. Lee falls instantly, embryonically asleep, shoes still on.

His father is nudging his back. —Lee, Lee. Wake up. Ice clinks in his father's glass. Now it is he who is weeping. —Wake up, Lee. We did it. Me and Harlon, we did it. We won. We saved the country. We took it, it's ours. No compromise! Never any compromise! Things will be good now, Lee. And know what Harlon said? He said Daddy was *essential*, that he played a *vital* role in our success. That's what he said, Lee: *Essential. Vital.*

He listens to his father on the phone with the General. —Where is everybody? We said oh-six-hundred hours and it's damn near eight. He listens, says, —General, this is the third time we're rescheduling this muster. It's like herding cats. I understand people have prior commitments but we've got to commit to *this*. *This* needs to be the prior commitment.

When he hangs up, his face is red and tight, but he looks more sad than angry. He scoffs to Lee, —General! He's not a *real* general. Never fought in a war. Never served a single day in the military. He's a daggone junior high school math teacher.

And soon the army men stop coming to the mountain and Lee and his father are not soldiers anymore.

For ninth grade he has to go to a special school for the stupid, because his father homeschooled him for seventh and eighth grade and he did not learn anything. After the special school for the stupid, his mother wants him to go to an elite boarding school in New Hampshire where, she says, people go on to Harvard and become senators and CEOs of Fortune 500 companies and Academy

Award winners, but his father says Abraham Lincoln went to school in a one-room cabin in the woods of Illinois and went on to teach himself how to become a lawyer and then a great president; those people at those schools think they're better than everybody and above everything even though they haven't earned their station, and he won't raise Lee to be like that, he won't have Lee thinking that way about himself, he will continue to be self-taught at home. His mother says the authorities won't allow that because what Lee's father seems to consider homeschooling they consider neglect. They fight about it through the lawyers. As compromise, Lee has to go to the local public high school. His father says it is an ultra-liberal hellhole, the machine of machines. —Just don't let them brainwash you, he says. —Don't let them corrupt you.

The school is terrifying. These strange people all seem so much bigger than he is and live in a chaos of unwritten social codes and arbitrary rules. How is he to know not to wear his Remington hat inside? Where was it stated that he would be laughed at for his clothes, which are mostly military-issue camouflage? Why is it considered any of their business that he prefers eating lunch alone in the back stairwell reading military histories instead of braying in the cafeteria with the other sheeple? Everyone appalls him with their frivolity and inane cheerfulness—what the hell are they always so daggone *happy about* when the country, the world, is how it is?

His first year there he does not say a word to anyone except in class when they make him. Joey Whitestone is the only one who is friendly to him but he does not like Joey Whitestone being friendly to him. He tells Joey Whitestone to leave him alone but Joey Whitestone does not leave him alone, so Lee Fisher tells him if he does not leave him alone he will blow his head off—and now Joey Whitestone knows to leave him alone and the rest of them know too.

It feels good to drive them off, to control people in such a way. You have no control when you let people change you. Blast them with coldness and it solves the problem, keeps them from hurting you. All people will hurt you. You must guard against them. When he gets home and is alone in his bedroom, he lies on the bed sobbing.

He is so lonely but does not know what to do about it, he wants people but he hates everybody.

In English class where they are taking a test on *To Kill a Mockingbird*, Joey Whitestone passes him a note: *I stole my uncle's smokes, we're meeting at the railroad tracks after school, want to come?* Yeah, right—it's a trick, Lee can see that, payback for what he said. Who knows what they have planned for him when he shows up? Humiliation. In some form or another, humiliation. He knows how to handle this: he raises his hand for the teacher, waving the note in the air. Joey serves ten days' suspension, the school administration tells Lee he did the right thing. It feels good. Right. He wants that feeling all the time. He will be a police officer, he decides, when he is eighteen and may leave. He will go to New York and be a police officer. With his mother. His mother is not there anymore and has not been for a long time but that does not matter, he does not need her, he needs no one. He will be in New York, alone. *Far away from here.*

The principal recognizes him as one of his own kind, not just another moron student. *Here is a boy with responsibility and virtue and values, a boy I do not have to worry about.* —If only I had a school full of Lee Fishers, the principal tells him, in his office, splitting a Coke, excused from that period of algebra class.

Lee takes it upon himself from then on to collect intelligence on all illicit activity perpetrated by students on school grounds during school hours—drinking in the bathroom, weed in the parking lot, cigarettes in the woods, sexual activity in the stairwells, unauthorized absences, cheating on tests—and deliver the evidence to the principal so that justice may be served and Lee may feel love. The other students start calling him McGruff the Crime Dog. They taunt him, threaten him, but most important, they stay away from him.

Someone writes on the mirror of the boys' bathroom: LEE FISHER IS A CHOAD. Lee sees it when he is in there washing his hands, sees his reflection looking back at himself through the insult, his hair close cropped with electric shears, done himself like a self-sufficient soldier. Does his face not reveal that he is unmoved, his eyes that he is unshaken? Is this not the reflection of a good guy being persecuted for his soundness of character, mocked for his having done the right thing?

Joey returns from suspension, does not look at Lee, does not invite him anywhere ever again, is always surrounded by friends, is always laughing or making them laugh, does not seem to have the problem with life that Lee has. Lee's problem with life is everything, everything to do with life and living. Lee sees Joey blowing smoke from a joint down Tamra Riley's throat in the parking lot one day after school. She is the prettiest girl who ever lived—Lee has been in love with her since the first time he saw her. He hates Joey even more than ever, for how he has taken advantage of Tamra Riley. He waits until they leave, goes and picks up the joint, and writes down the date and time and types up a report on the incident and delivers it to the principal. Tamra is suspended and her parents remove her from the school as an emergency measure to rescue her transcript for college applications, and Joey, having received his second infraction while still on probation, is expelled.

The day after their suspensions are handed down, Lee steals one of his father's Glocks and brings it to school in his backpack. Loaded. Not to hurt anyone—he would never do that—for self-defense. It's only smart—not everyone will like what he has done, not everyone appreciates those who do what's right. Walking around with the Glock having the ability to kill any bad guys who threaten him, or more so having the ability, the *option*, of killing anyone at all whenever he feels like it but *choosing not to, allowing them to live,* makes him feel much better about himself. *I am good,* he thinks. He finds he feels warmer toward people, is more forgiving, even feels affection toward them. He is more polite on crowded stairwells, gallantly allowing others to go ahead of him. *A cop,* he thinks. *A cop in New York.*

One of Joey Whitestone's friends, a big dumb moron named Bobby Pool—football, wrestling—stares Lee down in the hallway. He is surrounded by other gang rape mutants like himself. Normally Lee would stare at the ground and seethe as he pretends to ignore them, but today, knowing his gun is there, Lee meets Bobby Pool's gaze.

He says to Bobby Pool without breaking his stride, —What the fuck are you looking at? And Bobby Pool just looks away. Doesn't say shit. None of his friends says shit. No one says a goddamn thing to Lee Fisher.

—What the hell crawled up your ass? his father says when he gets home that day.

They are in the kitchen, pulling slices of pizza from the delivery box and slapping them onto their plates, which ordinarily they would carry off to their respective wings of the house, where they would remain for the night, ignoring each other. His father never notices anything about him, hardly ever talks to him anymore; he never talks to anyone and rarely leaves the house. Mostly he sits in his chair drinking and watching cable news. He has grown very fat and Lee is not far behind. They have not spoken to each other in days, and his now taking an interest in Lee is like one of those cable news people suddenly stopping midsentence, squinting out at you from the screen, and saying your name, saying hello to you. Lee says he's fine.

—The hell you are, you look like your dog just died. Lee looks away, but his father is peering closer at him. Puts his hand on Lee's shoulder and squeezes. It feels both good and repellent. —Whatever it is, his father says, —Let's take your mind off of it.

Down at the firing range, his father loads up the special gun, hands it to Lee. The firing range is the only part of the property his father still maintains nowadays, the rest of it is long overgrown with tall brown grass and weeds, including the farm they tried to live off of, the training course they once drilled on with the soldiers. Lee takes the gun, aims it at the targets, fires. Misses. Fires again, misses. Not even a nick.

—You're missing to the right, his father says.

Lee says, —As fucking usual.

—Hey, easy, it's all right, don't get down on yourself. You're doing good. You're a hell of a marksman. Here, try tightening up that right hand, kind of push against the gun with it, kind of brace against it on that side.

Lee does, fires, hits just on the edge of the bull's-eye.

—Beautiful! his father says.

Lee fires again, hitting the same spot, the exact same spot.

—Outstanding! his father says, slapping him on the back. —That's it! You and that gun were made for each other. His father suddenly looks at him, alarmed. —Oh no, Lee.

—What is it?

—Oh God. Don't move.

—Why?

—There's something on your face.

Lee's worried. —What is it?

—Good Lord, it's all over it, don't move. He wipes his hand over Lee's face and flings something away.

—Did you get it? Lee cries. —What was it?

—Nothing, just a smile. Been so long since I saw it, I didn't recognize it. Puts his arm around his son's shoulders and says, —Listen, something I wanted to talk to you about. That gun? It's yours now.

—Really?

—It's always been yours, I've just been holding it for you. Take care of it. Protect it. And remember: you're just keeping it for *your* son. It's already his, just like it was already yours.

(Sheeple I)

Jenny. I wake up, check my phone, and there is her face. This one's in Manhattan. Black boy, white man. Jenny is on the scene and raising hell; she has to act fast or she will lose the story to the civil rights activists. *This is not a black-and-white story but a gun story,* the story quotes her saying. *And gun stories are all-of-us stories.*

She likes to appear unbreakable. Like Joan of Arc. That's how she seemed the first time I saw her. It was in my hospital room where I lay sedated and suicidal in the aftermath of my own shooting. Her skin was dark, her bones big and heavy, and her high heels on the hospital floor sounded so powerful. She told me she had come a long way to see me. Said she knew exactly what I was going through. She told me about her Michelle, who died at her desk in a first grade classroom. She took out her purse, showed me a picture. *A nineteen-year-old young man with his daddy's gun decided Michelle and all her classmates and her teacher were going to die and so that's what happened.* Jenny shrugged, put the picture away. *After these things happen, everybody always says,* What do we do? How do we stop this? Why doesn't somebody do something? *Well, here I am. Now where are you?*

Our hero, I thought. I joined her. She moved into a nearby Embassy Suites but I don't think she ever once slept there; she was too obsessed, she was always strategizing, e-mailing, cultivating local ground operatives or playing politicians off one another. She went with me to Kaylee's memorial service, appeared by my side on the *Today* show couch. Our family home became a makeshift local branch of her organization, Repeal the Second Amendment. Under the guidance of Jenny Sanders we moved out all the furniture and replaced it with computer workstations and phone banks. She installed a small video production studio where the kitchen had been, equipped it with satellite linkup capabilities to enable her appearances on cable news shows. With her came a cabal of young women of color, inexhaustible little Jennys each with a specific role performed with unflagging optimism. Jenny Sanders was a charismatic prophet and innate executive genius. In another time and place she would have founded a major religion of the world. Every day Jenny and I met with major political donors and super PACs, and again and again, over pasta salad and little green bottles of water, I relived my shooting.

The movie was the premiere of the new installment of the action franchise I had grown up with and adored. My girlfriend, Kaylee, had no interest in seeing the movie but I convinced her. She and I camped outside the theater all night to get a seat. The previews ended and the lights went down. A door to the side of the screen opened and in from the parking lot stepped a figure. Kaylee whispered, *Who's that?* And then she was gone. I can only imagine people were screaming—if they were, I could not hear it over the noise of what sounded like a box of M-80s going off all at once by accident. I had already pulled Kaylee to the floor and lay on top of her. I could feel her heart beating against me. *She's still alive,* I said out loud. People were running for the exits at the rear of the theater. At the exits they pulled and pushed at the doors, not understanding they had been chained shut from outside. The shooter stood at the base of the screen emptying magazine after magazine, reloading several times with fresh ones he carried in the pockets of his black military contractor cargo pants. I remember his face as he sighted each shot through the scope of the assault rifle. It was blank. It might have been the face of someone driving alone a long distance. This was his life's great project. This was the only meaningful thing he had ever done. He had been carrying it inside himself for a long time, letting it come to life inside him the way others might carry a baby or music. The air smelled like sulfur. It was smoky, fire alarms were going off, sprinklers raining down on us. I remember seeing blood crawling down the sloped aisle from the exits where the bodies were piled. The massacre lasted forty-eight seconds. Two hundred forty-three were killed. They were dead in the heaps by either exit, dead in the seats they had carefully chosen, asking the ones they were with *Are these good? Can you see?* unaware this was the final decision they would ever make. They were dead with popcorn still half chewed in their mouths and dopey grins on their faces from the last preview, a raunchy sex comedy starring Jason Sudeikis.

Once the shooter decided he was finished and shot himself through the mouth with a Glock 19, I tried to lift Kaylee but her head lolled like it was made of dough and that's how I knew what I had been feeling was only my own heart. I hated my own heartbeat. It was a liar, a traitor—it meant that I was the only survivor. Can you name me? Can you name any of the other dead? No one ever can. But can you name the shooter? Of course you can—you can state all three names, they roll off your tongue: first, middle, and last. You can point at his picture and say, *That's him.* You can say what he did in his life. Can you say anything—*one* thing—those he killed ever did? Can you say one thing I ever did in mine?

Then Jenny would hit them with the economic data showing the benefits of a tax on all ammunition, the polling statistics indicating growing voter support in favor of repealing the Second Amendment in favor of a new amendment, *our* amendment, an amendment *we the people—not dead, slave-owning white guys from 250 years ago: us—* would write. —This is happening, Jenny would tell them. —It is *happening.* The tide turns quickly. Be on the right side of it.

I could almost see Kaylee there, in each meeting, watching me showing rich assholes her picture, watching CEOs and hedge fund managers take her picture in their small-fingered hands, pretending to care. I was using her smile and her youth and her utter perfect sweetness to try to garner votes for quixotic state legislation or small bits of money for Jenny's organization. I was using her lolling neck. Her silent chest. I was giving her to them.

A thousand meetings, a thousand howling escorts from the building. —I'm sorry what happened to you happened, said one Democratic state representative, —it breaks my heart. But, look, you're talking about guns. And if that wasn't bad enough, you're talking about *taxes*. In *Texas*. He looked at Jenny like he was going to cry. —Are you out of your mind? Do you want *any* Democrats in office in this state? Do you want *any* kind of future political life here, Jenny? There's a right way of doing what you want to do and a wrong way. And, darling, this is the wrong way.

—Fuck you, Jenny told him, and left. I followed.

People sent my family and me death threats all day every day, via phone or letter or social media or e-mail, even in person. They protested outside my house carrying guns, screaming at my family and Jenny whenever we left. A caravan of men carrying guns followed us around wherever we went, calling us enemies of the state, traitors to our nation. They called Jenny a cunt. Called me a faggot. Oftentimes walking through a crowd of these guys spitting at us and screaming, it was more terrifying than being in that movie theater. In the movie theater, I knew what was happening. By that point, it had happened so often I knew exactly what it was. And it was not personal. My and Kaylee's being there was a result of chance. With these guys, everything about it was personal. They hated *me*, wanted *me* dead, they wanted *me* gone, they wanted *her* gone. Jenny assured me not to worry, to stay strong, but her voice picked up a stammer, and I noticed her hands shaking whenever she lifted one of her half dozen daily macchiatos to her lips. —This is what is necessary, she'd say. —They're on the wrong side of history.

My family and I had to move after we found a bullet hole in the siding at the front of the house. Jenny found us a new one. To keep its location secret, its deed was signed by the manager of an LLC set up by one of her donors. It was in a town fifty miles away. I did not want to live in a town fifty miles away, I wanted to live in my town.

She and I kept giving interviews, kept writing letters and making phone calls to RSA members across the country appealing for donations to fight the Battle of Texas, in which Jenny assured them victory was close at hand but at the same time so was defeat, now more than ever their help was necessary if they wanted to save the lives of future Americans. I alone seemed to see the fight as increasingly hopeless. The more money she raised to fight the NRA, the more money the NRA was able to raise to fight Jenny. The stronger the candidates the RSA ran in local Democratic primaries, the more gusto with which the party shock-and-awed them with its vastly superior manpower, media influence, and money, tarnishing them as circus characters of the fringe Left with no chance of defeating the Republicans in the general election. Jenny and I were failing to get any lawmakers to even draft a version of the ammo tax just to get her out of their hair. The state assembly would not even hold a vote on whether to *consider* looking into the boxes and boxes filled with independent, peer-reviewed, rock-solid science showing the benefit of the ammo tax on the economy and public health in America. At the same time, the NRA was convincing its membership that victory for the RSA candidates in both the primary and general elections was a certainty, that Jenny Sanders's success at passing the ammo tax and ultimately repealing the Second Amendment was imminent and assured, and, as a result, new NRA memberships, donations, and nationwide gun and ammo sales all reached heights not seen since the aftermath of Newtown.

—Can you feel it? Jenny said to me the night one of her candidates lost a primary by thirty-three percentage points, as I sat slumped in the corner of the hotel conference room drinking, despondent. — What we're doing is *working*. We're making *big* progress. We've just got to keep doing what we're doing.

—Are you insane? I said. I sat up and began to rant, but she cut me off.

—Dude, shush. She pointed up at the ceiling, the music blasting now. —Beyoncé.

She spun and danced away to the center of the room like a drunk aunt at a wedding. I watched her dance alone, realizing what I had done. I had placed the last vapors of my faith in humanity into a callous lunatic.

Our daily schedule consisted of: meetings, phone calls, being shouted at, meetings, lunch, getting spit on, meetings, phone calls, having our tires slashed, e-mails, writing op-eds, TV appearances, campaign rallies, door-to-door canvassing, planning tomorrow which would always be the same as today—and over it all, an incessant looping sound track of the pop queen. After a major prime-time Fox News host called me a *sniveling, emasculated weasel* on live television, Jenny played Beyoncé to try to cheer me up. When a former Republican governor and presidential candidate called for my and Jenny's being added to the terrorist watch list, Jenny responded with some lyric from a Beyoncé song. And when another former Republican governor posted my picture on her Facebook page with a bull's-eye photoshopped over my face and the message *Lock and load*, the vast digital army of little Jennys blew up the page with pictures of Beyoncé until the offending former governor was forced to delete the whole thing. One time I caught Jenny staring at herself in the mirror in my house and she turned to me and said, —I kind of look a little like Beyoncé, don't I? I think the worst thing I could have done to her would have been, not joining the NRA, but confessing that I did not get Beyoncé, that Beyoncé meant nothing to me.

—Do you think she would like me? she asked once in the car as bearded men pounded on the windows on either side with their firearms. —I mean, if she met me?

Meanwhile every day a steady ticker tape of the day's dead: stray bullets killing mother on her front steps, toddler shot by older brother playing with dad's gun, road rage escalating to execution, failed news anchor shooting former colleagues on air, failed whatever killing ex-wife and her family and their kids, cop shooting unarmed black man in the back during a traffic stop, seventh grader shooting best friend in pre-algebra class, father mistaken for rival gang member shot on sidewalk, white supremacist sitting through entire service at a black church before taking out a Glock 19 equipped with a sixteen-round magazine and killing as many people as he could, then reloading and killing more...

That time for me was like being somehow shrunken down to the cellular level and injected into a human body—it could have been anyone's—right where the cancer is, and seeing the sickness breathing and eating and seething around me, tasting it, putting my hands on it, doing everything I could to try to stop it and nothing working.

I appeared in a video Jenny's marketing team produced, reading from cue cards she held up behind the camera, things she had written about what it was like for me being in that movie theater, what Kaylee meant to me and how in love we were, and what it was like having her die in my arms because of the NRA. Jenny did not know what Kaylee meant to me. No one did. Kaylee meant everything. Everything. But I could not remember her anymore. Now whenever I tried to remember her, all I could see was the picture I showed to men with all the money and power right before they told me there was nothing they could do. I did not even know whom I was talking about anymore when I said Kaylee's name. The reality— the real her, the real me, the real us—was gutted. I had gutted it. I should never have shown anyone her picture, I should never have told anyone about her neck, the heartbeat I thought was hers. I had turned Kaylee into something inhuman, I had desecrated her. I had desecrated myself. Because now I could not even remember Kaylee. I could not remember the girl I loved. I could only remember the politics, the men with guns. And Jenny.

Lawmakers stopped taking our meetings. Maybe now and again an aide with nothing better to do might come downstairs and meet us in the lobby, let me desecrate Kaylee for him, hear Jenny out about the science and the data and the tide, ensure us the administration was taking the issue very seriously before excusing himself.

—It's working! Jenny kept saying. —We're making progress! All we have to do is keep doing what we're doing and *not let up*!

Late one evening we sat around a table at headquarters, holding an all-night strategy session in advance of a big meeting (sleeping bags had been brought in for the staff), when Jenny began crying and did not stop. The little Jennys around us pretended not to notice. They said, —Thanks, Jenny! Thanks, everybody! and gathered their notepads and devices and scattered to their workstations, leaving me and her alone. I had never seen someone so lonely. Even her style of crying was lonely: hunched forward, curled small and tight into herself with her elbows on the table and hands over her face, shaking silently. I did not know what would happen. I watched her, the narrow hands with the veins sticking out and liver spots beginning to appear, her skinny frail wrists that looked anything but unbreakable, the strands of gray hair she had missed when she had dyed it herself in the bathroom of her hotel room.

—Jenny? I said. —Are you okay? She did not answer. I reached over, touched her shoulder. —Jenny?

—Get away from me! she yelled into her hands. —*Don't touch me!*

I jumped up and away, startled. I looked at the little Jennys. They pretended not to see. None of them looked away from her work. They just left her there at the table until they all went to sleep on the floor in sleeping bags. They turned the lights off on her. I covered her with a spare blanket. She was still shaking. Not crying, I realized. Shivering. Was I alone in seeing what it all was doing to her? That she lived on some kind of precipice and one day she would go over into the abyss, taking with her whoever happened to be holding on to her at the time? Would any of the others have believed me if I had told them Jenny Sanders, like any of us, was not the person she believed she was?

In the morning I woke to the sounds of Beyoncé. I found Jenny bouncing around with her disciples before a whiteboard, on which was written a day's full agenda. —We're making progress, Jenny shouted at me over the music.

I felt exhausted and useless. I told her I was done. She told me I needed to change my mind, but before long a former graduate student at a university in Washington State drove through campus in his Kia Sorento with a Sig Sauer semiautomatic pistol and a box of fully loaded sixteen-round magazines in the passenger seat (the gun and the bullets he had bought as part of the surge in guns and ammo sales resulting from Jenny's Battle of Texas), shooting at every woman and girl he saw, killing nine and paralyzing three and injuring twelve more before police could stop him. Jenny said good-bye via text from the airport as she boarded her flight to Washington. I tried calling her a few times over the next few months, but one of her little Jennys always assured me she was in a meeting or on a call or traveling and would absolutely call me back first chance. She never did. I never spoke to Jenny Sanders again. I saw her only on TV and in news stories like this I read now, today's shooting. Tomorrow will bring tomorrow's shooting, and like today's it will make me remember it all. All of it, that is, but Kaylee.

We're making progress! Keep doing what you're doing and don't let up! I did not understand Jenny's optimism in the face of completely contradictory facts until later, when hackers got into the RSA's servers and dumped its until-then-confidential financial and membership data and I learned for the first time how much money had been coming in to RSA during that time, how many new memberships, how the visibility of Jenny's movement grew like a second sun in the sky over the nation.

Victory at the Battle of Texas.

People ask me: *What is she like?*

I always answer: *There is nothing Jenny Sanders would not do to save us. Nothing at all.*

THE DOCTOR

They show up one day at his practice while he is in the middle of examining a ten-year-old boy with strep throat. Beefy bearded thugs with bleached teeth and Rolexes and firearms.

—We do not like your articles, they say, —we do not like your speeches.

He says, —Oh? Why not?

They say, —They do not give glory to God.

He says, —I do not know anything about God, I only know about treating people and their illnesses.

—The law says give all glory to God, they tell him, —you need to obey the law.

—No, he says, —I need more antibiotics.

—Recant all you have ever said and written, they say, —stop using Satan's medicine, disown science in favor of God's Scripture.

—I will not, he says.

They leave. A few days later he receives a letter from the state informing him his medical license is void and he must close his practice at once. He does not. The men with bushy beards and bleached teeth and Rolexes stand outside his practice informing all who approach that it is an unlicensed, ungodly facility and anybody caught receiving treatment here will be breaking the law and therefore arrested. Everybody knows what happens to those who are arrested. Still he treats patients at their homes, still he writes and still he speaks.

His colleagues admire him but also tell him he is foolish, suicidal, beg him to keep quiet. His wife tells him to keep going, that he is right. She tells him to not be afraid. He says, —I am afraid of no one and nothing and never have been. They are in bed when he tells her this. As soon as he does, they kick the door in and enter with guns, bandannas over faces, dusty civilian clothes, bulletproof vests. These are not the men with Rolexes and bleached teeth, these are men with darker skin and brown crooked or missing teeth; they speak a foreign language he has never heard before. They tie him to a chair in the bedroom, put the barrel of an AK-47 in his mouth.

—Are you the doctor? they say in his language but with very strange accents. He does not answer. —Are you? they say again. Through the greasy metal of the gun on his tongue he says yes, he is. They punch him, his teeth crack against the gun. —*Are* you? they say. He says he is and they hit him again and laugh, then turn their attention to his wife. They force him to watch everything. There are fourteen of them and each takes part. Their bodies reek of sweat and filth and the damp heat of the night outside.

When they are done with her they ask him again, —Are you the doctor? He can hardly speak. He whispers, —I am not the doctor. They leave.

All these years later now in New York, on wet nights in summer like that one, he will smell them all over again. He will be on the roof looking over the city, and the wind will bring him their smell and this new city will become that old city. He will be on the subway and it will be crowded and he will smell it wafting off the body of the man beside him, and at the next station he will force his way off the train and stagger along the platform to a bench, collapse on it, and sit huffing air, his head between his knees.

At the hospital they are afraid of him and will not treat her. They beg him to take her away, to forgive them. So he brings her back home, cleans and examines and treats her himself. Fourteen. Fourteen. There is little he can do but stop the bleeding and cauterize the tears and give her painkillers and sedatives from the illegal stash in the floor beneath the oven. He sutures her with the only thing he has, thread from her sewing kit. As he works she groans. She falls asleep and he puts one of her kitchen knives to his throat and pushes its point into the soft of his skin, puncturing it, dark blood trickling down over his Adam's apple to his chest, and is about to push it farther, but no, this is not the way, what will she do all alone?

The next night he puts her in traditional concealing garb the extreme religion of the regime commands its women wear and disguises himself as a cleric and they leave their home.

—Where will we go? she says.

He says, —I don't know. Maybe America. He thinks about it, then decides, —Yes. America.

—How will we get there? she says.

—I don't know. But we will. Have faith.

—You are not a man of faith, you are a man of science and fact and reason.

—I was. I do not know what I am anymore. I have nothing but you and, I suppose, if I want it, faith.

One of his patients tells him about a bus that will take them to the coast. It is carrying young, fashionable rich kids, foreigners on some kind of holiday trip. These passengers hide the former doctor and his wife beneath the luggage in the compartment below. She makes no sound at all over the eighteen-hour journey, though she must be in such pain. Then at the coast a cook on a tugboat sneaks them into his closet-sized quarters belowdecks, telling them if they are discovered the captain will turn them all in or just kill them all on board and throw their bodies in the water. He feeds them Coca-Cola and Pringles potato chips. They have nothing, not even a change of clothes. The cook has only two extra sweaters and two extra jeans and two extra pairs of socks, but he gives them to the former doctor and his wife even if it means he now has extra nothing. The former doctor never learns his name or why he helps them.

The tugboat takes them across the sea and out of the country. They sneak off the boat, and at a train station a woman buys them tickets and at the border a guard waves them through without checking their papers—maybe an oversight, but he seemed to look meaningfully into the former doctor's eyes—and six weeks later they are in a strange city in Europe, living in a homeless shelter under assumed names, safe from the reach of the regime. They are safe but it is a dead end—the American embassy refuses their requests for asylum. The former doctor looks for work of any kind. He does not speak the language here, knows no one. Buses tables at a café, washes dishes, sweeps and mops at a church, hauls debris at a construction site— they pay him in cash and food and not much of either. He teaches himself some of the language, asks people he works with about their lives, makes friends. Being friends with them and speaking to them teaches him more of the language. He is honest and works hard and people want to help him. The superintendent of the shelter lets him work as his assistant, teaching him the essential principles of repainting and derusting, the fundamentals of industrial cleaning and quick-fix plumbing. Unclogs toilets jammed with the shit and tampons of the homeless, mops their puke from the floor, kills rats the size of Komodo dragons, brings out the trash, shovels the snow, disrupts commercial fucking in nighttime stairwells. Medical school, residency, days-long shifts as a physician—these things have made him far more indefatigable than he realized and he is able to work and work, sometimes fourteen-hour days, earning a humble living for himself and his wife. The shelter is soon cleaner and runs better than it has since it opened thirty years earlier. Not a single burned-out lightbulb can be found, not one broken window or loose railing. He even plants a garden out front. The residents marvel at the paucity of vermin and bedbugs.

—Used to have to sleep with a sock stuffed in your mouth so nothing could crawl in it, one happy, toothless old man tells him, —but not anymore, not since you showed up.

The former doctor asks this man about the rattling cough he has, takes a look down his throat with his flashlight. Puts his ear to the man's pocked, crooked back and listens to him breathe. —Come with me, he says. Walks him quickly across town to the hospital, the emergency ward. —This man is dying of lung infection, he tells the nurse, who does not seem to like him because he is black and does not speak the language well, yet still has the nerve to insist and take charge. She makes them wait for four hours, the old man oblivious to the danger, watching the TV hanging from the ceiling and laughing at everything like a child. The former doctor returns to the nurse at her desk. He says, —Please. Antibiotics. Hurry.

She is impatient, yells at him like he is a dog. He waits until she is finished yelling at him like he is a dog, not understanding what she is saying anyway, then repeats himself in a calm and somber authoritative voice, the demeanor with which he spoke to his nurses and staff, which must push some button in her brain because her demeanor changes and she does what he has told her, she comes around the desk and takes the old man back into the examination area. Five minutes later she returns, bursting through the double doors, now white-faced and serious and moving very urgently, disappears through another set of doors, returns immediately tailed by a doctor. They both run through the first set of doors.

The next time the former doctor and the old man see each other, two weeks later in the hall of the shelter outside the showers, the old man has already put on weight and his cough is gone and his face has gained a lifeful ruddiness. Seeing the former doctor coming toward him, now a porter in musty coveralls on his way to attend to a wonky boiler, the old man does a little dance that ends with him lowering himself to his knees and kissing the feet of the former doctor and saying, —You save my life, you save it. This, the former doctor feels somehow, in a way he does not fully understand and cannot explain, but must believe, is the way to America.

She cooks the dishes from their home country in the shelter's kitchen; he trades them at the pub for bottles of wine and whiskey, makes friends with the people there. They connect him to two men who can help him, but it will require money. These men are from his home country, they fled the regime as well, they understand. He has money he has saved from working fourteen-hour days, gives it all to them, and they give him the papers. Triumphant, he takes them to the American embassy. They glance at the papers and order him arrested, hold him for four days in jail; they tell him he will be sent back to his home country. He does not tell them about his wife. He will be sent back and she will stay. He will be killed but she will live. As he is being led from the jail transport truck to the plane, his boss from the shelter arrives, tells the police he needs him, he is the hardest worker and most reliable, honest man he has ever known, he cannot be replaced, please, he begs them, and they let him go.

Works harder, replenishes his lost savings, gives it all to an American in a suit who is an attorney—processing fees for the necessary documents—never sees the American again.

Works even harder.

One night lying on their cots pushed together in the large, open public room beneath the fluorescent lights that never turn off, she in the crook of his arm with her face on his chest, now and again kissing her head and smelling her hair, stroking her back, thinking about that night again, she turns her face to his and her finger comes up to play with his lower lip.

—You have something to tell me, he says.

—How did you know?

—You always play with my lip like that when you have something to tell me.

—You know me well.

—I know you completely.

—You do, especially now, after.

—It's how I love you completely.

—You would love me more if it had not happened, if you did not have to see.

—I love you more because it did and because I did.

—But you cannot make love to me anymore.

—That will change.

—I am scared it won't.

—Don't be scared. What do you have to tell me?

—I think you know.

He is silent. Then he says, —Yes, I know.

She says, —All I have done is fail you.

—No, no, no, he says.

She says, —Will you fix it?

—I will.

—How?

—I'll find someone.

—I want it to be you.

—It can't be me.

—Why not?

—It can't.

Goes to the doctor's office located on a dark, wet, narrow road. The doctor is bent over his desk wearing a heavy wool cardigan sweater from Ireland. The doctor looks up, sees him, says to his nurse, —I'm seeing no more patients today.

—Don't snap at me, she says, —I know who you are and are not seeing, I make your schedule.

—I'm not snapping, I was merely stating.

—Well, then state what you would like me to do for him.

—Who is he?

—He lives at the homeless shelter.

—He wants money?

—No.

—He's drunk?

—No.

—How do you know he does not want money and is not drunk?

—Because the first thing he said to me when he walked in was: *I no want money and I no drunk.*

—Exactly what a man who is drunk and wants money *would* say.

—His wife needs treatment.

—What's wrong with your wife? the doctor says, addressing the former doctor. Before the former doctor can answer, the doctor adds, —Call emergency and they will take her to a hospital. What's wrong with him? He's just staring at me glassy-eyed.

The nurse says, —He doesn't know what you're saying, he doesn't speak the language.

The doctor snorts. —I wouldn't be surprised if there is no wife at all. Wife is likely just the closest word he knows in our language for what he means to say, which is that he is the pimp of a prostitute whose venereal disease is getting in the way of profits, so he expects me to fix it in exchange for God only can imagine what kind of depraved act so he may go back to peddling her and his ill-gotten profit stream may once again flow.

—Shame on you. That's not who this woman is and that's not who this man is and that's who *nobody* is.

—It is too.

—How do you know?

—I read the news. I pay attention.

—Who can imagine what this man's story is? You won't find out from the news. Think for yourself, Doctor. Think *of* yourself, back before you were a doctor, when you were a young man, a writer. Surely you were helped by people in the position you now find yourself.

—Maybe so, but I did not deserve it.

—And yet you still got it.

—Maybe so. But if that young man were to come to me now I would sit him down and chew him out until he saw how he was wasting his life. I started in medicine ten years behind my generation. I could have been a surgeon, I could have been a chief. But look, here I am instead, stuck in this dingy office draining pustules and fondling scrota and putting up with immigrant pimps trying to con me. Look at him now, what's he doing?

The former doctor is lowering himself to his knees. He has given landmark lectures to large theaters filled with thousands of doctors just like this one, each hanging rapt on his every word. He has mentored them, hired them, corrected them, improved them, supervised them, and, at times, fired them. He has fired dozens of doctors just like this one. A year ago, doctors like this came to him for advice, they groveled in his doorway and begged him for favors the way he begs now. —Please, he says in the language, humble and soft. The floor is cold and hard on his knees, and he is humiliated and he hates this doctor. —Please help me. Please.

The doctor shakes his head, exasperated. Now the former doctor is crawling across the floor on his hands and knees. Every cell in his being recoils but he still proceeds. The doctor flinches as the former doctor takes his hands in his own, begs. —Please. *Please.*

The doctor pulls his hands away. —Now that's enough of this nonsense. Leave at once before I call the police.

The nurse helps him to his feet and walks him out, holding him by the arm.

—Close the door behind you, the doctor says after them.

He visits every other doctor in the city. Every single one. None will do what he is asking them to do. It is against the law. There are, of course, disgraced physicians at the free clinic who could be convinced, but they are the types who could be convinced to do anything for money; he would never send her into a room with one of them. In learning how to ask them to do what he needs them to do, he picks up even more words and phrases in the language, becomes more conversant, which leads to more maintenance work beyond the shelter as does meeting sympathetic patients in waiting rooms overhearing him plead. Gets good contracts, becomes very busy. Develops a reputation as dependable, wizardly. Building owners fight over his services. He is making enough money to move himself and his wife into an apartment in one of the immigrant neighborhoods on the outskirts of the city. He thinks they could afford one with two bedrooms.

She is swollen and nauseated and depressed, cannot get out of bed. —Do something, she moans from the cot.

He says, —I'm trying.

—No, you're not, you're working, you're getting comfortable here, you're preparing for the baby, you want me to have the baby.

—I'm not, he says, not sure whether he is lying.

—You want me to have the baby and you want to stay here and raise it here.

—No, he says. He tries to think of more to say but only repeats, —No. Anyway we cannot stay here even if we wanted. Soon they will make us leave.

One night he finds a coat hanger among her things. —Please don't, please don't do that.

—If I have to I will, she says, —the clock is ticking and you're doing nothing.

—I am working on it. We'll find a way.

—How?

—I don't know. He kisses her damp head.

She says, —What do you think it looks like?

He says, —I don't think about it and neither should you.

—I can't help it, she says, —whenever I close my eyes I see it. She closes them. —There it is. The little demon. Hello, you ugly little disease. You are hairy like a chimp. Shit is smeared all over your mangy fur. One eye half closed, the other glassy and peering off sideways. You drool. Snot drips down your face. You've chewed through your own umbilical cord like a rat and suck my blood through it like a straw, that is how you feed. You feed insatiably. You shit and shit because you feed and feed. And then my whole womb is flooded with it. Instead of amniotic fluid you float and soak in your own shit. In your heart is only hate. You seethe and rip at the walls of my womb, you're so eager to get out and begin your wicked life of raping and ruining, just like your father. I see it all the time, I do not even have to close my eyes. And do you want to see what I do sometimes to help us?

She strikes at her belly with her fist.

—I do this.

She punches herself again. Before she can do it again he catches her wrist.

—You will have to do it, she says looking up at him holding her wrist.

He does not answer. He knows she is right.

—You know how, don't you? You've done it before?

—No, never.

—But you know how?

—Yes. I think so.

—How is it done?

—I won't tell you that. What matters is that it will be done.

—You will do it?

—It is either me or you, right?

—Right.

—Then, yes, I will do it.

He sets up in a secluded storage room in the basement. It is damp and dark and its door is kept chained shut; there are no security cameras, no one ever goes in. He has arranged several bright lamps. He searched for a proper table, but finding none he had to scrub the concrete floor with bleach and lay down plastic sheeting. He has bought gauze and rubber gloves and a surgical mask and gowns and antiseptics and a speculum and forceps and a thirty-centimeter-long sewing needle that he has sterilized. A plastic bucket sits empty. He scrubs his hands in the sink in the corner. She is lying on her back, silent. Her hands rest on her belly. He turns off the faucets using his elbows, comes over to her, clean hands dripping, holding the needle. Kneels before her as though in prayer. Spreads her knees apart. Her skin is so cold. In his other hand he holds a flashlight, shines it on her. He feels sick. Her belly rises and falls, rises and falls, its rhythm increasing.

—I love you, he says.

—I love you, she says.

She puts her forearm over her eyes, bares her broken teeth, grimacing. He begins to slip the needle in. Before he can, she sits up screaming. He drops the needle and the flashlight, holds her.

—What is it, are you hurt?

She is sobbing. —I lied before, she says, —I do not see a demon when I close my eyes. I see a boy, I see a little baby boy, I see our son.

She is walking down the street one afternoon when she becomes faint with hunger. Steps inside the first place she comes to, a pizza shop. The line moves slowly, she is getting more hungry, more light-headed; her face is icy, it is dire that she sit or she will faint. No empty seats. Lunchtime rush. Just in time a man notices her and stands to offer his seat, helps her into it. She takes it, feels much better, thanks him. He looks familiar. A little old man.

She says, —Where do I know you from?

He says, —I don't know if we've met.

—You look so familiar, do I look familiar to you at all?

—No, but tell me where you're from. She tells him. He says, —I've been there, it is beautiful, but a shame what has become of it.

She says, —Why were you there?

He says, —I was on a fellowship at a university.

—That is where I know you from. I was faculty there. We never met but I remember your lectures.

—Well! Of all the pizza places in all the cities in the world!

She tells him everything that has happened.

He is horrified, says, —Let me help you.

—How?

—Well, let me make some calls and we shall see.

He and his wife live nearby, they invite them for dinner. Martin and Monica are their names. Over dessert, Martin clears his throat and says, —I cannot tell you how moved I am by your plight. Monica has a cousin in New Jersey. He has agreed to sponsor you. We are working now to get you the documents you need. Once they come through, congratulations—you are going to America.

On the way home to the shelter after dinner, still stunned, giddy, he says to her, —You would never have met them if we had gone through with it.

She says, —Isn't it interesting? Everything is so beautiful.

He says, —I had forgotten, but yes, it is.

The papers come through. They are official, bearing all the right stamps and seals and watermarks. They take a taxi to the airport, board a plane, and suddenly they are standing in the United States. New Jersey is vast and new and clean. Monica's cousin is humorless and overbearing and expects them to go with him to a Christian church. Soon he resents them always being on his couch, the former doctor rubbing his wife's feet and feeding her macaroni and cheese, laughing, feeling their baby move in her belly.

The former doctor finds work as a porter for a nearby residential building. He does not want to become a doctor again. Now he is a handyman. In the blue distance from the rooftop he can see the skyline of New York City. That is where he wants to raise his son. Finds a better porter job there, in Manhattan, far uptown and hardly even on the island, but that is fine, and here he is, a New Yorker, married to a grand woman and with a son on the way. He loves walking down the perfect straight avenues passing American after fellow American, listening to all their languages, feeling the sun bouncing off the upper reaches of the gleaming towers down onto him, lighting his way through all that grit and pulp of striving, showing him all the free humanity, all the talent and opportunity and culture of the world distilled here and set loose, the whole spectrum of success and failure, goodness and immorality, beauty and ugliness, hope and despair. New York City, where you see a thousand faces a day yet know nothing about the people they belong to; there is an entire universe behind each one and so you must have faith in all people, you are forced to, the only other choice is to build walls around yourself and live afraid—what a fool is one who decides what is in another man's heart, what a vulgarian is one who ever presumes anything about anyone.

They live in Queens, an immigrant neighborhood on the outskirts, an illegal apartment: no electrical outlets, just a power strip stapled to the wall and leading to the apartment downstairs, no windows, no kitchen, they wash their dishes in the bathtub. The handyman makes sure she eats well— farm-fresh fruits and vegetables and premium meats and fish—but to save money he subsists on pasta and jarred tomato sauce. The manager of the building he maintains, Dave, tells him he also manages another building downtown in the West Village, a very high-end building; he needs a live-in superintendent on call around the clock seven days a week, would he be interested? He and she move out of Queens and into their new home, the basement unit of this building, down among its guts, with the trash and the rats and the laundry, exiled from the white people upstairs, but that is okay, it is a beautiful building in the heart of New York City—is there no end to their good fortune?

Their child is born. The handyman weeps when he first holds the swaddled fellow in his arms at the hospital, where one of his building's residents, a surgeon there, has arranged for them a private room. —He's so light, he keeps saying, —he weighs nothing, nothing at all, he's nothing to hold and nothing to be afraid of. Why were we ever afraid of you?

One of the first phrases the handyman learned to say in English upon arrival: *Tell me the story of your life.* He makes his new humble profession—often so exhausting and demeaning and stultifying—

tenable by chatting with the residents as he fixes their toilets and answers their beck and call. They are often unfriendly and unfeeling. Rather than resenting them he tries to see them as people who have experienced things he never has, who in pursuit of their success have known ups and downs, gains and losses, heartbreaks, humiliations, as he has, for everyone has, it is what we have in common with each other, and he likes to say to them as he sweats and grinds for them, *Tell me the story of your life*, then listens to them tell it and tries to feel it the way they have felt. Quickly he becomes respected and loved. They wave to him when they see him out on the street, invite him and his family to dinner, to parties, help him get loans and write him letters of recommendation.

When the new parents bring home their son the residents come through in a steady line, bearing gifts for the baby—a partner at the world's biggest law firm on floor six bearing a wardrobe of one-of-a-kind Hermès onesies, the Oscar-winning actor on sixteen bearing a custom-crafted crib made from two-hundred-year-old Bolivian wood—and Hector at the hardware store on the corner bearing diapers, other supers on the block bearing bottles and a high chair and a changing table, the owner of the drag queen bar one street over bearing a diaper pail—the entire city seems to want to meet the boy, help raise the son of the handyman they have come to love. The families of both the handyman and his wife are unreachable in that dark bloody world they have left so far behind, but the son nonetheless has a family. The handyman has nothing to one day pass on to him and probably never will—no money, no land, no pictures of relatives and ancestors, not even his own genes. All he can leave his son is his example.

They name him Clayton. Saw the name in the newspaper and liked it. The sleepwalking begins at age seven. No hardware is enough to keep him inside—he can undo any lock. It's as if, his wife says, he is trying to escape them. The handyman tries to mention it to the new residents after they move in. His wife makes traditional food from their home country, they bring it to them, welcome them, tell them about the building and Clayton's sleepwalking, tell them if it ever happens to not be afraid, simply call and he will come help Clayton back downstairs. Once an older woman, a cosmetic industry scion, forgot to lock her door and Clayton was able to enter her apartment. She found him in the morning curled on her sofa. She was forgiving, but the handyman was terrified of being fired and installed an alarm on his unit's front door. After three years without another episode, the batteries on the alarm ran out and the handyman never replaced them, and he stopped telling new residents about the sleepwalking.

None of the others know much about the man in the penthouse. Lee Fisher has lived there as long as the handyman has but they have never met. He seems to want nothing to do with anyone. The handmade dinner invitations the handyman's wife has left in his mailbox have all gone unanswered. The handyman never told him about the sleepwalking. Until recently the handyman has seen him only from afar, hustling out through the lobby to a waiting black Town Car. A woman lived with him for a short time, he believes. The residents below have complained of a baby crying. When there are repairs to be made in the apartment, Fisher always leaves or else locks himself in a back room and communicates through the door. The eccentricities of the rich, the handyman thinks. The idiosyncrasies of the brilliant and effective.

But one day when Clayton is fifteen, Fisher calls to report a leaking sink, and when the handyman goes up to fix it Fisher is waiting in the doorway, a short, pale, quite fat man with a gun on his hip, which is distracting, even alarming, and makes the handyman think he must be a police officer. As he begins to speak, Fisher cuts him off. —Please be quick, is all he says, then turns away and goes inside. The handyman goes inside to the sink, gets to work. Fisher stands across the room with his gun watching.

The handyman says, —I need part. I have downstairs. No problem. My son down there. I will call him, he bring part.

Takes out his phone, Fisher becomes very upset, yells at him, — Give me the phone! Give it to me! I said give it to me! Wrests it from the handyman's grip.

He says, —What's the matter?

Fisher says, —No photos!

—No photo, I call son, he brings part.

Fisher lets him use the phone to make the call but demands he turn it over to him after. The handyman does. He is sweating. He will be fired. He has had a fight with this rich white man, this police officer, and will now be fired and kicked out of America. This rich white man can crush him. They all can. Clayton comes, they fix the sink, get the phone back, and leave. Fisher closes the door behind them without a word. They hear his several heavy deadbolts clicking into place.

—Damn, Clayton says, —that dude a *dick*.

The handyman wipes the sweat off his face and laughs drily. He certainly cannot disagree.

(Sheeple II)

He wants to be a writer, a novelist, studies it at a university in Ireland. He will be a great writer. How does he know? Because something calls out to him from the sky telling him so. Reads, writes. No professors or editors think his work is as good as he does. But he keeps going. Rejection, rejection. Months, years, wasted at his desk with no apparent progress. Starving. Friends around him succeeding in other occupations. Writing begins to feel pointless. Absurd. Still he tries. Begins losing his mind. *It is not the work they are rejecting,* he decides, *but me. And it is not editors or magazines or the reading public rejecting me, it is the universe.* Will this be his life— poverty, pointlessness?

Thirty years old now. Nothing published. There is a con, a trick involved that he is not privy to. Something wrong with him. Tries writing some inartistic commercial bunk, cynical, but to make money and feel relevant. When the bunk too is rejected it adds a new degree of humiliation and self-loathing to the usual.

Thirty-two years old. Friends have five-year-olds, wives, one even has a vacation home. He feels like a five-year-old child himself. Why is he doing this? Why did he think he would be a great one? Cannot remember now. Cannot hear the thing calling out to him from the sky anymore. Quits writing, goes to medical school. A doctor is relevant to people. Makes a steady, unremarkable living as a general practitioner. He is not a great doctor by any stretch, but he has a five-year-old and a vacation home. Gets along. Life is gray. Sometimes it hurts, sometimes it does not. Often cannot recall details of days from a week ago. Moment-to-moment living. His heart beats, his wife stays, his car runs, his bills and taxes are paid. But he cannot shake a feeling that this is not it, this is not his real life. But everyone feels that way, do they not? A stupid feeling. Useless.

A pimp comes to his office, drunk, wants him to treat the venereal disease of one of his prostitutes. Nurse is pressing him on it. *Leave me alone,* the doctor says. *Not my problem.* Pimp buggers off. The doctor sits there thinking about it for a long while after. His nurse, when she was trying to convince him to help the drunken pimp, said, *When you were a young man, a writer, surely you were helped by people in the position you now find yourself.* He thinks, *Surely? No, I doubt that. No one helped me. I did not deserve help. Though,* he thinks but does not say, *there was the grocer. What was his name? Right around the corner from my little dungeon I lived in. How can I not recall his name? He would leave cans of food and bags of bread out on his back doorstep for me to come and take. Told the grocer,* I cannot pay you for this. *Grocer said,* Pay me when you write your first book and become rich and famous. Did not take the grocer seriously. Just a thing people say to would-be writers. But the grocer was otherwise a cheap, selfish businessman who never gave anyone else even a small one-time discount when times were rough. *If not for the grocer's help,* he thinks, *I would have starved.*

At the time he was ashamed about that, but now, sitting at his desk after the pimp has gone, he is very moved and appalled at himself for thinking he was on his own back then. He was not at all, he sees now. There were more. Suddenly they are so obvious. His friends who were always sure to invite him to their vacation homes for weekends to keep him company and give him a break from writing and relax with their families, who never teased him about his lack of success and never flaunted theirs—indeed, they always treated him as an exact equal, didn't they? They respected him for the sacrifice and dedication he had to writing. They inquired with sincerity about his work. When he went back to medical school and quit writing, the food stopped appearing on the grocer's back doorstep. The invitations to the vacation homes came less often. They stopped inquiring about his work. They respected him for being a doctor but not as much as they had respected him for being a writer. He did not need them anymore.

The universe had wanted him to be a writer, he sees now, after the visit from the pimp. It had helped him in every way. He should never have quit. Starts writing again. Sees fewer patients to give himself the time. Soon he is seeing zero patients and only writing. Life bursts into colors. The days are vivid and every detail sticks. The thing calls to him from the sky again. Sells his vacation home. Family okay with it, because he is clearly changed and they like being around this new man more than that bitter, unhappy one. Writes a novel. The decades of distance from the craft have made him a much more considerate writer. His writing now communicates directly and urgently with the reader in ways it never did when he was younger. First publisher who sees the novel accepts it. When it is published the reading public is agog. This great writer appearing fully formed from nowhere. Writes another novel. It's even better. Writes a third and it's better yet still. Astounding, unprecedented: three great novels in a span of seven years. Buys back his vacation home. Invites his friends who have suffered financial catastrophes and divorces and cataclysmic injuries and have therefore lost their vacation homes they once invited him to and have lost much of what they once had when they were younger and are as poor now as he was at thirty-two. Respects them, helps them. Locates the grocery store. It is still there, owned by the same man, who is under pressure because a national chain opened across the street, it will drive him out of business. Needs a lot of money to save his business, but no one will give it to him, because he has never helped them even with small discounts in times of trouble. But he gives it to him, saves him. Throws in a little extra for all the food he owes him for, from two lifetimes ago. Hollywood is making a movie of his first novel and gives him money and it is a tremendous amount of money, and he gives it to the homeless shelter where he remembers his nurse (now his research assistant) saying that drunken pimp was living at the time he wandered in out of the blue and changed his life. The pimp is of course long gone by now. He wonders what became of him.

An American judge reads his third novel in translation. He has read them all but this one is his favorite. The judge is an immigration judge, in New York City. The novel is about a husband and wife who escape war and certain death in their home country by coming to America on falsified papers. They live in America for fifteen years, illegally, raising a son. They are good citizens and contribute to society, but are found out, go before a judge who has no choice, he must send them back. The judge reading the novel stays up all night after finishing the final page, sick with the injustice of it. If he were in that position he would find a way to let them stay. There is always a way. Should such a family ever come before him in that scenario, he vows, he will not send them back. He will find the one way. He will protect them.

THE GUARDIAN OF THE FLOCK:

PART I

THE EDUCATION OF BOO RADLEY

Lee cannot wait to get away from his father and the mountain and become a police officer in New York—but to get his inheritance, he must first at least attend college. His mother says he should go to the school in New York she went to and his father went to and everyone else in the family went to, it is an excellent school, very prestigious. His father does not understand the appeal and derides the city and the school, but these days he does not fight for anything, so he gives in and agrees to pay for it. Lee applies and his grades are not good and neither are his test scores or his essay—but they accept him.

As Lee heads out the door to the taxi waiting to take him to the little private airstrip, his father calls derisively from his recliner in the living room, —*Have fun*—and that is it for farewell. And he leaves the mountain, flies to New York. The occasion calls for his nice shirt, the one with a collar, and the newer of his jeans. On the plane he sits there peering out the window from beneath the low brim of his Remington cap, clutching his military-issue backpack on his lap. The flight attendant tries to take it but he will not let her. One of the two other passengers on that small private plane arranged by the family company is a bald man with a mustache wearing a suit. He seems amused by Lee. He leans across the aisle.

—First time to New York, Lee?

Lee says nothing. How does he know his name?

—Don't be nervous. Nothing to be scared of. I've lived there all my life and I'm still alive, aren't I? He laughs, slaps Lee's knee, stands up, goes to the restroom, and never comes out.

After a while the other passenger, a woman, goes to the door and knocks. There is no answer. She looks to Lee, who stands and comes over. He knocks on the door, calls, —Sir, sir. He tries the door. It is unlocked. He opens it. The man falls out, right on top of the lady's fancy shoes. She apologizes to the man, kicks his body away, and hurries past Lee back to her seat. Lee stands there staring down at the man's open eyes, his meaty face pulled back revealing small gray square teeth in his mouth. Lee cannot move. The flight attendant comes, pushes him out of the way, and performs CPR. She looks up at Lee with the man's blood on her lips like she has been feeding on it.

—Gone, she says.

Lee's legs give out and he collapses into the nearest seat.

—Help me with him, she says.

He can only shake his head no.

—Come on, get his feet.

Lee keeps shaking his head no, unable to speak. She sighs and drags him off herself to the rear of the plane. Lee has his hands over his eyes. Through the space between his fingers he watches the soles of the man's shoes recede down the aisle.

He lands at another private airstrip somewhere in the middle of nowhere. An ambulance and a black car are waiting on the runway. He gets into the black car, and as it drives off he can see them loading the dead man into the ambulance. The driver asks how his flight was and Lee says, —That guy died on it. The man says, —Oh, and does not ask him any more questions.

He calls his father from the car to let him know he arrived okay and to tell him about the dead man, but his father does not answer, so he calls his mother, but it's the middle of the night in Africa so she does not answer either. Gets to Manhattan, finds his dorm. Everybody is fancier and more sophisticated than he can ever hope to be. He drags his duffel across the floor of the lobby to check in with the girl with the clipboard. She towers over him. Her arms are the size of his thighs. Metal piercings all over her face. Purple hair. Behind her he sees two girls holding hands. Holding hands. In public. Like they are boy and girl. And nobody seeming to care.

The RA does not even ask how his flight was, but he tells her anyway. He tells her about the man dying and how Lee performed CPR on him but it was no use, and how he dragged the man off to the back of the plane and put a blanket over him, and how the flight attendant was breaking down but Lee helped keep her calm and hold it together. The RA stares back at Lee blankly until it is clear he is done talking, then says, voice flat, —Yikes, and gives him a name tag with his name spelled wrong. He asks her to point him to the nearest McDonald's for dinner. —Ew, she says automatically.

He finds his room. His roommate has yet to arrive. Lee looks around at the white cinder block walls still dotted with bits of tape holding down the remnants of the previous occupants' wall hangings. The old gray carpeting has other people's stains still in it. He closes the door, locks it, takes off his backpack and places it on one of the beds, checks the door again to make sure it is locked, opens the backpack, and takes out the gun. It looks different here—smaller, older. Holding it in his hand makes it feel like his father himself is here, making a fool out of Lee. He has the sudden impulse to get rid of it, throw it out the window or bury it somewhere. The impulse is dispelled when there comes a knock on the door. Lee stuffs the gun under the bed's mattress, unlocks the door, opens it a crack. It is a girl, Chinese or something. She is beautiful. He feels his face turn red.

—Dorm meet and greet downstairs. Come get to know your neighbors!

He says okay and she smiles and leaves, and he closes the door, plugs in his portable stereo, plays his favorite album. The music makes him feel normal, stable. Can she hear it? Does she like it? Does she like him? His heart sinks when his roommate arrives with about eight hundred of his closest relatives. He knows who he is. He has never met him before, but that doesn't matter. Mr.

Fake. He is a tall prep school jock named Garrett wearing a blazer, for crying out loud, and is tan with broad shoulders—no doubt from the crew team—and he has perfect white teeth he seems to want to show Lee first before showing him anything else. He hates this person.

—Great to meet you, Lee. Garrett cocks his head and gestures to the ceiling to signify the music. —This is hilarious, what is it?

Lee feels his face get red again. He turns off the stereo and sits on his bed as Garrett's family trickles out, Garrett murmuring to them, —Ciao, ciao.

Then it is just the two of them. Lee watches Garrett looking at himself in the mirror, fixing his hair, obsessing over himself. It is quiet and awkward and Lee feels like that is somehow his fault, and Garrett is taking off the blazer and pulling down his pants and taking off his underwear and Lee looks away but not fast enough. Garrett says as he changes, as if he's not standing there bare-assed in front of another guy, —You going to that thing downstairs?

—No, Lee says.

—Why not? Might be girls there, you know? That one organizing it sure will be. You see her? That Asian one? Tits are kind of small, but she's cute.

Lee recoils, offended. —I got things to do around here.

—Like what?

Lee thinks it's none of Garrett's business and almost tells him so, but instead mumbles about unpacking and setting up his meal plan.

—Okay, well, if you change your mind, Garrett says. He clicks his tongue twice and leaves.

When he has gone, Lee sits on the bed staring at his stereo, hating it, and at Garrett's suitcase where it stands against the wall. He wants to drag it out into the hallway and leave it there. He tries his father again. Still no answer. He thinks about his mother. He hears fathers' voices and mothers' voices out in the hall and wishes they were his father's and his mother's. He lies on the bed, atop the gun, lies there listening to everybody. Waves of laughter and clapping rise up to his window from the courtyard below. *Nobody knows you here,* he tells himself. He sits up. He goes downstairs.

In the hall and stairwell he passes other students and their parents. The daughters look as old as mothers and the mothers look as young as daughters. The sons are all the same as Garrett. Everyone is browned and slim after a summer spent on quiet white beaches. —Howdy, Lee says softly to them. They glance at him, not sure if he has spoken, surprised to see a guy like him here at this renowned institution, sensing as well as he does that he does not belong here. He tugs at his nice shirt, his good jeans. Suddenly they feel so tight and rotten. Like he is wearing the clothes of a corpse. He can hardly breathe in them.

Outside he follows the hooting and hollering, finds a small crowd of people around the corner standing between his dorm tower and the neighboring one, fellow students including Garrett and the girl who invited him all gathered around a stepladder. A guy is climbing it, laughing nervously. The group chants something Lee cannot make out. The guys stands atop the ladder, turns so his back is to the group. The guy spreads his arms out and addresses the sky, his voice breaking, —My name is Steve? And I hate my father! The group cheers and chants, —Steve! Steve! Steve! and he sticks his tongue out of his mouth and screws up his face, leans back off the ladder, into the air, and drops. Before he can crack his skull and die, the group puts its hands up and catches him, eases him to the ground on his feet and high-five him, hug him.

The girl says, —Who's next? Come on, you guys, don't be scared!

No one is stepping up. Lee makes eye contact with her and puts his hand up and she smiles, and Lee's feet are heavy but he forces them to move forward. The crowd parts to make way. Lee is buzzing. Everybody watching him, watching him. Garrett drapes an arm over his shoulder like they are the best of bosom buddies and guides him to the ladder. —Know what to do? Just climb up, tell everybody who you are, then say a secret and fall.

—Say a what now?

—It has to be something you've never told anybody.

—I can't think of one.

—Don't think about it, just let it come out.

—What was yours?

Garrett says, —Nuh-uh, I can't tell you that, dude. You weren't here. You have to be here. That's the point. To *be* here. We're *here* for each other. Get it?

Lee climbs the ladder. He spreads his arms out wide. He knees shake. His fingertips tingle. He is giggling, giddy. —My name is Lee Fisher! he cries out in a wobbly voice. —And...

He does not think, he lets it come out.

—... and I might seem like just a normal regular kind of guy. But I'm just as rich as all of you.

His souls bursts from his chest. And he lets himself fall into the arms of these strangers. They set him upright on his feet. It feels good—nobody seems to care about what he said, and he makes eye contact, and nobody looks away.

—Nice! says Garrett, putting an arm around Lee and walking off with him. —Hey, man, that Asian girl? Sam? She's into you.

—No way.

—She totally is. She told me. I think you should go for it. There's a party tonight. She'll be there.

He looks over at Sam, imagining her and him in love; he is smiling, unable to stop, his face aching it is so unused to smiling, his whole body tingling it is so unaccustomed to being happy.

But later when Lee arrives at the party, Garrett has Sam cornered and is talking her ear off, oblivious to how bored she clearly is. Lee keeps going up to them and standing there like a moron, waiting for Garrett to take a hint and get lost, but Garrett never does, he just pretends to be oblivious to Lee's presence and keeps on talking to Sam, who keeps exchanging knowing looks with Lee. *Save me from him!* she seems to be saying. He tries, he really does, but it's no use, and after a while he can barely keep his eyes open any longer, it's been such a long day, and he decides the hell with this and leaves, waving good-bye to Sam, who waves back.

Hours later when the birds outside are beginning to chirp, Garrett returns to the room. He is very drunk, wakes Lee up.

—It was sideways, he says, —just like they say.

—What was? Lee sits up. —*What* was?

Garrett cackles. —I'm just kidding.

Lee says, —What the hell was that, man?

—What was what?

—Why did you tell me she liked me?

—I said that?

—Yeah, you said that.

—Huh, I don't remember.

—You lied to me.

—Hey, if there was a misunderstanding—

—There wasn't. You lied.

—This is stupid. I don't care about some girl. If you like her, I'll stay out of the way. I mean it. She's yours. I'd much rather we get along.

—Okay, Lee says, thinking about it. —Thank you.

Garrett shrugs. —Hey, something I wanted to ask you, by the way: Are you really super rich?

Lee does not answer.

Garrett says, —Because we were talking about it and—

—Y'all were talking about me?

—Just how funny you were. It was funny. What you said was funny. Lee does not believe him but Garrett says, —So are you?

Lee thinks about it and says, —Maybe like money-wise, yeah, I guess.

Garrett laughs and says, —*Like money-wise.* Where'd you say you were from again?

—Nowhere. You wouldn't know it. Garrett, listen, can you maybe not talk about that. I shouldn't have said it. I was just nervous. I feel so daggone dumb, opening my big mouth like that.

Garrett laughs. —*So daggone dumb.* I like you, dude. You're all right.

—Because that's not who I am.

—I know it's not. Don't worry about it.

He lets Garrett convince him to go with gaggles of dorm mates to brunch in the East Village and he manages not to embarrass himself. He goes with Sam to record stores and head shops and clothing stores; she picks out a pair of crazy blue sunglasses that she says look good on him so he starts wearing them. She shows him how to get a fake ID from Chinatown, and he goes along with groups of other freshmen to bars, he gets drunk, pukes, is a part of things. Garrett brings girls back to the room, and Lee lies in bed listening but only for signs of rape so he can intervene if necessary and protect them. He thinks of Sam—a girl like her wouldn't do what these girls are doing. He goes to parties in the dorm where Sam is, the girls are dressed like professional women in their thirties and the boys like people on MTV. They talk about politics and things—they're all liberal, of course—and he sits in a chair in the corner just listening to all the dumb liberal things they say, biting his tongue lest he say something that makes everybody mad, not understanding their jokes, feeling like everyone is making fun of him, though he keeps telling himself it's not true and that they are not even talking about him, and sometimes he finds himself in the middle of four or five people standing around talking and he'll screw up the courage to say something, and not only will they not be outraged by what he says and not think he's dumb and not make fun of him, but sometimes they even agree with what he says and seem to like him, or at least not mind his being there, and sometimes when he is talking to Sam he can tell she wants him to kiss her but he never can, he never can. Not yet.

One night after a party where he spent the whole time looking for Sam who never showed, he returns to his room and there she is, just leaving. —Howdy, he says.

—Oh hey, Lee.

—Good timing.

—What do you mean?

—You probably thought you missed me but here I am.

She does not seem to know what he's talking about and then Garrett opens the door and he is sweaty, his face is red. And then Lee can see the sweat on Sam's upper lip, the dampness around her hairline, and he turns and leaves without saying anything and throws away the stupid blue sunglasses. Over the following days, he tries to forget all about Sam and stops talking to Garrett, who keeps asking him, —What's wrong? What's wrong? as if he does not know, as if he doesn't just want to hear Lee say it.

Later that week Lee goes into his room thinking Garrett won't be there because he has class, but he is there and Sam is there and they're on Lee's bed, kissing. Garrett has his hand up her shirt and his tongue practically down into her stomach. Humiliated and furious but somehow managing to stay calm, he asks them to please get off his bed and Garrett tells him to give him ten more minutes, but Lee loses control and cries out hell no, what the hell's wrong with his own bed, or maybe he's broken the springs on it? And Garrett plays dumb, so Lee tells Sam about Garrett, all his girls, how he does not care about women, does not respect them, he will do it with anyone, he'd stick it in the gas pipe of a car and probably has, can't she see that Garrett is a disease-ridden creep who is just using her, can't she see that she means nothing to Garrett but everything to Lee? Garrett tells him to leave, but why should he have to leave? She's the one who should leave. He tells her to go. —Just go on ahead and get out of here, he says. —Because you broke my heart. You broke it. But then he changes his mind and says, —Know what? I *will* leave. You don't want a nice guy who respects you, what you want is an ape, so why don't you stay and enjoy your ape.

He leaves, stays away for hours, and when he returns Garrett and Sam are gone but right away he knows someone has been through his things. There is a letter on his desk. *Mr. Fisher,* it says. *Concerns. Anonymous reports. The welfare and safety of our students. Report to administration first thing in the morning,* it says. Lee realizes he has not breathed for some time and inhales. Not safe here. Not safe. Opens the door, pokes his head out quickly, the way they trained him back home on close-encounter warfare. All clear. Closes the door, locks it. Takes off his backpack, places it on the desk, opens it. He'd brought his gun with him today on impulse and good thing. It looks back up at him from inside the backpack like a stowaway pet. He zips up the backpack again but not before throwing more things into it: a change of clothes, rations, water. Essential. Then he hurries back out into the darkening city, a man alone in a hostile, soulless metropolis.

Wanted. An outlaw. Head down and hurrying, Lee checks into a hotel, paying cash and giving a fake name.

That night he stays up sitting on the floor of his room against the wall opposite the front door, the gun in his hand. It is silent out in the hallway. The streets too, even with their car horns and screams, are silent. Now and again there is an airplane passing thousands and thousands of feet overhead, making slow-motion noise, like a giant marble rolling overhead along an intergalactic wooden track that spirals down, down, ending atop the hotel, crashing down into the center of his skull. In a million years they will find him beneath the rubble, encased in mud. But even with the airplanes it is silent. He points the gun at the door, cocks the hammer. Places his finger on the trigger. He inhales, blood filling with oxygen, life. He exhales, pulling the trigger.

Click.

Click. Click.

He focuses on the sights, not the target behind the sights. Inhale, exhale: *click.* He's missing to the right. *Don't get down on yourself...* try tightening *up that right hand, kind of push against the gun with it, kind of brace against it on that side.* Inhale, exhale. *Click. That's it. That's it, Lee. Beautiful. Outstanding.*

You and that gun were made for each other.

He reports to the office. —Lee Fisher here to see the Ministry of Truth, he tells the lady. She does not understand. He shows her the letter. Her mouth tightens. —Right, she says. She shows him a seat to sit in while he waits to be thrown out of school. Why wouldn't they throw him out? What is he worth to them, to anybody?

But the meeting in the conference room consists of people talking about him as if he is not there. He understands some of them are lawyers and that some of the lawyers are his lawyers. His lawyers talk about all his family has done for the school, they talk about money, buildings. Throughout the meeting, a man with a buzz cut and university polo shirt glares at Lee across the table. It is decided that they will not throw Lee out of school, but he must leave student housing. They say, —How does that sound to you, Lee? and he says,

—Maybe I don't want to stay here, maybe I just want to leave this place altogether and never come back. I could if I want. And they say, —Do you want to do that? And Lee says no, he doesn't, he'll stay.

The matter is resolved and everyone stands up and pushes in their chairs and Lee does the same. At the door, Buzz Cut grabs Lee's wrist to stop him. He has yellow teeth, almost orange like a beaver's. His eyes are blue and almost unblinking. Pulls something out of his pocket and pries Lee's fingers open and places it into his palm and folds his fingers closed again and holds them shut.

—Where'd you hide it? Huh?

Lee pulls his arm away and does not look at what is in his hand until he is outside in the open air. A rag. The one he uses to clean the gun.

—Don't touch me, Lee says out loud to no one. He heads back to his hotel room.

He thinks of his father. He misses him very much. A good man, his father. He can see that now. A man's man. Capable and principled and willing to fight and die for his country's values. A patriot. They are not like that here. Here they have no values, here they believe in nothing except maybe behaving yourself, fitting in with the crowd. They are willing to fight and die for nothing. You cannot trust people like that. That is not how to be. His father is how to be. How lucky to be raised by him and not Garrett's father, because what values does Garrett have? He's a fraud, a backstabber. Slime. Everyone here is slime. Everyone but Lee Fisher.

Moves into an apartment. Uses family money. Just a little something, Fisher men do not need much, just a little peace and space to be one's self and believe the right things. It is small and quiet in a building with closed-circuit cameras and a doorman. In that apartment he has nothing but a mattress on the floor and a little television and a radio on which he plays loudly and proudly his *hilarious* music—*Ha, ha, Garrett! Ho ho!*—and his few clothes and a big US flag he had to order from a catalog because apparently the one thing you cannot find in New York City is a daggone American flag. And he has the gun. Keeps it now under his pillow. Eats McDonald's proudly, defiantly. Every day, McDonald's. Two times a day. Sometimes three. He luxuriates in each bite, moaning with pleasure. And, except for the night when he hears something outside his door—voices or footsteps of a stranger, someone rattling the knob trying to get in— except for that night, Lee Fisher sleeps like the dead.

Begins wearing a cowboy hat, the kind they wear back home on the mountain. Orders it from the same place he got the flag. Great big kiss-my-ass hat. Goes to class wearing it on his head, the other students make fun of him for it behind his back. They cannot comprehend the hat. A cowboy hat is not in line with the rules they follow, it does not gibe with their picture of the world, so they mock him, roll their eyes. *What a fool!* they say. The irony!

His history professor complains to the Ministry of Truth about him always interrupting his lectures to point out the entrenched left-wing distortions and institutionalized intellectual provincialism— for example that the War of Northern Aggression—or, as it's known on the coasts, the Civil War—was about anything other than states' rights. The rule is to not challenge, but Lee challenges. He will not sit back and be mindless. The history professor asks him to stop coming to class until he is ready to be a nondisruptive presence and Lee laughs in his face and says never.

They move him out of that history class and into another one, so he drops history, replaces it with physics. The physics professor is a Soviet who too resents Lee Fisher and his cowboy hat and his self-determination. He is not surprised to find so much in common between college professors and a Soviet. The Soviet dismisses everything Lee says in class, returns his papers with no comments or evidence of having read them aside from the letter D on top, does everything he can to make Lee feel like a third-class citizen. On top of that the Soviet is always calling out the wrong chapter to read for the next class. The quiz is always on a whole other chapter and Lee invariably fails it. The other students have no problem with the dysfunction, apparently, for they all mysteriously pass the quizzes. When they offer their comments the Soviet takes their comments seriously. Their papers are returned covered in ink, wrinkled and coffee stained from three readings, four readings. The Soviet, Lee surmises, may be some sort of foreign saboteur, sent by the KGB to wreak havoc on the physics educations of American students, to give Mother Russia a future scientific and military advantage. And the other students are all part of a cheating operation but are excluding Lee because of who he is and where he comes from, because he has the gall to be different, to think for himself in this day and age.

He fails yet another quiz and has had enough. Asks himself who he is, what kind of man. He stands up, closes the textbook, and, feeling the hard grip of the gun against his ribs in its underarm holster beneath his shirt, struts down to the front of the lecture hall where the demented old man hunches over his desk, gathering his papers.

—Howdy, Lee says, friendly, and tells him some ideas he has for improving the class, one of which is assigning the correct chapters to read for the quizzes from now on.

The Soviet looks up at Lee. He looks at him like he has no idea who he is or where he appeared from. He has only one eye and it takes in Lee's hat, his boots, his jeans, his double-breasted work shirt, and Lee can see the laughter in his eye, the derision. The eye settles on the textbook Lee carries in his hand and the Soviet says, —What is that book?

—It's your textbook, Lee explains patiently, raising his voice in case he is deaf too. —The one you wrote. The one we use for your class.

The Soviet looks astonished. Does he even remember writing it? Does he even know his own name? Then the Soviet chuckles, shakes his head, and says, —Let me explain something to you: you are idiot.

Lee says, —Now hold on—

—It's okay, the Soviet says, cutting him off, —you are young, you supposed to be idiot. That is why you are here. To learn from me how to stop being idiot.

Lee's father steps beside Lee. A big, strong, warm presence. *Ring his bell, son,* he says. *Go on.*

—Idiot? Lee says. —Now let me explain something to *you.* We might not be fancy where I come from, but when we write a textbook you bet your ass we assign the right chapters to read.

—Where you come from. Where you come from is past. Past does not matter. What matters is now. Now and future.

Lee takes a breath to keep his composure. —Where I come from ain't no past.

—It is prison.

—It ain't a prison either. And I don't appreciate you referring to my heritage that way. Who do you think you are? What's *your* heritage? Communism? Mass murder?

The professor is coming around the table now. He steps up to Lee, sticks his finger into Lee's chest, inches from the grip of the gun. He is six or seven inches taller than Lee, forty or fifty pounds heavier. He could step on Lee. He could crush him into the carpet and leave him for the janitor to scrub out. Lee looks up into the Soviet's dark hairy nostrils.

—You are not the biggest fool I have had for student, says the Soviet, —but you are close. The Soviet's breath steams Lee's face. —Do you know what number one important thing is? Not just in science but in life?

—Yes, I do, Lee says. —Access to firearms.

—No! Number one important thing is to never be tied to past! To never think you are right just because you follow past! To never put anything—anything—above inquiry, curiosity! To never make assumption about people! To never be afraid of unknown! Because the unknown is life! That is life! And the past is death! It is prison!

—That's more than one thing, Lee says.

—Are you understanding me?

—Hell no, I ain't got the slightest idea what you're raving on about.

The Soviet chuckles, nods, puts his finger to his own lip as though conceding defeat. —This is what I talk about. Look: you come, you make observation. Professor say chapter two, I read chapter two, quiz not on what I read. Yes? Okay. Observation, with unknown cause. Then you make *assumption*: professor is making mistake. No data! Now you are in prison. Try instead to collect data. Ask question. Question gets you out of prison! Go ahead.

—I ain't never been in prison, Lee says, —nor will I ever be. I'm a law-abiding citizen.

—Go, ask. Take it for the spins. See how much better life is when you stop being idiot making assumption about unknown and start asking question of unknown.

Lee feels the weight of the gun on his body. —If this were back home, he says, voice high pitched, —I'd take you out back and knock you sideways.

—There is no back home, says the Soviet. —And there never was.

Lee scoffs. —You're out of your mind.

The Soviet is now saying, —Come, ask question.

—Fine, here's a daggone question for you. How can I be expected to learn anything when you keep giving us the wrong chapter to read?

—Ah! Excellent first inquiry! Here is maybe a data point. The Soviet takes the book from Lee's hand, holds it up to Lee's face. — This, he says, slapping the cover, —what is it saying?

—It says *Applied Principles of Physics*.

—And what is edition?

—Edition two.

—Hmm, interesting data so far! Now here is question for *you*: Do you wish to learn obsolete theory of physic or current theory of physic?

—Current, obviously.

—And do you consider obsolete theory worth your time and moneys?

—Of course not.

—Aha!

—So what the hell then? I have an old version of the book or something?

—Perhaps a good focus of future study.

—Why don't you just tell me? Why won't you help me?

The professor raises his voice. —I *am* helping you. What do you think I do? I help you now more than anyone ever help you before.

—What do you know about me?

—I know enough, the professor says, lowering his voice again into a near whisper, gently reaching down and touching Lee's gun through his clothes. Lee recoils and runs away, out of the lecture hall, clutching the gun on his ribs like he has been stabbed there.

Goes straight to the registrar's office and tells the woman behind the desk, a black woman, not that he notices that, —I wish to inform you that the Russian allegedly teaching my physics course is a vicious, incompetent sociopath. I want him removed from the campus. I want him removed from the country.

She is unmoved, says without looking up from her work, — Sounds like you have Dr. Petrov.

—He disparaged my heritage. He said my past is a prison. Lee means it to resound as a powerful, devastating indictment of the man that sets the office aflame with indignation, triggers an earthquake of justice—but it sounds only like a child whining.

—He would know about prisons, the woman says, —he spent years in a gulag.

—The point is I don't have to put up with someone making me feel badly about myself.

—No? she says. —Why?

He wants to pull out the gun and say, *This is why*. Instead he says, —Because I don't. I don't need any of this. So, you know what? Why don't you just go ahead and drop me.

—Fine, have it your way.

—I will, thank you.

She reaches for some forms. —What would you like to take instead?

—No, I mean drop me completely. Drop me from the school. I quit.

He turns and leaves, shoving past the guy in line behind him, another insufferable snob, another cold, frivolous person.

When he returns to his apartment the family attorneys are already calling, telling him the university is begging him to reconsider. He asks them would he still get his inheritance if he does not reconsider and they say, —Yes, you will, so he says he will not reconsider, he is done reconsidering.

Leaves New York, flies home. They can have New York. May New York sink into a pit. In the cab from the airport going home he looks for the mountain in the distance but cannot see it through the overcast wintry day. The driver pulls up to a trailer standing alone in the middle of a field along the edge of, well, a pit, and says, —Okay, sir.

Lee says, —What's this? Where are we?

The driver says, —This is the address.

—Where the hell is the mountain? What's this hole?

The driver looks at him as though trying to figure out if he is kidding. —Ha ha, he finally says. —Right.

Lee gets out and knocks on the door of the trailer. His father opens it. —How's the gun, is it safe?

Lee says, —What the hell's going on?

—What do you mean?

—Where's the damned mountain at?

—This is it, his father says, confused, waving his arm around. The trailer is rotten with filthy food, flies. He is drunk. He is very drunk. His face is red and bloated from being drunk all the time. It looks like he has gained eighty pounds in the month Lee has been away. He looks like he will die.

Lee has to look it up to figure it out. Far underground beneath the mountain things shifted suddenly and drastically. They had never seen rock and dirt shift so suddenly and drastically. Because rock and dirt never have and never will. This was not rock and dirt. This was trash. From the tip of the mountain to nearly a mile below the surface of the earth— trash. The mountain was not a mountain and never had been, according to what Lee reads. Someone some time ago had the wicked idea of profiting off his overstuffed landfill by selling it as a God-made mountain to some fool and that fool was Lee Fisher Sr. of the industrial Fisher dynasty of the Upper East Side of Manhattan, the article purports. Over time, the decomposition and disintegration of the trash created a vacuum of space. And then, the article claims, one day three weeks ago, in a matter of hours all that trash was sucked down into the sinkhole, the entire house and land with it.

The stink. It all seems to be part of the same worldwide conspiracy against Lee Fisher.

Lee stays a few days in that little trailer with his father, but soon it becomes apparent there is no room for him. And it still irks him that they got the best of him in New York. That he let them get to him. *No*, he thinks. *I ain't done with New York. I got every right to live there. They can't just chase me off. Besides, where else do I have to go?* Late one morning while his father sleeps, Lee puts the gun in his waistband and leaves, returns to New York City.

$\left(\text{Sheeple III}\right)$

Garrett's roommate, Lee, was okay, but he acted like his worldview was already fully formed at eighteen years old and there was nothing anyone could tell him about anything. Those things made it hard for people at college to know what to make of him or how to interact with him. Plus the way he dressed you would have thought he was always just returning from digging a ditch or something. Until this summer Garrett looked the same way as Lee. It's just how people dress where he and Lee come from. They come from the same county out in the middle of the country. That's probably why the housing people put them together. But at Garrett's high school graduation party in his backyard, one of the rich guys in town, Mr. Hedlund, who owns most of the local Burger Kings and whom his father does some work for, shook Garrett's hand, slipping five hundred dollars into his palm, and told Garrett how damned proud of him he was for getting into that school but that if he showed up in New York looking the way he did, wearing jean shorts and a camouflage T-shirt, he would never stand a chance, they would laugh him right off the island.

Garrett went to the mall, bought all new clothes, the girls who worked there oohing and aahing as a new person began to emerge in the mirror. He went to the fancy salon to splurge fifty dollars on a haircut. When he was through he looked like someone who deserved his place in that school, who belonged in New York. When he arrived in his dorm room on move-in day, the first thing he did was look at himself in the mirror, to make sure that new person was still there, that he had not faded away on the flight over.

Lee had already moved in; he sat alone on the edge of the bed he had claimed watching Garrett look at himself. Lee had a frayed and faded cap that said REMINGTON on it pulled down over his eyes, and he was unshaven and shabby and wore old, baggy jeans and steel-toed boots with mud all over them and an overwashed, ill-fitting old polo shirt that made Garrett wince inside because he knew it was what Lee considered his fancy shirt, the one he wore when he thought he was rising to some sort of occasion. It was clear to Garrett that Lee had none of the advantages he had in life. *There but for the grace of God go I,* thought Garrett. *The grace of God or my father.*

Garrett's father. Whenever Garrett and his father stop to get gas it takes up half the day because his father is always getting into conversations with the Latino guys who hang around there looking for day work. It's always driven Garrett crazy, especially in high school when he was already late for his job at the grocery store, but after years of doing this his father has picked up decent conversational Spanish, some astounding chicken recipes, and carpentry techniques he has used to make small repairs on the house that has saved them money on a contractor and let them put away more for Garrett's college—but most important, it has given Garrett the example of how to get along with people, how to *try* to get along with them, the benefits of withholding judgment.

Garrett's family does not have a lot of money. His father paints houses, mows lawns, refurbishes furniture, messes around with murals and music. He used to be some kind of a musician. Almost had a record deal once, before Garrett was born. His mother is a middle school science teacher. The family is always surrounded by people. They host guests for dinner several nights a week at the house, throw frequent parties, lead donation drives for folks around town who have been laid off work or fallen ill or otherwise need support.

Garrett had a happy, stable childhood followed by as emotionally stable an adolescence one can reasonably hope for. He had a productive high school career in which he succeeded academically and socially. He had a beautiful young relationship with the sweet, smart daughter of family friends, had ecstatic firework times with her in the green field on school nights. He earned a spot at his reach school. A significant scholarship supplements the little bit of money his father has been saving since Garrett was born. Student loans fill in the rest. And here he is in New York. He has made it. He already misses Katie deeply, he has missed her since he opened the acceptance letter. He will always miss her. But he can see the good in anything, even the painful things. All things have some kind of good in them, somewhere. All people do. As his father has taught him.

Earlier in the day when Garrett arrived from the airport, he and a very cute Asian girl passed each other in the hallway and she invited him to the orientation activities downstairs. He was inclined not to go, but she smiled at him the way girls had been smiling at him since his new clothes and hair and he said he would see her down there. They continued on, he turned to watch her go, she turned back and caught him watching, she smiled at him, he smiled back. He almost said it out loud: Whoa. *Whoa.* He kidded with Lee about her a couple of times. Katie who?

A few weeks later, Garrett had some people over to his room, including Sam, the girl in the hallway, when Lee barged into the room, very drunk and screaming at them to get off his bed. No one was on his bed. Everybody was on Garrett's side of the room. But Lee was saying he had seen them from outside, through the window, he had seen Sam sitting on his bed. Garrett tried to calm Lee down by inviting him to join them, but that only made Lee angrier. He looked at Sam and called her an illegal immigrant, started ranting about how minorities had made this country fundamentally unfair and unbalanced until Sam got up and left. Lee told her as she opened the door to keep going, to just go on and get the hell out of his country. Garrett was right behind her, protecting her from Lee. They left Lee in his room and went downstairs. They were terrified.

Garrett called campus police. What else was he supposed to do? He told them what happened and how Lee had once insinuated that he had access to a gun, that if he ever needed one he could get one, something Garrett did not think much of at the time but now, after what happened, made him worry—maybe Lee had a gun in the dorm somewhere, maybe even in the room. It triggered an investigation. A campus security officer with a buzz cut came and searched their room while he was out. Found no gun or anything. But Lee was kicked out of student housing, though not out of school.

Garrett and Sam and the other students and their families were appalled that Lee was let off so easily. More drastic action should have been taken. They hired lawyers to convince the administration to remove Lee Fisher from the school entirely, but Lee Fisher's family was one of those New York families with all the money in the world, and they had better lawyers. Garrett and Sam fought the administration on it but got nowhere. Lee remained among them; they had to sit in classrooms with him, at his mercy, and they had to see him on campus and hope today was not the day. He showed up while they all lounged around Washington Square Park, wearing these bizarre giant blue sunglasses and a crazy cowboy hat. He said nothing to them, just sat nearby on a bench grinning at them insanely, staring Sam down, to intimidate her, to terrorize them all. It worked. —I don't think I can be here anymore, Sam said. —Not while he's here too.

She transferred to a very good private school outside Hibbing, Minnesota. When the time came for her to leave, he helped her pack. She had so many things. They were far too heavy for her to carry alone. He carried them all downstairs for her to the awaiting taxi. —What are you going to do once you get there? How are you going to carry all this alone?

—I don't know, she said, looking very sad. —I don't know what I'll do.

When she was gone he could not stand it. He visited her very often in Minnesota—one month he visited her every weekend—and the visits were never long enough and he did not need to see Katie again to know that it was Sam he wanted, Sam he loved. She wanted him to come join her. He applied for a transfer to her school. It was rejected. He did not care, he moved to Minnesota anyway. New York or the girl is a choice to end all choices, but this was not much of a choice. New York was not the same without her. It was not even New York. He and Sam moved into a mouse-infested apartment and knew nobody in Minnesota, had nobody in Minnesota but each other. That first winter back-to-back blizzards shut down the town. New York did not have winters like this. They fell in love, in the cold and the snow and northern darkness. When the snow melted Sam was pregnant. The baby was born in the fall. They went ice-skating on a lake and the ice beneath Sam broke and she fell in. She got hypothermia, and hospitals there were not New York hospitals and they gave her the wrong medication and she suffered a bad reaction, fell into a coma. When she woke after three weeks she was unable to speak and could not walk or use the bathroom on her own.

Garrett cleaned her and he cleaned their baby. He fed her and he fed the baby. He loved her and he loved their baby. He gave Sam and their baby everything. Everything. More than he even knew he had to give.

They moved back to where she was from so her family could help. Sam wrote on a notepad, *Why did we leave New York?*

She did not remember. He had to tell her over and over about Lee Fisher.

He had to tell her about their life since they left New York because of Lee Fisher: a series of doctors and bad news and medical catastrophe and arguments with insurance providers. He had watched the beautiful, outgoing young woman he loved waste away into a silent invalid. But there was also love. There was their baby. He would not trade them. There was nowhere he would rather have been than outside Omaha, with Sam, with their baby.

Sam's mom took a picture of Garrett one Christmas and Garrett was surprised to see that person in that dorm room mirror so many years earlier was long gone, replaced by a 250-pound man with a cheap buzz cut and an overwashed, ill-fitting polo shirt for special occasions. What a man he could have been if he had stayed in New York. What things he could have done, and what money he could have made. How impressive he could have been. What he could have contributed.

Tell me again why we left New York, she wrote one night. He told her one more time. Usually once he had told her she did not say much, just looked sad. But tonight—he and she and their child in their bedroom, crammed into her adjustable hospital bed with rubber sheets—once he had told her about Lee Fisher and about her leaving because of him, she wrote on her pad, *I bet you wish we had stayed. None of this would have happened if we had stayed.*

—Are you kidding? he said. —Think they live this good in New York?

She laughed, though they both knew he was not joking. When they were kids she would put her head back and laugh loudly with a big open mouth and it always sounded like music to Garrett. Now her laughter was only in her eyes. You had to know her to see when she was laughing. You had to love her to hear it.

The next day she died in his arms. She was twenty-nine years old. She lives forever in their child's eyes, which laugh tonight somewhere outside Omaha.

THE GUARDIAN **5** OF THE FLOCK:

PART II

GOOD GUYS AND BAD GUYS

When he returns to New York, he means to enroll in the NYPD first thing, but there is a backlog of applicants to take the entrance exam, he has to wait until testing resumes the following year. When it does, he finds out you have to be twenty-one to become a cop. He is only nineteen. But you can still take the test at least so he takes the test, he's been studying all year, he must have read the handbook four times, and he passes, he does very well, he almost aces the test. He asks them if his high score might inspire them to make an exception to the age requirement and let him be a cop now. They say it does not, and he says, —But that does not make sense, you have to be just eighteen to join the military, and they say then why doesn't he go join the military, and he says he does not want to join the military, he wants to join the NYPD, and they say he has to be twenty-one, and there is nothing he can do, he just has to keep waiting.

Two long years follow in which he does little else but prepare for the brutality of the academy, the demands of life as a cop in New York City. He trains with a former Navy SEAL he hires, loses twenty pounds. He can run and run. He has never been in better shape. He feels terrific. He looks great, catches women noticing him and, appallingly, men. At intersections, he watches women emerging from taxis and black cars—elegant, beautiful older women—and they all look like his mother, and he imagines saving each and every one of them. Hangs out in cop bars, hovering near groups of them pretending he's with them; lingers around cops on street corners, hoping they notice him and ask why an obviously natural-born cop has not been granted an exemption to the age requirement and offer to make some calls on his behalf.

On his twenty-first birthday, he arrives to apply at the high office tower in Queens hours before they open up. First they give him a medical exam, which he passes, then an interview—purely ceremonial, he knows—where they ask if he has military service and he says not *United States* military, no, but he did proudly serve in a militia, and he tells them how when America was first founded all there were were militias like that, no official army yet, so that's who fought the Revolutionary War, militias like the one he was in, so in that sense, he would have to say yes, he does have military experience. They write that down, not saying anything. He adds how comfortable around firearms he is, having grown up with them—how skillful and safe.

They ask more basic things: criminal history, substance abuse. No criminal history, he answers, no drugs. They ask about mental health history and he says none, he's perfectly sane. They say, — And your family? and since neither his father nor mother has ever been officially diagnosed as crazy he feels comfortable answering, —Them too.

They ask about college. He says, —A little college.

They say, —Minimum requirement is sixty hours of college credit, do you have that?

He says, —Yeah, I think so, yeah. They say he'll need to show documentation proving it before he can enter the academy. And he says, —Okay, but wait, what if I don't have exactly sixty hours?

They ask, —How many do you have exactly?

And he says, —I don't know, how long is sixty hours, like how many weeks?

And they say, —About four semesters, or two years.

He tries not to panic. They ask how long he attended college, and he tells them, —About three or four.

And they say, —Three or four semesters you mean? and he says, —No, three or four weeks. And they ask how many credits he has, and he says, —None probably, and they ask what happened, and he says he dropped out, and they ask why, and he says, —It was a horrible place, I couldn't stand it, I just couldn't stand it, hardly anyone could, that place was a sinking ship, and anyway what does it have to do with being a law enforcement officer?

And they say, —It's the requirement. Didn't you read the requirements? Don't you pay attention to details? Can't you follow basic instructions?

And he says, —Yes, of course I read them, I read everything there was to read, I prepared fully. I knew about the requirement but assumed it was not, you know, set in stone, that it was just something to keep certain people out, people with no other skills, to *dissuade* them. I thought maybe you would make an exception for a guy like me.

They say, —Why'd you think that?

He says, —My test scores.

They say, —Okay, let's just put this aside for the moment and move on to the next phase of the preinterview process, the character assessment.

He is relieved, that feels promising. —Okay, he says, —I'm ready, I think you'll find I've got ironclad character, so fire away.

Immediately they say, —The character assessment is complete and you've failed.

He starts to sweat, feeling his dream dying in his arms. He says, —Wait, no, what? What do you mean?

They say, —There was a clearly stated requirement that you disregarded because you decided it did not apply to you. We call that a character problem.

He says, —No, no, no. He is trying not to cry.

They say, —You have a character problem, and he says no, he doesn't, and they say he does and that you cannot be a cop if you have a character problem, and he laughs at that, he *laughs*, he says that's a good one, and he leaves, hating them—he hates the NYPD and he hates cops, he would never be one of them, never in a million years.

A position opens up at one of his father's companies. Lee applies and the interviews go very well and he is hired. That he is his father's son is never mentioned, never taken into account. He is hired solely on merit. He is never sure what the company does but the position is called "analyst." He is very respected here. He shares an office with a senior analyst, David. Lee does excellent work despite not having the prestigious education that David and all the others have. He is blessed with innate capabilities, as he's always suspected about himself. Feedback is excellent, his bosses tell him his work is absolutely stellar. He, they assure him, and the outstanding work he does are crucial, absolutely *essential*.

The accomplishment he is most proud of, however, is one that falls outside the responsibilities of his job description. It takes months to win over the C-suite on the matter, but eventually, with perseverance, he succeeds in establishing a mandatory office-wide drill in which once a week at lunch all employees must take the stairs the twenty-four stories down instead of the elevator so they will be familiar with the building's emergency escape routes in the event of a natural disaster or terror strike. They are grateful to him. *Excellent idea. One day it might save our lives.*

He has found his place.

One night after finishing a big project, David invites him for drinks. After several single malt scotches at a bar, Lee is quite drunk, and the prospect of going home alone to his empty penthouse makes him very sad. David stands, finishes his last one, squeezes Lee's shoulder, and says good night, but Lee says, —No, don't go. Come back to my place. Please. I want to show you something. Just come. I'll pay for the taxi. Please come.

David says okay and they go to Lee's place. —Whoa ho ho, says David, looking around. —Great place.

—It's okay.

—Where's all the furniture? Are they going to paint or something?

—No, I guess I just ain't got around to getting any yet.

—How long have you been here?

—Only about a year. Hey, stay here a second, I'll be right back. He leaves David and goes to the bedroom, the nightstand. His nightstand is an empty cardboard box atop a milk crate beside his mattress, which sits on the floor. Reaches into the nightstand, gets what he wants to show David, yes, David will want to see this. He brings it out into the living room where David stands at the floor-to-ceiling windows with his back to Lee, looking out at the city before him, all those lights in the night.

—I'm sorry, David says, —but your view sucks.

—Yeah, they keep building stuff and ruining it. I try to stop them, but—

—Dude, I'm kidding. It's *incredible*.

Lee pretends to laugh. —No, I know you were. But if you think that's a view, then you ought to see where I come from. I grew up on a mountain? Out in the country? Man, I'm telling you: *that* was a view. All these trees as far as you could see. I used to spend hours looking out my window just looking at them, they were so beautiful. Hey, David, check it out.

David turns to Lee and sees what he holds in his hand; he stares at it like it's a lion on a leash.

His face goes dark. —Whoa, Lee.

—Beautiful, ain't it? Here, take it. Holding the unloaded gun in his palm with the chamber safely popped and barrel pointed away, he offers it for David to take and hold and examine and admire and ask technical questions about, like how men, how friends, do with one another's guns. But David raises his hands above his shoulders, palms out, and backs away, nearly tripping over the coffee table. — What's wrong?

—No, thank you, David says.

—Why? It can't hurt you.

—Those things just go off on their own. Lee laughs at the insanity of the idea. But David flinches and says, —*Please* don't point it at me.

—I'm *not*, David. I thought you'd want to see it.

—I absolutely do not. Please put it away.

Lee feels a great sadness that quickly shifts into something else. —No, he says. —I won't.

—Please. I'm asking you to put it away and—

—Try and make me.

David sighs. —Lee...

—No. It's my home. It's my right. Come try and make me.

David glares at him. —You know what? They say you're weird but I always say no, he's cool. They make fun of your fire drills but I tell them it's a smart idea. You know they all think you're only there to spy on us?

Lee snorts, incredulous.

—They do. They think you're a spy to tell the bosses who should be fired, but know who stands up for you? Me. I stand up for you. I defend you. I really do. But if I had known about this.

—About what?

—Your *viewpoint*. That you have *that*. I mean, what have I been doing defending you? *Enabling* you?

—Enabling me how?

—Doing your *work*.

Lee says, —Doing my what now?

—Lee, come on. What did you think? It's never right, it's not even close to being right, of course it's not, why would it be, you don't have the qualifications, you're not an analyst, you're only here because of your father. So whatever you hand in to me, I redo it all first before passing it along so our team won't look bad.

—I don't get it, Lee says, —I thought I was essential. I thought we were friends.

David looks at the gun, then at Lee, then back at the gun, and says, —Jesus. Lee looks down and sees that without meaning to he has moved the barrel of the gun so it now points almost directly at David, who begs him, —Please don't.

Lee likes the way he says it. He wraps his hand around the grip of the gun and keeps the barrel where it is. —Know why you think I'm going to shoot you? Because you know you're a scumbag liar. Say it.

—I'm a scumbag liar.

—Say Lee Fisher is senior analyst and David is only here because of his father. David says it and Lee says, —Say I'm vital.

—You're vital.

Lee gestures to the door with the gun and says, —Go.

David does as he's been told, and after he's gone, Lee is depressed. Never has he been so depressed, so lonely. Never has he felt so unwanted and pointless. He closes the door and locks it again, all three titanium deadbolts, and sits on the couch with the gun dangling in his hand and he never goes back. He never goes back.

Then he is thirty years old and the woman on the stool next to him is speaking very loudly to the person on the other side of him and it is very annoying, and Lee is about to stand up and move but then he realizes the woman is in fact speaking to him.

—I'm Maureen, she is saying. —Tonight's my last night in New York.

She is beautiful. He realizes she is beautiful when she says tonight is her last night. She is beautiful, even if a certain kind of other man might dismiss her as overweight with greasy skin and obviously drunk, clearly a barfly. But Lee Fisher is a better man than that. *We respect women where I come from. That's the way I was raised.*

She says, —What's your name?

He does not want to tell her. Not yet. Buys her a drink. They talk. She is very funny. She is funny because she leaves tomorrow. And she does not mind that he cannot look at her or that she has to do all the talking. He wants to spend the rest of the day with Maureen. The rest of his life.

They go to her hotel room. It is the first woman he has been with. But that has been by choice. He is a man of standards and morals, he does not need to be with hundreds of girls to know what he wants. What he wants, what he has always wanted, is Maureen. Oh, Maureen, Maureen. Everything he has become melts away like wax in the flame of Maureen.

They lie in bed together. —Come with me tomorrow, she says. — leave with me.

He says, —Where?

—Wherever, she says.

He says, —I don't even know you.

She says, —Then get to know me.

—We don't know what will happen.

—We never do.

—Too many things can go wrong.

—If they do, we'll make them right. Don't you see? This is your chance. We only get one and this is yours.

He says, —Chance for what?

—To be saved.

—I don't need saving.

—Yes, you do.

He says, —Why do you say that?

—Because it's obvious.

—What is?

She smiles playfully and does not answer, pushes herself up to her hands and knees and crawls away from him down to the foot of the bed, and he watches her. She reaches down to the floor where his clothes lie in a heap and digs through them.

—Maureen, he says, voice rising, becoming tense, —don't do that.

She ignores him.

—Stop it! he shouts. He sits up and dives for her, grabs the wrist of her hand that grips the handle of the gun, squeezes it very tight.

—Ow! she says.

—Let go of it. Let go.

—You're hurting me!

—Let go of it!

—*You* let go of it.

—Take your fucking hands off it. *Now. Now*, Maureen.

She does. He gets up, securing the gun by placing it on the desk and standing between her and it. He's naked. She lies there looking at him naked. He covers himself with his hands, then dresses urgently, holding on to the desk to balance himself.

—What's the matter? she slurs, still playing. —You don't like me anymore?

—No, he says, —I don't think I do.

She becomes serious and says, —I'm sorry. She rolls onto her back and looks at him upside down. —Come back to bed.

He says, —No, thank you.

—*No, thank you,* she mimics in a terse man's voice. —Why not?

—I gotta get.

—You ain't gotta get, she says, mocking him and the way he talks and who he is.

—Please don't tell me what I gotta do and what I don't. Because you don't know. You have no clue.

She goes quiet, chastened. He sits in the desk chair and ties his shoes, keeping an eye on her. At the bar he thought her eyes were kind and compassionate but they are not kind and compassionate—they are just hungry. She covers herself with the blankets. But he can still smell the alcohol wafting out of her oily skin. He can still taste the bacteria in the folds of her unwashed flesh. He stands, desperate for air, desperate to leave.

—I'm sorry, she says, sincere.

—Me too.

—Aren't you even going to tell me your name at least? she says.

—Hell no, he says, holstering the gun, opening the door, and leaving.

She leans across the table at Per Se, places her hands over his. Her hands are small and dry and clean, like the rest of her. Her skin tanned, almost cured. Eyes sparkling, wrinkles at their edges. The lids of her eyes have grown puffy. Bands of tendons push out from her neck and her chest is covered in freckles, as are her breasts, most of which he can see down her loose shawl, silk or something like it, something he imagines you could drape over one of those statues with no arms or legs.

She is in town to receive an award from the United Nations. She has done something to dirt. The dirt is in Africa and the thing she has done to it is very important and the dirt in Africa is now doing very well, much better than it was doing before, so thank God for her, thank God for what she has spent all these years doing for the dirt of Africa.

—Babu, she says. —How are you? How have you been?

He signals to the waiter for another Budweiser. He wears jeans, boots, a J.C. Penney sport coat, a cowboy hat. —Me? Great. I've been great.

—Tell me more. Tell me everything. Tell me absolutely everything.

—What do you want to know?

She looks at him heavily, like she is trying to convey something without using words. He does not know what. He does not care.

—Well, I don't know. Have you missed me?

What do you think? he wants to say. *What the hell do you think?* — What are you talking about? he says, —I see you all the time.

—It's been three years, she says.

—No, it hasn't.

—Three years and three months.

He looks away. He does not like meeting her eyes. They make him feel like she needs things from him and maybe he has them but he does not want to give them to her.

—Anyway, she says, —how's work?

Work. She always asks about work. He does not have a job. He has done his best to find his place, his purpose. He tried to be an investigator for an insurance company, uncovering frauds. Then he tried to be a security consultant to corporations, tracking down sources of leaks, thwarting data breaches. For a time he was a guard at an office building but quit when they would not allow him to carry a weapon. He taught a self-defense class at a gym, but the clientele were all models and the admen trying to copulate with them and it was disgusting to watch, and trying to get these foolish people to understand the importance, the absolute dire necessity, of self-protection was futile and depressing. The problem has always been the same: the people he works with disdain him. They disdain him on sight. They disdain him for who he is and what he wears and whom he votes for. They disdain him for his sense of humor, of which they have none. They disdain him for everything. Everything. They do not like him. He likes them, but they do not like him. They want him to change, to be more like them. Then they might like him. But he does not ask them to change to be more like him. Yet they feel entitled to asking him to change. And, as he has found himself explaining a hundred times in a hundred meeting rooms to a hundred soon-to-be-former colleagues, if he were to change, if everybody were to abandon who he is and what he believes just because others wanted him to, what would happen to this country? What would happen? Who would be left to stand up for what is right? This country needs guys like Lee Fisher. It needs him. He is the keeper of the flame.

—Fine, he says.

Whenever he speaks she nods enthusiastically and happily to whatever he says, holding strong eye contact and smiling, like every word from his mouth is music and everything in the world is just wonderful. As he does every time he sees her, he has the impression she is not listening at all to what he is saying, and if she is she does not care, that she is interested only in how she looks to him, whether he thinks badly of her. She does not need to hear about his life, what she needs is to look good for him and for him to tell her that all the things she suspects are her fault are not her fault and that there was nothing she could do. The only thing she ever really thinks about, he knows, is how guilty she feels. Not him, not his life—how guilty she feels. That is his job, as far as she is concerned: to keep her from feeling bad. So he could say anything right now, anything at all, and she would not hear it, she would just nod and smile enthusiastically and happily.

—Yeah, he says, —these days I'm more and more in the necrophilia space.

—Wonderful, she says brightly, nodding and smiling.

—Necrophilia and bestiality.

—Hey, do what you love and you never have to work a day in your life. She lifts her white wine to her lips. He watches her open her face and pour the wine into it.

—You act like you're the first person who's ever said that.

—Well, it's *true*. So where are you *living*? Where do you *live*? Still on the Upper East?

—No, I was living there but now... He trails off, looking at her hands. One is wrapped tightly around her wine stem like she is afraid someone will try to take it from her, and the other is on the table beside her plate and it is opening and closing in a fist over and over. He suddenly does not have it in him to finish. —Now I live somewhere else, he says quickly.

—Where?

He does not want to tell her. —Greenwich Avenue.

She claps her hands, gasps. —The West Village! Do you rent or own?

—Own. I bought it last year. Late last year. No, two years ago. Wait, three years ago I guess.

—How many bedrooms?

—Six, but seven if you count the office.

—Oh, she says, surprised. —Is it just you?

—Just me, he says. —Me, myself, and I.

—That's a lot of space for one person.

He wonders if she is angling to move in with him, if something has gone wrong for her and she needs somewhere to live. —I have a lot of things. It was available and I could afford it. It's the penthouse. Privacy, you know.

—Your father and I met in the West Village. Did you know that?

—No.

—It used to be so different. It used to be beautiful.

—It's still beautiful. I mean, I like it. It's quiet.

—Have you heard from him?

Lee shrugs, not wanting to talk to her about his father.

She points to Lee's hat. —He used to wear one just like it.

—I doubt that.

—No, he did. He looked just like John Travolta in *Urban Cowboy*. He was the hottest thing. Gay men hit on him *constantly*. She laughs. —Do gay men hit on you *constantly*?

—Hell no, he says, shifting in his chair.

—You're not their type anyway. You look way too hetero.

He feels insulted without understanding why. —Thank you, he says.

—Anyway there probably aren't many of them left down there these days, are there? It's all Wall Street guys and the drugged-up children of international tycoons. Most of those homes are empty because rich men buy them only to park their money. It's a ghost town now. They've gutted it, gutted it. I hate it.

—When were you here? She tries to wave it off but he says, —No, you've been here? You've been in New York, you've been to the West Village, and you haven't... He lowers his voice because he realizes he has been almost shouting. —... and you haven't *called* me? You haven't *seen* me? *What the hell is wrong with you?*

—I've *read* about it! In the paper! The *Times*! My God!

He does not believe her. —Well, I *like* my neighborhood, he says, pouting. —I *like* the West Village. I *like* what it is now. Nobody bothers you. Nobody needs you. Nobody wants anything from you. Nobody expects anything of you. That's the way I like it. It's quiet and calm, and I'm so high off the ground that on cloudy days I can't even see the daggone street, I can't see nothing but the sky above me. Reminds me of back home.

—Back home, she says, flip. —That dreadful place.

—It wasn't dreadful. I don't like you calling it that.

—You hated it there.

—No I didn't. It wasn't bad, in retrospect. He wasn't either. I mean, in comparison.

—In comparison to *what?*

—To people here. At least he has some kind of moral center, unlike people here. She laughs. Lee shrugs. —Back then, I was just a kid and I just didn't understand his values or appreciate them like I do now.

—I can't believe you're *defending* him. All I've ever heard you say about him are terrible things.

—That's not true.

—It is.

He suddenly feels cruel. —What do you tell them about me?

—Who?

—People. People you know, people in your life, people in Africa. The African dirt people.

—I don't know what you mean.

—When they say, *Where is your son, don't you have a son?* What do you tell them?

She is starting to cry. —Lee, please.

—When they say, *Why aren't you with him, why did you leave him with that man? Why don't you miss him?* When they ask you that, what do you tell them?

She says something into the napkin she holds to her face to hide. He cannot hear it.

—What's that?

—They don't ask, she says.

—They don't ask. And why not? Why don't they ask?

—We're busy over there, it's very serious work, people are *dying*, we're not on vacation—

—You don't tell them, he says. —Right?

She falls silent.

—You don't tell them about me. You don't talk about me. You talk about your other kids, but you never even mention me. The people you know don't even know you have another son.

—Oh no, you're so wrong.

—You're ashamed of me. I embarrass you.

—No.

—Your life with him was a phase. Just a phase. A person you once were. You grew out of it and moved on and got another husband and had other kids, and now you look back at him and me with regret.

—No.

—With regret. Don't you?

—No.

—Yes, you do. Yes, you do.

She stares at him with her mouth open and eyes red and wet. Then she laughs, once. It is like a death throe. —Lee, she says, —I hope one day you learn it is better to be kind than right.

He has come into possession of many other properties around the world—Madrid, Miami, Los Angeles, Chicago, Manila, Kuala Lumpur, a few more here in Manhattan—but he has never gone to them, he rents out some but most remain empty, beautiful places you pass like tombs and wonder who lives there. He always preferred this property, the West Village penthouse. The highest and quietest. The safest. It is home. He never sees his neighbors. The building staff does not bother him.

One night, late, he is on his laptop in the living room near the front door, where he sits to work on his various pursuits—an online bodybuilding publication, an urban survivalist resource teaching post-civilization skills to a world on the brink of imminent global societal collapse, but most often doing nothing more than searching for her, again and again, all he has of her is her first name and her hometown and a vague memory of her face—when he hears the door to the staircase out in the hall open and then ease shut, followed by the shuffle of several pairs of feet hurrying their way up to his door. He reaches for the gun, always nearby. He puts aside the laptop and stands and tiptoes to the door, and he is pointing the gun at the door while he stands there holding his breath and assessing, wondering if this is it. Then giggling and more whispering: —Do it, do it, no you, no you!

Children. To confirm he peeks through the peephole and sees the tops of their heads. Their skinny little shadows stretch on the wall behind them, and he can almost feel the children through the door, their frantic little heartbeats inside their bony chests, the wind through their throats as they whisper to one another, fast and high pitched, —Do it, do it, no you, no you. Without meaning to he leans too close to the door and taps the gun's barrel against it and they run away, silent, terrified. He watches them through the peephole. He counts four of them—one girl, three boys, one boy taller than the rest, one shorter, three white, one black. A black boy. The black boy is the smallest one and the only one smiling, the only one laughing. The only one not afraid. The super's son. Lee must be some sort of myth to them. The mysterious recluse. The building's very own Boo Radley. And what does Boo Radley do in the book? He saves the children. He is weird and marginalized and misunderstood and he saves them.

Though he is seduced, hypnotized by the solitude of his home, the new Boo Radley begins forcing himself to go out and spend the nights in the rain and cold, on patrol, vigilant in the face of the random and uncontrollable, circling the block on foot with the gun, keeping an eye out for those who want to hurt kids.

Soon the children no longer come whispering and giggling outside his door anymore. It occurs to him that they have grown, that it has been seven years and they are not kids anymore.

He still patrols the block at night. Whether there are children who live here these days he does not know, but the people of the building are still good people, he believes, though he does not know them, they are good people and he is still Boo Radley, he is still the hero.

To keep his skills sharp on patrol—bad guys do not stay stagnant, their weaponry and tactics are forever evolving to keep a step ahead of the good guys—Boo Radley of the West Village attends self-defense seminars around the country. The seminars are educational and necessary but also healthy, for they satiate the irritating human need he has for socializing, communing. The seminars also provide a good deal of entertainment—some real weirdos attend these things. He gets a kick out of checking them out. The seminars are also important for business, not that he has a business, not a real one; he is still looking for *it*, his calling and purpose, the big thing he will do that will connect him with his world in meaningful ways. Also, the seminars give him something to do, somewhere to go where he is expected, his name printed out on a badge waiting for him.

The chitchat with sales reps and firearms instructors and NRA marketing guys and fellow Boo Radleys he recognizes from previous conventions—there is a whole roving circuit, a shadow army of citizen patriots convening along interstates in Radisson Hotel ballrooms, always ready for muster—and UFC fighters and international shooting champs making appearances to sign autographs and pose for pictures in the apparel and gear of their sponsors are the closest thing Lee has to any kind of social life, though he is quite well known and very respected, even feared on several online forums. He can subsist for months afterward on the nourishment of sales pitches and new weapons demos and bull-shooting over soda water at the hotel bar.

At one such bar, at a seminar outside Scranton, Pennsylvania, there is a woman. Such rare phenomena receive due attention. A crowd of men surrounds her. Lee does not bother trying to elbow his way in to join them. It is a very distasteful display. A woman should be able to learn self-defense skills without being dry-humped, in his personal opinion. He stands instead on the edge of the crowd, drinking his soda water, heart swollen with affection for himself for how much respect he has for women. Finds himself talking to the sort of person he for some reason always finds himself talking to at these things: Tim, with a flattop and a red face and long nose hairs, his gun in its underarm holster bulging beneath his cheap sport coat. Tim keeps leaning in and saying things to Lee like, *Look at this, look at all these dipshits bending over backward to appease this woman. And yet you know she'll still cry about unfair treatment. Oppressed. Wish someone would oppress me like that, buying me drinks, offering to take me in and pay my way, then give me half their shit, give me the house, give me the kids. Oppressed. Know who's really oppressed? The most oppressed person in American society today is the straight, white, hardworking Christian male. Me. You. Us.*

Lee is trying to pay no attention to Tim, he is instead zoned out on this woman. This woman. Whenever the cloud around this woman moves in such a way that she becomes visible to him again and her voice breaks through the din to reach him, Lee becomes a little happier. They make eye contact. Usually they look away. Or he looks away. Someone always looks away, ending whatever moment that might have been. But then this woman, at this convention outside Scranton, does not look away. Neither does he. And for a brief moment she pauses whatever she is in the middle of saying, her lips hanging apart as though she recognizes Lee, and then she resumes her conversation, still looking at Lee as the cloud swallows her up again.

Tim tells him to come on, let's go rejoin the convention, but Lee declines. Because the woman is pushing through the cloud and coming his way, and she is walking right up to Lee, for God knows what reason, and she is saying, —Hiya! Lee feels Tim's resentment as he peels away on his own, muttering, —*Jesus...*

Lee does not know what to say to the woman. Or to any woman. What do they like? What do they want? Food? Things? With the exception of one freak night years ago, he has never known how to be with them, what to do. His mind always goes blank and they realize how boring he is, how irrelevant, and they lose whatever misguided interest they might have thought they had. But that night. That night. It was years ago. Another woman, another bar. Another life. He was a maestro, he was Don Juan—a brash, cocky stud. Maureen melted for him. Hardly had to say more than a few words to her before he brought her to her room and played her body like an instrument. Afterward she begged him not to go. She wanted more. God, to recapture the confidence he had as a younger man, when everything was so much clearer!

Now he is just a man in his midforties to whom nothing is clear, a man with a mind that now, as this woman speaks to him, goes blank. But this time it is okay, because she is doing all the talking. Laura is her name, she says. This is her first time at one of these things. While he stands there listening and doing his best to smile, having read somewhere that women like you to smile, Laura goes on and on about what she has learned today about strangulation techniques, knives. All he has to do, he finds, is stay quiet and keep smiling and she will continue talking to him, to the tangible dismay of the jilted suitors all glancing over from the bar. So this is what he does, feeling like the most handsome, most desirable man who has ever lived.

She wants to eat, so he takes her to the hotel restaurant, called Smooth or Silk or SoHo or something, and they wait for a suitable table. A suitable table is one located in the corner, where you can sit with your back to the wall and have unobstructed visuals on all entranceways. Demand for such a table at these conventions is very high, and Lee and Laura have to wait nearly two hours for one but it is worth it if you wish to dine safely. Laura is a big, tough woman in hiking boots with thick wool socks even though it is summer. Her hair is in a ponytail, and she wears no makeup. Her big, clear voice is unrelenting. So is her self-certainty. She eats voraciously and without apology, like she has been starved. She is from Michigan, she says, and now lives outside East Germany. East Germany? Scranton, she clarifies. She lives outside Scranton, which she calls East Germany because of all the regulation and taxes and wanton violations of its citizens' American freedoms. She works in IT for the county. She calls it the Stasi.

She asks where Lee is from. Lee tells her about his childhood. The mountain. The outdoors. Big green trees to climb, blue sky, his daddy teaching him how to change a transmission and mend a fence and stay true to his word and do unto others and respect women, how to shoot a gun, how to take care of a gun. How to be safe with a gun. He tells Laura about him and his daddy taking care of themselves, making the most of rough circumstances, namely his mother up and leaving. Children were free back there, at home, he tells her. They ran barefoot through the grass and were happy. Folks were Christian, they went to church.

—Did you go to church? Laura says.

—Of course we went to church, he says. And he and his daddy, he remembers, lived off the land, they ran a little farm for some time, raised all kinds of animals—chickens, pigs, horses. Needed no one and nothing. Self-sufficient and independent. They had a barn—he laughs just thinking about it: he remembers how he used to hide in that barn for hours, his little sanctuary; he loved it there, he would go there to disappear into his little-boy fantasy worlds and his daddy always let him be. Then high school where he had his rowdy group of buddies and his little sweetheart. He and Tamra Riley were two fools in love, he remembers, it was always him and Tamra and his best friend, Joey Whitestone, raising hell and having good times and getting out of trouble. He will never forget those wild-hearted American nights out there, back home on the mountain. They would cruise that little town for hours in Lee's pickup truck. They did not want much—folks back there were modest—just to be safe and happy. His father was his hero and still is, he tells Laura. Taught him how to be a man. And now he finds himself living in New York City, of all places.

She snorts. —*New York City?* Guess you like being told what to do and how to do it and paying out the behind for the privilege.

He tells her he has to be in New York for work. The family business. His presence is crucial. He is a crucial asset. Without him, he doesn't know what would happen. He's also a small business owner. He thought he would hate it in New York, he tells her, but he finds everyone's so daggone busy screwing each other over and being up their own you-know-whats that you can find real privacy and solitude there.

She thinks about it and stuffs more meat into her already full mouth and says, chewing it, —I do like Times Square. Got those Elmos.

Then she talks about how she has hiked the Appalachian Trail twice, all by herself, with no help. And when the check comes and he tries to pay it she will not let him.

—We split it, she says, reaching into her side pocket and pulling out a man's leather wallet.

He thinks she is just being mannered and in fact expects him to pay, so he holds out the bill and the money for the waitress to come take, but Laura reaches across the table and twists his thumb back until he shrieks in pain and lets go. She takes the bill, looks at the total, and counts out her share in cash. She winks at him as he tends to his throbbing hand. —I've never taken a handout and I don't plan to start now.

They go upstairs to his room. —Take off your gun and trousers, she says, standing hands on hips in front of the television. He does so, then sits on the bed. —Well, that was dumb, she says, bending down to pick up the gun and holding it in her hand. —Never listen to anyone who tells you to put down your weapon unless it's a police officer, and even then demand to see his badge first.

She undresses where she stands, then comes over. Beneath her hiking shorts and old T-shirt her body is soft, her skin white and smooth like milk, breasts beautiful with bright pink nipples as fat as the tip of a pinkie. He barely gets past her fistful of bright orange hair before crying out with pleasure and relief. She says, —Whoa, baby, I'll get some TP.

She unsaddles, lifting one leg high, and waddles to the bathroom, her hand cupped between her legs. He listens to her urinate. She urinates for a long time and very heavily. Then he listens to the toilet paper roll going around and around and around. She must use the entire roll. Toilet flushes, she comes out with more toilet paper and wipes him down. She returns to the bathroom and he hears the toilet flush several more times, then she reappears, stands at the foot of the bed, spreading her feet apart wide and squatting, stretching her leg. —Got a cramp in my groin, she explains cheerfully.

—I'm sorry, he says.

—It's not *your* fault. I should have hydrated more.

—No, I mean I reckon that I was kind of faster than you probably expected.

She twists up her face. —You kidding? It was great. Who has the time to futz around all night like California yoga yahoos?

—It's been kind of a long time.

—How long?

She stands up straight and bends her left leg up behind her and holds it, stands like a flamingo, leaning on the TV for balance. Then she does the other leg.

It has been fifteen years but Lee says, —Maybe about a year. I've been so busy. With work.

She puts her underwear and hiking shorts back on and, still nude from the waist up, comes over to the bed, the nightstand, bends over the clock radio looking for the conservative talk station. Lee watches her breasts dangle, sway.

—Shouldn't have answered that, she says. —It's none of my business and now I know more about you than you know about me. Puts me in a position of advantage over you.

—Then let's even it out. Tell me something about you, he says. — How long has it been for you?

—Nope, she says, joining him in bed. —Never give up ground already gained. Fundamental principle of self-defense.

Before he can answer she is instantly, deeply asleep. She snores, sweats, her body draped over his like a Great Dane's. His hand is falling asleep beneath her and he tries to move her off it but she will not budge. It is like she has not slept in weeks.

Later she wakes up with a start, bolts upright, and looks at him. She seems different. He feels like he is looking into the eyes of a different person. Then she blinks and that different person is gone and the Laura he knows returns. —Hiya, she says.

—Howdy, says Lee.

—What time is it? She reads the clock radio and grunts. —Don't worry, I'll leave you alone now.

She starts to rise but he puts his arms around her and pins her to him.

—No, he says. —Please don't go.

Laura comes back with him to New York, moves in. Says she does not own anything that is not in the giant suitcase she brought with her to Scranton, so there is nothing to go home and get. She has, she says, no loose ends to tie up, no one to say good-bye to. —I'm a loner, she says. —I prefer it that way.

—What about your job? he asks her.

She waves off the question. —I can do what I do from anywhere.

Every day she goes out into the city and returns with a small broken electronic or kitchen appliance: a dusty obsolete printer, a coffeemaker. She says, —We'll sell them. All they need is a little tinkering and they'll be good as new. But Laura never tinkers with and never sells anything, and after a few months the junk has only piled up. Lee asks her to please start fixing things or else get rid of them and to stop bringing in more.

—I won't get rid of them, she explains. —I'm building a business, I'm nesting.

—What do you mean? he says.

—Lee, she says, coming toward him, smiling, hands on her belly, —obviously I'm pregnant.

Lee is outraged that she has known this but not told him.

—You should have noticed, she says. —I thought you're the kind of man who pays attention to what's going on around him.

—I *am* that kind of man, but *Christ.*

—It's a beautiful thing, Lee. There is no greater love than the one you're about to know.

For days he thinks about it. A family. Lee Fisher, a daddy. A man raising a child and loving a wife, doing his best to support his family.

The responsibility of it. The respectability. It would give him something in common with other people. He would be an excellent father. He has wonderful virtues to pass on to a child. It would be a beautiful family. Yes, this is what men do: they have families. He will have a family and he will protect his family. It will be his duty. He will be needed. He will have a place and a point at last. He cannot be happier. There is nothing more than Laura and their baby.

She will give birth in the penthouse: the bathtub, candlelight, and silence and space and control. Just the two of them. Like a frontier family. They do not need harmful, inhuman hospitals. Where they come from, they birth their own.

—Hospitals give your baby autism and allergies, Laura says, — and those doctors get off on it, you know, looking at women with their legs spread all day.

An hour into the delivery her tough facade evaporates and she screams and cries and begs for a hospital and doctors and drugs, but they agreed beforehand that no matter what she said or did she wanted to deliver her child without drugs, so Lee keeps her in that tub. All those black-red plumes of blood and brown-gray plumes— Lee almost loses consciousness several times.

The baby is born safely. A boy. A son. He is perfect. Lee kisses him and wraps him in soft fuzzy blankets and will never put him down. Lee hands Laura her baby to hold. She does not want to hold him. Nor does she want to look at him. She keeps her eyes closed and head turned away, face covered in one hand.

—Laura, Lee says, —it's your baby, it's your son.

But she will not turn her head to look at him. She climbs out of the tub and plods out of the bathroom and locks herself in one of the spare bedrooms, the one with all the junk she has hauled back from the garbage, and refuses to come out or open the door, not even to use the restroom or eat. The care of the newborn falls to Lee and he is very dutiful, waking to prepare every bottle, change every diaper. Lee gives every bath—twice, three times a day he bathes his son.

One afternoon while the baby naps, Lee searches for Laura's name online. He has done so before and, as then, no meaningful results come back. In her dresser beneath her underwear and socks he finds a health insurance prescription card with her picture on it but the name Caroline. Knocks on her door.

—Go away! she yells.

—Caroline? he says.

He has the gun in his hand. Silence from inside. Then her footsteps come across the floor. The door opens a crack in which she places some strange, dark, exhausted, and small face—shriveled mess of tangled hair and acne and glowing bloodshot eyes—that he has to strain to recognize as hers.

—Is that you? Are you Caroline?

—It's me, she groans.

—Who are you?

She sighs and says as though defeated, —Just wait one minute and I'll tell you. She eases the door shut and he hears it lock and he waits several hours but she does not come out.

Eight hours later she emerges, somehow cleaned up and fresh, strong and bounding and loud. She wears the hiking boots and heavy wool socks and T-shirt she wore when they first met. She is Laura again.

—Hello, young man! she bellows, strutting into the kitchen and reaching out her arms to the baby, who is feeding in Lee's arms.

—He's eating, Lee says, —please let him eat.

She says, —That's okay, and plucks the bottle from the baby's mouth and sets it down, lifts the now crying baby from Lee's arms, swings him around, kissing him and kissing him. —Look at these muscles, she cries. —Strong man!

Lee watches from the table: his terrified son, his son's insane mother. Now what is he supposed to do?

—Are you feeling better? he says to her.

—Much! Postpartum is no joke. Being cooped up here in this city sure doesn't help. But see? No meds, no bellyaching, no whining about my problems to some shrink. Right? You take it, you deal with it. You deal with life. She is addressing the baby now. —You roll with the punches. It makes you strong. That's the kind of people we are. Right, Dad? She looks to Lee, waits for him to agree.

—That's right, he says. She hands the baby back to him. Both he and the baby are relieved to resume the feeding. He asks her, —Do you want breakfast?

—No thanks, I ate.

—What the hell did you eat in that room? Computer parts?

—Don't forget, Lee, she says, retying her boots to tighten them, hiking up her socks, —you're talking to a survivalist. I can survive anywhere, on anything. I need nothing and no one. She stands up.

Lee says, —Where are you going?

—For a walk. Need to get the blood circulating again and start reconstructing my muscle mass.

—Please no more printers or anything.

—That's a potential fortune we're sitting on in that room, Lee. That's our son's inheritance.

—I already have a fortune. He already has an inheritance.

—You never know what will happen. The world economy is just a shell game. The bottom can drop out overnight, any night. And when it does your fortune will vanish right along with it and you won't have a pot to piss in. That equipment in there will be good as gold. Can you believe how wasteful people are? Just walk a couple of blocks in this town and you see all the good stuff we just throw away. We'll throw away anything. One of these days I'll probably find a human out there in the trash. A kid, some child they decided they didn't want and just threw away.

She gets her phone, opening the maps app, and then goes to the door, opens it, looks back at Lee and their son. —What a beautiful sight, she says. She closes the door.

Laura goes up to Central Park, Lee later learns. Fifty blocks on foot. She removes her belt from her khaki shorts and hangs herself from a tree in the broad daylight. A jogger finds her.

One of his drivers takes him and his son to the gun range. The gun range is in Pennsylvania. There is a gun range in Manhattan, but like everything else in Manhattan it is overpriced and overcrowded and overregulated and crawling with cops. The range in Pennsylvania is located in an isolated corner unit of a business park. From the outside it looks like it could be a dentist's office. Lee's driver waits while he goes inside, baby hanging from his chest, gun in a carrying case. As he approaches the entrance a tall, strong, bearded man is leaving. His flushed face drips with sweat. A semiautomatic pistol is holstered on his hip and earmuffs hang around his neck. He still wears his protective eyewear. It is fogged with perspiration. His smile is a postcoital smile. He swats Lee on the shoulder as he passes, like they know each other, like they're old friends. It sends shivers up Lee's spine. He opens the door. Already he can hear the shooting. *KOOM! KOOM!* He feels a little kick—he always gets a little kick.

Inside, more of his people—safe, responsible gun owners. It's like a bowling alley, but instead of knocking down pins and guzzling pitchers of beer, everyone is present-minded and focused on the world around them, considerate first and foremost of everyone else's well-being. *A gun range is maintenance of the democracy,* Lee thinks. *Ordinary Real Americans executing their most essential right. This,* he thinks happily, *is what makes us exceptional. This is how one is an American. We are doing it right.*

The firing takes place in a soundproofed gallery in back. There are windows through which you can watch from the waiting area where they also sell firearms and firearms accessories and knives and double-breasted heavy-duty shooting shirts. *KOOM! KOOM!* It is so visceral and exciting, like the drums at a rock concert. He smells the gunpowder and he is on the musty green hills of Gettysburg in the early morning. He is charging a position at Bull Run, picture of his mother pinned to his breast beneath his uniform. He is at the Battle of the Bulge with his fellow marines, his brothers, having killed for one another today, having survived today's battle to fight tomorrow's.

KOOM! KOOM! KOOM!

The shooters are men, women, girls, boys, college kids, couples on dates, black and white, skinny, fat, rich, poor, all cultural backgrounds and every apparent tax bracket and personal style. Lee is more accepting of people who are different from him here. No one is staring down at his or her phone. No one is jostling anyone else, no one is cutting in line or arguing, no one is cheating, no one is lying, no one is daydreaming. This is the way we once were, here at the gun range. It feels new only because modern life has become so vicious, our values so deranged. This, Lee feels, is the way things should be. The way we should be. When is the last time Lee looked around a room filled with people—his fellow countrymen—and felt not grim alienation and disdain and distrust, but deep affection and appreciation?

He enters the shooting gallery. It is hot and concrete and loud. He has his earmuffs and eyewear on, his son wears little baby versions. Lee sits him on the high chair the staff leaves out for him against the wall out of the way of flying shells, one of the perks of his platinum club membership.

The universe wants to take it all from him. It took his mother and it took his father and it took his home and it took Maureen and it took Laura and one day it will try to take his son as well. He knows it will. At the doctor's office for checkups, the pediatrician tapping the door and stepping inside, studying the test results over the top of his glasses—Lee knows he is in fact preparing to deliver the terrible news of a rare, fatal genetic condition. Crossing the street pushing the stroller, every car waiting at a red light is driven by a drunk, or an immigrant so desperate he's become heartless, or a lost and incompetent out-of-towner whose foot, as Lee and his son pass across his bumper, will slip off the brake and onto the gas and speed forward to crush the stroller, rip it from Lee's hands, and drag the baby's little body down the street until nothing remains but streaks of white and red. —Didn't see him, the driver will explain to the judge, and the judge will exonerate him, he will walk out of jail and get back behind the wheel of his vehicle and drive home, stopping first at the car wash to clean off the skin, the bones. And sidewalks—anything or anyone at any time might fall from a high window or roof and land atop the stroller, crushing his son to death. An air-conditioning unit or a human body. Passing a construction site—nothing but construction work in New York City!—a worker's circular saw will break and the blade will spin loose and go shooting dozens of feet through the air and sever his son's head. There will be a car bomb. A stray bullet. Collapsing scaffolding. Lee gushes with sweat always, face red and chest tight, hands sweaty and knuckles white around the stroller handle, making no eye contact with anyone lest they want to take from him what they have not already.

But not here. Here is safe. They all are.

He unzips the gun case and takes out the gun. It is the only thing that gives Lee and his son half a chance.

He pushes the button to call in the target holder, sticks a bull's-eye sticker onto a three-by-five card, clips it to the target holder, and sends it back out twelve feet. He assumes proper shooting position. Inhales, exhales, pulls the trigger. Bull's-eye. *That's it, Lee,* his father says. *That's it.* He inhales, exhales, pulls the trigger. *Outstanding, Lee.* He empties the cylinder and, feeling pride at his acumen, confidence at his capability, he reloads. Inhales, exhales, pulls. His mother is watching. *Oh, babu.* His *KOOM*s sing out among the others, harmonizing with them, accepted as one of them, like children in the park chasing a puppy, running toward trees.

He is smiling, shooting. His face hurts, it has been so long since he smiled this big.

Here it is. This is it.

At last.

He is in bed in the middle of the night one night—maybe a Tuesday, maybe a Wednesday; it could be any night—when he wakes to a noise out in his living room. He sits up, listens. There it is again. What could it be? Nothing probably—he locked the door. All those deadbolts and chains. Of course he locked the door. Didn't he lock the door? After getting his son down, he spent his evening the same way he spends every evening since Laura died: drinking a six-pack and watching Netflix, but instantly he feels completely sober and he cannot remember locking the door. And he hears the noise again. He knows exactly what to do, he has practiced it a thousand times, imagined it a million times. He reaches for the gun. It is already loaded, always is. He goes to the bedroom's doorway, right hand on the grip with forefinger extended across the trigger guard, left hand cupping the right.

—Is someone there? he calls out into the dark apartment.

No answer. Finger moves to the trigger and he goes down the hall, toward the threat. He passes his movie theater, his game room, his recording studio, his gym, his conference room, the gun pointed ahead, trying to steady his shaking hands and to keep focused and to breathe but in fact doing none of these things, he has not breathed in thirty seconds, his chest burns. Passes his son's room, looks in on him; he is asleep on his back. Continues on. His knees shake. He is the only hope. He is Boo Radley, protector of children.

—You better get the fuck out of here, he shouts in the black void ahead. —Do you hear me? You better get out right now.

He wants to sound big and mean but his voice is not big and mean, it is weak, it is a voice that breaks like an adolescent's, and it comes out so fast the words all meld together. He comes to the living room, freezes at the threshold. He sees nothing. Gropes for the light, cannot find it.

—Hello? he says.

Then he hears the noise again. And he knows what it is. It is a voice. A human. Someone chuckling, someone muttering. Lee has never been so terrified. His flesh is cold. This is evil that has come for him in the night. He is in the barn in the dark and the heat and he cannot get out, and the voice says something to him and he does not know what but yes he does, he knows, it is saying, *HEEEE! HEEEE! HEEEE! HEEE!* Lee raises his toy gun and says, —Let me out!

YOU AIN'T NEVER GETTIN' OUT!

And Lee pulls the trigger. He pulls it again and again. Four times he fires, maybe five, maybe six. It must be six because soon the gun is not firing anymore though he still pulls the trigger. He is so deaf he cannot hear his own blood rushing through his head and he is so numb he cannot even feel his own heartbeat though it kicks like a caged gorilla. He touches his ears, expecting to find blood gushing out of them. Everything smells burned and sweet. Finally he finds the light.

On the floor, just inside the closed front door, in fact right up against it, lies a kid. Not a home invader—just a kid, wearing Air Jordan sneakers and jeans and a hooded sweatshirt. His hand opens and closes, opens and closes, as though grasping for something. The other arm is draped over his face. Then the arm moves, drops away. And Lee sees the kid's face looking up at him. Blood all over it. Blood everywhere. Lee keeps the empty gun on the kid, trying to figure out where he knows the face from.

The kid says, —Where am I? Then he stops talking, stops grasping.

—No, no, Lee says to him.

But he's gone.

$\left(\text{Sheeple IV}\right)$

Maureen is in town for work. One day she knocks off early and stops in at a bar for a glass of wine. She never goes to bars alone. Nor is she much of a drinker. But today the constant, throbbing low-level insanity of New York makes her feel resigned and hedonistic, makes her feel French, though she has never been to France. Likes to imagine that in Paris they think nothing of wandering away from the office at three P.M. to drink wine with the sun still out, letting whatever happens happen.

It is awkward to be alone at a bar. There are some young people from either the college or Brooklyn, and there are old men, probably alcoholics. A man comes in. He is about her age. Says hello to him, they chat, fall in love.

She is successful at work but does not think much of herself. She is not small or cute or bubbly and does not feel compelled to charm or flatter men. Her teeth are not great and she is afraid of the dentist. Her clothes on her look nothing like they do on the models. Is fine without men or romance. She is far from alone. Many friends. Family. Her work. Was in love once. Darren. Long time ago—college. She told him, *I love you,* and he responded, *We are at a point in our lives where we should be casual and have fun, not saying I love you to each other.* She told Darren to get lost. Three days later, drunk on her doorstep at two A.M., he was saying, *I was dumb, I do love you.* She closed the door on his face.

Father was a drunk narcissist. Mother was gone. Could not or would not stand up to her husband, who was cruel and called Maureen dumb and fat and lazy and a dyke. A woman who does not stand up to her husband, Maureen believes, is a woman who is gone. *Why did you marry him?* she once asked her. *Why don't you take me and leave him?* Maureen was eleven. Her mother answered, *Because I love him. And he me. We are in love.* Grew up from then on to believe love is a myth. Darren changed her mind. Then he changed it back. Years later in a bar in New York a man comes in and changes it again.

Between her parents and then Darren, it has taken her fifteen years to teach herself to trust people. Where at twenty-five she would automatically assume everyone she met must be a danger to her, at forty she looks at new people and whatever their race or gender or class and sees not danger but help. She sees them as being capable of somehow helping her in ways she cannot necessarily conceive right away. And she them. It does not matter what her first impression is, what her visceral reaction is. Even when she feels repelled by a person or situation she tells herself, *Let them help you,* or *Let it help you...* She read this in a self-help book after Darren when she was just out of school and beginning her work life. Thought, *What the hell, try it.* It has worked. Since she has been doing this her life has been very successful and rich. Sees the world very calmly and clearly, as how it really is, free of the influence of news media or her father's warped myths or anyone else's myths. Sees the truth: that people are good. They are sweet and kind and lonely and want to do right, and the last thing anyone wants is to hurt anyone else. Everyone, she sees, is doing only their best. So she gives everyone the benefit of the doubt, no matter how she feels about them. Because you never know. People like to think they know. It makes them feel smart and in control. But there is no such thing as either smart or in control. Her many friends she has made from choosing to see people like this protect her when she needs protecting. She is never alone. They protect her with love. Real love.

At work she trusts people enough to ask for help and to give help, to admit when she is confused about something everyone else assumes to be obvious. People appreciate these things about her. She is a voice of reason. Catches problems others are too worried about appearing dumb to speak up about. She trusts that they all love her and will never think she is dumb. It makes them trust her in return. And to want to help her. They recommend her when positions open higher in the company, and in networking scenarios they mention her and recommend her; she has developed a good reputation in her field and is constantly fielding attractive recruitment offers from rival corporations, is often poached, never has to interview for a job, people throw money and responsibility at her and she is still unafraid to ask for more because she decides that the people she is asking, whether she likes them, are good people who want to help her. Earns an excellent income yet works steady, reasonable hours with unlimited vacation and ample perks, alongside people she respects and enjoys working with, because she is unafraid of refusing to settle for less. Owns a lovely home surrounded by neighbors she cares for and who care for her and who know her and she them and whom she can depend on if tragedy should ever strike.

Has made good with her father and mother. It took a big leap and maybe a little whiskey, but she sat down with them and explained her side of the experience growing up and its effect on her and asked them with sincere interest to talk about their own side, so she could have an idea of where they were coming from when they acted how they did so she would no longer see her childhood as irrational and monstrous and would therefore not see life in general as irrational and monstrous, which she did, at the time she had this conversation with them, early on, when she was having tough luck getting her first job out of school and had just read this self-help book and was bitter about Darren and pretty much everything. And they did talk about their perspective. Her father, she learned, was not a monster. He was a man who wanted to be good but was frustrated with his work and could not figure out what to do about it and who felt in general obscure and meaningless and alone and did not think he was worth much. He felt he was being a good dad by being so critical, so Maureen might turn out better than he. He was aware he was an alcoholic and had secretly tried to quit dozens of times, including going to AA meetings, but just could not quit and this made him hate himself more, which he projected onto his family, for they seemed to love him, a man who was not worthy of love, and therefore they were stupid and worthy of ridicule. And her mother's father was also an alcoholic, so an alcoholic man is what made sense to her, what she was drawn to, if only because it was recognizable, which she mistook for attraction. She learned as a little girl how to be passive and deferential to alcoholic men to avoid setting them off into a rage. For Maureen's mother, the choice was either be quiet and accommodating or be responsible for what happened as a result: things being broken, emotional hurricanes. That is what a man meant to her and that is what love meant. What family did. All she wanted was to be a loving wife and a good mother who contributed to her family. Maureen left that conversation changed. Understood them now. Trusted them. Began training herself to trust everyone else. Did.

Knows plenty of people from fucked-up families—whose isn't?—and she helps them get over it by telling them how she dealt with hers. *Get yourself trusting your folks,* she tells them, *and you trust life and you become free. Then you can do anything. Best thing you can do for yourself.*

In town for work, New York, stops in at a bar, meets a man. Bald, overweight, dour, and introverted. Suspicious, scared eyes. She wants him, she needs him. Everything about him she hungers for. She says hello. Hit it off, go back to her hotel. He is quick about things from his end and the wineglasses on the end table are not exactly shattering from anyone singing alto soprano, but it is very good, still, somehow. Lies there afterward listening to him talk. He talks mostly about his father. At one point he cries very hard talking about him. *I have always loved this man,* she realizes.

The next night they are going out to dinner with her friends from work. She meets him at his place. His place is incredible though he has no idea what he is doing with it. Or, worse, maybe he does. The mattress is on the floor. He has, for some reason, an old portable washer-dryer in the middle of the kitchen hooked up to the sink faucet. —Got that out of the trash, he says, —someone was throwing it away, can you believe it? They'll throw away anything in this country.

She says, —You don't have laundry in a building like this?

He says he does not like to use it ever since someone stole a pair of his underwear.

Hot dogs and nothing but hot dogs in the fridge.

Big television, way too big for the space.

In the bathroom she paws at the empty toilet paper cylinder in the dispenser and washes her hands in a sink coated in a layer of long-ago-hardened shaving cream, kicking aside an NFL towel grown mildewy on the floor. When she comes out he is standing there holding a gun.

—What do you think about this? he says.

—Not much, to be honest. It pulls to the right so bad you have to push against it, otherwise you won't hit the side of a barn. She explains, —My granddad had the same one.

He smiles, baring yellow teeth. She kisses him.

On the way to dinner he wants to know all her friends' names and backgrounds and Social Security numbers. They are all seated at a table in the middle of the restaurant and he makes the staff move them to one in the corner where he can sit with his back to the wall, facing the door. Her father used to do the same thing. He is polite if quiet with her friends, and she can see how much he enjoys the rare company, how lonely he has been.

Trip ends. He is at her hotel to see her off.

—Why don't you come with me? she says.

—Ha ha, he says.

She says, —I'm serious.

—What are you talking about?

—Lee, I think you need someone. I think you should come with me.

—That's completely irrational, he says. —I can't just leave New York.

—Why?

—Because I have a life here. A whole company depends on me. My community needs me. I am *vital*.

She puts her hand on his face and says gently, —Honey, no, you're not.

His face grows red and he says, —I don't even know who the hell you are. You're just a lonely woman. You've misunderstood all this. It's lust, nothing else. You were drunk at a bar probably hitting on every man there and I was just the first who said yes. And now you want me to think it's love and move to God knows where with you and change me.

—You're such an idiot, she says.

—You're the one trying to get the man you threw yourself at at happy hour to run away with you.

—You should listen to me, Lee.

—I can't even believe I'm still here talking to you.

—That makes two of us, she says, and turns away, falling out of love with him. She leaves the room with her suitcase.

He follows her down the hall to the elevator, not saying anything. He follows her all the way out front to the sidewalk, where she gets a cab. He watches her get in. The cab pulls away and he stands there watching her until they are out of sight of each other. Lee. Never even knew his last name.

She spends most of that flight home from New York in the bathroom. Her body has gone haywire. She is so sad.

Back at home, to cure the grief she works. And spends time with friends. Works harder, becomes an even better friend. Her ambition burns even hotter, after Lee. Maybe it's anger and it probably is. To think he had all that power to destroy all they should have had. Works harder and angrier. Finds new space for her company to expand into, has the guts Lee does not have and she uses her guts to take big risks on new products for unexplored markets. The risks pay off and revolutionize the space. Company grows. She is promoted to C-level executive. A Fortune 500 multinational approaches her to put her in charge of its North American operations, headquartered in Chicago. Dream job. More friends.

Late one night being driven from O'Hare following a trip to Beijing, a stray bullet shatters her window and hits her in the head. Emergency surgery saves her life. Blind in left eye. No feeling on left side of body. Left corner of mouth droops. Shooter never found. Could have been anyone, from anywhere. Nothing happens legally as a result. She just has to live with being mangled. Is anyone doing anything about this? Becomes obsessed with counteracting gun violence. Hears about a woman out of Ohio trying to start a movement to repeal the Second Amendment. Getting nowhere of course. Meets with this woman, Jenny Sanders. Has to fly to South Dakota to find her. She is there failing to get voters to turn on state senators in the pocket of the NRA. Meet at a Starbucks. Jenny Sanders is pretty if a bit cross-eyed and aggressive and unlikable. That's cool to Maureen. Maureen says she wants to help Jenny Sanders however she can. What can she do? Stuff envelopes for her? Make calls to voters? Canvass neighborhoods? Start a gun buyback program? Stage a rally outside a sporting goods store that sold the bullets used in a shooting?

Jenny sits forward and shouts, —They've been doing that shit for decades and know where it's gotten them? *Nowhere. Absolutely nowhere.* We need votes. And to get votes, we need money. Can you get me money?

—How much money?

—More money than *they* have.

—How much do they have?

—A whole lot of fucking money.

Maureen goes to her board. They refuse to get involved in politics, let alone radical ones like this. However the company is European owned, not American, and Maureen is a star who is excellent for its stock price but could leave for a rival whenever she chooses, and she makes the firm way more money than she is asking for, so they agree to start contributing to a shell company that contributes to another shell that funds Repeal the Second Amendment. This funding allows RSA to absorb the various extant and ineffective gun control groups. Jenny sneers at the very term *gun control*, saying society cannot control guns, it must annihilate them into extinction. RSA can also now buy advertising on national television, hire top marketing talent. It poaches some of the NRA's own lobbyists. Deluges neighborhoods with direct mailings and phone calls to create the image of a popular grassroots uprising, which then helps create a true popular grassroots uprising. In South Dakota voters remove two of the NRA's state senators in favor of dark horses who vote against gun rights across the board, no exceptions. Maureen silently becomes the largest financial supporter of anti-gun America. The ammo tax gains traction.

There is a shooting in Kentucky. Little girl playing with the family shotgun. Then there is one in New York. White guy emptying his revolver into the black kid next door just for knocking on his door. She sees the shooter's picture in the news, finally learns Lee's last name. Jenny goes off to New York. Maureen pays for the ticket.

THE BOY

Seem like there something crushing people like him. Boys like him get sent to fight the wars, get exploited to make the colleges money on the basketball court and football field, get murdered by cops, get put away in jail, can't get no jobs. The game seems rigged. He don't understand it but that's okay, he only fifteen, he gonna keep doing well in school and keep his head down, get into college, not one of those podunk ones advertised on the subway, he want *Harvard*, he want *Yale*—and Dr. Fallon at school tells him he's *on* that path, just gotta stay at it—and learn about how all this shit work to make America run as unfair as it do for people like him, and his mom and dad. And then once he figure out how it all work, he gonna fix it. Somehow. So boys like him coming up behind him have it better. Why not him? No one else seems interested in doing it.

His skin black. His lips thick, plum colored. Eyes: they brown, narrow, with swollen lids that make them look even narrower. Five feet eleven inches, 165 pounds. Fifteen years old but white people think he look older, they assume he gotta be twenty, twenty-one. His hair tufted. Voice loud. He walk around with his hood up and his head down. Obsessed with his Jordans. He does not necessarily step aside for you on the subway stairs. He like girls, loud music. He live in Manhattan, one of the dwindling few people of color for which that is true anymore, not counting those stuffed into the housing project towers in the Lower East Side and Chelsea. His friends live there, Raul in the LES and Kenny in the Chelsea ones. Raul's Dominican, Kenny's Trinnie. He himself lives in the West Village, like a white dude, like some gay actor, in a rich-person building but down in the basement, door next to where they keep the trash, his dad the super there, on call 24/7 to unclog the superrich folk toilets or scrub the superrich folk dog pee out of the hallway carpet or anything else the superrich folk don't want to do for themselves.

Sneaking out tonight with Raul and Kenny, parents think he sleeping over at Kenny's and technically he is, but first they getting pizza, and then they standing in line outside the store waiting for those new Jordans to drop at three A.M.. Raul's giving an in-depth account of this girl who let him fingerbang her last night, this pretty Jamaican girl named Tiyah—*she was moaning all loud and I had my hand over her mouth because her grandma was right out there in the living room*—but Clayton thinking about nothing but getting those shoes on his feet. More accurately, he thinking about getting them on his feet and seeing Stacey tomorrow night. She invited him to her friend's birthday party. He gonna take the train across the river and he thinking maybe he'll get a cab from the station and pick her up in it. Like a man. Yeah, he gonna hold her hand back there while he give the driver directions. He gonna pay for it using some of that money he buying these Jordans with, scratch his dad been throwing his way out the Christmas gifts the tenants give him each year, and supplemental scratch he himself been earning delivering for the diner on Greenwich Ave. weekends, and then when they get to the birthday party he gonna get out his side, hustle around to hers, and open the door for her. He gonna help her out, close the door behind her. He gonna tell her she beautiful and offer his arm and walk her into the party.

Stacey. Stacey Magnolia. Met Stacey Magnolia at her dad's hardware store on the corner where she was working the counter. He and his pops were painting 13F and they ran out of paint, Pops sent him to the corner for more. That apartment nasty. An old rich dude name Max been living there alone forever. Max act like a little kid, Clayton first thought he retarded or something, but Dad said that just how you get when you drink too much. Max used to make commercials, but now he just sit around his house smoking cigarettes and drinking and watching TV and telling whoever there to listen about when he used to make commercials. Dude smokes so much that the once-white walls were now brown, so Clayton's pops had to come paint them. Dirty dishes in the sink, old fuzzy-ass food up in the fridge (Clayton peeked). It was middle of the summer. *Hot. Humid.* The paint took *forever* to dry. What should have been a two-day job took three days, then four days.

—Shit, Clayton said in the middle of the third day, taking a water break and toweling off his dripping head, —this is stupid, we shouldn't be doing this.

His dad didn't answer.

—Ain't our fault dude smoked so much his damned walls turned brown.

—No, it's not.

—We could hire it out, send Dave the bill. He won't mind, we've done it before.

—We could.

—Then what we doing it for?

—I don't know.

—What you mean you don't know?

—I mean, there is reason. I just don't know what reason. It has not made itself apparent. But it will, when it wants. Now get yourself to the store before it closes, we need that paint.

His dad. Straight up batshit sometimes. Used to be a doctor, back in his home country. They won't let him be one here. Has to be a janitor instead. Who knows why he left. Things couldn't have been that bad over there to go from doctor to janitor, could they?

He bounced down to the store, feeling like a doofus in his painting clothes. He was dressed like Samuel L. Jackson in *Pulp Fiction*, after they clean up the bloody car and trash their suits, and the Wolf sprays him and John Travolta down with the garden hose and they put on random T-shirts and old gym shorts. *You guys going to a volleyball game or something?* People in this neighborhood are fancy, dress *nice, always,* everyone always looks like some sexy person from the movies.

When he got to the store, instead of ugly old Hector behind the counter there was this *banging* girl. Body incredible. Face so pretty, with these big, shiny, dark eyes and juicy lips. Clayton could barely look at her, she so fine, but from what he could tell she was about his age. One thing he learn from his dad aside from how to be a doormat for the rich and the white is to never be afraid of anyone. So as she rang up his can of paint, who care if she outta his league? He chat her up, ask her about herself. —What's your life story? he said. Something else he picked up from his dad. His dad always saying that to people. She seem so sweet and nice and smart, and they were definitely vibing, you could feel that. When Clayton returned with the paint, he must have had a big dumb grin on his face because his dad looked at him all suspicious, came over and got real close and started examining his eyes and smelling him. —What did you do? Who got you high?

—I ain't high, Dad. I'm in love.

And his dad turned back to the wall he was painting and, smiling a little, said, —Aha. Now we know reason for job.

Hippie-ass dude.

That was last summer. She live across the river in New Jersey, they been talking on the phone all year, writing letters and chatting and texting. She had a boyfriend for a little while and that hurt, he was depressed for a week, but then they broke up. Every Saturday he find a reason to go in there in case she there. Went to see *Fast and Furious* together. Kissed for the first time during it. Few weekends later her parents were going to be out of town the whole day, did he want to come over? She hadn't gotten the sentence out her mouth before he was outside her house knocking on her door. Took him two hours on subways and PATH train and buses and it felt like four, but he'da gone to Mars if that's where she lived. They got naked together. *Naked.* It was the greatest thing that ever happened to him. When he left they were a couple, it was official, boyfriend and girlfriend. That journey back home felt like it took eight seconds.

—My friend, she said on the phone that night when he called, —he gonna have a birthday party end of summer. His parents are gonna be gone. It's gonna be real. And, baby? That night? I want to do it. With you.

—Do what? he say.

She laughed. —You so stupid.

Then he understood. He a real idiot sometimes. For real. He go, —Really? All excited, voice all high.

She say, —Really.

He wanted to run around outside telling everybody: *She wanna do it with me, she wanna do it with me!* Ever since then, whenever he sees them, he been grabbing handfuls of those NYC condoms they put out on counters in bodegas. He must have fifty of them stashed in a shoe box among his Jordans.

—You ever done it before? he say.

—Nuh-uh. Have you?

—Nuh-uh.

—Yeah, right.

—I'm serious. You believe me?

—Yeah, I believe you. You believe me?

—I believe you. I'm kinda nervous.

—Me too.

—It'll be all right.

—I know it will. I can't wait.

He on the phone, playing some game he addicted to. Kenny brought a lawn chair and Bluetooth speakers, playing Kendrick on repeat; Raul think Kendrick trash, he call it white-girl shit, he say street niggas don't listen to that skinny-jean motherfucker, but Kenny can't get enough of it and Clayton agree with Kenny but act like he agree with Raul. It two A.M. Shoes drop at three. Kenny and Raul are gonna turn around and sell theirs, already have buyers lined up online, but Clayton would never sell his—well, maybe he would if the birthday party wasn't tomorrow.

Drunk white people stumble by, asking what everyone standing in line for. Smiling men, pretty women. Raul answer them with a straight face, —Gang bang, and Kenny and Clayton crack up, white people continue on they way, not knowing if they serious or not. They a little high, taking out Kenny's one-hitter when they sure the coast is clear. This city ain't nothing but cops. Everywhere you go a cop telling you what to do, trying to ruin your life. Last spring Raul got popped with a joint and they arrested him and everything, nearly broke his wrist doing it. They put him in jail for the whole weekend. On a little weed. It was only juvie jail but Raul still said it was the scariest shit he ever been through. And Raul the biggest, hardest dude Clayton know. And now Raul supposed to get into school, supposed to get a job, with that shit on his record?

Something, man—something trying to crush boys like them.

There are things Clayton can tell Kenny that he could never tell Raul, and things he can tell Raul that he could never tell Kenny. One of the things he can tell Kenny is that he scared for tomorrow night. Another is that sometimes he stand around looking at things, like the world, for example right now, out here on the street, in the heart of New York City, watching everyone, watching cars, seeing the people and the cars in the glow of all the lights, and he can't tell where they come from, the lights, he know there are streetlights but the lights don't seem to come from just the streetlights, and he know there are lights on stores and from windows, but the lights don't seem to come from there either. Like what is supposed to be making light don't in fact make it. Like in fact it make darkness. And the darkness make light. And he don't understand it, he don't understand life, why people are how they are and do what they do, but he want to, and he just know he can, one day, he think once he do he can make things better somehow, like maybe he has something to offer all this. He want to live a big magnificent life. He got this vow he made to himself. It seem like everyone between his age and his pops's age, somewhere along the way they get so tied up doing what they think they got to do that they never do what they *really* got to do. And they get crushed. But he ain't gonna get crushed. He gonna survive. He'll be the first. Like his pops always say: *You just never know.*

If he told all this to Raul, he'd just grunt and be all quiet and awkward, not knowing what the fuck he talking about. He and Raul once got busted at Atlantic Center in Brooklyn for trying to steal Blu-rays from Target to sell for Air Jordan money. Clayton don't like to steal but Raul do, and Clayton too afraid to stop him. Raul all, —Stop acting superior, nigga, and stand here in front of me so they can't see. Clayton don't like being called *nigga* or calling other people *nigga*, but it one of those things you have to do sometime, along with standing guard while Raul peels off the plastic from copies of *Poseidon* and *Transformers 2* and *Taken 2* and shoves them down his pants to bring them back to sell around the project.

Five security guys came, white dudes in red Target polo shirts. Clayton froze, Raul ran—both were caught. Took them into some little room in back of the mall that smelled like beer and made them sit there for hours, saying how the cops were gonna lock them up for years and years and what a good thing that would be for everyone. Four of the guys lost interest after a while or their shifts just ended and they left, leaving Clayton and Raul with just the one who seemed to be in charge, old white dude in his fifties or something, clearly a cop moonlighting. Had a gun. It was in a holster on his hip. Cop sat there the whole time with his back against the door, his hand over the gun like he might pull it any second and start firing. Clayton never been so scared.

—Let us go, yo, Raul said.

The cop gestured with his chin to the door and said, —You want to go? Go for it. Please.

His hand on the gun, making no effort to move aside to give them space to pass. They weren't idiots. They stayed. Stared at his gun the whole time. Clayton started losing it, was begging forgiveness, mercy. He could tell the cop enjoyed it. Clayton even cried a little— cop *loved* that. Raul scowled at Clayton, disgusted with him. But when Clayton was done, the cop took his hand off the gun, opened the door, and said, —All right, get outta here.

On the D train back home across the river into the city, Raul was saying, —What you beg him like that for, C? I was 'bout to *fuck* a nigga up, man. *Fuck* his badge and fuck his gun, nigga. He not on duty, and think I scared of a gun? Think I ain't neva seen a gun? Think *I* can't get a gun? I can have a gun *tonight. Tonight.*

And Clayton just staring out that train window. It was the part where you come up from underground into the daylight, and you going over the bridge and can see on one side the gray river going up the side of Manhattan and all the bridges and the water towers like pinecones on all the rooftops and the wall formed by all the towers of Raul's housing project greeting you into Manhattan, and on the other side of you the open horizon, endless water, like an old painting, and the sun on the water, the Statue of Liberty visible way out there but only if you know where to look and only if you squint hard enough and only if you look past all the rusted spray-painted steel beams of the bridge and all the big cranes and all the other ugly things blocking it. And if you ever get out there to see it up close—ain't no boats to take you, you gotta swim—you gonna find it ain't even really there, you gonna find that all this time it's just been an illusion projected from one of those big skyscrapers, some kinda prank or advertisement or something.

That night he went sleepwalking again. First time in years. He must have got out of bed, opened his front door, went out into the hallway, and gotten in the elevator and gone up to the sixth floor, started trying to open the door of this family who've lived there as long as his has, the Mendelsohns, white people, rich. Lawyers or something. They know him and his condition. They've had him and his parents over for dinner, always stop to chat when they come across him in the building, asking him about his life, trying to be nice, he guesses, but coming off like just more cops. That is what must have happened. As far as he knows, one minute he falling asleep in bed, then next minute he waking up to Mrs. Mendelsohn's voice gently saying, —Clayton? Clayton? Wake up, Clayton... and looking at Mrs. Mendelsohn's face. She was standing in the open doorway in her pajamas, she was putting her arms around him, putting her head in his chest, he was so much taller than she was, and he was sobbing, he was so scared—it scary enough when it happens, but he also scared because he think now his dad gonna get fired. And Mrs. Mendelsohn was saying, —It's okay, Clayton, it's okay. She helped him back down to his apartment and would not hear it when his dad thanked her and apologized and thanked her again, and when he begged her not to tell his boss she assured him she would not, and his pops say of course she kept her promise, but Clayton wonders, to be honest he don't know.

His phone rings. His dad. Seeing that name on the incoming call screen drive him crazy. Such an intrusion. It's embarrassing, he know what he gonna say and he gonna say it, that man always the same, predictable as a dog: *Hello, how are you doing, where are you?*

Where am I? Where I told you I'd be—at Kenny's, sleeping over.

Okay, so that's not where he is, but it's still annoying as what.

What did you have for dinner? What time will you be home in the morning? Why are you still awake, you should be in bed...

Whatever, man.

Be home early tomorrow, we need to fix dryer. Be home at eight.

And Clayton will say, *Eight o'clock? In the morning? On a Saturday? That's too early, Dad, come on, Dad. Ten, I'll be home at ten. Me and them maybe gonna get breakfast.*

And his dad will say, *Okay, ten, but ten sharp.*

It's astounding how easy his pops is to lie to. He feels guilty about it but it's what you gotta do. His pops believe everything he say. Sometimes it makes Clayton mad, like, don't he care? But what he gonna do, press the issue? Say, *Be tougher on me, Dad*? His dad a trusting type of dude, he trust everybody, he believe everything everyone tell him. To a fault. Always saying, *You gotta have faith in people, you gotta trust people.* Why he gotta be so damned weird? Why can't he just be a normal dad? Like the kids Clayton go to school with. Those rich white kids. Their dads never say that kind of shit. Those dads never just believe whatever people tell them. They ain't naive. They're suspicious and smart and that's why they CEOs and attorneys and hedge fund managers and have money and power— and why they ain't no *maintenance men* always scared of getting fired and deported. Always the same voice, the same tone, the same words. *Faith. Trust. Fearlessness.* You get tired of it after a while. You want your dad to be different. Especially when you with the crew, puffing weed and talking shit in the middle of the night in the city. You feel like your life with the man is a lie sometimes. Studying, working, all that Eagle Scout shit—it all feel impossible and fake sometimes. That ain't you. This is you. What you are right now, tonight, with the crew. Clayton hits IGNORE, puts his phone back in his pocket.

A bunch of preppy Upper East Side *Gossip Girl*–looking dudes roll up in a taxi all wearing tuxedos and drunk. They like the kind of kids he go to school with, those swooshy haircuts, cocky, strutting around like big men, like they think they they dads. They try to cut in line. They act all nonchalant about it, first just acting like they standing *near* the line, then slowly drifting closer and closer until they right in it, right up in front behind where Clayton and them been camped out for hours.

—Yo, Raul say to them. —Line end back there.

They act like they don't hear him so he repeat himself. Then they act like they can't understand him so he repeat himself again and they say, —What are you talking about, bro? We were here. We've been here.

Raul smiles at them. —Come on, now. We all just *watched* you roll up in that taxi, don't try to tell me y'all been here.

—We were here, bro.

—No, you were not.

—Bro, why don't you mind your business?

—Do what?

—Turn around, bro. He make a little swirly motion with his finger like he can control Raul with it, and he say again, —Turn around.

They talking in some bullshit fake voice, like they're plumbers from Long Island or something, the way they must think real men talk. Clayton thinks, *It's because they scared, they want us to think they're like us.*

Raul is grinning broadly now, like he's watching a magic trick. — You seriously trying to tell me to turn around?

—Turn around, bro.

—Would you like to discuss this further? Raul say.

Clayton panicking now. He panicking because Raul being formal. *Discuss this further.* When Raul start being formal to you, you know he about to start wailing at your head with them giant roast-beef fists of his. And if Raul fight, that means Kenny fighting, because Kenny think he can fight, and *that* means Clayton gotta fight, because Kenny can't fight for shit, and if Clayton don't help him Kenny gonna get hurt. Clayton don't want to fight, especially not these dudes—he feel sorry for them, the way they think they have to talk like contractors from Long Island. He don't want to fight nobody.

—Raul, he say, gently pushing Raul away from them. —Don't worry about it. Fuck it.

—Don't tell me not to worry about it, say Raul. —It ain't fair. We been here *hours*. And these motherfuckas just show up? Raul is seething, big chest moving in and out, sweat on his fuzzy upper lip.

—Just chill, he say to Raul. —Chill.

One of them say something and the rest of them snicker. Raul tenses and Clayton puts his arms around him. —Chill, chill. Clayton can't help but see them all as babies. Like, infants. A tick he has. Can't help it. When he get anxious sometimes he calms himself down by looking at the people around him—even cops—and imagining them how they were when they were babies, which makes him think about how they *were* babies once, everyone was a baby once, and then he feels better about everyone, less anxious, less scared. Everyone a baby once. He cannot imagine hitting a baby, even a very old one, one so old it don't look like a baby no more. Which is what adults are, if you think about it.

Raul mutters, —How they say they were here, man? How can they say that?

—I don't know, Clayton say. —Don't worry about it.

—Man, that's *bullshit*, C. That's a pussy point of view, yo. That some fucking subservient shit, man, and you know it is. You know it is.

—Maybe so.

—You a pussy, yo.

—No, I ain't.

—You a pussy. That time in the park? I *knew* you weren't gon stand up for me. I knew you didn't have my back. I knew you were gon do what you did. I knew it. I knew it.

Someone stole twenty dollars from Raul and Raul was going to fight him, so of course Kenny and Clayton had to go with him to meet the kid in the park to fight, and the kid brought his friends and shit was about to get crazy. But Clayton couldn't help but see them all as babies and convinced Raul to forget the twenty dollars and walk away.

Raul says, —You can't let niggas do what they want to you. You gotta defend yourself. Protect yourself, man.

—I don't want to fight.

—Ain't your choice sometimes. Niggas jump you, what you gon do, you just gon shrug? Say, *Wulp, that's the way the cookie crumbles, I suppose*? You gon tell me with a straight face that you not gon fight back?

—Raul, we fight those niggas and police come, we get locked up. Think *they* get locked up? Man, all I want is my damned *shoes*. I got a big night tomorrow.

—A pussy with nothing but pussy on the mind.

—Call me from jail tomorrow night. I ain't gonna answer. Imma be with *Stacey*.

—Whatever you say, *pussy*.

At that moment, one of the *Gossip Girl* dudes break off the line, wander out in the street, flag down a cab by yelling at it, making his voice all deep, trying to be all assertive and commanding. The others all follow him into the cab and off they go into the night, to other worlds behind fortress walls. Clayton turn to Raul with a look on his face and Raul say without even looking at him, —Shut the fuck up.

—I didn't even say nothing.

—I don't want to hear it, Clayton. It don't mean nothing.

—You'd be getting locked up right now if it weren't for me.

—Yeah, well, you still a pussy.

Clayton smiles, reaches out, pinches Raul's substantial nipple, twists it. —Ow! Quit it, yo!

—I want to kiss you sometimes, Raul, you know that?

—Try it, Raul say, smiling too but trying not to show it.

In the morning, sprawled on the floor of Kenny's room, Raul's rank-ass foot all up against his face, Clayton wake up early and dip out, stopping in the kitchen to say hi to Kenny's mom and little sister, Gabriella. Kenny's mom wearing a bathrobe and making pancakes.

She work at Flashdancers, but she so pretty she could be an actress. He can tell from her glittery skin and her makeup that she ain't been to bed yet after work. The TV blares cartoons, Gabriella lying on the floor in front of it watching them. —Good mornin', baby, say Kenny mom, —sit down, have some breakfast.

Clayton both trying and trying not to look at her tattooed titty showing through where her robe don't close all the way. —No thanks, I gotta be out. My pops need me at the building. We fixin' one of the dryers today, the rotator blew out and— He cuts himself off, seeing her eyes glazing over. —Anyway, thanks for letting me stay over.

—You welcome, Clayton. You welcome any time. You such a good influence on him, I don't know what his problems is. Idolizes his daddy, God help him.

—How his daddy doin'?

—*That* motherfucker.

—He out yet?

—He out. Again. Know how I know? Nigga show up drunk the other night banging on my door. Just like he say he gonna before he got locked up. Told me as soon as he get out he gonna come break my neck. He mean it too. He's beat my ass black and blue all over this apartment. Gonna kill me one day. I know it. Not the other night though. She lowers her voice to a whisper so Gabriella doesn't hear, leans in close to Clayton, very close, —My friend Tony got me something to keep under the mattress. She raises a finger with a crazy-long purple glittery nail to her lip to tell Clayton to keep that between the two of them. —I put that shit in his face and say, *Get the fuck away from me and my babies.* Poof! Dude gone like smoke. Without that, who know what woulda happen.

—Damn.

—Damn's right. I shoulda fallen in love wit a nigga like you. Anyway, say hello to your momma for me, baby.

—I will.

—Roll by the club some night, she say.

His face burn up and he grinning and he say, —Okay. He go to Gabriella in front of the TV, bend down and kiss her on her head, say, —Bye, dweeb, and she say, lips stained with red drink, —Bye, *dork,* and he sneak one last shameless glimpse at Kenny's mom's titty then he out.

A cool summer Saturday morning. He skip the train in favor of a long walk, first down Tenth Avenue, then making his way over to Seventh, carrying his Jordans in their box under his arm. No way he gonna put them on now and get dirt all over them before tonight. Brown dudes stand in front of bodegas spraying down the sidewalks. Outdoor produce stands are filled with green and red and orange, all of it wet and shiny and alive. Sirens still echo out across the fresh new concrete of Chelsea. Rumpled white people in sunglasses and four-hundred-dollar T-shirts stand over squatting, quivering dogs, the dogs looking at Clayton, the white people scowling into space. White people with nice hair stand in hordes outside French cafés, taking photos of each other in the sun.

Fine women pass this way, that way, this way again, every which way there is. None compare with Stacey though, who he dreamed about last night after texting with her until almost five A.M., his grinning, stupid face glowing blue from the screen as Kenny and Raul snored and whimpered in their sleep. He feel her out there to his right, across that river. It's a wide, wide river. It is a river a thousand mile wide. New Jersey, with its driveways and front lawns and parking lots and big houses, might as well be eight rivers away, eight oceans. The wind coming from that direction is warm and sweet because it come from where she is. Every car coming from the right, from that direction, is a good car. Every person walking from that river is a person to know and to welcome. He want to stand on the corner shaking each of their hands. Then he want to slip past them and go to the river. He want to run to the river. He want to feel her pulling him into it, he want to feel her hips, her skinny soft upper arms, soft gentle cheeks. His heart speed up, his tongue salivate. He want her wet lips, her hot minty breath; he want to tear off his clothes and dive into that river and swim across it, climb ashore on the other side, sprint down the highway and across the parking lots and through the yards of the big houses all the way to her and never leave.

He duck off the avenue onto Twelfth Street, lean against a wall recently painted to cover up writing. Take out his phone. He text her: Can't wait for tonight. Watch the nice town house across the street, the front door is closed but they left their keys in it. Flowers are in tree beds out front. The brick is bright and stoop is clean, heavy black iron railings painted recently. Stacey write back, Me too ;). He lift the phone to his mouth and he kiss her text. Then he dash across the street and up the steps of the town house, ring the bell. No one come. He ring again. Still nothing. Ring a third time, knock too. He lean over and look in the window. Inside, someone standing at the top of the stairs. Seeing him looking in, they duck around the corner to hide.

—Yo, he call through the glass, tapping on it. —Your key in the door!

He tap again, ring the bell yet again. They keep hiding. He like, *You for real? Maybe I'll crack the door and toss the keys inside and close it, that'll at least be better than just letting them dangle like this for anyone to take.* He put his hand on the knob, turn it, it open. Before he push it all the way open he thinks, *Hold up*—the fuck you doing? *This how you gonna get* shot. Sometimes he forget what he is to them. It hard to always keep it in mind, to keep track of their perception of you, to consider how you are seen by them. That something he learning better and better: you can't just live. They can, but you can't. You can't just behave naturally, as a human, and just do things you naturally do, like tell someone they motherfucking keys in the door. You always got to remember that you exist as two people—the *you* you and the *they* you, meaning the thing white people want to see when they look at you. You don't get to just live. Not if you want to live. Okay, then. He remove his hand off they doorknob, he turn and hop down the steps.

Has a thought as he walks away, a sort of moment of clarity in which he see everything in ultrahigh definition, a million megapixels per inch: That sums a lot of people up right there, don't it? Crouched inside they house, holding they breath, scared out their minds of whoever is knocking on their door and they don't even know who it is.

Get home, Pops's out front the building sweeping up other people's trash off the sidewalk, just where Clayton expected him to be. He hate when his pops's exactly where he expect him to be. And he's *always* exactly where he expect him to be.

—How are the rugrats? Pops say.

For a minute Clayton has no idea what he talking about—rugrats?—but then he remember he told his parents he and the boys were volunteering last night as counselors at an overnight church camp for little kids.

—Oh, it was fine, he say, enjoying the image of Raul trying to chase after a bunch of little kids. —Those brats though, man, they exhausting, they never get tired.

—Don't take nap yet.

—I know, I'll be right there, I just need to change and wash up.

—Hurry up.

—I *will*. Damn, why you gotta tell me to hurry up? Do I ever not hurry?

—Don't stop to use bathroom. You'll be in there all day.

—What are you even talking about?

—We should take a look.

—At what?

—Your digestive system.

—Why?

—Something wrong with it maybe. Always in bathroom. Hours and hours and hours. Your mother is concerned.

—Oh my God, you need to stop. For real.

His dad's grinning but trying not to, tip of his tongue sticking out from between his rows of teeth.

—Ain't even funny, Clayton say.

—It start beginning of last summer, no? Your medical condition? The day we painted apartment. After you went to store to get new paint. Met Hector's daughter.

—Ain't even funny, Clayton say again.

—You caught stomach virus there maybe. His dad snickering, going back to his sweeping.

—Whatever you say, Clayton say, opening the door, going inside, mortified.

He go in, holding the door for Ms. Larson coming out, a tall pretty lady always dressed up and whose high heels always clack. She had cancer a few years ago, almost died. His pops had Clayton water her plants and take care of her cats and keep the place clean for her while she was in the hospital. Momma cooked for her. Ever since then on Clayton's mom and dad anniversary, Ms. Larson make his mom a new dress to wear to dinner. It ain't just a dress either—it's a *gown*. Like *Oscars* shit. Mom look like Halle Berry in them. He tell her that too and she smile and you can tell she love it. Mom's friends always telling her to turn around and sell them after she wear them. Custom-made, one-of-a-kind Elana Larson gown? She'd get *thousands*. She always say no way, my friend made me this, a gift from my friend. Nobody else knew Elana Larson had cancer, only Clayton and his folks. She told nobody else in the world, not even her assistants. As far as the fashion world knew she was off on some crazy-ass Buddhist retreat where she had to keep a vow of silence, so she couldn't talk to or see anyone for months. It helped explain how skinny she was when she came home.

Always say she going to write Clayton a college recommendation when the day come he start applying, just let her know. He got three years to go still and it might as well be thirty, but she went to Yale and knows a lot of rich people who went to other schools like that and serve on advisory boards, and knowing she in his corner inspired him to boost his GPA last year from 3.1 to 3.6. She say, — Clayton, I encounter a lot of very successful, effective people in what I do and I see in you the same qualities that they have. You can be one of those people. You can live that kind of life. Just let me know if there's anything I can do to help you get there.

She always seem lonely, Ms. Larson. Whenever he see her, like now, for a second before she see him, when she in her own world stepping off the elevator, rounding the corner, she look sad, like she a million miles inside herself, like she crouched down in a great big empty house with her fingers in her ears, praying no one looking in through her window ringing her bell to tell her her keys in the door. Then she see him and, whoosh, she light up, burst out of herself, smile, call to him in her rich loud voice, —Good morning,

Clayton! He can't imagine what it must be like to feel like you can't tell nobody but your super that you dying. Why do people live like this? He always want to be like, *Why you like that? All you adults, all you grown-ups: Why you like that? Why don't you just stop?*

The doorman Lucien standing behind the counter flirting with Frank the UPS guy again, Clayton say what up to them. Lucien got hair like *Saturday Night Fever* but it graying. When Clayton first met him when he started working here three years ago, Clayton assumed the man was an actor who couldn't make a living at it or a recovering drug addict or an ex–drag queen or all the above, but his dad found out Lucien was in the Secret Service for twenty years, protecting President Bush, then Clinton, then the other Bush, that crazy one who fucked up all kinds of shit and nowadays just sit around all day painting pictures of cats. Lucien saved his money all his career and retired here to NYC, took this job to have something to do and a way to meet people. Chose NYC because, as Lucien say, it the greatest city in the world. —I never want to see a gun again, let alone carry one, Lucien say. —I just want to live and love, baby. Spends his off nights at bars in Chelsea doing exactly that. Dude got game. For real. Clayton gotta hand it to the man.

Some odd creatures show up in that building lobby off the street sometimes, there are some scary cracked-out drunk people out there, but Clayton feel safe knowing Lucien down there keeping everything on lock. He a bad muthafucka. Clayton seen him wrestle a big ol' drunk dude to the ground, must have been six-foot-six, 350 pounds, and keep him down until the cops come, and he also seen Lucien break up fights between girlfriend and boyfriend that look like they about to get violent, but charming them, talking to them and listening to what they say, keeping the peace.

Clayton take the stairs to the basement. Down in the basement he pass the laundry room where Art stands scowling in his underwear, no pants on, growling at the washing machine like an animal.

—What's the matter, Art?

—Damn thing ate my money again, he say.

—Pssh, Art, man, I told you, it didn't eat your money, it just don't start till you put the lid down. See? Look. Clayton go to the washer trying not to look at Art's nasty-ass dirty laundry in there, shuts the lid. It's now supposed to switch on and start filling with water but it don't.

—Damn thing, Art says. —Damned *conmen running this place.*

—No one's a conman, Art. These buttons probably just aren't pushed in all the way. You never push them in all the way.

—I push them.

—Not all the way though. Clayton push them, nothing happen.

—Classic con, say Art.

—Okay, what about your money, Art? You put money in it, right?

—Hell no, I didn't.

—Art, you didn't put any money in it?

—Why would I do that? It's only gonna eat it.

—You crack me up, Art. Here. This one's on the house. Clayton pull out his keys, there's a special one that opens up the maintenance panel on the washers to get at the circuits. He pop the panel open, hits a button to turn on the machine. The washer comes to life, water comes pouring out.

—Temperamental machine, Art grumble.

—Sure is, Art. All right, I'll see you. And Art, man, you gotta put pants on, man. For real.

—Don't tell me about pants.

—I won't tell you about pants, Art. I won't. I'll see you, Art.

Clayton go down the hall to his door at the end of it, near the freight entrance and the trash. He unlock it, go inside. His mom making breakfast, he smelled it from down the hall, *fit-fit* and *fatira,* damn his stomach *growling.*

—Is that you, baby?

—What up, Momma.

His mom wild, she still have that thick heavy accent and always bungling her words—she ain't making breakfast, she's *making the breakfats.* Clayton pretty sure sometime she do it on purpose, just because she think it funny, but over her fifteen years in America, in New York City, she assimilated into her vocabulary all kinds of ways of talking—from kinda street or hip-hop like how he talk to little bits of Spanish, some Korean, even Arabic she pick up from the bodega man. She that quiet kind of smart, the kind where she don't have to say nothing smart for you to know she smart. You wouldn't be surprised to learn she was a professor back in the day in their home country, before they had to leave.

His folks don't tell him much about all that. When he ask how they did it, how they got out of there alive—that place is *still* on the news, satellites keep turning up secret concentration camps, people still going missing, seem like there always war going on or an entire village getting slaughtered—and how they made it to America, how they got in, because you can't just show up at JFK and get made an American, you need papers, you need connects—but all they ever say is *Strangers. We were not afraid of strangers. Including you.* He never know what they mean by that: *including you.* He always ask, they never tell him.

—Clayton, do you want the breakfats? she call from the kitchen as he duck into his room to sit on his bed and open the shoe box and look at his Jordans.

—Gotta help Dad.

—Don't be punk. You have to eat.

He put his hand over his face. *Don't be punk.* That some funny shit. He take his phone out real quick, tweet that, toss his phone aside, pull his shoes off, take out the new Jordans. Damn, they smell *good.* They all stiff and bright and the insides are soft like something an astronaut would wear. Yeah, these are engineered by the elite, man, and you can tell—they feel like they should be part of a spaceship. He smell them again. He addicted to that scent, that new Jordan aroma. Laces them. Even the laces are premium, got these glittery woven flourishes that seem like would hold up a suspension bridge for a hundred years without breaking. Now for the big moment: he put them on his feet... *Oooooooooooo-we!* They feel *gooooood,* they grip that foot, they wrap that foot in comfort and warmth and softness, it feel like a girl, it feel like *Stacey.* He put on the other one. Shivers are going up and down his spine as he tie it and stand up in them. They so light, he feel like nothing on his feet. He feel powerful in these shoes, *indomitable.* Like he can go outside on the court right now and drive the lane like LeBron, drop eighty-foot threes like Steph Curry.

Wears them into the kitchen to show his moms. —Check it out, he say.

—Where did you get those?

—Bought them.

—When?

—Last night. She narrow her eyes, knowing something up. —I mean, last *afternoon*, like, on my way to the church. I had some time to kill. I had money saved up from making deliveries. These are limited edition, Mom. Only a thousand in existence.

She raise her eyebrows, turn her mouth downward, nodding in approval. —They bang, she say. He bend over cackling. —What's so funny? she say, pretending to be confused, but she smiling too.

He put his arm around her, smooch her cheek. He go back to his room to get his phone. To his tweet Kenny say: lol. Stacey say, awww she so adorable. hi clayton's mom! and a little blinky smiley face with flowers. He say back, I kno right? love her. Then he take the shoes off, wipe them down with the piece of cloth that came with them, stuff the paper and plastic form holders back in them, place them carefully into the velvet bag that came with them too, and set it in the box, place the box in proud top position on his dresser, next to his chess tournament trophy. The rest of his Jordans are in the closet, in their original boxes, precisely stacked according to release date. Five pair. Each one worked for and earned dollar by dollar. That's why he take such good care of them—appreciates them more than those rich kids do. But these, these new ones here, these his favorite. The prize jewel in the crown, for sure. He kiss the box and change, brush his teeth, eat breakfast, then hustle back out to help his pops.

In the laundry room, Art still there, still in his undies, sprawled in a plastic chair engrossed in an old issue of *Cosmo*. Clayton's pop shows up, rubbing his hands together, sleeves of his work shirt rolled up, glasses secured to his face as usual with the little black plastic elastic band that go around his head. The dead dryer is the one at the end. —All right, he say, putting his hands on his hips and considering the dryer. For a second, Clayton can see him as a doctor, like how he should be. It look right. Like when you're making music on your laptop and struggling to find the right beat, and then you finally get that kick where it should be and the snare sound just right and it all settles in on itself and becomes its own little being that has lived forever and will live on forever. —All right son, he say, pointing to the unopened UPS box in the corner. —Open box and get new belt.

Clayton squat over it, pull out his keys, use one to split the shipping tape and open the box, take out a black rubber loop. —This right? Clayton hand it to him, he study it.

—That's it. It's a beauty.

—Yeah, gorgeous, Clayton say, sarcastic. His pops don't pick up on it.

—Manufacturer uses cheap belt, his pops say. —Cheap belt snap. If they make with high-quality belt, like this, these machines lasts forever. What a beauty.

—Dad.

—Mmm.

—You serious? It's a piece of rubber. It's a washing machine. Nothing beautiful about no washing machine.

—Dryers.

—Whatever. I mean, you don't get sick of pretending like you happy? Like you satisfied?

—I am happy.

—You *can't* be.

—Why not?

—Because this ain't where you supposed to be.

—Sure it is. This is where I am. So this is where I am supposed to be. Clayton shake his head. —But you a *doctor* though.

—*Was* a doctor. Now a handyman. There was purpose for me as doctor and now there is purpose for me here.

Maybe he feeling a little cocky because he got Stacey waiting tonight, but Clayton sneers, —Purpose. What purpose? To be these people's minion?

His dad ain't looking at him now. Clayton know he want to, but he pretending to be very focused on unscrewing the side panel on the dryer. Clayton feeling bad now. He want to hug him. He want to cry and he want to kiss his dad and make him feel like he given him the greatest life anyone could have. He want to say, *I know what you mean about purpose, I do, I know exactly what you mean when you talk like that.* But he can't say it. It ain't like there a *reason* he can't say it—he just *can't.* So he don't say it. He stay where he is, standing there, watching his dad unscrew screws, the last word he said still hanging where he left it: *minion.*

—Hand me crescent wrench, his dad say, all curt and weird now. When Clayton put it in his hand, he suddenly look up at him over his glasses, staring at him, and something much more serious comes into the air. —Clayton, he say. —You know how we always say, *We were not afraid of strangers, including you?*

—Uh-huh, Clayton say.

—And you always ask what we mean?

—Uh-huh.

—Well, his father say, —you probably guess there is more to our life before you than you know.

Clayton don't want him to keep talking, he don't want to hear whatever he about to tell him, he know he don't before he hear it. But Pops already saying it. He saying all kind of shit that Clayton can't believe. Horrible shit. Things that happened to his mom. —No, stop, stop, Clayton say, feeling sick. None of this making sense, it too crazy and he don't want to hear no more. But his pops keep talking. He hardly hear him, he can't be in the room with this man saying these things.

He don't know where to go, he just walk out the basement, up through the lobby, head down, past Lucien who ask what's wrong, out the front door, down the street, and he *gone.* And then he just wander, riding the subway back and forth, going from crying to laughing in disbelief to imagining giving big speeches to his parents: *Why didn't you tell me? Why didn't you* tell *me this? How long were you going to wait? Why did you... ? How come... ? How could you... ?*

He go to the park. Ain't never going home again. Never. He can't. He done. Done. Everything he know is a lie. A *lie.* Why didn't they tell him? Well, now they gonna be sorry because he gone. He on his own now. They ain't never gonna see him again. Where he gonna live now? He don't know, out here in the park. Why not? Get a tent and live off hot dogs he steal from vendors and, he don't know, fish he catch in the pond or something. They'll be sorry then. They'll come see him there in the park. *Please, Clayton,* they'll say, *please come home.* And he'll be like, *Nope. Shouldna lied. Sorry.* That's right, he ain't never going home. Never ever. Never. Over his dead body.

He go home. After a while there ain't a lot to do in the park, and he forgot his phone so can't call nobody. He tried going to Kenny's, but once he got all the way down there, he was close enough to his house, he figured might as well just go get ready for the party. When he come in they sitting on the couch waiting for him. He like that they're waiting for him. Yeah, he gonna twist that knife. Make them sorry. *Liars, man. Fucking liars.*

—Just came for my phone, he mumble, all cold and steely, to make them feel it.

He walk past, not even looking at them. Lock his bedroom door, take his clothes off, throw them toward the hamper, kick the hamper over loud so they hear it. Then he crying again. Face burning. He so damned motherfucking mad. Never felt like this. A chained beast. No place to put his rage. It boil inside him. He pace back and forth, growling, hitting himself on the head. Then that start to hurt too much, so he sit on the bed, face in his hands.

His momma knock on the door. —Baby? she say.

—Go away. But he thinking, *Don't go away. Please keep knocking. Please kick down the door and hug me, please, Momma, kick down the door and hug me.*

—Can we talk? She sound like she been crying. He feel bad but she lied.

—No. I gotta be somewhere.

—Where, baby?

—None of your business.

He get dressed and walk out past them again, out the front door, still not looking at them, feeling they eyes on him and kind of enjoying that. His mom don't want him to leave, just fly out into the city like this, not telling them where he going—*a party? Whose party?*

Where? Where are the parents? I speak to them. I speak—but his pops put his arm around her and say, —Let him go, it's okay, he okay.

Clayton go outside, he already going, it don't matter whether they allow him or not, it ain't up to them no how, they lied, they liars. He wearing his hoodie over his head because he can't stand to look at the world right now and he can't stand to be looked at by it. He go up to the train station. Crosses the street, cab honks at him to get out of the way. Cops on the corner staring him down. — Where you going, buddy? they say. He don't answer. Can feel them watching his back. He don't give a fuck, not tonight. He got all his shoe money, a big grip of cash in his pocket. He got his phone. He got Stacey Magnolia, across the river, waiting for him. He keep walking.

Three kegs, countless bottles, maybe a pound of weed spread across the kitchen counter, Adderall and ecstasy going around, a band playing Prince covers in the basement, sweaty giddy girls wiggling and bouncing all over the dance floor, no parents, no neighbors for a mile—these rich white kids know how to make a dude forget his worries. They got a half-pipe out back, kids are skating it; there a pool all lit up turquoise, kids gliding naked through it. The host of the party, Stephen, lives on a serious spread, like a farm, with its own *pond* on it. Down by the pond they got a bonfire going strong, and all around it are tattooed white boys without shirts, tattooed white girls in bikini tops with their hair tied back, and they got beer and they got guns. God*damn* they got guns. You can see all them scampering around in and out of the light from the fire, carrying this gun or that gun, bending down to load this gun or that gun, then standing upright and pointing it across the water and firing— *CRACK! CRACK!*—drawing on a cigarette and firing again, handing it to a girl, putting their arms around her to show her how to shoot it right—*CRACK! CRACK!* Clayton saw them down by the pond when he and Stacey rolled up in the backseat of her friend's car.

—They crazy, he said. —They gonna get arrested.

Stacey said, —No, they allowed.

—I'd like to see a bunch of black kids doing that. National Guard be down here.

He still feeling upset. Bitter. She ask what wrong, he say nothing. She rub his arm and kiss his shoulder.

Inside the party they make a little pretense of walking around saying hello to people, but they both have one thing on their minds. He so nervous. Mouth all dry. Hands cold. Legs trembling. They find a couch in the corner. They kissing on it. Stacey's friends keep walking by saying smart-ass shit.

—She choking?

—She need the Heimlich?

She swats at them. —Y'all need to quit.

—And *y'all*, they say, —need to *get a room*.

She say to Clayton, —They so ridiculous.

He say, —I don't know, do you want to?

—Want to what?

—Get a room.

The answer is obvious, it's in the air with the weed smoke and the music and the energy of the party, she just waiting on him to stand up and take her hand and lead her up there. But before he can do it, Stephen, the rich white dude who live here, come through with no shirt on carrying some crazy-ass machine gun like it's nothing.

—What up, porn stars, y'all trying to shoot dis?

—What is it? Clayton say, spooked but also kind of fascinated.

—What the SEALs used to kill bin Laden. Got it for my birthday. Dis shit's *dope*. I got an eighty-round drum on it. When thugs roll up on me, I can chill up in my position and pick them off all day long. Stephen act like he shooting it, going all, *Blatblatblatblatblat!*

Clayton staring at it in Stephen's hands. He still kind of feeling like how he felt in his bedroom. Like he boiling.

Stacey laugh. —Stephen, who gonna roll up on you on your farm? They gonna steal your cow?

Stephen snorts. —Whatever. Shit's real out there. Y'all coming or what? He say it staring straight into Clayton's eyes, like he know something about Clayton. He has to struggle to meet Stephen's stare.

Stacey got herself propped up on one arm, hand in her hair that she has done special for him tonight, like it's prom or something.

She say she spent all day getting ready. *Wanted to look beautiful for you tonight.*

—No, Clayton say. —I'm cool.

—You sure?

—Uh-huh. Stephen leave and Clayton *relieved.* He say to Stacey, —Still want to go upstairs?

She smiles at him all shy, goes, —I don't know, do you?

—I don't know. He smiling too, he can't stop.

He take her hand, lead her to the stairs, go up, find a bedroom. Can't get her clothes off fast enough. He take in everything he see and feel, to remember it later. Outside he can hear them shooting. *CRACK CRACK CRACK!* He on top. Can't get it in at first. Hard to see what happening. Then she say hold up and reach down and do *something,* and he in. He *in.* It feel *goooooooooood.* It feel even better than he imagined. *Feel* ain't even the right word for it, it like he acquired a new sense. He kiss her. She breathing heavy. He come. —I came, he say. She smile, all gentle, and say nothing, just stroke his hair and look at him. He lie with her naked for what feel like hours, and then he tell her about what his dad say today. After he tell her, she just smile and kiss him and keep kissing him, and she just love him and it's perfect.

—Is that why you used to sleepwalk? she murmur.

And he say, —I don't know, maybe.

She quiet for a moment, then she say, kind of to herself, —Your poor momma.

And he say, —Yeah.

When they go back downstairs, they are new people, it is surprising anyone they knew from earlier still recognizes them. They find food in the kitchen and just *eat* like they high. They both *starving.* —Why are we so *hungry*? she say with her mouth full of Tostitos.

All he can do is laugh. —I don't know! He still can't stop grinning. Face hurt.

She gotta go home, her ride's leaving. He put his hoodie up, walk her out the front door, to the car. —Come on, get in, we'll drop you at the train.

—Nah, he say, —they ain't running no more.

—How you gonna get home?

—Imma just call a cab.

She looks like it blows her mind. —That's expensive.

He shrugs, casual. —It ain't bad. It's reasonable.

She laughs at him. —*It's reasonable*. Look at you, all Mr. Big Time now.

—That's right.

When she gone he sits on the curb and call a cab and wait for it, thinking about his momma some more, his pops. The night feel different now. Everything seems brighter, more vivid. But it taking *forever* for that cab to come. Finally after, like, thirty minutes it come. But it see him and just keep driving past. He call again and wait another half hour for another one and same thing. He call a third time, saying, —Yo, send someone who cool with a black teenager in a hoodie. He laugh.

Dispatcher go, —Say again?

—Black kid in a hoodie, Clayton say, —that me. I got money. Cash. I ain't gonna rob you. I just want to go home.

Dispatcher quiet for a second, then go, —Five minutes. And exactly five minutes later, a black dude roll up in a cab and Clayton get in.

Driver say, —What's a boy your age doing out this time of night? but he ain't even trying to talk about it. Driver ain't got no idea. Words cannot explain. He put his head back and look out the window, thinking of her legs, how her thighs felt. That warmth opening up all of a sudden and him going in that first moment. Then he see his momma. And he look around and he see all sort of dudes with machine guns, and he see his pops tied up in a chair screaming and his momma bloody and she crying, and there blood all over him and he holding Stephen's gun in his hand and he down by that pond shooting it with them and a spirit comes out of that pond and it his dad. His real dad. And it coming toward him and Clayton shooting at it, but the bullets ain't doing nothing and the spirit crawls inside him and next thing he know, cabdriver yelling at him: —Wake up! Wake up!

He wake up. He ain't in the car no more, he outside. Everything is orange and concrete and cars fly past. The cabdriver standing in front of him, he terrified, he has his hands on Clayton's shoulders and he screaming: —Wake up! *Wake up!*

—What? What happened?

Driver see he awake and say, —*Gah-damn!* You damn near gave me a heart attack!

—Where am I?

—You in the *Holland Tunnel, son! Gah-damn!* We stopped in traffic and you start screaming and banging on the window. Next thing I know you out the gah-damn car, walking down the middle of the Holland gah-damn Tunnel.

—I was sleepwalking.

—*No shit* you were motherfucking sleepwalking. *Gah-damn.*

—I'm sorry.

—You need a hospital or something?

—No, no, just take me home, man. I'm sorry.

—You ain't gonna jump out again on me?

—Nuh-uh.

—You lucky traffic don't move but three miles an hour in here. You lucky we weren't on the West Side Highway or somewhere. Try that on the West Side Highway, you're roadkill, son. Happened last *week* to a guy.

—I'm okay.

—You gonna stay awake?

—Yeah. I'm awake, I'm awake.

Cab pull up behind his building. Clayton pay him, giving all of it, all his savings. Driver take it all, just snatch it like it pennies, shoving it into his pocket.

—You got a condition or something? driver say.

—Yeah.

—Gotta be careful.

—I know.

—Take care of yourself.

—I will.

—Can't never be too careful.

Clayton get out, cab drive off. He fish for his key, unlock the building's back door, slip inside, then go through the basement and inside his apartment. He know his mom awake in her room, listening for him to come in. That feel good. She'll be relieved hearing him come home. Now she'll finally let herself sleep. In the morning they'll talk about everything. It don't hurt so much now, after Stacey. Nothing hurt now, because of her. Now he only thinking about his momma, what they did to her, and he feel sick, he feel guilty, but he also feel so proud of her. He got so much love for her. Dumb ass feeling sorry for himself. When his dad told him, what he shoulda done was run and hugged her and never let go.

He got so much love in his life. Maybe it don't matter who your father is, where you come from. Maybe he gotta learn that. Maybe that the most important thing: not your past, but how you deal with your past. If you don't deal with it right, your past can be death, it can be prison. For real. There so much to learn. *I'm so young,* he thinks. Can't wait to learn. Wanna learn it all. Wanna be a good man, have a good life.

Can't wait to kiss my momma in the morning, my pops. Can't wait to call Stacey, hear her voice. Wonder what she look like right now, sleeping. Pretty as hell, no doubt. Damn, he wish he were there with her. *Remember last night?* he'll say when he call her. *Remember what?* she'll say, teasing him. He'll laugh. *The band,* he'll say. And she'll say, *Oh yeah, they were great, they were the best part of the night.* Then her voice will get soft and whispery and she'll say, *Of course I remember, Clayton. I'll always remember.* He go to his bedroom, falling onto his bed atop his sheets in his hoodie and his Jordans. He out before he know what hit him.

(Sheeple V&VI)

A girl is ignored. Old teacher was good. But this new teacher—the girl can tell this new teacher just gives no kind of shit. She just yells at them, tells them to sit still and shut up and do what it says to do in the book.

Fuck the book. Nothing to work for and be excited about. The girl tries to read the newspaper but the words don't come right, they are in some kind of different language, the words that are supposed to be at the end are at the beginning, and the words that are supposed to be first are second and sometimes third. It takes her half an hour just to understand a single sentence. Better when someone reads it out loud to her, but who is she going to ask to do that, her teacher? She'd just say, —We ain't readin' da newspaper, we readin' *da book*, now do what you told and read *da book*. So she does not read the newspaper. And she does not read *da book* either.

Nothing is simple in her life or makes any kind of sense. She doesn't understand why shit is the way it is. Why does no one she knows have a job except her teacher? What is the point of learning what's in *da book* when there is nothing out there but jail and drugs and alcohol and death? Nothing makes sense but boys. Boys make sense because you got it and they want it. You make it look a little better, you stick it in their faces a little then take it away from them, they want it even more. They notice you and ask you things and try to make you laugh, if they want it.

This boy from the block want it, he's wanted it since she turned eleven years old. He isn't a boy, more like a man. He buys her candy and soda, and he has a sister, he says, who does hair and maybe she'll do hers for free. And this man has a spot in the basement of this building he can get into whenever he wants. It's scary down there and she doesn't like him, but she wants her hair done. And it feel like she can't say no to his attention. It's like she cannot tear herself away. And no one else gives a fuck about her. So she starts going to this spot with him almost every day. Gets pregnant. Tells him. He looks mad at first but then he says it's okay, don't worry about it, no problem, we'll handle it. And she feels better. Few nights later he wants her to meet him at a different spot, way out in the park where there's nobody else, and she goes. He takes out a gun and puts it in her mouth and pulls the trigger.

She thinks, *I'm dead.* He is saying, —Shit, shit, and trying to fix his gun. The gun *jammed.* He says he was just kidding around but she runs away and he doesn't chase after her. She tells no one anything. Gives birth to the baby. They say, —What do you want to name him? She says the first name that comes into her head: Kenny. Quits school, gets a job. The job is being talent in a gentlemen's club in the Meatpacking District making all kinds of money. The lady who runs it says she makes movies, maybe she will put her in one. Are they porno? No, they're not porno, they're real movies. Holds on to that, when dancing gets too tiresome and too fucked up. Real movies. I'll be in a movie. One day, one day.

Years go by. Still dancing. A second baby—Gabriella. She's seven now. Kenny's fifteen. She has moved them into the project in Chelsea. Getting in was like winning the lottery. Works while they sleep, is home while they're awake. Kenny's father has been locked up for something she had nothing to do with, but he gets out and she hears he's looking for her. She gets a gun from a security guy at the club. Kenny can't read the way she couldn't read at his age, but his best friend, Clayton, who's a sweet good kid, sits with him and helps him, and Clayton's momma talks to the school Clayton goes to, arranges for Kenny to take an admissions test, and Clayton helps him study so hard for it and he gets in, with full scholarship. Clayton gets killed, shot by a white man for no reason. They make a movie about it. Lady at the club knows them, says they're using real people in it to make it more authentic, puts her in touch and they like her, they want what she's got, and put her in the movie playing Clayton's momma. This definitely ain't a porno—it blows *up* and everyone recognizes her and now she's an actress, she gets a role on a TV show, she's making drug dealer money, she moves Kenny and Gabriella out of the project into a white-people building with a doorman next to the park. She pays for Kenny's college and can put Gabriella into a good school with teachers who recognize her brilliance and talent and who pay attention. Gabriella grows up with everything in the world to be excited about.

Weighs four pounds at birth, almost dies. Mother has no insurance, can't afford the checkups she needs while pregnant. While Momma's out working, Kenny feeds her, changes her, sits with her around the clock until she can breathe without machines. She's seven now and Kenny's fifteen. Kenny's at school, Momma's out doing nails at this salon, latest stab at getting legit because she feels like she needs to quit the club. Kenny's dad has been in prison, but he's out now and comes up banging on the door, calling Momma's name. Gabriella tiptoes up to the door to listen, careful to do it to the side so he can't see her toes under the door. He is trying to twist the knob.

—Open the door, Gabriella, he says.

How does he know her name?

—Open the door, he says.

She does not open the door. Calls her momma on the phone—no answer. Calls Kenny—no answer. Calls Ms. Debby across the hall—no answer. Her momma has a gun under her mattress, thinks she doesn't know about it. It's so heavy. Points it at the door holding it with both hands. *Please, God,* she prays, *please, God, make me disappear, make me a ray of sunshine so I can vanish.* Like a magic wand, when she points the gun at the door the knocking stops. Then Kenny's daddy is talking to somebody else outside in the hall. She knows the other voice. It's God, answering her prayer. Kenny's dad is mumbling something and she can hear him leaving. Then there is knocking again, but this time it is the one with the good voice, the God voice.

—Hey, nerd, God says, —you in there?

She puts the gun back, opens the door. Clayton. He comes inside, closes the door. How did he know? She wraps her arms around him and he says, —What's going on? Who was that? She is crying. He strokes her head and says, —Shh, everything's okay, you're safe, I'm here. Next time it happens call the police, do you understand?

She says, —What are you doing here?

He says he is on his free period from school and Kenny didn't show up today, so he's checking up on him to make sure he isn't sleeping or playing video games. Then he says, —Why aren't *you* in school?

She shrugs, says her momma don't make her go.

He says, —No, you gotta go. You gotta go every day.

She says, —Do you go every day?

—Yeah.

—Then I'll go every day too.

Sometimes he stays over in Kenny's room and she gets to hang around them for hours, sometimes all night, listening to them talk about things and people she does not know, and asking, *What? Huh? Who said that? What happened? What's so funny?* until Kenny yells at her to go sleep on the couch and leave them alone, but Clayton always says, *Aw, Kenny, it's cool, let her stay.* He is so nice and smart and works so hard and never lies, he is what she wants to be when she grows up. If she is like Clayton, she knows, she will fall in love with a boy like Clayton and not a boy like Kenny's daddy. And she will not have to work the way her momma works. She will have nothing to be afraid of, like Clayton has nothing to be afraid of.

He says now, squatting down in front of her, hands on her shoulders, —You promise, Gabriella? You promise to go to school every day and do all your work and pay close attention so you can get out of here one day?

And she says, —I do.

He laughs. —I do? Are we married now or something?

She says, —Yes.

Goes to school every day. Then one night Clayton stays over with Kenny and in the morning kisses her head good-bye.

—Bye, dweeb, he says.

—Bye, dork, she says.

Last time she ever sees him. He leaves and never comes back. They take him. It's how she first learns about death. Keeps going to school, for Clayton. Straight A's, perfect attendance, like Clayton. Turns thirteen, starts looking like a woman, men want what she's got, but they are not like Clayton so she does not care about them, their attention means nothing, they can go ahead and want it but they'll never get it. Gets into college, meets a man like Clayton, they fall in love, he becomes a pediatric neurosurgeon, she becomes a public junior high school teacher in Brownsville, Brooklyn, looking for little Gabriellas she can be a Clayton to.

THE HANDYMAN

She was shouting, —How could you let him go? How could you? It is your fault! Why did you tell him? Why then, why in that way? Her voice was rich and throaty. It tore through the ceiling up into the apartment of the young woman upstairs. Certainly the young woman was listening.

He said quietly, —Because he was disappointed in me.

—He was not, she said.

—He was. I could see it. I felt like he needed to know the truth.

—No one needs to know the truth, she said.

He said, —He needed to know where he came from. So he knows who he is.

—So he knows who *you* are, she said, —or who you *were.*

—That's not it.

—It was pride.

—No, not at all. He was standing with arms crossed, speaking as softly as he could, wondering if she was right. He hoped his speaking softly might influence her to do the same, for she was really shouting very loudly. She was going into the bedroom, taking off her shirt, pulling on another one. She was taking off her pajama pants, putting on jeans. She was sitting on the edge of the bed pulling shoes on to her feet.

—What are you doing? he said.

—I am going to go get him.

—He just wants to be alone, let him be alone.

—Too bad. It does not matter what he wants. He does not know what he wants. He needs us. He needs to be with us. We cannot let him wander around alone out there late at night.

—He will be with his friends. His friends will be there for him. He will lean on them and have fun and take his mind off everything, and when he comes home he will have blown off his steam. The shock will have worn off. And in the morning, we will talk about it. Really talk about it. He will understand.

She said, —But I am afraid. He's not answering his phone.

—Of course he's not, he does not want to talk to us right now. That's all it means. He knows how to take care of himself. He is very smart. He grew up in this city, remember? And this city is not what it was when we first came here. It was very dangerous then. Now it is nothing but rich white people. Which is good. It is safe.

He went to his wife, put his arms around her and kissed her on the forehead. The scent of her hair made him feel much better. As it always had. He was acting very calm but only because she was very anxious, because that is how he is with her—her counterbalance, and she his—but in truth he was just as anxious as she. They could not both be this way, one had to be calm. And her hair made him feel more like the way he was pretending to be. Her hair has always done this to him. On the bus that night so long ago, with Clayton already forming inside her, as they cowered under the coats and luggage of those cheerful rich kids on holiday risking their lives to hide them, as he cleaned her after the monsters, as he sutured her, all along the way since, he had stolen greedily luxurious scents of her hair. It had been all that kept him alive for her and, he did not know then nor could he have known, for Clayton.

—He will be fine, he said again.

—The things you tell yourself, she said.

—We have to tell ourselves things.

—Stories? Lies?

—Whatever you want to call them.

She agreed to wait until midnight. They lay in bed waiting. It was a standoff. Again and again he felt her about to speak then not speak, doing it only so he would suffer the tension it created, letting him writhe in it. Her way. To enhance the effect she changed position again and again, huffing and puffing, muttering angry little things at the mattress, kicking the sheets off, pulling them back over her shoulders. She wanted him to say, *What is it, what do you want to say?* This would allow her to uncork. And he would know she is right and it would make him angry at himself and his mistake, which would be painful, and when he gets hurt he gets mean, so he would then snap at her. *Well,* he would say, *what the hell are you doing about it, besides lying there huffing and puffing? How is that helping anything?* And this would make her so mad she would not say anything. That is how he knows she is really angry. Then she would kick the sheets off one last time and, muttering about him now, get out of bed and put her clothes on. He would do the same. *Fine,* he would say, *we are getting up and putting our clothes on, let's get up and put our damned clothes on!*

Now he would be as angry as she was, a hurt man who knows he has made mistakes and the problems are his fault and now is responsible for fixing them. But there would be no good way to fix them. So he would fix them using the only tools at hand, which are meanness, impatience, childish ham-handed gruntling apences. Of course those tools do not fix anything. He would not let that stop him. He would be mean to her, mean to the unfortunate cabdriver who would happen to pick them up and charge them a fortune to go to New Jersey. And, once they humiliate Clayton by ambushing him in front of all his friends, the only ones left tonight in the whole world whom he trusts, he would be mean to Clayton too. He would rip Clayton apart. He knows he would. *How dare you leave like that? Do you know how stupid that was, how dangerous it is out there?* He would rip her apart too.

He did not want to rip them apart. He did not want to be mean. Mean was not the way. It would fix none of the problems he had caused. So when she huffed and puffed and kicked the sheets off only to pull them back on and made him feel like she might say something but never did, he did not ask her what. Instead he let her be. It was better to let things be.

Her vise grip tightened. The more he ignored her the greater the pressure she put on him, the more she pushed him. She kicked the sheets off herself with more hostility. Muttered a little louder. He rolled over onto his back. Looked up at the ceiling. He could not stand it anymore. He said, —What, goddammit, what do you have to say to me?

Before she could uncork, the front door opened. Then it closed again. And at once the home was warm with the presence of Clayton. They listened to him walk past their room, go into the bathroom, and close the door, turn on the water. They heard him pee. She was no longer tense. She lay still. He still heard her breathing heavily but it was not her huffing and puffing—she was asleep. He put his hand on her back and kissed her. She was very hot and damp. Buried his face in her hair and fell asleep with her, it came so easily now, all the worry dispelled like it had been nothing.

Knocking on the front door. He wakes. Sits up.

—Who's that? she says, rousing beside him.

—I don't know.

It is hard, rapid knocking. Banging.

—Don't answer it, she says.

He gets up, leaves the bedroom, goes to the door. The deadbolt is not turned. It is always turned at night. Clayton's bedroom light is off but his door is open, and he feels a vacancy in the bedroom and knows Clayton is not in bed. *It's happened again,* he thinks. His sleepwalking was very disturbing. It represented deep psychological trauma, in-born wounds that break the handyman's heart. The boy was conceived in horror and now lives his life in it. Through the door now, between the pounding knocks, a voice is yelling something. He opens the door. It's Lucien, the doorman. Clayton is not with him.

—Where is he? the handyman says.

Lucien says, —There's been a shooting.

He knows. He runs to the elevator, and when that does not come quickly enough he takes the stairs, two at a time, all the way to the top floor where he runs into the police with their guns out. They put their guns into his face.

—GET DOWN! GET THE FUCK DOWN! SHOW ME YOUR HANDS!

He does, they cuff him. He is coated in sweat. Past them, as they lift him to his feet by his arms, he can see through Fisher's door into his apartment and he can see a basketball sneaker and he can see blood.

—CLAYTON! he is screaming. —CLAYTON!

He is struggling to break free from the cops. His son. They wrestle him down the stairs. He fights them every step. They will have to break all his bones. All he can do is scream his son's name. It explodes off the stairwell walls. Then he is again in the basement, cuffed and escorted down through the basement hall to the rear exit of the building, and she is standing there, outside their apartment. He cannot tell her. But he does not need to—somehow she already knows. —No, no, no, she is saying. He feels the officer's grip on his right arm loosen and twists away, or tries to, to run back to the stairs and up to Clayton.

—Stop resisting! this cop squeals, a twenty-two-year-old white man.

—No! he says.

Something wet on his face and orange on the wall and then his face is burning, like the cop's fingers are shoved into his eyeballs, a fork stabbed deep into his tongue. He is set on fire. His fight is taken from him. They drag his burning limp body out the door. He is slobbering. He does not care about the pain. He could take more of it than this. Do they think this is all he can take? Outside he cannot see but hears voices and sirens.

—Let him go, that's his father! people are shouting.

Lucien's voice is saying to the cops, —He had nothing to do with it, it's his son!

—Stay here, bro, the cop shouts at him. He does. Water is poured over his head. The fire is extinguished. Hands are touching him, trying to pull him away. His friends, his neighbors. Protecting him. —Why are you fighting me, bro? the cop voice says.

He does not care about the pain and he does not care about cops. The cops could nail his hands to a wooden cross and hoist it up and stab him in the ribs, and he still would not care about the cops.

—Clayton! he is screaming, throat still thick and raw from the fire.

—There he is! someone cries.

He thinks they mean Clayton. —Clayton! he says. He is blinking his eyes, can open them now, but everything is very blurry. Out the same rear door they brought him through they now bring Clayton. Thank God!

But it is not Clayton. It is a white wad of a human, a fat short chunk. The devil. Here is the devil. Here is the monster of the world, it is the monster of tonight, here are those monsters from that night and all nights. He opens the doors for monsters knocking at night and in rushes hell. The cops could not inflict real pain but now the real pain comes. He roars. The real pain begins at his feet—no, it starts in the dirt beneath the concrete he stands on, then rises through it into his feet, up calves to thighs, through groin, rips up into bowel and stomach unleashing shit and poison into his blood and then it keeps going, snaps his ribs one by one, slaughters his heart. It slaughters it. He collapses into the arms of his friends roaring in his handcuffs, even the cop now letting go of him as Fisher is shoved past into a police car and taken away. The handyman's wife then runs out the door and no one stops her as she chases the cruiser.

—Go, he says, —run.

She runs in silence, robe flapping behind her. He hopes she runs faster than anyone ever has and never stops running so it never gets her. He hopes she runs faster than hell.

But it gets her. No way it will not. It gets her at the hospital. At the hospital they expect to sit with their son while he recovers from the shooting. But you do not recover from a shooting. They tell them this, at the hospital. You do not recover. Not from this one. And that is when it gets her. It gets her worse than it got him. She turns to him and takes his head in her hands like she could bash it, and in her eyes is pleading, desperation. *Fix this,* her eyes says. *You fix things, so fix this.* He can do nothing. All he can do is catch her when she loses consciousness. It is her only recourse in the face of hell, when it gets her. He helps them put her into a bed.

—Keep her this way, he tells them. —Give her what she needs to stay like this.

Everyone is very nice. He feels guilty that they are so nice. They give him water, tell him what to do. Ask him what they can do. He does not know what they can do, but they tell him what he must do now is talk to the police.

He talks to the police. Tells the police everything he knows, which is very little, and the police in return tell him nothing they know, which is very much. Their questions are designed to figure out what Clayton did to deserve this. *Did he get into fights, have trouble with anybody? Did he run with gangs? Did he have any sudden, unexplained income? What kinds of drugs did he do? How often did he go to school? Did you ever know him to carry a gun?* They keep asking about a gun: *He had a gun, right? Where'd he get it? Come on, what kind of gun? You never saw a gun? You'll be in big trouble if you knew your kid had a gun and didn't do anything about it. This is your one chance.* He is to answer these questions, he is to take these insane questions seriously. He is to tell them everything they want to know, and he does, but they are to answer none of his questions, they are to tell him nothing he wants to know. Realizes in the middle of the conversation with the police that he is wearing jeans and a T-shirt, but they are not his and he does not know whose they are and has no recollection of ever getting dressed. Whose clothes are these? Where did they come from?

And then the police allow him to stop answering their questions and he is told what he must do now is identify the body. The body. Someone from the hospital brings him into a room where there is someone on a table completely covered by a sheet. He focuses on this someone from the hospital instead of the someone under the sheet. She is a young woman, not much older than Clayton. She asks if he would like water. He has water. Can't she see it? It is in his hands. Can't she see? She asks if there's anything she can do. How is he supposed to know? He is not her boss, he is not a doctor anymore—how is he supposed to know enough to tell her what to do? He hates being with someone who is only pretending to be somber, only approximating the display of pain. She is a barnacle. None of this means enough to her. It is insulting to think he would not see through such bad acting. She is quiet with her hands folded in front of her and speaks gently. —Mr. Kabede, is this your son? And she pulls back the sheet. How dare she pull it back? She does not know how his bedroom smells or what he likes to eat or about his stuffed turtle, which you had to make sure was in his crib with him or he would cry. She has never seen him cry. She has never loved him. How he hates this person, with fervor, without end.

—Sir? Is this your son?

He can barely spit out that it is. She has tissues. Of course she does. Hands him one. He throws it off to the side and it drifts down like a feather to the floor. Silent now, she puts the sheet back over Clayton. He grabs her dainty wrist, stops her.

—Is this what we went through it all for? he asks her in his language.

She does not understand. She is nervous—he is squeezing harder than he means. She yanks her wrist away and hurries toward the door and opens it. —Our grief liaison, Michael Kapper, she says, — will be more than happy to go over the many resources we offer, if you would like to wait for him in our waiting room.

He ignores her. He pulls the sheet back again.

—Sir, she says, not knowing how to handle this.

He touches his son's face. Blood in his hair they missed when they cleaned him. His last bath. He remembers bathing him as a baby. Eyes wide open, mouth grimacing in terror. Small hole through his cheek. Lips pulled back. Teeth shattered. He remembers when those teeth came in. Clayton was so proud of them. Now they will soon be dust. He kisses his son. His son, Clayton. His baby, who will soon be dust. Feels her about to speak, to try to get him out of the room away from Clayton. —I stay, he says before she can speak.

—I'm so sorry, sir, but we do have a policy, we—

He says to her, —I stay.

She leaves, returns with security and a man in a suit. —He won't leave, he hears her whisper to them.

—Okay, okay, the man in the suit whispers back to her. Then the door closes again and does not open, and he stays there all night, undisturbed, with the body of his son.

A knock on the door. He sits up in bed, puts his feet on the floor. His wife beside him in bed says, —Who is it? Who is knocking at this time of night? He is standing up, saying, —I don't know. He is leaving the bedroom, she is saying, —Why are you going to answer it if you do not know who it is?

He walks across the living room to the front door. The banging is very insistent, urgent.

—Hello? calls a voice he does not recognize. —Doctor?

Maybe someone is ill or injured. He pulls aside the curtain to peek out the window. It is someone he does not recognize, a short foreign man. The accent he speaks in is very heavy and strange. Looking out beyond the man, all he sees is darkness.

—Yes? he asks the man, through the window. —Yes? Are you sick?

The man does not answer. He looks very nervous. —Yes, he finally says. —I am sick.

The doctor steps away from the window, makes sure the door is locked, then returns to the bedroom. —It's nothing, he tells her. — Kids playing around.

—Are you sure? she says.

—Yes. Something should be done about them. They're hooligans. Where are their parents?

—It is them, isn't it?

—No.

—Isn't it?

—I don't know.

—What will we do?

—Just wait. They will go away.

The knocking stops.

—See? he says. —Now let's go back to sleep.

He lies down on his side, his back to her. She lies down on her back, facing up. He sleeps, she does not. In the morning he makes contact with an organization that helps people at risk of death at the hands of the regime, which demands religious extremity and are known to behead in public those who represent Western culture, which is unholy and evil, even those caught practicing Western medicine. Somehow to them he has become the symbol representing Western medicine. The organization says there is little they can do, the regime has won control of all borders and travel in and out is near impossible, but they are working to find him and his wife passage out. They wait. Neighbor tries to give him a gun, a thirty-year-old Soviet AK-47.

—I can't take it, the doctor says, —these are very hard to come by, you will need it yourself, you already have very little.

—That is true, says the neighbor, —just a small home and a cow and a bicycle and my family, but they are not coming for me, only for you, you must take it. I saw them last night. I do not know where they are from but not from here. See?

The neighbor points at the dirt where there are seemingly hundreds of boot prints.

—These are in front of no one else's house, Doctor. Please. Take the gun.

He does. That night they come again.

—Don't answer it, she says.

He does not. They shatter the window and are climbing in through it. She is screaming. He has the gun. How does it work? He goes to the doorway of the bedroom and points it and holds the trigger down, it comes to life, squirms and jolts in his arms like a small pig. In the flashes it makes in the dark he can see their faces, their bodies hunching and falling and running away and dying. He fires until it does not fire anymore. When he stops his home is filled with smoke and the smell of eggs, and his hearing is muffled and his ears hurt. Bodies lie all over. They are kids—eighteen, nineteen years old. Outside through the shattered window he can see one more running away into the night. Then he sees his neighbor run out of his house and chase him and tackle him and wrestle him to the dirt and bash him in the head with a rock. Goes to his wife who is under the bed and screaming. As he is attending to her one of them appears in the bedroom doorway. He is very small and very young, maybe twelve or thirteen. He holds his hands over his bleeding torso. He is crying.

—Help me, he says.

The doctor puts him in the empty bathtub and fetches his medicine kit stashed under the floorboards of the kitchen. Cauterizes the gunshot wound and tries to get the bullet but it is impossible, too deep inside his chest cavity.

—I am not a surgeon, he says. —There is nothing I can do for you but try to prevent infection. Take this. It is an antibiotic. You will probably die anyway. You are probably bleeding to death inside right now. It is good if you are. You deserve to die.

He leaves the boy in the tub dying, God willing, while he and the neighbor drag the bodies out and line them along the front yard.

—It was like killing a goat, the neighbor says, —killing that man.

—That's because these aren't men, the doctor says.

—That's right, the neighbor says, —they are animals.

But that is not what the doctor meant. Back inside he has to stop his wife from slitting the boy's throat with the scalpel in his medicine kit. In the morning the boy is still alive and the doctor and the neighbor start burning the ones who are not. They burn them in the same pit they use for burning their trash. In the fire are burned their penises and their testicles and their sperm. One of the testicles burned contains genetic material that would have created half an American boy named Clayton. The whole town comes out to watch the bodies burn. Children peep through the doctor's broken window hoping for a glimpse of the one they caught alive. The men of the town are impatient for the boy to heal so they can execute him.

—You will not touch him, the doctor says.

He delivered most of their children, has cured each of them of something at one point or another. They listen to the doctor. The boy does not die. The doctor's wife feeds him. The doctor insists on tasting the food first, to make sure she does not poison it. They talk to the boy. Learn the story of his life. His brother convinced him to join the mercenaries. His brother is everything to him. They were starving to death in their home country. No farming, no work of any kind. Both parents dead. No reason to live. *Here,* his brother told him, *is our chance for a good life, to make the world a better place. If you are not fighting to save the world,* his brother told him, *you are fighting to ruin it.* Made him choose one or the other. His brother was a murderer. He had watched him slit three boys' throats for smoking hashish. He did not want his throat slit, he did not want to ruin the world, he wanted to have a good life. —It all made sense before, the boy says, crying. —Now it makes none. What have I done?

One day the bullet pushes itself up from beneath the boy's skin in his armpit. The doctor cuts it out. Soon the boy is able to walk around. Flips through their books. —Will you teach me to read? he says. The doctor begins giving him literacy lessons. Then arithmetic. He learns very quickly. He is very smart. Helps repair the damage from the gunfire, helps the neighbor with his cow. Stands guard at night with his gun. The doctor and his wife become used to caring for him. It feels very good. His wife, he can tell though she tries to hide it, enjoys cooking meals for him and checking his arithmetic and looking after his health.

—What will we do with him? she says.

—I don't know, he says.

The boy makes friends with the boys his age in the village. He is very funny and kind. People flock to him. He begins wearing his pants with one leg rolled halfway up the shin and soon all the boys in the village are wearing their pants with one leg rolled halfway up the shin. The doctor thinks, *He could be prime minister one day.* The organization gets in touch. A position at a hospital in Alberta, Canada. Transport out of the country tonight on a military truck under the direction of an officer who has been bribed.

The doctor tells his wife, —Pack only one small suitcase, everything else must be left behind.

She says, —Good riddance to it all.

The boy is standing there listening. —What about me? he says.

The doctor and his wife look at each other. —What about him? the doctor asks her. She sighs, groans; she cries out in frustration.

And when the military truck comes in the night to the intersection in the field as arranged, all three of them stand there waiting for it. The soldier driving, who is very nervous, says, —What the fuck is this? There are only supposed to be two, who is this?

The doctor says, —This is our son.

Soldier gives in and they hide under greasy metal equipment. The truck is extremely bouncy and the roads very bad, even the doctor vomits from the motion. But when the truck comes to a stop, after two days, and the back door opens and hot white light spills in and someone bangs twice on the outside signaling they are to get out discreetly and never look back, they are free, they are new. They fly to Calgary. He practices at a beautiful hospital, out in the country. The boy goes to school for the first time. Catches on very quickly. Makes friends here too, even without knowing the language. Soon he learns and soon he is speaking very well. And when the doctor thinks this is all a miracle, how did he get so lucky to have been given this salvation, a job offer comes from the United States. New York City. A clinic for the immigrant community and other uninsured, impoverished people. Who can say no? He goes. They move to America, into a lovely building in the West Village neighborhood. And he is safe. He is free. In America. His American family is.

The people in this building are very rich. Often he looks up at the penthouse and wonders who lives there. The richest of them all.

His adopted son has never slept well. Clayton, they name him. Even when they were treating him in that bathtub he would sleepwalk at night. They had to put a chair outside the bathroom door to stop him. So many things to hurt him out there, back in that place. They do not treat people so brutally here in America. They respect life here in America.

One night in bed, Clayton fifteen years old, a knock on the door. He goes to answer it. Notices as he passes his bedroom that Clayton is not in it.

Knock on the door, he does not open it. They come back, he shoots. Nurses the boy who has survived. Get to Canada, bring along the boy, whom they have adopted as their own, named him Clayton.

—Your new name, they say. Beautiful, peaceful life in Canada, practicing in the hospital outside Calgary. Clayton learns English, how to read. Once he is introduced to formal education, he excels brilliantly. The doctor makes many friends, is accepted among his Canadian peers. Job offer from the United States. Declines it. Is fine here. Clayton sleepwalks. No one is afraid of him. Therefore he lives. Graduates high school, goes to a small local college. Does very well, transfers to McGill in Toronto. Meets a woman. Graduates. They are in love. Moves in with her. She is white. The doctor and his wife like her very much. Clayton goes to law school, changes his mind after two semesters, goes instead to business school. Marries her. Goes to work for Nike, in the United States. Comes back to Canada shortly after when he locked himself out of his house one night and so tried to break in through a window, and his white neighbors called the police thinking he was a criminal, and when he could not find his lease he was arrested, booked, and everything, held in jail until his wife could come prove he lived there. Starts a shoe company in Canada. It fails. Works for a Canadian fast-food company, in the corporate office, not ideal, his childhood dream was not this but his own shoe company. But he supports his family. The doctor and his wife babysit. The babies call them Goo and Beeb. On the doctor's deathbed Clayton, his own hair gray now, takes his hand. —Thank you, Pops, for not being afraid of me.

When the night is over and it is morning, he lets them take Clayton away. He checks on his wife. She is still sedated. She is surrounded by flowers and cards people have already sent. He hates that people know. He kisses her lips. She murmurs something in her sleep.

He meets with the grief liaison Michael Kapper not because he wants to but because that is the direction in which things next push him. He is floating and things want to push him in certain directions and he wants to say yes to them, he needs to say yes to things right now, to people. Life has become a tire bursting on the highway, and he wants it all to stop and saying yes is the only way he can think of to try to make things stop. The grief liaison Michael

Kapper has papers for him to sign, information to get from him, information to give him—psychologists, counselors, medications, support groups. There is literature to receive from Michael Kapper and hold in his hand and even to pretend to read and pretend to not want only to tear it to bits and open the jaw of Michael Kapper and shove all the bits inside his mouth. Then the meeting with the grief liaison Michael Kapper is finished. —Thank you, he tells Michael Kapper, —this has been very helpful. Michael Kapper smiles, he seems very relieved.

Then immediately after or hours later or it could even be days or weeks later, he and his wife stand on the sidewalk outside the hospital with air blowing over their faces and through their hair with no son. What is air but theft and murder? For every breath they take is one that Clayton does not. He sees Clayton everywhere. He tells her to stay there, then wanders into traffic. It is heavy traffic, major Manhattan avenue though he does not know which one, he is unsure where he is. She does not stop him, just watches as the cabs all swerve and slam their brakes in the darkness. All around them darkness. What day is it? Is it night or early morning? How long has it been? He stands in the yellow beams of the headlights coming toward him. He will let them crush him if that is what they want.

The people stagger around muttering, —I can't believe it, I just can't, it is so horrible, it's unreal, I just saw him, he was just here, why does this keep happening, why won't somebody *do* something?

His home is filled with people—all their friends from the neighborhood, many of the building residents, at least those who have not fled to second apartments or vacation homes to escape the hoopla—it is filled with people but void of the one who matters and therefore the home is empty. But more than that—it is sinister and everything is pointless. The people are not Clayton and so they are no one. His relationships with them all are founded on constructs that existed only because of Clayton, which means they no longer make sense. He does not like that they are all here, but he does not care enough about anything to bother turning them away.

She sleeps in Clayton's bed, in the dark, mercifully entombed in the effects of sedatives. The pills were part of the hospital's all-inclusive grief and loss package. Your dead child, your police interrogation, your grief liaison, your medications—good-bye, come again. She sleeps, he plays host. It is something he can do and it is maybe better than the other option, which is swallowing all the sedatives at once. He stands there saying hello to those who come, thanks them for coming, shakes their hands, hugs them if they hug him first, nods at whatever they say, tells them Clayton loved them though he recognizes none of them—he knows their names and who they are, yes, and the things they have shared, of course he does, these are his friends; he trusts them, they are what he and his wife and Clayton have had in place of family here—but he does not recognize them anymore or know why they are their friends, and the reason he does not recognize them is because they all wear the mask of Clayton. He offers these once-family now-strangers a drink from the sodas people have brought, scares up more chairs for them to sit in, directs the endless parade of Clayton-aged boys delivering flowers and food, boys who live while Clayton does not. He and she will never eat it. They will never water the flowers. They can nurture nothing. They could not keep Clayton alive so how dare they try to fool themselves that they can keep a flower alive, or their own bodies?

The once-friends now-strangers here include contractors he has worked with—Ken, Victor, Marlon, Buley—and former residents who moved out long ago but now return to express their grief and show support—Dilbert and Janet, Danielle—and the mailman Shaun and the UPS guy Frank and the owner of the Italian restaurant on the corner, Veronica, and several of her staff including her chef, Robert, and one of the busboys, Xiang, from China. Ahni and Paula and their kids are here, along with Sonny and Ben, Hassids who attend the synagogue across the street. Some of these people are black and others are white and some are gay and others straight. There are rich people, poor people; there are people who talk on TV and there are people who do not speak a word of English. A Babel of languages and cultures and lifestyles.

It is what he dreamed America would be but never was until now when he has lost everything.

Charlie corners him. Charlie is a landscape architect who lives in 6B and has a cable television show. Charlie hugs him and says, — Oh my God. The handyman does not know what to say to Charlie. But Dilbert and Janet are approaching him now, retired financial executives, white, a little drunk, especially Janet, and they tell him they own a condo on the Upper West Side that he and his wife may stay in, they should not have to stay *here*.

—Thank you, he tells them, —but we go nowhere.

—What? Janet says, aghast. —But you *can't* stay!

He starts to explain himself, how this is his home, they live here, here is where Clayton lived, where Clayton's bedroom and his things are, but then he understands that this makes no sense to anyone but him and his wife and that Janet and Dilbert do not actually care whether he takes them up on their offer, all that is important to Janet and Dilbert is that they have thought of it. People need things from you when you lose it all. He gives Janet and Dilbert what they need. Takes their hands, tightens his face up into a grimace, looks deep into their eyes, then kisses their creamy white hands, which are like his hands when he was a doctor, and says, —Thank you, *thank* you.

Janet and Dilbert look like puppies given a biscuit, and one of the residents, an actress on Broadway and in movies, comes in from outside, excited, saying, —Do you have any idea what's going on outside right now? She turns on the TV. CNN. Live coverage of a city block on a pleasant late-summer day. —That's us! someone says. Only then does the handyman recognize it as outside the building. Media are everywhere. Onlookers. It looks like a movie shoot, a scene in a feature portraying media hysteria flocking to the scene of a spectacle: news vans, their microwave antennae stretching high into the air; coffee-clutching producers hurrying about; gorgeous white on-air talent in business casual leading the camera guy around and speculating.

But it quickly becomes clear that what has brought them all here is not what happened to Clayton but the power and charisma of a particular woman among them. She is the object of the cameras. She could be another pretty reporter pulling people aside for interviews, and she is doing just that, she catches whoever emerges from the building's front door, but she is not doing it for news to report but to ask them, —What are you doing about this? Gun-owning white males are responsible for mass death and they must be left behind and they *will* be, but only if you start the tidal waves of change!

She is handing out sheets of paper. The network cameras are surrounding her, pushing their microphones close to her mouth.

—These are the phone numbers of your representatives. *Call* them! *Do* something! Call them right now! Write them letters! Show up! Bombard them! Tell them you will not stand for children being slaughtered so privileged white men can play cop! Tell them the lives of our children trump their so-called traditions! Tell them we must leave behind the reckless, bloodthirsty Second Amendment that trumps out children's right to life, liberty, and the pursuit of happiness! Tell them to vote in favor of the ammo tax or you will replace them with someone who will!

The woman's name appears on the screen: Jenny Sanders, Founder, Repeal the Second Amendment.

Now this woman is leading the hundreds of people gathered around her in chants, a sea of people compelled by her. —Justice for Clayton! she shouts.

Her mob echoes it: —*Justice for Clayton!*

—Justice for Clayton!

—*Justice for Clayton!*

A boiling energy. Police are lined up on the perimeter in riot gear, they carry machine guns and wear body armor like soldiers; there are small armored personnel carriers. Then she has all these people chanting the word *justice*, over and over, pounding the word like a drum: —*Jus-tice, jus-tice...* It sends shivers down the spine. People's eyes are misty. —She'll get him, someone says, —she will.

The handyman looks over to the couch where Stacey sits. Hector's daughter, Clayton's girlfriend. The poor girl. She sits with Hector and Kenny, Clayton's best friend. She has her arms folded over her stomach, rocks back and forth. He goes to her, sits down beside her, puts an arm around the young girl. She starts sobbing and puts her head on his shoulder and he pulls her close, wrapping her up. She sobs into his chest. He kisses the top of her head. The little child. Her little heart. —He loved you, he tells her, and she sobs harder. —And he knew you loved him too. You were his love, his love.

He puts one of his arms around Kenny too. Kisses Kenny's head. —He loved you too, Kenny. You were his brother. You'll always be his brother.

It is the first time today the handyman has known what he is saying, the first time he has said something and meant it.

On the television the woman has the crowd chanting, —Re-peal! Re-peal!

It means nothing to him. What can she do with her chants? What can she do for Clayton, what can she do for his wife? He squeezes Kenny again and hugs Hector then gets up, leaves them all, goes into Clayton's room and closes the door behind himself, locks it, lies down in Clayton's bed beside his wife.

He opens the door, answers the knock. It is Lucien. —Clayton, says Lucien. The handyman pushes past him, down the hall, up the stairs to the penthouse. Cops block the way. They pull guns on him. He pushes past. It is easy, all he has to do is be harder and tougher than he was the first time. He runs down Fisher's hallway and inside through the open door to where Clayton lies with his sneakers on and his hoodie covered in blood. The cops there try to stop him but he fights them off. Who knew he was so strong? He can lift them and throw them, he can make them disappear just by wanting it. He bends down to Clayton. Checks his pulse. Still alive. Rips open his hoodie; it tears easily, like paper. The handyman's hands are smooth as cream again. He is a doctor again. He can save Clayton. Runs his smooth hands over Clayton's flesh, smearing the blood, looking for the entry wounds. Finds them, sticks his fingers inside each one. He is so capable and effectual. He slides out the bullets from Clayton's body, wound by wound, and tosses each aside. When he plucks out the final one, Clayton coughs and opens his eyes very wide, and the doctor can see the life return to them like headlights approaching at high speed. Clayton jolts and seizes. The doctor holds him. Clayton is very scared.

—There, there, the doctor tells him, —you will be okay. Lifts Clayton in his arms, carries him back down the hall to the elevator. Brings him home.

—Oh my God, she says, —what happened?

—It's okay, he tells her, —it was very close but he will be fine. I pushed, I was tough, I saved him, I would not be denied, I did not let anyone keep me from him.

In the morning he joins them for breakfast. Then he goes to college. Begins work. Falls in love. Finds peace.

He hears her wake up, sit up, and look around, startled. She puts her feet on the floor and stands, opens the door and looks out and listens. He watches her then close the door again and come back to bed.

—You forgot, he says.

She says, —I did not know why I was in his room or where he was. I did not know why all these people are out there. For a few seconds, I forgot. And it was wonderful, it was so wonderful. But I did not know it was wonderful until I had remembered again and those few wonderful seconds were already gone.

—Take another pill, he says.

She says, —Let's take them all.

He does not say anything in reply. It is too good an idea. His not agreeing that it is a good idea is all that prevents them from doing it.

She takes one pill, then drinks water while he rubs her back watching her. She swallows, puts down the glass on Clayton's night table, and says, —Don't touch me.

He stops touching her.

—Everything feels horrible. Everything tastes horrible. She pulls her feet into the bed, curls her knees to her chest. He is careful not to touch her. They lie on their sides facing the door through which Clayton might walk in in his pajama pants, shirtless and grumpy, groaning, *What y'all doin' in my bed?*

She says, —The air. My tongue. My teeth. The water. Horrible, horrible, horrible.

He says nothing.

—This will never not be happening, she says, —will it?

He says, —No.

—It will always be, won't it?

—Always.

—And they won't even tell us what happened. Then she is silent again. The sedatives have worked quickly. Now that he has taken care of her, his pain may come. It comes searing. The bones hurt deep in their insides, their marrow quivering and cut. *It is your fault*, a voice tells him. *You have killed him. Now kill yourself.* Lies there hurting and crying until he hears cars and voices outside on the street, which he takes to mean it was night and now it is morning and here is another day they must live through. He kisses her and gets out of Clayton's bed and leaves the room, taking the bottle of sedatives with him.

Everyone has long ago left and cleaned all the dishes and put away all the chairs and packed away all the food and arranged and watered all the flowers in vases. They even vacuumed and mopped. Their home has not been this clean in years. All the curtains are closed. Voices and activity and light are behind them. He goes to one, peeks out. Hundreds of people are out there, even more than yesterday. A little boy holding a sign that says JUSTICE FOR CLAYTON: REPEAL THE 2ND AMENDMENT with a picture of Clayton on it. It is one he has never seen before. Where did it come from? The boy sees him in the window and points at him and says something to his mother, who looks too, and the handyman closes the curtain and steps away from the window.

Takes a shower. Uses Clayton's bodywash, the heavily perfumed kind that gives him a headache but Clayton uses because the advertisement reveals that girls are unable to control themselves around boys who use it. Clayton's razor hangs beside his own, from the hook. He began shaving just last winter. They went to Duane Reade together to pick out the razor for him, then went home and he showed him proper technique. From then on Clayton has been shaving every morning; it does not matter that there is nothing to shave, he does his neck, jaw, chin, cheeks, over and over the same spots to make sure he did not miss anything, *using all my shaving cream up too,* the handyman thinks, *keeping his mother and me locked out of the bathroom. Drove me out of my mind some mornings. I should use the razor to open my wrists,* he realizes. But her. He turns off the water, dries, dresses, returns to his wife.

A knock on the door. He gets out of bed, opens it. Two people stand in the hall, looking around. Strangers. Nobody else out there now. A pretty, thin woman with tangled long brown hair and glasses and a young man who is short and thick with a purple T-shirt and glasses. The man takes his picture. The woman smiles at him like she has come to bestow a gift upon him. She clasps her hands, hunching her bony shoulders and turning her body from him humbly.

—*Hiiiii,* she says in a throaty, hungover morning whisper. —I work with NBC News? I'd love to chat with you about what happened.

—I don't know what happened, he tells her.

She says, —You haven't heard about the shooting?

—I know about shooting, yes, of course. But what happened, I don't know, they will not tell us.

She looks at him, trying to understand but failing to. She says, —Did you know the victim?

—Of course.

—And what were your *impressions* of him? Like, what *vibe* did he give off?

He stares at her mouth, goes in past those teeth that remind him, actually, of Clayton's when he was seven or eight and began losing his babies—yes, she has baby teeth doesn't she?—and he keeps drifting in over her tongue to the back of her throat, which is inflamed from sleep deprivation, then out the rear of the skull, exiting with a geyser spray of brain and blood and cerebral fluid all over the face of the other one, the male she is accessorized with, who, face covered in gore, continues staring back at him through the camera with the same smirk he has now, like he is impatient to get what he feels he deserves, which is everything.

—Sir? she says.

He says, —How did you get in here?

Over her shoulder he can see the answer to that himself. They found a window in the alley he forgot to lock and crawled through it. Just then at the end of the hall appears another woman, moving swiftly toward them. —Out, this woman tells the reporters. It is the woman from television. The chanter. The chantress. She is smaller, more delicate in person, but her voice is even louder and more commanding. What a voice it is. It obliterates.

The woman reporter says, —Absolutely, Jenny, but care to chat with NBC News for a story?

Jenny answers, —This man has just lost his son, can't you understand that, doesn't that mean anything to you?

The reporter looks at him anew and says, —You're the father?

Jenny says, —He will issue a statement in due time, but until then you will respect his privacy, and if you don't then you get nothing from us ever again, how does that sound?

Before they can answer Jenny takes the male reporter by the arm and leads him back to the open window, calling over her shoulder to the other, —You too, Britney.

Britney is staring at the handyman. —I'm sorry for your loss.

—Thank you, he says.

She leaves her card and follows Jenny to the window, where Jenny hurries them back out through it, saying, —Out we go. She slams it shut after them and makes sure it is locked. Then she comes to him. She embraces him. She smells like cold rain in the summer sun.

$$\left(\begin{array}{c} \text{Sheeple} \\ \text{VII, VIII \& IX} \end{array}\right)$$

The career I've ended up in, I've ended up in the only way people end up in careers they love: totally unexpectedly. What I studied in college was art history. Did art history prepare me for this? I suppose it did—the history of art is the history of grief.

I moved to New York City after college to be an art dealer and one day own a gallery. I had no reason to believe it would work out. I had only barely earned my degree and knew nobody in the art world and had no start-up capital. This was supposed to be the part in my life story where, somehow, using wit and grit, I beat the odds and made it, but within six months I was down forty-eight pounds and my money was gone and I was desperate and lonely and failing. The only job in art I could get was at a gallery in Alphabet City. The owners called it an internship but that was really a way to get away with not paying me. Hardly anybody came to this gallery. My job was to sit there behind the desk staring into space, straightening the stack of price lists that never needed straightening because nobody had touched them, and after closing sweeping up, even though most days the only shoes that had walked on the floor were mine. The owners, I assume, used the gallery to launder money. The art was wretched. I have forgotten all of it.

So I got a new job selling timeshares. Selling art, selling timeshares— after a desperate year the delineation had narrowed. I turned out to be an excellent timeshare salesman. The company was very pleased with me, very encouraging. I hated it. I resented them for providing me work I was so easily good at. So I quit. Got evicted. Fell ill with pneumonia. Kept chasing art, it kept pushing me away. The people at the timeshare company begged me to return, offered me a higher commission, health benefits. I was disgusted with the whole universe. I was, I realize only now, very young. Homeless and sick and ridden with debt, I gave in and returned to timeshares. I made sure they all knew, every minute I was there, how much I resented them and how little I thought of them and how much I hated it. After work each day I would swing down through Chelsea to the galleries where art, my love, was slipping away. It all felt more and more unrecognizable to me, and me to it. Every time I swung through Chelsea after work, the following morning at the timeshare office—a dingy little hole in midtown—I would be even angrier and more resentful of them all. It must have oozed from my skin. I see now I was grieving. For the future that would never be, for the life I would never live.

One night, the gentleman sitting at the phone next to me was reading from the script they gave us to the potential client on the other end. —Full access to the state-of-the-art gym and sauna, he said, then died. He fell forward onto his desk with the phone still up to his ear and died. Right there. He was maybe forty-five. I went with his body to the hospital. I don't know why. It just felt like I should.

At the hospital I found myself in the position of greeting his family and telling them what happened. Wife and two daughters maybe twelve and ten. When I told her, his wife screamed like I had never heard before but have heard often since. As I embraced her, my blood was surging and my heart pounding and my head was pulsating and I was in love again. Art had once made me feel this way but now it did not. Now this did, whatever this was. I prayed with her even though I was not someone who prayed. She barely spoke English and, I think, could not read, so I helped her with paperwork and navigated her through the hospital's procedures, asked questions for her, located a priest of the proper denomination to come meet with her and the children. I became this woman's friend and helped make the funeral arrangements and, since I was doing so well with timeshares, was able to give her money for groceries and pay her rent until she figured something out, which I would help her do as well. Helped the kids with homework. Made sure they went to school and found a counselor for them.

I went back to school soon after for a master's degree in psychology, paying for it with the timeshares. Volunteered at every hospital and hospice that would have me, read all the literature about grief. In time I was hired to do this by a hospital and here I am, doing what I am supposed to be doing and what I love after all. I met my wife here, she is a nurse, and we have two children, and what I do helps people. And still on weekends I go into that dark midtown hole, which, I see now, is anything but soulless and dead and represents everything but failure and rejection, and I sell timeshares to make money I use to buy art from galleries in Chelsea. I even patron artists directly. I champion artists who need it, sell their work to make them money they need, money that changes the tides for them, brings the ship back to shore.

This is what New York means to me. What our country does.

But lately over the last few months I find myself again in a rut. No matter how much you love it, grief work will wear you down. The constant death and relentless tragedy, so much of it the same. We just do not think certain people matter. They are disposable to us. It is a virus that infects our entire society. I have been feeling like a fraud, reciting from a rote clinical script to these families, knowing there is this illness out there we are not doing enough to cure. I feel like I am selling them timeshares. I keep expecting the mother of one of these boys to stop me in the middle of my pitch and tell me how full of shit I am.

And tonight I am in bed dreading going in to work tomorrow, when I get a page from the hospital. I go in. Black boy, fifteen, dead from a gun. His neighbor shot him, a millionaire white guy. Father's the guy's super. I do what I can for the father, while the mother is sedated. In the chaos, I provide an order for him to hang on to. Papers to sign, information to provide. Things to read and do. Tangibility.

It's mostly bull, but concrete objects and tasks are vital when you have been crushed. And this man interrupts me in the middle of my pitch. Here we go. What I have been bracing myself for. He is the one who will tell me I am full of shit and I will not even wonder if he is right, because I will know he is. I will see my work for what it might truly be: a crutch that I, a luckless man, have fashioned for myself out of death and debris and desperation the way rats make homes out of society's feces and trash. And I will fall out of love with it the way I fell out of love with art. My wife will not recognize me anymore, after I've fallen out of love with it. The foundation of our relationship will become weak. We will grow apart. I will lose her and my family and never help another widow who cannot read and cannot understand English fill out paperwork or locate the right minister. I wait for it.

The man, the father, speaks. He says, —Thank you. This is very helpful.

And I am very relieved. My work feels valuable again and worth the emotional grind. I am not a con and I am not selfish. I help. The work wants me. I will not fall out of love with it. I will keep going.

I go home that morning, after he and his wife have gone back out into the city, to wash up and eat and refresh before heading back in a couple of hours to start my workday, and I have more energy for helping those crushed than I have had in months. New ideas for grief counseling bubble into my head, exciting new ways to be more effective for others. I follow these bubbles, see where they go. They take me into new universes. I apply for research funding, get it, work with Yale and Harvard; our research dispels flawed best practices, establishes newer better ones. We learn for once, at last, how to grieve. Our way works for everybody, like a vaccine. We learn how to grieve and we teach the world and at last our broken hearts may begin to heal.

She takes the order for the new door, writes down the address. —
Hold on, she says, —ain't this where that boy got hisself shot? Tell
me something, where the hell were that boy's parents, what kinda
child did they raise, why weren't they watching him? Ought to lock
them up.

Hangs up. She's so angry. That poor child. Thinks of her own
son. Giving birth to him, breast-feeding him, him pointing at
cars and dogs and airplanes, how good he was at Legos, thought
he would be an engineer for sure. Single mom, had to work. Not
home enough. He grew up, put away the Legos, started running
around the neighborhood. Didn't know what he was getting up to.
She heard things, didn't believe them. He followed a young woman
into her building, tried to take her purse. It was on the stairs. Young
woman fell over, cracked her head. He ran off with the purse while
her brain swelled through the crack in her skull. Coma, then death.
Son put away. Could not look at herself. Knew it was her fault. So
she looked elsewhere. Whenever she sees a black boy get in trouble
she sees her son and sees herself failing him and she gets disgusted,
has no forgiveness for the parents who failed him, as she has none
for herself.

She has never let her son know she is harder on herself than she
is on him, makes him think she hates him for what he did to that

girl. When your mother hates you you hate yourself and everyone else too. So he gets in fights, inside. Fucks with the guards, gets his ass beat. Does not do school or anything inside, only fights. Will get himself killed. Doesn't give a shit, for he thinks his mother hates him.

Next day on the way out to Rikers to visit her son, she is still fuming about the boy who got hisself shot. She tells her son about how she got an order at work to replace the door where that boy on the news got himself shot. She says, —His parents got him killed, oughtta lock *them* up. Where were they for him? Where was I for you? That boy needed them and you needed me. I been making you feel like dirt for what you did, but I want you to know I was only talking to myself, you understand? Everything mean I've said to you I meant it for myself so I shoulda been saying it to myself. Every harsh coldblooded thing I've done, it was me I should have been doing it to. I love you endlessly, baby, it's myself I hate. Understand? From now on I'mma be different to you. I'mma be different.

And from that day, she is. And he stops fighting, stops hating himself and everyone else. Gets interested in school, completes GED, then bachelor's, then master's, then law degree. Finds Islam, the love of God. Peace. Paroled. Leaves prison a better man than he entered. Does paralegal work for the Innocence Project. Has a brilliant attention to detail, a methodical relentlessness that leads to full exoneration of dozens of men on death row for things they did not do but were convicted for because they were not born with the ability to defend themselves. Saves these men's lives.

Jenny Sanders throws the reporter out the window, she lands atop her partner in the alley below, does not get anything useful to report, cries—she will be fired, this was her last chance, her boss told her so, and fired she is, cannot get another job in news, goes broke, starves, is evicted, wanders the city digging through trash to eat, ridden with worms and lice. Family will not help, they are disgusted with her, always have been; they are luminaries and genius capitalists, looked down on her for going into news out of Princeton instead of international commerce like them—money and power are important, not "infotainment," as they call it—that she has failed at it disgusts them further, cut her off, all alone, winter coming. Has developed a tremor in her left hand from the trauma, rides the subway begging for money, no one gives because the tremor is disturbing, it looks like she is making male jerk-off motions at them, riders try to ignore her walking up and down the aisle making her male jerk-off motions at them until she passes through to the next car where they try to ignore her too. She used to ignore as well, when beggars on the subway said it could happen to anyone; one in particular she remembers now, *Please, mang, I been out since six o'clock this morning, mang, looking for a job, mang. I'm tired, mang... this ain't no joke, this could happen to anybody, mang.* She did not believe his spiel, decided it must be a hustle; now she believes it, and going between two subway cars she falls, lands on the tracks, train slices off her legs at the knees. At hospital an infection, dies, meets God, God sends her back, staggers out of the hospital, or not staggers, because she does not have legs below the knees, must roll, rolls out of the hospital, in a wheelchair, cruises into a chain burrito place, gets a job—should have done this a bit sooner maybe, she realizes—moves into a spare room in a Queens apartment with seventeen undocumented Guatemalan men, only place she can afford, they teach her Spanish and how to cook Guatemalan food, she teaches them English and how to cultivate news sources. Soon she is cooking the food better than they are, no kitchen, has to do the dishes in the bathtub; on a wall someone has scratched MR. + MRS. + BABY KABEDE and a date sixteen years earlier. From the back office of the burrito place she steals the direct lines of the chain's corporate executives, calls, pitches them a Guatemalan restaurant, they bite, so to speak, invest, very successful, becomes a national chain, millions of dollars, tens of millions, gets artificial legs, gives much of her new fortune to subway panhandlers, especially those with unfortunate tremors, and helping undocumented people avoid deportation by funding an underground railroad for them to get to safe haven in nations friendlier to the poor huddled masses, for example Iceland. And whenever she sees Wayne LaPierre of the NRA on TV in the aftermath of a school shooting praising the glories of guns and tsk-tsking that no kids or teachers had one and saying the only thing that stops a bad guy with a gun is a good guy with a gun, she donates another million dollars to Jenny Sanders and Repeal the Second Amendment, for throwing her out the window so her life could go so well.

THE MYTH

What have I done? What did I do? —I shot someone, Lee tells the 911 dispatcher as he stands in the baby's room, baby in his arms and the kid still out in the living room. He cannot look at him, he cannot bear to see his blood. *No wrongdoing,* he thinks, *no wrongdoing.* The baby is very calm and Lee inside is screaming. The dispatcher asks what happened. He tells her.

—And you *shot* him? she says. She sounds incredulous.

—*Yes,* I shot him, *of course* I shot him.

—Why'd you *shoot* him? she says.

—What do you mean *why* did I shoot him? Lee says. —He was *in my apartment.* And the dispatcher asks who the person is. —I think he's the super's kid, he says. The dispatcher asks what age, what race. Lee does not want to say what race. —I think he's twenty-two, twenty-three? The dispatcher asks again what race. —He's black, Lee says.

Police come. Gun is unloaded on the ground far away from Lee in another room. When they arrive he starts to explain, but the cops scream at him and have guns out and they tackle him even as he still holds his baby, the baby is screaming now, his face red and twisted up, little fists clenched and shaking—maybe his baby has been hurt, his leg pinned beneath Lee's, his little ankle broken—and they are trying to take his baby, have guns in Lee's face, there is the barrel of a gun pushed deep into his right eye, they are shouting things he cannot understand, they are animals. They are prying the baby from his arms, he holds on as tightly as he can but they are so much stronger and they take him, they take his son. They turn Lee over and put a knee into the back of his neck and he cannot breathe. They are twisting his arms, punching his kidneys, his head. They are screaming in his face, —WHERE'S THE GUN? WHO'S HERE? WHERE IS IT? and they are running through his house, one kicks his son's jumper out of his way like it's trash. They are taking over his home.

He remembers his father. It has been four years since he has seen him, maybe five. Or it could be more, it could be as many as ten. Not since his father's third wedding has he seen him. *You will understand,* he tells his father now. *They are breaking my arms and taking my baby and you will understand that.*

Only temporary, he hears his father say back. *Protocol. Relax. They will investigate and see there has been no wrongdoing on your part and you will be cleared.*

They put him on the couch in the living room, about a dozen uniformed cops standing over him. They are jacked up, sweating and red, eyes so all-seeing they seem unseeing, heads darting around, huffing loudly through their noses like fighting dogs. He is cuffed at the wrists and ankles. Behind the uniforms across the living room against the front door he can see the kid's feet. He is wearing Nike Air Jordans. They are bloody. When the cops pushed their way inside the kid was against the door and he was shoved aside against the wall. So much blood.

—What will happen to my son? Lee asks them again and again. They do not answer. He keeps asking them again and again, he keeps telling them that he is a good guy, that it was self-defense, but they say nothing, just stare down at him.

Stay patient and calm and do what you're told, it will all get straightened out, he hears his father telling him. The voice of a father in the ear of a child. Familiar as if he heard it yesterday. Remembers now his mother too, her high heels clacking, her smile as she bent down to him; she was orange, she smelled like tangerines: *Good-bye.* He sees his son vanish through the door in a cop's arms and he sees his mother getting into the car and Laura's hiking boots dangling from the tree branch and he cries out, —Don't go!

Then they bring him out past the body. The kid's eyes are still open.

—You're not just going to leave him there, are you? Lee says to the cops.

Still they say nothing. And Lee says nothing more because he wants the cops to see that he respects them and is on their side, that he will let them do their job and get all this straightened out. Someone has pulled the fire alarm, he only now realizes in the hallway. It has been going off the whole time and he has not noticed it. They bring him downstairs, through the basement, to take him somewhere away from the chaos and talk to him, he presumes, so he can explain. But when they take him out through the rear entrance and he sees a cruiser waiting with lights on and the door open and the backseat apparently ready for him, he becomes terrified. Things have escalated, seemingly of their own accord, he has no control. —No, no, no, he says. He says it just like he said it to the boy. And adding to the realization that his fate and his life are not in his hands anymore—that his self-determination is null—a crowd of people has materialized, stark and silent, with their phones held up, videoing him. The dozens of red record lights are like laser sights from sniper scopes. Their expressions are void and sinister. Heartless. Inhuman. It is a mob. It does not matter to the mob what is true—they will rip Lee apart. They have been here this whole time just waiting for him, needing only a reason.

My son, he realizes, staring into them. *My son is in danger now. Real danger.*

Dangerous, crazy people out there, his father says.

—What will you do with my son? Lee is crying out to the cops as they bring him through the crowd, which now shouts violent, hateful things at him, spitting on him, calling for his imprisonment, his execution. It does not matter—*imprison me, execute me, just don't hurt my son.* Still the cops pretend not to hear him. —They'll come after him, he tells them. —You understand that? Don't the cops see that he is not asking what will happen to himself, that he is not complaining about being arrested, that he is not concerned for himself—don't they see that he is not a criminal but a father whose sole concern is for his child?

They put him in the backseat and close the door. Off to the side in handcuffs is the super, the kid's father. The cops are pouring water over his face and he has no shirt on, and when the water gets all over him it catches the police lights and reflects them, making him look supernatural, wicked in red and blue. Lee knows they are pouring water over his face because they have pepper-sprayed him. And then he understands. Since the moment he turned on that light and the home invader became just a boy and he felt his own body go cold with guilt, he has been looking for the way in which he is not a murderer—and here it is.

Don't you remember, his father says, *when they were in your apartment not long ago to fix the sink? Did they seem right to you? Me neither. Made you very suspicious, didn't they? And apparently for good reason. Your instincts have always been spot on, pardner. You can always tell a bad guy, no matter how nice they might try to act to you. Remember you spent the entire time very anxious, ready to spring if they made some kind of move? They were taking photos, weren't they? And they kept murmuring to each other in their language. You thought maybe it was Arabic. Whatever it was, it was clear they were up to something. And now this, handcuffs and pepper spray—it can only mean he was involved in what happened tonight. And what happened was a break-in. An attempted attack on you and your infant son. And you thwarted it. The police will see this. Welcoming them into your home was where you made your mistake. Trusting them. Bad guys take that as a sign of weakness, seeing the nice things you had and how good-natured you were—it must have given them an idea. The super leering at you as he worked, sneering at you but pretending to be polite, and the kid saying darkly in English,* Cute kid, *and taking a picture of your baby with his phone. They saw your baby as their ticket to wealth, didn't they? That's all anyone's looking for here. And so they began forming their plan—their heinous, sick plan—in the elevator on the way down. You did not have the gun on you that day, did you? It was in your nightstand, wasn't it? If it had been on your hip instead. If they had seen it there. That was your first mistake, Lee. Thinking for once you were safe. Your next mistake—God you have made so many—was letting yourself drink too much tonight. You somehow forgot to lock the door. You thought the baby was down for the night, but he woke up screaming and you could not figure out why, and as that was happening the pizza you'd ordered arrived and you could not handle the confusion, the situation overwhelmed you—maybe if you were sober you could have handled it, but you were a bit drunk, and you hurried to the door with the baby screaming in your ear and writhing in your arms and you grabbed the pizza with your one free hand and closed the door with your foot, no hands free for the deadbolts, but you would come back for them, and you hurried off to check his diaper again, and while changing it he spit up a bucketload all over himself and so now you needed to put him in a new onesie or he would never go back to sleep, and after that he was still crying, so now you had to try feeding him, and when you finally got him down again all you wanted was another drink and you forgot to come back and lock the door. That is the way life is. You keep your guard up all your life and the one time you slip up... But while you might have picked the wrong night to lose control, those two picked the wrong guy to come after, didn't they?* Lee can almost feel his father's hands on his shoulders as those words come and it feels good: *The wrong guy. They picked the wrong guy. Lee Fisher is not a murderer. Lee Fisher was simply the wrong guy to come after. And they paid the price for it.*

The cops leave him in the cruiser for what feels like hours. The super writhes in the hands of the police where, Lee sees now, he belongs. The neighbors are trying to get between the super and the cops, demanding they let him go. They do not know the truth yet, Lee thinks. They will. It is not their fault. He fooled us all. Then Lee and the super meet eyes through the cruiser window. Lee sees nothing in them. Nothing. Chills go down his spine. *Cold blooded.*

At last they take him away. He asks them again as respectfully as he can if they know where his son is. They say nothing. He asks them with so much respect and humility that it verges on inferiority that they are not treating this like a murder, are they? That they understand what happened, don't they? Because he—They interrupt to tell him to shut up and he apologizes and does so, then apologizes again and hopes the truth about who he is and what has happened radiates off his essence and off his apologies and makes them understand, so when they get to wherever they are taking him they will enter him into the machine appropriately for the man who he is and this will all be straightened out.

When they turn the corner up Hudson Street, a black woman in a ratty old bathrobe jumps out in front of the cruiser, forcing it to stop. She looks homeless, emaciated from drugs, obviously insane. She slams both her hands on the cruiser's hood and stares through the windshield at Lee, then comes around to his window. The cops are doing nothing about it. Red eyes and woolly hair stand from her head in unwashed tufts. White spittle is hardened in the corners of her cracked lips, between which stringy goo stretches as she opens them and yells at Lee in a foreign language. To Lee she is like a witch. She punches the window, trying to break through it. The cops just keep letting her do it. He does not understand. It is like they do not see her. And then the one in the passenger seat turns halfway around to Lee, showing Lee enough of his face to see the smirk, and says, —Bro, aren't you gonna say hello to her? Common courtesy, you murdering her son and all.

Lee's voice cries out, —No! I'm not a murderer. I'm not.

The woman punches the glass. Lee jolts back, yelping. She screams. She punches the glass again and again, she will not stop until she breaks through it and grips him around the throat and tears out his eyes. He turns his face away and ducks his head, almost feeling her blows striking the back of his skull. The cops pull away, closing up back into their impenetrable silence, and the witch chases after them down Hudson Street for an entire block before collapsing to her knees in the middle of the street and that is where she is when they turn the corner and at last put her out of sight.

At the precinct, because he is wearing nothing but underwear, they give him an old oversized FUBU T-shirt from a storage bin. The tail of the FUBU T-shirt comes down to his knees, the sleeves come down to his wrists, it smells like mildew and cigarette smoke and stale body spray. Such an insulting, degrading thing to make him wear. Humiliation. He is furious now, thinking of the witch, the cops. The super. The kid. Inside him, the cold guilt is leaving, replaced with a hot, rumbling anger. *Guilty?* his father says. *Why should you feel guilty? You should be furious. First you were the victim of evil and now you are the victim of injustice. Everything is in confederation against you.*

He is no longer being polite and respectful. He tells every cop he sees that he is not a murderer and he demands his attorney, and that is all he says to them. They make him wait for hours before letting him call the multinational firm that represents the Fisher family interests. Hours after that, an attorney arrives. John Potter talks too quickly, keeps interrupting him, makes too little eye contact, is too impatient, is interested only in legal procedure and does not make Lee feel like he understands what has happened—the bigness of it and that he is not a murderer; he does not understand how the media will misinterpret this.

—Where is my son? Lee asks urgently. —Who the hell has him?

—For the time being, emergency care.

—What's that mean?

—Means the cops have him.

—People are going to think I'm racist and want to hurt me. They are going to want to hurt him.

—He's fine, he'll be there a few hours until a friend or relative can take him. So give me some names and numbers.

—My dad'll be here, he'll take him. Does he know yet, do you know?

—I don't know.

—He probably does. I bet he's on his way now, I bet he's already on the plane. That's the kind of guy he is. When do I go home? We have to post bail, right?

—We're working on it. Tell me what happened.

Lee thinks about it for a moment. Face still in his hands.

—Lee?

—I don't *know*, he says.

Potter is quiet. Lee can hear him breathing, he can hear the ink on the point of his pen sticking and unsticking on the paper of the legal pad as he waits. He can hear sirens outside. Then a cop's voice in the hall saying something about football and laughing. Then he can hear his father and his father says, *You know what happened. You know. So tell him.* And Lee tells him. His father tells Lee, then Lee tells Potter. He tells how in the middle of the night he heard a noise and got up to investigate. He tells how he grabbed this dinky old gun he has, a family heirloom he keeps around only for decoration and was not sure even worked. He tells how he hoped just the sight of it would be enough to scare off the intruder because he had no intention of using it, could not even remember if it was loaded. He tells how he encountered the intruder in his living room. It was dark, he could not find the lights, he could only barely see the guy. He made to retreat and call the police, but before he could, the intruder was speaking. He was saying, *I got a gun and I'm going to kill you and everyone who lives here.* Lee tells how this made him fear for his life and the life of his son. He then thought he saw the intruder point a gun at him. Terrified, reasonably believing he was facing imminent death, Lee did the only thing he could and raised his own gun and pulled the trigger. It did in fact work, it was in fact loaded. He fired only until the intruder was no longer a threat and then he called 911. Then he attended to the intruder to see if there was anything he could do to keep him alive until first responders came—but there was not. And that is what happened.

Potter nods his head and stares at his notes, clicking and unclicking his pen. —Okay. Okay. He reads it over then says again, —Okay.

He and Potter speak with a detective. The detective is a chubby blond guy with a buzz cut and a sport coat similar in style to what Lee likes to wear. The detective starts by looking at Lee's FUBU shirt and apologizing for the limited selection of men's apparel available here but, he says, their fall line has not come in yet. A little joke, Lee guesses. He does not laugh. The detective says anyway he just sent someone to swing by Lee's place and grab him some clothes, they should be here shortly. The detective waits for Lee to thank him and at last Lee does and the detective waves him off, humble. —Least I can do. You've been through hell tonight. He stands, takes off his sport coat, drapes it over the back of his chair and sits back down, sighing. —How you doing? You holding up?

—I'm okay.

—I'm sorry you had to go through this. I know where you're at right now. I've had to fire my weapon in the line of duty. No one understands what it's like. No one gets it. Not unless you've been there, like we have. Even when it's someone who gave you no choice, it sucks, right? It sucks. All I can say is, what you're feeling right now never goes away, but it does get easier with time.

He goes quiet and looks at Lee like he's waiting for him to say something, but Lee does not know what to say. Lee looks at Potter, who looks straight down at his notes.

The detective says, —I know you want to get out of here, but my job is to ask you some questions first. Don't worry, it's all just basic stuff. It's not a test, you won't be graded on it or nothing. The detective chuckles, winking at Lee. —It's just protocol. I think we can probably knock this out in a few minutes, then get you back home with your family, which, God knows, is where you want to be tonight. How's that sound to you, Lee? The detective looks at Lee closely, then suddenly laughs, shaking his head and looking down at his papers. —I'm sorry, you know, I just got to admit here, it's a trip looking across this table and seeing a guy like you. It's kind of a breath of fresh air. Obviously something has gone wrong here because usually I'm sitting here across from, you know, crackheads and gangstas. People who, well, they're bad guys. They usually look more like that kid than like you. You understand? And they sure as hell don't like *me* much. Even getting them to tell me basic information like name and address is like pulling teeth. I swear. Makes things much more difficult than it needs to be. Very time consuming, very frustrating. It makes me not want to help them much, to be honest. They just don't understand that the system relies on guys like me who know the ins and outs and who to talk to, know how to *help* them, to keep them from getting locked up for twenty or thirty years. Or worse. If not for me? Hoo boy. And I enjoy helping them. I do. I see it as my duty, as a matter of fact, being a Christian. It's a relief having you here because I know a guy like you understands the process and will get me home at a decent hour tonight so maybe I can take my kids to school for once. So thank you for that in advance.

He sits back in his chair, opening his body to Lee, and, again, waits for Lee to speak.

—What do you want me to say? Lee says.

Potter says, without looking up from his papers at either of them, —Just tell him what you told me, Lee.

Lee tells the detective what he told Potter. Disappointment comes over the detective's face.

—Lee, he groans, —I know you're scared right now, buddy, but lies do neither of us any good.

—I'm telling the truth.

The detective shakes his head. —I mean, I want to see it, Lee. I'm really trying to. But I just don't. This kid walked into your house, okay, and you got scared and shot him, right? Of course. Who wouldn't? Perfectly reasonable. I would have done the same thing. That's what they train *us* to do. I mean, you did everything right, Lee, tactically speaking. I mean, Jesus, what the hell did that kid expect? You can't just walk into a man's house. Especially not in New York City. You're a single father, you've got your baby, you see someone—you don't know who—come through the door, you get your gun and go after him, right? So you have a gun— as is your constitutional right. Nothing wrong with a law-abiding citizen owning a firearm for self-protection in his own home. It's not like you're outside waving it around or nothing. So you get your firearm, right? And you creep out into the dark silently, and you sneak up on him, right? You have no idea if this guy's got a gun and you're not going to wait and find out. You have to assume the worst. You've got to go after him. You know you gotta be aggressive. You gotta neutralize the threat right away. Right? You get the first move on him. You shoot him before he can shoot you, right? That's what I would have done. That's how they train us at the academy. You know that. You're competent. You're skilled. It's not like you have a character problem or something.

He looks hard at Lee. Lee seethes, humiliated, flashing back to his academy interview decades ago. Could the detective know about that?

—That's not what happened, Lee says firmly. —I told you what happened.

—Tell me again.

—Go ahead, Potter says. —Tell him again.

Lee tells him again. He knows he's trying to trip him up, catch him with discrepancies. But all his life he has imagined someone breaking into his house and what he would do, what he would say to the cops after. His father always taught him that the first part of responsible gun ownership is knowing the law. And criteria for justifiable homicide in the state of New York, in the event of a home invasion? Duty to retreat, reasonable fear of imminent death, rendering of aid. His father taught him to be a man who knows things and is prepared, a man who knows how to take care of himself and his family. He can tell the detective what happened as if by muscle memory, despite the chaos, the hurricane of worry for his son ripping through his head and heart.

—Now just hold on, says the detective. —This guy just *stood* there and let you *shoot* him?

Lee looks at Potter, who says, —It happened fast.

—I'm not asking you, says the detective.

Lee says, —It happened fast.

—If it was me and I saw you had a gun, know what I would have done? Run. He saw the gun and ran, right? He ran for the door.

—No. He kept coming.

—Dude, look, it's okay, it's been a chaotic night. I'm not accusing you of lying to me, I'm just trying to help you remember accurately. I cannot accept him seeing your gun and then *advancing* on you. That's not what people do. Okay? If he saw your gun, he would have done one of two things: pull his own gun or run away. So try again.

Lee shrugs, helpless.

—Need help? Want my theory? My theory is he walks into your house, for whatever reason. You don't know who it is, it's too dark. But he sees you, he sees your gun, or maybe you tell him you have it, he says holy shit and runs for the door. But when he gets there, he can't get it open right away, he kind of struggles with it, probably because he's scared or cracked out or drunk, right? We'll know for sure when we get the toxicology results. You tell him to freeze right there, because you're gonna call the cops. As is the right thing to do. But, ha, what's he gonna do—*wait?* And these motherfuckers, man, these thugs, you know if he gets out of your house he's never gonna get caught. Us cops, we try, but Christ, you know what we're up against, you know if you let this kid leave we ain't gonna find him. You know that. And he'll go off and he'll hurt someone else. No way, forget it, you can't let him go, you've got to be a good citizen here. And that's what you did. You did what you had to do. As a good guy. To keep society safe. We just want to clear that up for you, it will help you later. I got it right, right?

John Potter puts his hand on Lee's arm to make sure he says nothing.

Detective says, —Lee. La Cuzio? The DA? I know him well. He's my boss. If I give him what you've told me, he's just gonna look at it and see the gun and say, *Fuck this guy,* and charge you with murder. But he's very sympathetic to good guys being good citizens the way you were tonight. If he sees that, he'll see things differently. Just confirm I got that small detail right just now so we can get it in there and it'll make me feel much better that you'll be taken care of later.

John Potter says, —He's told you what happened.

—He's given me a rehearsed story that makes no fucking sense.

Potter says again, —He's told you what happened.

The detective sneers at them both, first at Potter, then at Lee. He laughs helplessly and says to Lee, —You're so full of shit it's coming out your ears. I know you were the aggressor. I *know* you didn't have to kill that kid. I know as soon as you saw him you decided he was dead. What you are trying to pull is going to hurt you in the end. Your lawyer here is getting you into serious trouble. This horseshit story you've given me is going to get you charged with murder. *Murder.* Now is there anything else you want to tell me? Last chance.

Lee says nothing.

The detective shakes his head sadly and leaves without another word, forgetting his sport coat.

But then another detective enters. A black guy. —Why you lying to us, dude? he says first off. —Why do I have witnesses saying they heard *you* screaming you were gonna kill the kid? Why do I have witnesses saying you're some NRA white supremacist motherfucker, some ticking time bomb wandering the streets of New York ready to go Dirty Harry on whoever looks at you wrong? You wanted to kill that kid, didn't you? You think you're a cop. You think you can enforce law and order, right? You hoped that kid would come through your door. You smoked him right off the bat, didn't you? You didn't check to see who it was first. You went out into your living room with guns blazing. That's what my witnesses say.

—What witnesses? says John Potter. He says to Lee, —He doesn't have witnesses.

The detective says, —Tell me the truth right now, bro, or the hammer's gonna drop on you. You're looking at *life in prison*. You ever been to Rikers? You gonna get *fucked* up. And I got buddies who are COs over there, they tell me it's way too crowded, they got nowhere to put new motherfuckers, the only place to put them now is with the craziest, gnarliest, blackest-ass motherfuckers who they ain't wanted to put with nobody else because these dudes got dysfunctions, man, they got disorders.

John Potter says, —This is great stuff. Coercion. Intimidation. This on the record? I hope so, I can't wait to read it aloud in court.

—Fuck the record. Tell me the truth. This is your last chance.

Lee says, —He said he had a gun and he was there to kill me. I retreated. I rendered aid.

—He was sleepwalking. You know that? You killed a fifteen-year-old boy in his *sleep*. How that feel? Feel good? You *hard* motherfucker. The one through the face is probably the one that killed him. Got his brains all over the door. How that feel right now, to know that? Feel pride? You proud? Proud to kill your own neighbor who grew up right downstairs from you? Who all his life lived right downstairs and you didn't even know who he was? I have a question for you, tough man: How many times it take for you to recognize a black person's face?

Lee is sick, knows from how dizzy it makes him that it is true.

No wrongdoing, his father says. *His fault. Not yours.*

It goes on like this for hours, the rest of the night and into the morning. Four more detectives separately try to break him. No one ever shows up with the clothes the first detective promised.

The last detective throws up his hands and leaves the room, and cops in uniform come and tell Lee to stand up and turn around.

—What's going on? he says.

—It's okay, says Potter. —Just do what they say.

—Where are they taking me?

—I'll be down there first thing, Potter says.

—Are they taking me to jail? Y'all taking me to *jail?*

One of the cops says as another cuffs him, —No, we're taking you to breakfast. What do you feel like? Pancakes?

They take Lee outside and put him on a bus. It is so confusing and horrible, everyone seeming to know what is next but him. As the bus pulls away he can see Potter and the black detective standing on the sidewalk outside the station comparing iPhones, side by side. Potter lightly taps the detective on the chest with the back of his hand and says something, and the detective leans back and laughs, hand on his belly. It is like they are friends. Like they have always been friends. The bus is filled with other prisoners, mostly black but some Hispanic. Lee cowers, makes no eye contact. Takes a seat next to a young Hispanic man, a kid really. He has dried snot and blood on his face. —Don't sit next to me faggot, Snot and Blood says. Lee apologizes, stands to find another seat. Guard at the front of the bus screams at him to sit back down. Lee sits back down.

—Said don't sit here, faggot.

—He told me to sit here.

—You can't, mang.

—But there ain't no one else sitting here.

—That's right. Including you, bitch-ass faggot.

Lee says nothing, stays where he is. Snot and Blood keeps staring at him.

—Said fuck up out here, mang.

Lee does not. Snot and Blood puts his face up against the side of Lee's. Lee can feel his breath on his skin. He can smell it, hot and foul like he hasn't brushed his teeth in months.

—Fuck up out here. Now. You wanna get stabbed? Punk-ass faggot bitch. He spits on him.

Lee is trembling, trying not to cry. He stands up. Guard yells at him. Driver looks at him in the rearview mirror and pumps the brakes, bus lurches, Lee tumbles, face lands in the seat, presses against the vinyl fouled with decades of New York City criminal ass and sweat and piss. All the prisoners are laughing at him. —*Bwa ha ha ha ha!* The guard is screaming at him to get up off the floor, — Why you on the floor? Sit down, inmate, or I'll break your head. Lee pushes himself up without the use of his hands, which are cuffed behind his back. He tumbles sideways onto the bench, driver pumps the brakes again, Lee rolls facedown into Snot and Blood's lap, Snot and Blood says, —The *fuck*? and thrusts his pelvis violently to get him off and spits on him again and keeps spitting at him even when he has gotten off. Everyone laughing, laughing. Lee sits upright.

—*Fuck* up off me before I kill you, says Snot and Blood.

—I'm sorry, he tells Snot and Blood.

—Fuck you.

—Please, he begs the guard, —please let me change seats.

—Fuck you, says the guard.

—I told you not to sit here and yet you still sitting here, says Snot and Blood.

—Come on, dude, Lee says, voice breaking, —you understand my predicament here, what am I supposed to do?

They all love that: —*Bwa ha ha ha ha ha! Dude! Duuuuuuuuude!*

Snot and Blood spits on Lee one more time, then loses interest, falls silent and sullen.

Outside the windows covered in steel mesh the city goes about its business with no regard for what has happened. The city absorbs everything. It is omnivorous. Its capacity is infinite. It is lonely to see people going into coffee shops right now, going in and out of subway stations. Wearing work clothes. Talking on the phone. Chuckling as they walk alongside each other in conversation. Walking children to school. Loneliness has not been loneliness until now.

The bus enters an underground garage and one at a time the prisoners are ordered off the bus. They are brought into an old labyrinth of green fluorescent-lit cages and low-ceilinged halls that seems to twist miles and miles beneath Manhattan toward the center of the earth. He is disoriented and covered in Snot and Blood's spit. Correctional officers tell him, *Shut up. Stand here. Walk there. Bend. Stand. Turn. Walk. Shut up.* He is forced to undress in a roomful of strangers. He is raped by a guard's fingers while several others watch, including women, all peering up with flashlights into his stretched rectum as they chat idly about car stereos. Something tears, he feels hot liquid. —*Ooooh, a bleeder!* They stick paper towels in his ass, tell him to pull his pants up and stand here, walk there, turn, sit, stand, shut up, don't look at me. A doctor looks at him and says he's fine. Humiliated and in great pain, he moves along with the rest of them like bovine in his prison garb—it smells like industrial disinfectant and old semen—and ill-fitting laceless sneakers into a large room, where he finds a bench far away from everyone in the corner where he can sit with his back to the wall. What now? What will happen? When can he post bail and go home and be with his son? When will the system work?

It is extremely cold. The walls are cinder block coated in cheap white paint, with graffiti all over it. The lights are flickering greenish fluorescent tubes behind protective steel cages. The other prisoners slump depressed against the walls with heads down on their knees or pace and slobber and shout gibberish over and over. They fight, threaten each other. They are on all kinds of drugs, in various stages of intoxication and detoxification. Prisoners are screaming, fighting, writhing around crying, slumped on the floor and maybe dead. There is a large light brown coil of human shit in the corner, it *stinks*, it makes you gag. The COs laugh at it, leave it there. *Stay aware, Lee. That is the thing to do right now. Stay aware and try to be invisible and wait to be called and released.*

—Hey yo, a black prisoner calls to Lee from his own seat on the other side of the room. Burns all over his neck. —That's mah seat you sitting in.

Lee tries ignoring him.

—Look at me, motherfucker.

Lee looks at Burns. He grins, teeth all fucked up. —That's *mah* seat.

—But you already have a seat.

Burns stops grinning. —What you say? *What you say to me, motherfucker?* He stands up, he must be seven feet tall and three hundred pounds. He comes toward Lee. —*What you sitting in mah seat saying to me?*

—Nothing, Lee says.

Three other big black giants flank Burns now, materializing from who knows where to back him up on the matter. —That's right, they say, —that's *his* seat.

—*Mah* seat, says Burns.

—*His* seat, say the giants.

—Fine, Lee says, —you want the daggone seat? Take it.

He stands up, paper towels in his pants crinkling as he gives up the seat, furious and terrified and completely powerless. The only other place left to sit is near the shit, and he's not about to sit there. So he has to stand, and the only place to stand is in the middle of the room where he is vulnerable to attack from all sides. Now everyone seems to be eyeballing him, talking to each other about him. Plotting. Do they know what he has done? He hears his father say, *What have you done? You've done nothing.* What will he do if attacked? What defense does he have? He has never been in a fight before. He likes to think he knows what he would do—he has posted long, detailed instructions in online forums about how to fight, where to attack a gang of street thugs to most efficiently neutralize them when they jump you in a parking lot, close-encounter hand-to-hand tactics to use when someone breaks into your bedroom through the window and you don't have time to reach for your gun, and he has even demonstrated these methods at self-defense seminars, but inside he is afraid that if someone were to actually strike his face with a fist he will just immediately lose consciousness the way chickens do when you hold them down on their back. *Hell you will,* his father says. But he will, he will panic. And fuck up. Like last night. *You didn't.* Yes, he finally had his chance to be who he believes he is and he panicked, he fucked up.

Go easy on yourself, you're always so dang hard on yourself. You did what you had to do to protect your son.

At his feet space opens enough for him to sit on the floor and he does.

—Yo, says a massive thug with braids and tattoos, standing over Lee now. —They busted the Pillsbury Doughboy! What they get you for, Pills? Messing with kids, right? I always suspected that about you.

Lee has learned his lesson now; he avoids eye contact, says nothing. But he can see enough to know that this one is better groomed than the others. He hears his father say, *You know what that means, don't you?* Lee does. Kingpin. A high-ranking gangsta who deals in weight and has soldiers do his enforcing and street-level dealing.

—Said what up, Pills?

Plans to frame you for something, sell you contraband, trick you somehow into inescapable debt. You know what guys like this are like, no values, always scheming and manipulating and exploiting. You know.

—Hello? says Kingpin, snapping his fingers in front of Lee's face.

Lee peers around for a CO, there are none to be seen. *Stay sharp— Kingpin has paid them to look the other way for a few moments while he does God know what to you.*

He leans in close to Lee. —You know they saying you kill brown-hair girls. Young girls with brown hair. That true?

Despite himself, Lee scoffs, insulted. —Hell no.

—What about shooting up your office. They saying that too.

Lee says nothing. *Wait him out, maybe he'll go away.*

—What about going vigilante on a kid? That one true? Kingpin reads Lee's silence and nods and says, —Thought so. How it feel? Feel good?

Lee says nothing.

—What's your name?

—Leave me alone.

—Your name's Leave Me Alone? Your parents antisocial or something? Well, hi, Leave Me Alone, my name's Joseph. Plain old Joseph. My parents are boring, I guess.

Joseph holds out his hand. Lee lets it hang. Joseph chuckles but seems to file the slight away for later. —What's the matter? Don't want to talk to me? Don't like me? All right, that's cool. Just don't shoot. He puts his hands up and backs away, laughing but without smiling, and with deep, deep anger in his eyes. He wanders off across the room and Lee notices how no one talks to Joseph, everyone stays away.

Hour after hour passes. It is like a DMV in hell, one where everyone wants to kill you. Now and again inmates get called out to meet with lawyers or face the judge, but Lee is never called. *Forgot about you. They made an oversight, you mean nothing to them, and now you will die in here.* At one point, despite his efforts not to, he drifts off to sleep. Last thing he hears is the kid next to him hissing at another, —Gonna kill you, gonna *kill* you.

When he wakes up there is a blanket draped over his shoulders. He throws it off. Cannot imagine what nasty substances are on it. He brushes his arms and face for lice and bedbugs and fleas, looks across the room and sees everyone has one, which makes him change his mind and think maybe he should use it, but then he sees Joseph there watching him and he understands and does not touch the blanket again, stays cold instead.

The next day he is still there in the bullpen of the Tombs, still waiting for Potter, still waiting for his father, for justice. He is very sick—being cold has made him acquire what must be some kind of new super rhinovirus that has mutated in here over the years. His head feels like a balloon filled with Elmer's glue. He is the only one who is sneezing and sweating and breathing through his mouth. Joseph says, —Feel okay, Pills? and chuckles drily. He can hardly stand when at last he is called to meet with his attorney.

—What the hell is going on? Lee asks Potter. —What's taking so long? When do I post bail and go home?

Potter says, slathering Purell on his hands, —This is homicide and a gun.

—I know that.

—There's no bail.

—Sure there is.

Potter just shakes his head and says, —No.

—There's got to be something we can do.

Potter says, —There's not. It's homicide and a gun. They don't grant bail for homicide and a gun.

—Jesus Christ, they understand I'm not a criminal, right? I mean, what do they have? What are they basing their decision on? What information? Is it just a piece of paper they're looking at, with my name and what the cops say I did? Maybe they need to know more, maybe if they had the full picture. Maybe if they knew who I *was*. Who I *am*.

—What do you mean?

—*You know.* I'm not like *them.* He gestures over his shoulder back toward the bullpen, the other prisoners.

Potter is just looking at him. He has made a name for himself by defending mobsters accused of murder, IMF officials accused of raping hotel housekeepers, professional athletes accused of both. — Being rich, he says, —isn't a viable defense.

—No, I know that.

—Nor is being white.

—I *know* that, that's not what I'm saying. All I'm saying is, maybe if they see that I'm a guy who has never been in trouble, who has respect for traditional American values—

—I know exactly what you're saying. And I'm telling you: in the eyes of the court it makes no difference.

—That's not true. Come on, everyone knows it's not. What are they always complaining about? Double standards, white privilege. Right?

—Bail will be denied. I'm telling you. So plan accordingly. Now let's talk about your son.

—I told you, my dad'll take him. Is he here? Why hasn't he come? They not allow visitors or something?

Potter looks at his notes and shifts in his seat, uncomfortable. — Maybe there's a backup plan.

—What do you mean?

—Your mother says she's tied up overseas but is trying to come as soon as she can, she says she's worried sick and wants me to tell you she loves you and stay strong. She says one of your brothers or sisters would be more than happy to take him.

—Half brothers and half sisters, Lee corrects him. —And no way, I hardly know them, they might as well be strangers, I don't know who they are or what they're about. If they're anything like her, absolutely not. But what are we talking about? Where's my dad?

—He's not an option at this point.

—Why not?

—Lee, he said no.

—I don't believe that.

—Then don't. He said no. He's not coming.

—What? Why? Is he okay? Is he sick or something?

Potter has no answers. It's irrelevant to him. —We need to find someone else. I have investigators looking at his mother and, boy, she really had no one, no family to speak of. Look, he's headed to a shelter unless there's somebody, anybody, you trust to take him. A friend, a coworker, a neighbor—anyone at all, Lee. Is there *anyone* you trust?

Lee can think of no one.

Potter says, —There is an option. There is a woman in Washington Heights. Court-appointed guardian. The court knows her, she takes in children in cases like this all the time and she's stellar. The best in the city. I know her, I've used her before. I'd let her babysit my own kids. I've called in some favors and, well, that's actually where your son is headed right now.

—You *what*?

—At least he's out of the shelter, Lee.

—Washington Heights? My God, have you ever been there?

—Yes, have you?

Lee has not, but he does not say so. —My God, do you understand the risk he is under? Once the media gets ahold of this, there are going to be people out there who will want to kill me. *And* him. And you're sending him up to God knows where, with God knows who.

—Lee, she's a saint.

—She does not know how to protect him.

—And you do?

—Absolutely not will my son live with some welfare queen.

—That's not who this is at all. She's fine, she's lovely. Really.

—Yeah, I'm sure. Fine to *you*. Don't be so gullible, John.

—You think you know better than me?

—I'm not saying I know *better* than you, but I do *know*.

—What do you know?

—I know... *things*. Okay? I pay attention. I read.

—What do you read?

—I read the news, the real news. I read between the lines. I think for myself and pay attention to the world around me. And I know all about your homegirl up in Harlem.

—Washington Heights.

—I know all about her. People like her hoard babies like cats. They smile at whoever they need to smile at to keep their checks coming from the state each month, and then they turn around and stuff the babies into closets.

—She's qualified.

—Is she a trained security expert? Because if not, in this case no, she ain't qualified. They are out there, John. They will be coming for him. They will come for my son. And when they do, your homegirl will be zonked out on the couch covered in Cheetos dust, high as a kite on painkillers and... Lee cannot even finish. It's too terrible to imagine. He is sweating and shivering. He is so tired. So sick. God, how he just wants to sleep. —Tell me this, he says. —Have there or have there not been death threats?

Potter sighs and says, —They're being taken very seriously.

Lee puts up his arms in morbid victory.

—Law enforcement is on top of it.

—Yeah, I'm sure every cop on the NYPD is bleeding internally over it. Look, I'll call my father and talk to him and figure this out. Meanwhile, just keep working on it.

Potter smiles, irritated at being ordered around. —Yeah, okay, sure, I'll keep on working on it. What I *am* going to work on, because it's a *wise* use of my time and your family's resources, is getting you a fucking antiviral before *that*— he points to Lee's face, signifying his cold —turns into pneumonia. You look like death. They're supposed to provide you a blanket, didn't you get a blanket?

—There's a guy in here? Big criminal.

—*Really*. In *jail*?

—No, I'm talking real big, *whale big*. Okay? He's one of these guys who acts nice and charming, but really he's a bad dude, he's wicked. And he's got it out for me. He knows why I'm here. He's got eyes everywhere. He's going to hurt me.

—What's he done to you?

—Well, for one thing, I was asleep when they were handing out blankets but he made sure I got one.

—I'll have him hanged.

—No, you don't understand. He put some kind of virus on it. That's why I'm so sick.

Potter smirks and picks up his pen and pretends to make a note of it.

Lee says, —John, what about the gun? When do I get it back?

Potter mutters, still looking at his legal pad, —The gun.

—I'll get it back when this is all over, right?

Potter says, —I should put in an insanity plea. Lee, you're going to prison for that gun.

—No, I'm not.

—You had an unlicensed gun in the city of New York.

—Any law that contradicts the United States Constitution is an unjust, immoral one and I do not recognize it.

—Well, this unjust, immoral law says you face two to five years automatically. No bail. No nothing. Even if bail were on the table, no judge would grant it. Not to you. Look at yourself. Look at your life. You have no ties to your community.

Lee starts to protest but Potter cuts him off.

—You have nothing keeping you here. No work. No friends, no family. You don't even have anyone to take your kid.

—I have those things, Lee says, wondering if he has those things. —I have ties. I have work.

—Fantastic, Potter says, getting ready to write it down. —What do you do?

—Gosh, a lot of things.

—Give me one.

—Well, lately, I've been painting.

Potter laughs at him and does not write it down. He looks at him and says, —Yeah?

—Yeah, Lee says, offended. —I paint. I'm a painter. Write it down.

—You mean, what, like, house painting?

—*Art* painting.

—Okay. What do you art-paint?

—Lately? Mostly American flags and patriotic things like that.

—Make any money doing that?

—You'd be surprised, Lee lies.

—What do you do with them?

—Sell them on eBay. Got some on there right now.

—Great. Maybe I'll buy one.

Lee ignores the vicious sarcasm. —Point is, I do things. Things are important to me. Not just my gun. I know there are other things that are important. I *know.* I'm not dumb, I'm not crazy. The gun is a means to things that are important. Okay? Like freedom. It worries me that you don't see that. I'm kind of worried. I thought you were a good lawyer, but if you don't see that my gun is about freedom, then I'm kind of starting to wonder here what I'm paying you for.

—I am a good lawyer. And you're not paying me. One of your family's shell corporations is. And very well too. I'll be able to take the rest of the year off. I'm thinking Ibiza.

He returns to the bullpen. He does not believe he said no. He does not believe he is not coming. Then again, maybe Lee might have said the same in his position. They do not talk much. He likes to think of his father as frozen in time—the same guy he was when Lee was small. That is how he thinks of him, that is how he dreams of him. He's not a man or a person to Lee but a set of sensations bonded to the time and place of childhood. When he saw him at the third wedding he was alarmed that the black hair on his head was all white, and all the muscles he remembered were gone to flab, the broad shoulders were slumped, and his face was dried up and withered with wrinkles, desiccated here and there with pale brown spots. Sometimes he gets a terse, enigmatic e-mail from him on his birthday (*Happy Birthday, I think. Or as they say in Katmandu... . ??*) and he does not feel the need to respond to them, because it does not take a psychologist to understand they were written drunk. Lee has his address but has never been there. He knows the third wife left him, and he knows none of his other kids talk to him, but other than that Lee does not know much about what the man's life is like now. But he can imagine: a big house completely isolated from anybody else; maybe some sad romantic misadventures; a general corroding loneliness, a kind of living death.

There was a cancer scare, he knows. Years ago, back before his father and his other kids fell out. One of Lee's stepsisters e-mailed to tell him about it. Not serious, completely routine procedure, nothing at all to worry about, even if from the way his father was acting you would think he'd been diagnosed with the plague. Lee asked if he should come and was relieved when she said there was no need, they all had it covered, there was nothing he could do. So he did not go. Should he have gone? It's different when it's the son, isn't it? The son does not have to go when it's the father, but when it's the son the father must go—always, absolutely. *You just have not heard about it yet, is all,* he tells his father now. *Otherwise, you'd be here. Once you hear about it, you'll come.*

At last Lee's name is called for court. A tattooed gang of five steroid-ridden correctional officers brings him upstairs, treating him so rudely and handling him so roughly it is like once they get there they will put him against a wall and execute him. It has been thirty-six hours in jail. He is filthy and exhausted. He has grown even sicker. Tortured with helpless worry for his son. No one in the bullpen but Joseph has seemed to recognize him yet, which makes him think what has happened has somehow escaped the media.

But this hope is decimated when the elevator doors open on the lobby of the court and through the big glass windows at the front he can see the sidewalk outside, the festival of hatred under way, the throng of murderous humanity gathered there. It is a wall of vitriol. Protestors pound the glass and scream at him. They want him dead. He is not human to them. What he has been through and continues to go through, how bad he feels for what happened, what he was forced to do, and the consequences he now suffers do not matter to them. Only the gun matters to them. They would be glad to see him dead, because they hate his gun so much. To them he is just a symbol to be destroyed. Lee is stunned by the fury in their faces smashed against the glass, contorted in unhinged rage for him. It is like a science fiction movie where a plague has turned ordinary people into monsters. Who is responsible for such madness? Who has stirred this up in them? Who has hijacked their minds, exploited their emotions and fears, and turned them into a private battalion; inflamed the worst parts of them and put the life of a man and his family at risk for political gain? Who would do such a thing?

His father says, *You know who it is. You know. She's here. Of course she is.*

In the courtroom he looks for his father even though he knows he is not here. For a moment he panics—dead, maybe? Maybe Potter is lying to him, doesn't want him to know his father died weeks, even months ago, and nobody thought to tell Lee.

He stands next to John Potter before the judge, trembling and sweating and coughing, so overwhelmed and ill he feels like he might pass out. He can hardly follow what is being said about him. They are discussing something far removed from Lee Fisher. They could be discussing mutual bonds, or the human microbiome. He can feel a brittle tension on his back, knows it is the parents, they are here. They have let the father out and the one they're keeping in jail is Lee Fisher. The dread that comes with this realization numbs him so that he hardly hears it when the prosecutor announces homicide and gun charges and the judge remands Lee Fisher into custody without bail. And that's it. Thirty-six hours in hell for that. There is cheering behind him, taunts and heckles from what sound like thousands of people. He does not turn to look into the noise, the thunder. He does not dare. Potter is gathering his briefcase, cops are taking hold of Lee.

—I don't understand, Lee says to Potter, —what happened, what's happening?

A woman's voice behind him says, —*You're getting locked up, that's what! And I hope they throw away the key!*

More cheering, laughter. Lee turns and sees who said it, and there she is, Jenny Sanders, and now the dread consumes and the dizziness overwhelms him. The judge barks at them through his microphone but it does nothing to silence them. The hecklers are stomping, chanting: —*Re-peal! Re-peal! Re-peal! Re-peal!* and it is the last thing Lee hears as he loses consciousness and collapses.

He comes to alone in a room in the court and then he is examined by a nurse—he has a bump on his head from where he hit the edge of the table on the way down—and herded onto a Department of Corrections bus waiting in an underground garage beneath the court. Waits hours on that bus. Has to use the bathroom. Where the hell is his father? Why is *she* here and not him? One after another a new prisoner is brought out from the court and loaded onto it. Black, invariably. He has the impression they all know each other, that they have all been through this before and know what will happen. Joseph boards the bus, walks past Lee not making eye contact.

Hours and hours he waits. His bladder and colon are on the edge of bursting. Burns is here, begging like a little child to use the bathroom. —*Please, man. Please.* Snot and Blood is here too, staring sullen and unreachable out the window. Won't somebody tell Lee what is happening? He knows not to ask, not to speak.

Two more hours pass. Burns starts moaning, —*Man, I didn't even do nothin'. My baby, man. Where my little girl, man? Where my momma, man... ?* and then Burns goes quiet and then Lee can smell urine.

Joseph in back complains, —Yo, you did not just piss yourself. You did not just piss yourself. He calls to the CO up front, —Yo, this nigga pissed himself.

The CO ignores him. They all sit in the hot stink of Burns's piss, the hotter stink of Burns's humiliation, until, for no apparent reason, the driver puts the bus into gear. Lee Fisher is taken across town—the free people outside in the streets glancing briefly at the bus as it passes and seeing nothing, seeing no one, and then forgetting it altogether—then up FDR Drive to the Queensborough Bridge, then up to another bridge, this one long, gray, and solitary, on the other end of which is Rikers Island.

Spends his first night on Rikers listening to a lunatic compelled by the Spirit of Jesus Christ, hollering: —NO FAITH, NO LIFE! NO FAITH, NO LIFE! People screaming at him to shut the fuck up, their screaming only adding to the noise, so other people screaming at *them* to shut the fuck up.

His father's voice says, *Potter is incompetent, a vacuous celebrity. What difference does it make to him what becomes of you?*

And Lee says back to him, *And what about you? What difference does it make to* you? *Where are you and where have you ever been?*

The bitterness he feels makes the claustrophobia even more nauseating than it already is. Inmates steal his shower flip-flops, they steal his replacement shower flip-flops. They steal the socks off his feet as he sleeps, or, rather, as he tries to sleep, for the tube lights remain on twenty-four hours a day, buzzing and flickering like the inside of his head. Yet again he has no idea what he is waiting for. Or how long he will be here. No indication of what is going to happen to him. No one will tell him anything. Not Potter, not the COs.

—Yo, Pills, Joseph calls to him from the TV area as he passes through. —Come see who's on TV.

Lee ignores him, continues walking.

—No, come here. You wanna see this.

Warily, Lee goes over, sees who is on TV. Lee Fisher is who is on TV. His home too. And the kid. And the parents. And her. *Her.* —Oh no, he says out loud. How can she be allowed to sashay into this situation she knows nothing about and make pawns of them all to capitalize on a kid's tragic death?

She shouldn't be, his father says. *She shouldn't be allowed. She is laying waste to our way of life. She's asking for it. She's pushing us and pushing us and we will only be pushed so far.*

And she is calling Lee Fisher an enemy of the peace, a polluter of the public health. —*A dangerous, radical conservative gun nut, a wannabe cop, a domestic terrorist, who for no reason other than he was white and male felt he was entitled to take the law into his own hands and kill with impunity. This is gun culture,* she says. —*This is the so-called tradition we bend over backward to protect. In fact it's all a myth. This is the reality: Lee Fisher was influenced by an inborn sense of white supremacy and cowboy fantasies that were inflamed by the irresponsible, fear-mongering rhetoric and lobbying of the NRA, whose loyalties lie not with the American people but with the gun industry. And this is what you get as a result of that: a society saturated, absolutely saturated, with guns and gun worship. You get death. You get dead kids. You get more dead Americans each decade than all the terror attacks, all our wars combined.*

And now they are playing audio of someone speaking on a telephone. Takes Lee several moments to recognize the voice as his own, on the night of the shooting. They have edited out all the 911 dispatcher's questions, leaving only Lee's out-of-context responses. —*I shot him,* America hears Lee Fisher say. —*Of course I shot him. He's black.* There are subtitles to make sure no one misses the shocking, blatant racism. All the prisoners watching TV are looking at Lee now. Black faces, black muscles.

—They edited it, Lee says.

It sounds like a lie. Even he does not believe himself. Now his mug shot appears. It is not him. It is the Face, the one representing everything: slavery, lynching, Jim Crow, economic disparity, mass incarceration, Rodney King, Ferguson, Eric Garner. Here is who we can blame for it all: Lee Fisher. Now go forth and avenge. The news goes to a commercial for Dulcolax and no one speaks. No one is looking at him anymore. That is worse than when they were. Then Joseph says, —Better be careful, Pills. His father agrees, *Be careful.* Fisher staggers to his cell, now feeling every eye in Rikers on his back.

He wraps his towel and his little thin pillow and some magazines around his torso and around his wrists and throat beneath his jumpsuit and goes to the phones. Calls his father again and again, he does not answer. Calls Potter, who is aware of the situation, has already been in contact with Rikers authorities about getting Lee out of general population and into protective custody, but they are saying there is no space.

—That's bullshit, Lee says, —I'm in *real, imminent danger,* don't they see that? What do I do?

—Stay safe, Potter says.

—Brilliant advice, man, thank you.

—Your case is with the grand jury. If they don't indict you in five days, they have to release you.

—I won't last five days, I won't last five hours. *Please.*

Guard comes by, makes him hang up, gives no reason. Lee starts to argue, guard pulls out his baton and more guards show up also with their batons, so Lee hangs up the phone. Joseph is there in line behind him. There's a menacing twinkle in his eye. Lee keeps his head down and walks off, feeling Joseph's eyes picking the spot in Lee's kidneys to stick the homemade knife into.

In the cafeteria he cannot eat. Too nervous. Throat dry and constricted. He can hear every utensil sink into every small mound of wet, mushy food. Every time someone stands he flinches. After dinner he returns to his cell. On his bed, folded neatly and somehow not yet stolen, is a blanket. Lee was given one when he first arrived, but a guy with shoulders the size of a bull's walked up to his bed and helped himself to it. Lee hears his father explain, *If you are an idiot, you'll use it. Someone's done something to it. And you'll get sick and they'll send you to the infirmary, where you will get an infection from the unsanitary conditions and the inept doctors there will misdiagnose you and you will die. If you are an idiot, that's what will happen. But you aren't an idiot, are you? You know what to do.* Feeling like his father is watching him somehow, from somewhere, wherever that is, Lee uses a cardboard toilet paper roll to poke the blanket off his bed onto the floor, then drag it into the hall and leave it there. The inmates all see, stare at him blankly. *Underestimated you, didn't they?* Starts to feel better about himself again and who he is and where he comes from.

Calls his father, no answer, leaves a message babbling semi-coherently about the toilet paper roll, hangs up. That night he does not allow himself to sleep. Blanketless, he shivers all night long and wakes up even sicker than before. Out in the yard he stands in the shade watching others run laps and lift weights and shoot hoops. He is coughing, mucus streaming from his nose, feeling much worse now, utterly terrible. *Doesn't matter. Small price for safety. Almost over.* His back is against the wall to prevent a sneak attack from the rear. *How will they do it? Belt around my throat? Cardboard blade forged from a box of Cracker Jacks bought in the canteen? My skull bashed in with a weight?*

Joseph jogs by on the dirt track, dreadlocks flapping behind him. —Get that thing I left you? Lee ignores him. Joseph comes around the track again and stops before Lee, running in place, eyes sparkling. He asks again, —Get that thing I left you?

—Don't know what you're talking about.

—Aw, someone stole it? Don't worry, lady CO in charge of blankets here knows my momma. I'll get you another one.

—No, thank you, Lee says, playing it cool.

—You have a thing against blankets, don't you?

—I like the cold. It's invigorating.

—Yeah, okay. You look like hell.

—I'm fine. I'm great.

—You sick as hell. Or maybe it's just guilt eating away at you? Lee shakes his head, says nothing.

—You don't feel guilty?

—Of course I do.

—But you don't think you did anything wrong, right? You think it's unfair you being here with us, right?

Lee does not answer. He is afraid to.

—Well, don't worry too much. You gonna get off. You'll be out of here before you know it.

—I'm facing life in prison.

—Right. Rich dude with big-time lawyers. Yeah, you in real trouble. They're gonna *nail you.* If there's one thing they don't tolerate it's a dead black teenager. Joseph shakes his head. — Walking around looking like the damned Michelin man. You look insane, you understand that, right?

Lee does not answer. He is afraid to. His eyes scan the vicinity, in case Joseph is trying to distract him while an accomplice strikes.

—You gotta try running or exercising or something. Better than standing around going crazy.

—I'm not.

—Bruh, you even starting to smell crazy.

Encouraging news to Lee. He has not showered once since he has been here. In the shower line he lets criminal after criminal go ahead of him, delaying long enough for the COs to think he must have gone already and to tell him to get back to his bunk. Thinks if he can manage to avoid showering long enough he will reek so badly that no one will be able to tolerate being near him long enough to hurt him. —Just stay the fuck away from me, okay?

Joseph just laughs in response.

Lee goes back inside to lie down on his cot and relish a rare moment or two of solitude and privacy. He collapses onto the cot and, despite his efforts not to, falls into his first real sleep since the shooting. He dreams of it, sees the boy's dead body, wakes later that afternoon soaked in sweat, his fever broken and his illness cured. Goes to dinner. Appetite comes roaring back. Cannot resist, takes his chances to stand in line for food. His jaw juices at the sight of the rehydrated meatloaf and instant mashed potatoes and shriveled frozen baby carrots. He flashes back to his boyhood, the little hard potatoes. He can taste them again. They were horrible, weren't they? *They were delicious, they were pure.* No, they tasted like filth because that's exactly what they were growing in. *You're ungrateful. You're letting them get to you, bully you into changing. This is how they do it. Don't feel guilty. You did nothing wrong. It was your house. He came into your house. Don't let them bully you into changing...*

The skinny guy scooping the meatloaf says, —Hed da buh bumduhuh, and Lee makes the guy repeat himself but he only says the exact same nonsense. Lee says, —I don't understand you, but look, I'm watching you, so don't even try to spit in my meatloaf or anything.

—I *said*, the guy enunciates absurdly, nearly shouting, the guy beside him on the carrots cracking up, —I... got... some... thing... for... you.

He puts down his meatloaf spatula and is bending down for something stashed on the floor by his feet. A weapon. Lee drops his tray to the floor, his food spilling across the tile. Prisoners jump to their feet—something happening, something to see—all hell breaking loose as Lee pushes through the line behind him and shoves aside prisoners and tables, running for his life to the door. Covers his head and stays low, bracing himself for gunfire. How did they get a gun in here? Does not matter. The COs, not understanding he is the victim, or, more likely, involved in the plot themselves, tackle him, punch him in the ribs and head, kick him in the stomach, cuff him, drag him away, the prisoners behind him cheering and heckling, stomping their feet.

Lee spends the night and next day in punitive isolation. Even colder here. Feels like a walk-in freezer. They even take his underwear. He sleeps. Wakes a short time later shivering and sweating and hurting deeply. Sickest he has been yet. Sicker than he has been in his life. When they come for him, he begs them not to return him to general population. They ignore him, put him back in his cell to be butchered. Folded atop his bed is yet another blanket. He vomits into the toilet, then sits on it, simultaneously weeping and shitting a fiery liquid stream, sweat rushing down his face like he has come up from underwater.

—Awwwwww, man! his cellmates cry, springing up from their cots to bolt from the cell, waving their hands before their faces, covering their mouths and noses with the crooks of their elbows.

—Get it out of here, Lee cries, pointing to the blanket, —get it out!

They don't know what he is talking about and don't care, they're running. Uses the remainder of his toilet paper to more or less wipe himself down, washes his hands in the sink, splashes cold water on his face—it seems to hiss when it hits his burning flesh. Again and again he fills the little plastic cup with water and empties it into his mouth, which sucks it up like dry summer dirt. Weak and losing consciousness and clutching his beaten ribs, he staggers to the bed, falls atop it, blanket and all. Cannot muster the strength to even lift himself off the blanket and throw it to the floor. He killed that kid. Killed him. His young body, the blood. Dead eyes staring into his. The black skin, the hoodie. He murdered him.

He does not hear his father. His father says nothing. He is not here.

Wakes up later clutching the blanket, body clinging to it. It is morning. He is very hungry, eats gratefully, his body fighting off the disease and injuries. Steps out into the yard, the sun, watches Joseph run around the track. When Joseph can't see, Lee swings his arms back and forth. It is difficult to do with all his body armor. Maybe he will remove it. Maybe he will begin exercising. Maybe he will begin right now. Hops a third of an inch off the ground. Coughs, cannot stop coughing. It is the most exercise he has done since he was training for the NYPD Academy twenty-five years ago. *Twenty-five years.* Jesus, where did his life go?

Sleeps that night again with Joseph's blanket pulled snug over his body, mouth agape, dreaming of his father, the grocery store parking lot, Lee's eye oozing and swollen, and the awful horror in the faces of the people passing by them, his father sweating and drunk, the gun on his hip. A kind, concerned woman coming up to them in the parking lot, *Sir, his eye is in trouble, you need to take him to a hospital,* and his father saying to her, *You need to mind your own business.* A truck backing out, Lee on the pavement, back tire crushing Lee's leg. His father pulling Lee to his feet, both of which are mangled. *Apologize to him, Lee. Apologize to me.* His beery sardine breath on Lee's face as he leans in with bushy gray-black beard. *Your pets are dead.* He wakes up soaked.

That day he waits in line for the phones to call him again, but when he gets there and lifts the receiver and begins to dial, he just hangs up and calls no one. He goes to the yard where he stands in the sun for longer, closer to the track, swinging his arms a few more times than yesterday. He looks down at his belly, the fat of his perspiring throat squeezing sideways on either side of his chin, pressing down like a finger on a toothpaste tube. Puts his hands on his ample lard, jiggles it. Those little goddamn potatoes.

Maybe he is not who he believes he is and never has been. Maybe his father too. Is it possible?

Meets with Potter. —How's my son?

—He's fine, I checked in on him yesterday, she's taking great care of him.

—He's safe?

—He's safe. And if you're not indicted by tomorrow, they have to let you out. For now. I can't believe they haven't indicted you yet, to be honest. I don't know what's taking so long, it makes me think La Cuzio's struggling. I'm sensing weakness. I'm smelling blood. You never know with a grand jury. You played it well with the detectives, you gave a beautiful statement. I wish I could have been there when La Cuzio read it and saw he has no choice but to forget the dead kid. *I feared for my life, he said he had a gun, I rendered aid.* No witnesses to contradict it. There's no way he'll try and take that to trial—he won't risk the embarrassment of an acquittal. No, he won't touch the shooting. You'll get off on that. All he can do is go after you on the gun. If the gun goes to trial, it's a slam dunk conviction and he looks good, the city looks good, the protestors lose their steam. Which La Cuzio needs. They've been relentless. Jenny Sanders has them all stirred up, they've been clogging up the streets, the trains, embarrassing everybody, bringing the media everywhere, being up everybody's ass, cops are roughing them up, looking like the Red Army, and it all just stirs up the other side and *they* start protesting and doing the same thing. It's a mess out there. A spectacle. La Cuzio convicts you on the gun and all that goes away. So that's his strategy. Well, here's what I'm gonna do. It's a long shot, to put it mildly, but we have nothing to lose and it's our only option, so why not take it: I'm going to put you in front of the grand jury tomorrow, and I want you to tell them your reasons for having that gun, make them think long and hard about locking up a citizen for exercising his constitutional rights, for protecting his family. You never know who you'll get on a grand jury, I've seen surprising things happen. Three-fourths of your jurors see it your way, then technically—and I stress technically, because this really has almost zero chance of working in your favor—they could decide not to indict on the gun. And if that happens, you walk. For now. It won't be over. You won't be clear. La Cuzio can still take you to trial if he wants—and he will—but without the grand jury it will take a bit longer and be a bit more difficult for him. But it will buy you time. It will get you out for the time being. So if you have somewhere you want to go, Potter says meaningfully, —you would have enough time to go there. For a vacation. Understand?

Lee says, —You're saying leave my country? *My* country? Be a damned fugitive?

Potter says, —No, I can't advise that. But if we're talking theoreticals? Potter shrugs. —People do things, they do what they have to do. And right now, just know that beating this grand jury is what you have to do. So for your sake, I hope you can give a good speech.

Tomorrow. He lies awake all night counting down the minutes, thinking about the grand jury, his father. Leaving the country. Where could he go? Venezuela? Russia? North Korea? It makes him ill to think about: in prison in a free country, or out free in some prison country? He does not want to tell them about his reasons for having the gun. Because suddenly he is thinking, *They were the wrong reasons attached to the wrong values. The values themselves never existed. The country they were supposed to have come from never did either.* And the only significant thing he has ever done in his life is murder a boy. That is not true—his son is significant. So he has taken one boy and given another. His life is a zero sum. All he has done and all he has been adds up to nothing. He was tested and he panicked, he fucked up. That is the truth. Is that what he will tell them?

In the silence that comes after that question a small voice speaks. He can barely hear it. He has to listen very hard, at first, but then he does not have to listen hard at all. *One thing about me, pardner?* it says, *I'm as real as they come.*

And he knows what he will say.

They bring him out to the bus. Take him across the bridge, through Queens, down the length of Manhattan, through his neighborhood—they pass his building, European tourists are taking photos of themselves in front of it—and to the courthouse. This time it is calm. No media or protestors or police. No signs calling Lee a racist or a murderer, no one holding up pictures of the kid. No *her*.

—Where is everybody? he asks Potter.

—They took over Union Square and Bryant Park today. Grand juries are secret, they don't know you're here.

They sit on a bench in the hallway outside the grand jury room waiting to be called inside.

—They're in there talking about me?

—Yes, they are.

—How long's it been going on?

—Four days. And now here you are. The headline act.

They call him in. He goes alone. His attorney has to stay outside. It is silent. There are a bunch of people who must be the jurors and a court stenographer and armed bailiffs and a bald-headed guy in a suit who must be La Cuzio. And that's all—no one else. No judge or anything. La Cuzio seems to be in charge. It feels somber and pious in here, like church. The jury sits in cushy theater-type chairs staring at him, the man La Cuzio has been telling them about, this callous, evil, murderous, racist demon. He sits in the chair on the witness stand at the front of the room, and one of the members of the jury, a woman in her fifties, swears him in. —*Do you swear to tell the truth, the whole truth...* He nods somberly and says he does.

He notes the holstered pistols of the bailiffs. That one there must be a Glock 19, modified with a twelve-pound trigger pull the way most New York City law enforcement service weapons are. There are also a Smith & Wesson 5946, a Sig Sauer P226, and another Smith & Wesson, judging from the shape of the grips. He can feel each gun in his hand, its weight, its texture, the thickness of the polymer. He can feel each nine-millimeter hollow-tip round between his fingertips as he shoves one after another into the clip. Eight, nine, ten... He can feel each gun kicking tight and hard in his hands as he fires, like choking a coyote; he can feel the sound of the shots split his ears, see the casings flip end over end in the corner of his vision up toward his shoulder, some landing warmly on his wrist. He can smell the gunpowder. Can see the iron sights, his target blurred beyond them. He can enjoy the silence that falls when the gun stops firing because you have shot all there is to shoot.

La Cuzio comes up to him and, using his hand to cover the little microphone in front of Lee, he mutters, —I'm gonna enjoy this.

He turns and wades back out among the jurors.

—Mr. Fisher, welcome.

He waits for Lee to reply. Lee leans into the microphone and says loudly, —Thank you. The sound booms out the speakers and the jurors all flinch, hands going to their ears.

—Not so loud, Mr. Fisher.

—Sorry, Lee says.

—Just try calming down. Take a breath. Are you nervous? You want a glass of water?

—No, thank you.

—Sure you do. La Cuzio approaches him, picking up a pitcher of water and a plastic cup from a table on the way. He stands in front of Lee and pours the water into the cup all the way, until it brims over. Then he hands it to Lee and says, —There you go. Drink it.

—I don't want it.

—I can hear your mouth sticking together, it's so dry. You must be very nervous.

—I'm sick. I got sick in jail. It's horrible there. I got very sick. As if on cue, he sneezes.

—Suit yourself. La Cuzio reaches out and takes the cup back from Lee and returns with it and the pitcher to the table. He sets both down and says, —Mr. Fisher, you shot Clayton Kabede, correct?

—Yes, unfortunately I did and I feel terrible about it and wish to God I hadn't had to.

—What did you use to shoot him?

Lee hesitates. —Is that a real question?

La Cuzio raises his eyebrows, indicating it is indeed.

—I used a gun.

—Where'd you get it?

—I kind of inherited it. It's kind of something I inherited.

—In your statement to detectives you say it was a decoration. Is that correct? Do you remember saying that?

—I don't remember much from that night, to be honest. It was too horrible.

—Do you keep all your home decor loaded and oiled and capable of destroying human beings?

—No.

—You did not own a decoration, you owned a firearm, correct?

—I owned a firearm, yes, sir. I never intended to use it.

La Cuzio tells the grand jury, —At trial, the court will hear testimony from forensic firearms experts proving that Mr. Fisher's so-called decorative family heirloom was in fact fired very often, even as recently as three days before the shooting. The illegally owned gun was a fully functional, deadly weapon kept for one purpose and that was *shooting*. Mr. Fisher, did you have a license for your gun?

—The Second Amendment of the United States Constitution says nothing about a license.

—Yes or no, please.

—I applied for one. They took my two-hundred-dollar fee and rejected my application without even considering it. That's how the process works in New York. It ain't nothing but a charade.

—*Was denied a license*, La Cuzio translates for the grand jury, nodding as though mentally checking some box. He turns to them. —I remind you that New York City law requires a license for a gun. Owning a functioning firearm without a license—even if it does just look good on your bookshelf—is a felony crime. A *felony crime*. And Mr. Fisher has just told you he did not have a license. And, Mr. Fisher, when your application was rejected you decided you would just go ahead and have a gun anyway because laws don't apply to guys like you, right?

—Not at all, Lee says. Then he says, —What kind of guy's that?

La Cuzio does not tell him. It feels like the grand jury knows what he means. La Cuzio says, —You feel you are above the law, don't you?

—No, I do not, Lee says, speaking directly to the jury now. —New York decided *it* was above the United States Constitution. They make you have a license but they have no intention of ever giving you one. Unless you're a cop. So it's an illegal gun ban. A violation of our basic rights. We have rights we are born with, and one of them is the right to self-defense. But somewhere along the line, politicians like this one here decided they could violate those rights and throw us in jail if we take issue with it. And if you ask me, that ain't right. That ain't right. La Cuzio starts to say something but Lee interrupts him. —Do *you* have a gun?

—Please simply answer my questions, Mr. Fisher.

—You do, don't you? La Cuzio protests but Lee talks over him, —He does. I know he does. Know why? He used to be a cop. Know how I know that? I read the news, I pay attention. I read between the lines. So he gets to throw other guys in jail for doing the same thing he does? See, that's not fair to me. The same cops we read about in the news every day killing unarmed people without justification and without consequence, they get the guns and the rest of us don't? Cops get to protect their families but the rest of us don't? Normal, everyday people: our children aren't as important as cops' children? Is my son's life less important than Mr. La Cuzio's kids? That just don't seem right to me. It don't seem right.

La Cuzio is staring down at papers in his hands as he says, —You think you're a normal, everyday person, huh?

—That's right. Just a normal kind of guy.

—How many homes do you own?

—Well, eight. No, nine, technically.

—He doesn't even know, ladies and gentlemen. He's such a normal guy he doesn't even know. I wish I had inherited so much money I could lose track of how many homes I own. Maybe then I could do whatever I wanted too, without consequence. Mr. Fisher, how much did you inherit? Before Lee can even answer, La Cuzio says, —Doesn't even know that either.

La Cuzio is visibly disgusted with Lee. It's so personal. Lee is wondering if they somehow know each other. La Cuzio puts his hand to his eyes and rubs his forehead. The people in the jury look very uncomfortable. One woman keeps looking at the door. La Cuzio points to Lee without looking at him. —Born rich, white, and male. Doesn't get more privileged than that, does it? He grew up in a time of peace and economic stability. He fought in no wars, he lived through no political upheaval, he suffered no famine, he faced none of the dangers faced by eighty percent of the world. Clean water. Access to education. Top-notch doctors. Medicine. He had every privilege, every advantage; he was given every benefit of the doubt. He had wealth. He had property. It still wasn't enough for him. He wanted more. He wanted to feel *important*. And *heroic*. He felt it was part of his entitlement to feel like a soldier without putting his life on the line for his country. To feel like a cop without putting his life on the line for his city. To *feel* tough without actually *being* tough. La Cuzio looks over at the jury. — At trial, the court will hear testimony that Mr. Fisher is known in his community as a reclusive racist, a cold, paranoid person who wants nothing to do with his neighbors.

—I am not, Lee says.

La Cuzio says, —In fact he even once *viciously* screamed at and chased the young children living in his building for having the nerve to play in the hallway outside his door. One of those children? A young Clayton Kabede, who Fisher would go on to one day slaughter in almost that exact same spot.

—Now hold on, Lee says to the jurors, —I don't know what he's talking about. I remember the kids who lived in my building thought I was Boo Radley, you know, from *To Kill a Mockingbird*? They used to come up to my door and knock and try to get me to come out. It was kind of a game. And once or twice I thought it would be nice to kind of play with them and so I gave them a little knock back. When I did they all shrieked and ran away. It was a game.

La Cuzio ignores him and says, —If you want to put this entitled man and his gun away, now is the time to do it, folks. If you want to make an entitled man who thinks he is above the law finally, *finally for once in his life*, face the consequences the rest of us have to face, now is the time to do it. The power is in your hands. The choice is yours. Put him away. Don't let another entitled guy with a gun get away with murdering someone. La Cuzio stops abruptly and looks at Lee. —Mr. Fisher, you're shaking your head. Do you disagree with what I'm saying?

—Well, yes, sir, I reckon I do.

—*I reckon I do,* La Cuzio mimics. —You think you're a real cowboy, don't you?

—It's just the way we talk, is all, where I come from.

—Is it? And where's that?

Lee tells him about the mountain.

—Was it a real mountain?

—Yessir.

—Does it still exist?

—No, sir.

—It never really did, did it? It was fake.

—I grew up on it, so it was real to me.

—It was a landfill. Are you *sure* that's the kind of guy you are? A cowboy?

—Yessir.

—But that kind of guy is not real, is he? He's never existed. He's a myth, isn't he?

Lee's answer is immediate but calm, —He ain't a myth. He's real.

—Uh-huh, well, which part do you disagree with? By all means, explain to these hardworking people who have real problems, explain to these people of color, explain to these women, these people who work full-time, *more* than full-time, these people who have gone through hell and high water to come to this country, these people who are sick and can't afford treatment, these people who grind themselves to the bone each and every day just to keep their heads above water, who live in neighborhoods where bullets whizz by their heads, where they get mugged, where kids shoot each other to death outside their door, explain to *them* why you have it so hard that you need a gun. Please, by all means, do what you have foolishly and needlessly and dangerously been trying to do all your life: defend yourself. La Cuzio sits on the corner of the table with an expectant smile like he is about to watch stand-up comedy.

—I don't know. You keep saying I have so much, but I don't feel like I have a whole hell of a lot.

La Cuzio laughs out loud, turning toward the jury as if to say, *Are you getting a load of this guy?*

Lee says, —I mean, my father's a piece of work, he ain't never been much of a father to me. My mother never cared about me as much as herself. Neither of them have been in my life since I was a kid. So no family. Several properties, yes, but never a home. No love. So really I ain't never had nothing at all. Until my son. Now that I have my son, I have everything. Everything. The rest of it—my property, my money, all that—go ahead and take it, I didn't earn it, it's never meant much to me. But you've already tried to take my ability to keep my son safe, and now you want to lock me up to keep me away from him altogether, just for doing what I have the right to do? You do that, you're taking everything I have. You're taking it all. Does that seem right to you? They tell me it's up to y'all: if you think I did something wrong that deserves going to jail for, then go on ahead and indict me. But if you don't, then you're free not to. So I'm asking: Does it seem right to you?

$$\left(\begin{array}{c} \text{Sheeple} \\ \text{X \& XI} \end{array}\right)$$

I wander from car to car throwing the fastball: —Please, mang. I been out since six o'clock this morning, mang, looking for a job, mang. I'm tired, mang. I got sick, mang, I lost my job. I ain't got no family, mang, I'm just trying to get something to eat, mang, I can't even afford a cup of coffee, mang, please help me out, this ain't no joke, this could happen to anybody, mang, y'all don't know how easily, mang.

Car after car and they all ignore me so I get mad, and at the next stop when doors open I steal a white lady's phone out her hand, book it. Doors close, train continues, white lady still looking at her hand like the phone still in it. Cop chasing me. Shit, they was one right there on the platform, saw the whole damned thing! Now to run the bases, inside-the-park homer, mang! Bounce up the stairs and out to the station, up to the street. Cop chasing. Run into the street, through traffic, cabs almost killing me, cop yelling. Turn real quick, use the phone to snap a photo of him! And then still running, text them shits to all the white lady's people! Get away, hide out in NY Public Library. Read books, or look at them at least, I can't understand them shits, mang, foreign language. Looking at teenage tourist ass. I can be charming with the *chicos*. —Hey, dude, hey, bro, where you from? Why am I so dirty, you ask? Aw, mang, I'm in a band, mang, we been on tour, living that rock 'n' roll lifestyle, mang, we been in Japan, Paris, Los Angeles. Where you staying, bro?

Go back with two of them. Skinny Oklahoma Justin Biebers, fifteen or sixteen. I use their computer to find some music, say it's mine, they believe me. One of them's more into me than the other and it's the other who's finer one but you take what you can get, and this one and I start trying to fuck and the finer one sees what we doing and acts shocked and says, —Oh my God, dude, and the one says, —What's the matter? and the first asks if he's serious, then leaves.

Then there's a knock on the door, mang, a mean cop knock. And I'm pulling my pants on and yanking up on the window, but them shits don't open but an inch or two, mang. I'm trying to squeeze through anyway, mang, and a stern white man voice outside is saying, —Kevin, goddammit, open up this instant!

It's the dude's dad, mang, and he got hotel security with him, and I know firsthand that hotel security beat you worse than the cops, mang. And they do, mang. They take me downstairs, beat the fuck out of me, tell the cops I did it to myself and cops believe them, mang. Arrest my ass for rape, mang, they saying the kid fifteen years old, mang, like I'm some old man, but I'm only eighteen, mang.

Put me on the bus with blood and snot dried all over my face and some white fat dude sit next to me and I'm in no kind of mood, mang, and he just look like one of them security guards who was calling me faggot and beating my ass in the basement. So I want this dude out of my sight right now, for real. I want him ejected from the game, mang. I know my life fucked now, mang, I ain't never getting out, and I'm trying not to cry, there ain't no crying in baseball, and the only way to not cry is to spit at this dude and scream at him and tell him he is what those motherfuckers told me I was, mang. So I call him that and he ain't leaving like he need to, so I keep calling him it. And I can see that he going to cry now too, and that feels good, not being the only one. And he says, voice breaking and shit, —Dude, you understand my predicament here, what am I supposed to do?

That make me go off harder on his ass, but when we get to the Tombs, mang, all I'm thinking is *Predicament? What the fuck is predicament?* I don't know the word. I get obsessed with it, mang. I gotta know what *predicament* mean. It's like a bug in my ear canal, mang. I ask everyone I can inside: —Hey, bro, what *predicament* mean? They think I'm crazy. First thing I do they put me back up in Rikers, I don't even wash the snot and blood off my face, I go to the library, find a dictionary, look that shit up. Definition of *predicament* is a bunch more words I don't understand, mang, so I gotta look up each of them too. Now all I'm doing is looking up word after word. Truth is, I like it, mang. I like looking up words. And I start reading. And understanding that shit too. It all clicking for me right now, mang. And I come to realize, mang, my life a whole big goddamned predicament—of my own making, mang.

I start writing, mang. Using the words I'm learning now. I write about baseball, mang. I love baseball, but baseball, mang? Baseball? Back when I played Little League there was this kid on my team and I was in love with him. And I told him that, mang, I told him *I love you*. It was stupid but I didn't know, mang—I didn't know. And he said, *You faggot,* and he raped me, mang. He beat my ass and raped me. That's what I get, mang, for not knowing better. And I write about that and people like it, my writing teacher inside here, mang, he sends it to *Sports Illustrated,* mang, and they publish that shits, mang. And all these dudes start sending me letters up here saying it happened to them too and that what I wrote helped them, mang. And that feel better than anything I've ever experienced before in my life, mang, and I decide I want nothing from life but words and helping people, mang. And that's all I been doing in here ever since, mang, and that's all I'm gonna be doing rest of my life, mang, either in here or out there but most likely in here, mang: helping people like me out of our predicaments.

Joseph came tearing down the stairs, baseball bat in hand, and beat the old man coming through the door.

He was a sweet baby, rarely cried, became very happy when laid out on a blanket on the floor having his diaper changed. His mother was sixteen, his father was either sixteen too or forty-six, depending on which man it was, Spoon or Spoon's father, James. Bensonhurst, Brooklyn. James denied responsibility, family could not afford to pursue the matter in court. When Spoon found out about his girl and his father, he went and stood on the Manhattan Bridge to jump off it. Looked down into the winter gray of the East River. Thought about how long it had been gray like that, how even a hundred years ago it was the exact same color, even two hundred years ago, even a thousand, even ten thousand. While all these buildings were going up and coming down and all these people were being born and suffering like how he was suffering right now and dying like how he was about to, this river had been gray.

Did not jump, went home, and on the way saw her and the baby, she was pushing him in the stroller. It was a slushy winter, baby was bundled up and grinning out at Spoon; evening was coming on, the lights on the storefronts starting to glow, the block strangely deserted but for the three of them in that moment in time, and she said, —You know I didn't want to, you know I love you, let's be together, just the three of us. He could never tell any of his friends this or even say it out loud, but *just the three of us* sounded like poetry to him, it was perfect and right, and he chose to believe that she was telling the truth. —Just the three of us, he said, and leaned in and kissed his baby, Joseph, his son, no matter what anyone else said.

The next day went around to get a job. He'd have to provide now. But no one in the neighborhood trusted him—used to run with these dudes who ripped people off and broke into cars and sold heroin, everyone thought he was still like that—and they knew about what his father did and don't want anything to do with anyone whose own dad would do that to him. After being turned down at a grocery store, he saw his father on the corner playing dominoes with some old cracked-out islanders, and he decided he would kill him. He'd kill him. Couldn't get a job but he could easily get a gun. So many guns here you were just about tripping over them in the street. Went into the city, to Central Park, walked up to a white lady, said, —Give me your purse. She did. He took out the cash, gave her back the rest. Went up to another white lady, did the same thing. Counted what he had now. Five hundred dollars.

Went back to the neighborhood, by that evening he had a loaded semiautomatic nine-millimeter in his hand. Found his father coming out of a bodega scratching off lottery tickets. Followed him. Stayed a half block behind. Twice his father sensed something behind him and turned, but Spoon would duck into the shadows so he didn't see him. Then on a long block, it was just the two of them. *Just the two of us.* Spoon sped up. Now he was close enough to slip the gun from his pocket and fire as many bullets he wanted into this motherfucker's head.

But then he thought of his son. He thought of how bundled Joseph was in his stroller when he saw him and her in the street, and Spoon felt her lips on his and heard how she laughs when it's just the two of them being stupid. And he realized that it didn't matter what his father says or what any tests might say: she loved him and that baby was his—these are facts that belonged not to the world but to him, they did not need the world, they were truth without it, all they needed was him—he, Spoon—to believe they were true and they became true and stayed true, and believing they were true was better than the world telling him they were true. This is something he would never even try to explain to anybody else, because if he were to have tried, if he were to have taken it out from inside himself like that and exposed it to the air, it would have died. But having it within himself made him better than his father, he realized, and killing the man was suddenly meaningless. So the same way he kept the truth inside himself, he kept the gun inside his pocket and he just said, —What up, Pop?

His father jumped, terrified. —Shit! Sneaking up behind me. Gonna kill a nigga.

—I wouldn't do that, Spoon said.

He went left, father went right. Spoon had no idea that up above a woman was watching from her window and she could see Spoon's face clearly in the streetlights, had just gotten a fresh prescription on her eyeglasses, recognized him too, knew his name, where he lived, had called the cops on him before for loitering on her stoop with his friends playing music at all hours. She'd have called them again in a heartbeat. Testify as a witness in court. Put him away for life.

Next morning Spoon went into the city—no one knew him there— got a job at Radio Shack near where he was robbing white ladies day before in the park. Saved every penny he made for Joseph, for *just the three of us.* He was not Spoon anymore at his job in the city, he was James, his real name, not James like his father but James like himself. Did the job well and boss liked him, promoted him to shift supervisor, then assistant manager. Soon he was making enough money to get a place for *just the three of us* out of the neighborhood. Got married, he went to night school, first GED, then work toward a bachelor's in business. Baby grew. Suddenly he was a little boy.

Spoon-James went in with his boss on a new Radio Shack franchise outside Union Square, it was successful, moved *just the three of us* to a white neighborhood with a great public school—Joseph could avoid the kind of people Spoon-James ran with at his age, instead ran with children of architects and writers and attorneys and entrepreneurs. The influence paid off, Joseph was second in his class at his high school, one of the best sprinters in the state, worked nights and weekends at his dad's stores, of which there were now three in the city. Got into Boston University on a full scholarship for track.

Few days before classes were to start, Joseph was at home packing when there was a bunch of noise downstairs. It was his grandfather at the front door arguing with his father. Joseph had never seen the man up close before, only at a distance when his dad pointed him out on the street to say, *Stay away from him, that man's a bad dude.* Went down now to help his father with the bad dude. Brought a baseball bat. Stood on the stairs. His father was trying to close the door on the bad dude who was yelling, —Lemme see my muthafucking son 'fore he go, that my muthafucking child, that my baby! Joseph found himself jumping from halfway down the stairs and pushing his father out of the way, father saying, —No, no, no, and the bad dude coming through the door, which swung open so hard it put a hole in the wall. Joseph started swinging the bat and will never forget the look on that man's face when those ribs cracked. Cops came, arrested Joseph, put him in the Tombs to await arraignment.

Where he sits now looking at the floor, which is gray and ten thousand years ago it was also gray. *Like a river,* he thinks. Life is ruined. Trying not to cry. Scholarship gone. *Should be on my way to Boston right now, meeting my roommate, meeting my teammates, meeting girls.* There's a white guy in here, one of the only ones, they're saying he killed a kid tonight. Black kid. *Guaranteed he'll be out before I am.* Fat white guy. They're calling him Pillsbury Doughboy. Joseph hates him. He hopes somebody fucks him up, so when he walks out of here and gets off for what he did, at least he'll be fucked up. It feels good to focus his hate on this motherfucker. They're saying when he made his one phone call he had no one to call so he just called the time.

Joseph doesn't know what to do, there's nothing to do here but sit and wait and hate yourself and feel guilty but try to think of ways you're not, because even though you feel guilty, you know you aren't. Freezing in here too. They're trying to give everybody pneumonia, hoping they can kill some of them off so they don't have to deal with them. Well, his father knows one of the COs, so Joseph gets him to bring a bunch of blankets and goes around handing them out, because he wants one for himself and figures if everybody has their own, then there's less likelihood of them stealing his. He's saving Pillsbury Doughboy for last, hoping he runs out before he gets to him. He hands them all out, and then he has one left, for himself, but on his way back he walks by Pillsbury, almost steps on him as a matter of fact, dude's curled up on the floor whimpering and shivering so bad his lips are purple and Joseph feels bad, can't help it, he can even hear his teeth clacking.

But fuck him. If he were a black dude who did what he did, you think anyone would feel bad for him or try to help him? Think they'd give him their blanket? Nope—they'd carry him off to the lethal injection chamber fast as they could, saying, *What's wrong with the black community and what should black leaders be doing about it?*

Joseph's stepping over the man but then Pillsbury wakes up and looks Joseph right in the eyes. And Pillsbury's eyes remind Joseph of a baby's eyes looking up at you from the crib. And before he knows what he's saying, Joseph goes, —Want a blanket? And he's already regretting it. But Pillsbury says no, he tells Joseph to leave him alone, he looks at Joseph like he thinks Joseph is going to stomp him in the head. So Joseph leaves the man alone. Happy to. And he finds a spot to lay down.

At least, he thinks, *I am warm under this blanket.* Everyone else in the cell is warm under theirs too—everyone but Pillsbury the Killer. Joseph lies there all night listening to the man's teeth chattering. He gets curious about it, listening to the big man becoming a little animal, crazed with animal fear. *Matter of fact,* Joseph thinks, *maybe I could be like him—I could be scared to death. It's how I got here, isn't it?*

From then on, when they get to Rikers, where he and Pillsbury are in the same place, everything Joseph does he does with the intent of being not like Pillsbury. What Would Pillsbury Not Do? Pillsbury would not run in the yard, so Joseph does run in the yard. Pillsbury does not talk to anyone, so Joseph talks to people. You have to talk to people in here, you have to be a little friendly, you might try to keep to yourself, but if you are too closed up they will notice it and take it the wrong way and pick on you. So Joseph tries to talk to people. His father always says you get what you give, so in times of sorrow, go help another's sorrow. Joseph remembers that and tries it. It's all he's got. In talking to people he learns something: nobody's a monster. Like anyone. Even the meanest, most fucked-up ones just want to be safe. And he tries to help, doesn't know if he does or not, but he tries. And Joseph does okay there. He sees guys go in one of two directions: either they act like him and try to help people, try to find some kind of good to give, or else they go all interior and fall apart, get dark, go crazy.

Pillsbury is one of the second kind—you can tell. He starts smelling real bad, he gets real skinny, he's sick as a dog, because though Joseph can get blankets in Rikers too and does, Pillsbury refuses one because he decides Joseph's trying to poison him with it. And during yard time he just stands against the wall staring into space. And the worst of it is, Joseph talks to him one day and it's clear the man feels no kind of guilt for what he did. Just out of curiosity—call it an experiment—Joseph tries one last time giving him a damned blanket, but Pillsbury throws it away into a trash can. Fascinating—until the next day, when the man walks. He walks after just three or four days inside.

Meanwhile Joseph is in there a year. A year. But the difference between guys like him and guys like Pillsbury is that once Joseph's served his time he gets out, he's not in prison anymore—but guys like Pillsbury never get out, even after they've served their time. They're always in prison. But Joseph gets out. And when he does he goes right to Bensonhurst, Brooklyn, finds his grandfather.

—Who are you? Joseph asks him.

Grandfather tells him: a man who has done bad things he is sorry for.

Joseph says, —Why don't you apologize then?

Grandfather says, —What I did was too bad for apologies.

Joseph takes his grandfather to his father's house, grandfather begs father for forgiveness. Decades of hurt all come out. Father forgives grandfather, mother forgives grandfather, grandfather forgives Joseph, Joseph forgives grandfather. Father and grandfather start talking every day, become very close. Joseph goes to college; it's not Boston University, it's one that advertises on the subway, but he meets a woman there, to be honest she is one of his professors, but they fall in love, and when the course is over they get married, have a child together, a girl, and the child is beautiful and is born into a beautiful family. Joseph's daughter grows, comes of age in this beautiful family. Grows up trusting and unafraid, lives with faith.

FAREWELL  TO ARMS

They meet Jenny Sanders in her suite at the hotel uptown. She tells them about who she is, what she has lost, and what she now does about it. On the wall above the television she has hung a picture of what she has lost: a little girl with missing teeth in a checkered dress. Says she travels with the picture, puts it up in every hotel room she stays in. All she does, she says, is travel and fight. He looks at the picture and all he sees is Clayton. She orders lunch from room service but they still cannot eat, cannot even think about eating. She expresses sympathy, vows justice. Second Amendment, she says. NRA. Gun culture. Says those are the things that slaughtered Michelle, the girl in the picture, as she sat in her classroom drawing in her journal. The topic was "My Plans for the Weekend." Michelle had just finished drawing the horse she was supposed to ride that Saturday when the young man armed with the assault rifle his lifetime-NRA-member father had taught him to shoot responsibly and safely stepped into her classroom and blew her brains out and tore the fingers off the hands she raised to her face to protect herself and then, in the ensuing fourteen seconds, killed all the other five-year-olds in the classroom and their teacher, Ms. Mary, a twenty-four-year-old girl in her first year of teaching. Then he moved on to the next classroom and the next, killing thirty-two children in just over three minutes. Three minutes. When the cops came he shot himself. His father was charged with nothing. He was within his rights in giving his deranged son the means of mass murder, we as a society decided. Nobody was ever arrested or charged with anything related to the massacre. And nothing legislative or political came of it either. Nothing. America decided to stay the same. It reaffirmed that the right to bear arms came before the right of children to be alive.

Jenny is saying all of this calmly, almost sweetly, her voice maintaining a low volume. She says, —This has been the story, massacre after massacre: dead babies, politicians in the pocket of the NRA, more power and money for the NRA, no lasting changes, more dead babies. Nobody really cares until it happens to them. And then they say, *Why isn't anyone* doing *something about it?* Well, I'm doing something about it. I'm here. I'm going nowhere. What happened to Clayton is not some tragedy—it is just what happens now, it is who we are. But who we have been is not who we have to be. It will take a war to change us. It's already under way. I'm already fighting it. I'm fighting the war for Clayton.

It is a relief to sit with someone who has clarity and answers. He is nothing he used to be—not the handyman, not the doctor, not the father, not someone who loves people and has faith in them. What he is now is flesh and hair and pain and hate. Pain and hate are holes. They are cold windy spaces inside you. He fills the holes, the spaces, with her. *Here,* he thinks, *is our hero.* He is crying. She puts a hand over his.

His wife says, —Every day we call police, every day we say to police: *What happen, do you know he was sleepwalking? You do not think he criminal, you do not think he rob, he* sleepwalk, *you* know *that, yes? Why did that man shoot him?* We say, *What does he say, how many times he shoot?* We say, *Tell us, did Clayton die quickly, did he suffer, did that man warn him, did he give him a* chance? *What. Happen?* What? And every day police say, *We investigate, we tell you when we tell you, sit down and shut up and go away.* It is not fair. Do you understand?

—I do, Jenny Sanders says.

His wife says, —They take Clayton from us and say, *Clayton ours now. Not yours. Police's. Not son, not boy—police's. He is evidence. Just evidence. And he is theirs. Theirs.* They say, We *decide what he do to get shot.* We *decide who your son was.* We *decide whether he criminal.* They think we have no right to know. We must sit and wonder and let them decide the truth when we *know* truth. He was sleepwalking. He was a good kid. Not a criminal. Not dangerous. It is not right.

Jenny Sanders says, —I can get them to talk to us. I'll get them to see the truth, that he was a good child, he was an unarmed sleepwalking boy, mowed down in cold blood by a gun nut who thinks his life is worth more than Clayton's. I'll get the world to understand. I have lawyers on it already. We'll find out everything there is to know and get the police to understand the truth so justice is served.

They visit Clayton every day at the city coroner's office. He lies there in a freezer while Lee Fisher relaxes in bed in a cushy private cell, reading and eating food and tasting and showering and meeting visitors and breathing air and chatting and stretching and working with expensive attorneys to build his defense. Jenny goes with them to the city coroner. They will not let them inside beyond the lobby, so they stand in the lobby all day long until the office closes and security makes them leave. When security makes them leave, they stand outside on the sidewalk. In the morning, when the office opens again, there they are, waiting to go inside and stand in the lobby and be as near to Clayton as they can. A small group of reporters begins hovering around them. They bring coffee and bagels and film them for the news. They demand a statement, they demand an exclusive interview. Jenny tells the reporters, —In due time. Please. Privacy for now. They'll talk soon, I promise.

People begin showing up. They are fragile and quiet. Women, mostly, but some men too. They wear T-shirts that say JUSTICE FOR CLAYTON: REPEAL THE SECOND AMENDMENT. Stand in grim silence holding signs and candles. They seem like they have done this before, like they were ready for this; they seem to know Jenny. With them come more media.

The concern, Jenny says, is that the story of another black boy killed by a gun in New York City will be turned into a race story, not a gun story, or else buried entirely and they will not have leverage with the authorities for getting information and making sure the investigation is a priority. —You have to push these people. You have to push them very hard. Embarrass them. Shame them. Cost them money. Make them fear for their jobs.

The Justice for Clayton people chant and march. Cops show up in military gear with heavy artillery vehicles, make some arrests. Jenny captures it on her phone, puts it up. There is a hash. It is a trend. (*Hashtag, Dad,* Clayton would correct him, laughing. *Trending.*) His wife brings Jenny a photo of Clayton in the park. She took it when they picked him up after his last day of freshman year of high school, to take him out to celebrate. They went to the steak house he likes. Growing Clayton ate a steak as big as he was, then he reached over and finished his mom's.

I'm gonna be bigger than LeBron, he said, his mouth full.

His wife said, *Oh yeah? You take care of us when you're rich basketball star?*

Hell yeah, said Clayton. *I'll buy you a dope house with acres and acres of land.*

Your father is a city man, he doesn't want a farm.

He said, *What would I do out there? Who would I talk to?*

I don't know, Clayton said. *Your cows.*

I don't want to talk to cows. I want to talk to people.

Why? People can be annoying. Cows just stand there and moo. They gotta listen to you. They don't interrupt or talk back or disagree with you or nothing.

Disagreeing is okay, he told Clayton. *Annoying is okay. You must understand. Pain? Inconvenience? Unpleasant? All that is okay. All that is good. Because it is human. With human? You can never know. Animal? You always know. Human? Never ever ever.*

I don't even know what you talking about right now, Dad. How much you have to drink?

You don't understand.

Let me try that whiskey and maybe I will.

Sure. Are you twenty-one?

Yeah.

Show me ID. Show me your fake ID.

Clayton smiled and said nothing, ate more of his mom's steak.

Do you understand what I mean? When I say annoying okay and disagree okay?

I think so.

Tell me what I mean.

You mean life ain't about just avoiding pain and surviving. Sometimes good things can come from bad things.

What else?

I don't know. I guess that there ain't nothing to be afraid of really. Life, people—there ain't nothing to be afraid of. Don't try to control it. Because you can't. You just gotta embrace it.

He laughed and said to Clayton, *Nothing to worry about with you.* Put his hand on the boy's shoulder and pulled him toward him, kissed his head.

Jenny's group puts the photo on their signs and T-shirts. Clayton in the park, proud of his good grades and scholarship, handsome, tall. Jenny says he looks just like his father in it. This is how Clayton should be known to the world, she says. Not the images the media has been using. The media has been using pictures Clayton took goofing around. The pictures show Clayton holding up money he made selling his sneakers and making imaginary gang signs and looking tough. Dangerous, in other words. A rabid animal that should have been better controlled. A thug who had it coming.

Almost told him, at that steak house dinner. Almost told him. Clayton said, *Good things come from bad things, right?* and he almost said, *The* best *things. The* best things *come from the worst things.* Clayton would have said, *What you mean, like what?* And he would have looked at her and put his arm around her, and she would have been looking back, wondering if he was really about to say it, and he would have said, *Like you.* And he would have told him. Clayton would have stood up from the table. *What? You ain't my real father?*

He would have grabbed his arm. *Sit down,* he would have said, very sternly. Maybe he would have yelled it. Not meanly— passionately. To illustrate how deeply he loved Clayton. *Sit down.* And pulled Clayton down into his seat. And pointed his finger into Clayton's face. *Now understand me: I am your real father and don't you ever question that again. Understand?*

Clayton would have understood. *You right, it's just that it was a shock, you know?*

And he would have said, *I know. We were waiting for the right time. And this was it. It seems like it might change everything but it does not. You understand that, right?*

And Clayton: *Yeah, I understand.*

And he: *And you see the bigger lesson, son? With every reason not to, without even knowing you, we let you in. And it was the best thing we have ever done. The best thing came from the worst thing.*

And Clayton: *It's the best lesson I have ever had. I love you both so much for that, for having such guts like that, for waiting until you got to know me to decide about me. For giving me a chance.*

And they: *We love you.*

And Clayton: *I love you too. I'm glad you said it. I'm glad you told me now and not later.* And he would have gone home with them that night and woken with them in the morning and every morning since, including this one. He would be alive if he had told him then.

He does not understand how or why he once believed that: that the best things come from the worst things. He believes in nothing he once believed in. Being brave, having faith, trusting people—he was wrong. The man who believed that is gone with Clayton. Now what is he? Now what does he believe? He believes nothing. For he is nothing.

Others begin showing up at the city coroner as well, white men in black T-shirts and baggy jeans. Sunglasses, black baseball hats. They smoke cigarettes, strut around. They have signs that say WE ARE LEE FISHER and signs that say SHALL NOT INFRINGE and FROM MY COLD DEAD HANDS. —Get! A! Job! they chant at the Justice for Clayton people. —Get! A! Job!

His wife says, —What is *their* job?

Jenny says, —To be assholes. She seems happy the men have come. She looks very intently at them, scrutinizing their waistbands.

—What are you looking for? he asks her.

—Guns.

—Get out of our country! the men shout.

Police in riot gear form a barricade between the two groups.

—Do you think they shoot? he asks Jenny.

She says, —Yeah, of course they will.

He looks at her. She is crazy.

—Don't worry, she says, —it won't be at you. They want me.

She signals to one of her people, an alert young woman named Becky who is wearing a backpack. Becky takes it off, unzips it, pulls out an American flag—it is very large—she unfolds a collapsible pole from the backpack and attaches the flag to it upside down and raises it, waves it back and forth as though signaling to the sky for rescue.

The men boo her and shout, —Fuck you! Respect my country!

Becky does not back down. Cops push one large gun man back and take him to the ground and cuff him. More sirens are arriving in the distance. He watches these men chant USA. The man he used to be would have ventured to understand these men. Find the goodness in their hearts. But now he just hates them. He would like to make them have to grow up in his home country, he would like to see them intimidated and threatened by the monsters who intimidated and threatened him. Would they have resisted, like he did? He would like to put those mercenaries on their doorsteps. Would they have survived it, watching their wives attacked? In the morning after, would they have still wanted to live? Would they have still had faith? Could they have kept living? Would their wives have been as brave as his? Would they have had the courage to flee their homes, would they have made it to the USA they think is theirs because they inherited it? Would they be here if they had not been born here? So who deserves to chant USA? Whose country is this?

Jenny puts a hand on his shoulder. She seems very excited, thrilled. —They don't even know what an upside-down flag means, she says, —they think it's an act of disrespect. You guys okay?

He nods and so does his wife. —It's cool, don't escalate it.

She is holding a video camera up and recording them as they shout, —We're the reason y'all have your damn freedom!

The Justice for Clayton people are chanting louder, to drown them out.

—What do we want?

—Jus-tice!
—When do we want it?
—Now!

It is a beautiful thing. He gets goose bumps. All these people, for Clayton. He holds his wife. She is crying. They shout so loud and there are so many of them that now you cannot hear what the gun men are even saying. You can only see their faces contorted, their mouths twisting and screaming but nothing coming out. Jenny holds her camera with one hand, extends her other arm as much as she can, with her old injury. She gestures toward herself to them. *Come on,* she seems to be saying to the gun men. *Come on.* He does not understand.

She puts up the video, hundreds of thousands of people see it in the first few hours. The networks rebroadcast it. *We're the reason y'all have your damn freedom!* Donations to Repeal the Second Amendment hit $400,000 overnight. One hundred thousand new memberships in the first twenty-four hours.

They lie in Clayton's bed, watching the video. He tells her about what Jenny said about them shooting, about the way she gestured with her arm, as if inviting them to shoot. She does not believe him. She says, —Maybe you misunderstood. Why would she do that?

—I don't know. I think maybe she is trouble. She's lost her mind. She is using us to get herself martyred.

His wife looks at him like she does not know who he is. He does not know either. He has never said anything so cynical.

—Jenny is good, she says. —She is the only one here for us. We have to trust her. In the worst times, we must keep believing in people, we must keep living with faith. Like you have always said. Remember?

—I remember. I was wrong.

—Do not say that.

—How can we have faith in anything anymore? In anyone?

—I don't know. The same way we did before. The way we always have. It is what got us through. If not for it, we would not be here.

—Here. Is this what it was all for? To get *here*? To suffer through *this*?

—I don't know.

—I don't remember now how I did it, how I had faith. That man seems like another lifetime.

—Please. I need that man. I don't need this one.

—That man is gone. Gone.

—Get him back. Please be that man again. Please.

At the coroner's office the next day, Jenny says that her organization's chief attorney, Howard, has finally extracted information from the NYPD.

—What do they say? he says.

—They say Lee Fisher shot your son, and your son died of those gunshot wounds.

He waits for Jenny to continue but she does not.

—Yes, and?

—That's it.

—But we already know these things.

—I know, it really cracks things open for us, doesn't it? Aren't they unbelievable? Just sit tight and stay tuned. Jesus, look at this, she says, pointing to a pickup truck approaching, large speakers on the back, an eagle painted on the side clutching a black assault rifle in its talons. From the speakers plays a white man's voice, murky with false folksy sincerity. —*This hoodie-wearing thug,* says the voice, —*comes kicking down your door in the middle of the night, dressed like he was, carrying himself in that gangsta kind of way, with that snarling indifference—do you know by the way why they carry themselves like that? Do you? To intimidate you. To show you what a big, dangerous thug they are. They want you to think they might hurt you. That young man—and face it, folks, they use words like* boy *and* child *but this was a six-foot-tall male, 170 pounds, that is a man—that young man was completely enthralled to hip-hop culture, a culture which worships crime, which praises murder, which equates casual, out-of-wedlock sex with masculinity and status... Folks, if you hear a noise in your house at two in the morning with your infant asleep in his crib and you find a guy like this standing in your living room, well, what would you have done? What did he expect? To be greeted with open arms? He messed with the wrong guy that night. Lee Fisher is a hero, and don't forget that. He is a great father and a true American. God bless that man. If everyone were more like Lee Fisher, thugs might start thinking twice about entering our homes, raping our wives. Violent crime in this country, folks, is rampant, it is out of control, and our politicians do nothing to stop it. But if more of us were man enough to be like Lee Fisher, crime would stop tomorrow. It would stop tomorrow. Please stay vigilant out there, patriots. Be ready. We need you now more than ever...*

His wife says, —Who is that idiot?

Jenny says, —Biggest talk radio host in the country.

The police are making the truck turn off its speakers but it does not matter.

His wife says, —That's not what police think too, is it? That Clayton is a thug? That he is a criminal?

Dread overtakes him when she says this. He feels dizzy. *Yes*, he realizes, *that is exactly what they believe.* He has to sit down. He sits on the curb. Someone gives him water but it does nothing.

They meet with police in an office. —Clayton is not a thug, he tells them.

The police stare back at him blankly and say, —Our investigation is ongoing.

Jenny says, smiling, —Gentlemen, I know you are doing your work, we respect that, but these folks have suffered so deeply, and any information you might offer to help them understand what happened to their son—what Fisher is saying happened, what you think happened—anything to help them in this terrible, confusing time of unspeakable sorrow...

The police say nothing, do not even look at them.

—Have you received the testimonial letters we sent?

—We don't conduct our investigations via what kind of letters we receive.

—But you will talk to these people as part of your investigation? she says.

The detectives kind of roll their eyes and look at each other and start to ask them to leave.

She interrupts them, still smiling. —You know, I'm good at using pressure to get what I want. The spotlight is hot now but this is nothing. Want me to turn it up? Or do you want to talk to twenty-seven reliable people standing outside right now about the Clayton they knew, the real Clayton, who was a good kid who did not deserve to die.

The detectives ask them to leave. They leave. On the way out, the desk sergeant stops them to fill out a form. There is a manila folder on the counter.

—What's that? Jenny says.

Desk sergeant says, —Property of the NYPD. You touch it, you go to jail.

But the cop walks off, leaving the folder. Jenny takes it. They go outside where all their friends and supporters wait. Jenny opens the folder, looks through it. —It's from the case file. It's Fisher's statement.

—What does it say? he says.

Jenny reads it and says, —Piece of shit.

—What.

—He's claiming self-defense.

—No.

—He says Clayton said he had a gun and that he was there to kill him. She reads it. —This is tight.

—Oh my God. His wife puts her hands to her head.

Jenny says, —Clayton's last words, according to Fisher, were: *I have a gun and I'm going to kill everyone here.*

—No, he says, —how can he say it? It's not true.

—Of course it's not, Jenny says. —It doesn't matter if it is, there are no witnesses to contradict it. If I'm La Cuzio, I'm very nervous about taking this to trial. Not with the kind of lawyers Fisher's got.

Dread fills his belly. His wife says, —I don't understand.

—He's going to get away with it, he says.

—Not necessarily, Jenny says. —That's going to be up to a grand jury. It'll be up to the people.

—Yes, he says, his voice flat and vacant, —they will let him go.

His wife looks at him closely, horrified. —*Why?* she says.

—Because they do not want Clayton. They want Fisher.

Jenny says, —Fisher knows the law. Of course he does. All these guys do. They're weasels. He knows what he has to say to escape responsibility. He's been fantasizing about it for years, killing somebody, shooting a home invader. He has been imagining for years how to handle himself with police in the aftermath, what he has to say to meet the criteria for justifiable homicide. *Fantasizing.* But look, they have him on the unlicensed gun. No way to weasel out of that. He'll serve time for that.

—How much?

—Two years at least.

—Two years, he echoes.

Jenny sighs. —I know. Two years for Clayton's life, right? Unacceptable. That's why what we do now is crank up the heat on La Cuzio not to let up on homicide. A prosecutor has a lot of sway with a grand jury—little things he does will affect the outcome. Who to call as a witness, whether to blow them up or make them look credible on the stand. So we get everyone who knew Clayton to bury La Cuzio with letters, fill his inbox with e-mails, jack up his voice mail with calls, day and night. His phone will not stop. He will never even consider that what Fisher is saying could be true, that Fisher is anything but a cold-blooded murderer. We need to make La Cuzio and the city and the country see Fisher for what he really is: a scared, mean little idiot whose unfettered access to firearms murdered a boy. Make him fear for his job. Make him see that the people who put him in office demand Lee Fisher be tried for murder.

Jenny moves to a hotel downtown to be closer to the courts and police and prosecutors. There she establishes the headquarters of Justice for Clayton. Phone banks, letter-writing stations, computer terminals. Every morning Jenny and the Justice for Clayton people show up at La Cuzio's office to dump across the receptionist's desk a new sack of letters begging him to go whole hog toward bringing Lee Fisher to trial for murder.

I had the pleasure of having Clayton as a student in my freshman history class last year... if I could have a classroom full of boys as well behaved, inquisitive, kind, and bright as Clayton...

Clayton was my best friend since 5th grade & I ain't NEVER seen him get mad or get in a fight or NOTHIN, hell NAH, there ain't NO way Clayton woulda had a gun, he wouldn't even know where to get one in the

FIRST place, that dude shot him is LYING, he think just cause he a white dude he get away with it...

As a counselor the last two summers, Clayton has exhibited nothing but the most persistent patience and largeheartedness with the kids who attend our church camp, many of whom come from challenging backgrounds. Those kids looked to Clayton as a role model. They are devastated. The man who took that from these kids deserves to be punished to the full extent of the law...

Clayton AIN'T NO THUG! Ain't no drug dealer! Everyone know that! He made his dollar buying and selling those Jordans, I seen him make five hundred in one afternoon on eBay. He make BANK doing that and he use that bank to buy more shoes. He don't steal shit, he don't sell drugs, he don't use drugs. Everyone know CLAYTON A DORK ASS BUSINESSMAN TYPE DUDE.

I have been a resident of this building for nineteen years and have known Clayton Kabede all his life, as well as his family. As COO of an international headhunting firm, I like to think I have a knack for sizing people up. Clayton was rock solid, a stellar student who was always helpful and friendly. My family and I trusted him with our house key so he could walk our dog. Not only was there never any incident, but Lucy, our spaniel, learned several new tricks, including how to "speak." Lee Fisher was looking for trouble that night, and he found it. I fervently, desperately hope you will put all resources toward charging him with homicide and seek the maximum punishment in our state. He has taken the promise of a stellar young man and broken all of our hearts.

Jenny says she needs them to do a commercial. A blistering ad spot for television, radio, and computers to raise the ire of the people. — Our only hope is to put this to the people, she says. It will be quick. Her production team can shoot it in the Kabedes' home. Show Clayton's bedroom, his yearbook photos, the picture of him in the park. He and his wife will sit on their couch and simply talk about Clayton and how he was murdered. They will mention that Fisher will get away with it and continue to walk the streets unless people watching at home take action. They tell her they will think about it.

That night in Clayton's bed, clinging to each other, her back to his chest, his hand cupping her underarm, her belly, feeling each other breathe in the dark, she says, —We should do it.

—No, he says, —never.

—Why not?

—It does not feel right.

—Jenny says what's not right is how no one talks about it, we need to make people start talking about it.

—Jenny just wants to make money for her organization.

—Money equals votes equals change.

—You sound just like her. I do not like it.

—Good things can come from things we do not like. You said that.

—Don't tell me what I said, I have never said anything true in my life.

—You have said you love me. You have said you love Clayton. Were those things not true?

—Of course they were.

—Then you are wrong, you have said things that are true.

Jenny has them meet with Al Sharpton, Michael Bloomberg. Sharpton pledges the support of his group and says he's already been down there at La Cuzio's office, getting their word that they will do all they can to indict Fisher and bring him to trial. On the way to the Bloomberg meeting, Jenny tells them he might still be mad at her for absorbing his anti-gun group, but what did he expect? It was laughed off Capitol Hill before it even got there. Jenny says, —I told him, *I have ten times your membership and am growing fast, Michael. We need a united front for this war. You're either with me or against me. Do not be against me.*

At the meeting, Bloomberg dominates with a monologue about how much money he spends on gun control. —Fifty million this year, fifty million last year. Year before that? Fifty million. Next year? Fifty million. I give Jenny more money than anyone else. Right, Jenny? If there is an afterlife, I'll be let in through the pearly gates on the express line. The NRA paints me as an out-of-touch big-city elitist, but people *love* me! Wherever I go, people shout at me through the window of my limousine, *Go Michael, go!* I'm a rock star!

At precisely the thirty-minute mark, an aide breaks up the meeting, saying the former mayor has lunch with Warren Buffett in fifteen minutes. Bloomberg says to them as he stands up and leaves the room, —Per Se. Have you been? Go. *Go.*

They leave, go down in the elevator and out into the street to the car Jenny has waiting for them. They are looking forward to going home now, but Jenny has a last-minute meeting she confirmed during the Bloomberg meeting. —It's a huge one. Very important for us. This guy's a huge donor, with, like, a jillion followers on social media and he's been tweeting about Clayton.

He says, —We are tired. No more meetings. We go home.

—Just this one more, then you can go home. Jim is very excited to help and he's only in town today. And like I said, huge donor. He's about to start shooting a movie and I think I can get him to donate his salary to us and talk about it on the press tour. So, you know, pound a coffee or wheatgrass shot or something and be gracious because this meeting is important.

They go to a restaurant on the Upper West Side. He and his wife do have coffee but it does not rejuvenate them. —I am heartbroken, the odd man, Jim Carrey, says. He says he wants to go further than just donating his money; he says he wants to produce a film about Clayton's story. It will be the *Roots* of gun control, he says, the *To Kill a Mockingbird*, the *Uncle Tom's Cabin*. He even knows who will direct: it's this young filmmaker who has made several great difficult films that no one saw; he lives out in Brooklyn, has been working on a film about guns, and Clayton could be the missing piece. This filmmaker is ripe for his breakthrough, this will be it. —This movie will change everything, Jim Carrey says. At one point Jim Carrey seems to cry very hard, his head in his hands and bony elbows knocking a knife off the table as they watch in confounded silence. At the end of the meeting he gives them his personal cell phone number, they give him theirs. He asks if they have considered doing an RSA commercial, because if not, they should.

—Good work, Jenny says in the car heading home. —That's really going to help Clayton a ton.

On the radio is this: —*Whether or not it is true that this known thug was* sleepwalking—*what was Fisher supposed to do in that situation? Was he supposed to ask him,* Oh, hello, Mr. Thug in a Hoodie Standing in My Living Room at Three in the Morning, how may I help you tonight? Are you by chance sleepwalking? Are you on Prozac? Did your mommy not hug you enough? Can I get you a cup of warm milk? *No! No! No, Lee Fisher owed that thug nothing. Nothing.*

Jenny apologizes and tells the driver to turn it off, but he says, —No. Leave it on. He can feel his wife staring at the side of his face but he does not care.

—If you are in that situation, you are a man and a father and you must take action, you must advance on the threat, your child is depending on you to protect his life, this is what you have been training for at the range, you must be a man and protect your family. Call me a bigot, call me a racist, and they always do, because they *are racist,* they *are hateful, but this is a matter of individual liberty, this is a question of accountability and freedom. That they are even considering charging this man who behaved heroically in nightmare conditions with murder is an outrage, an injustice, it is sick. If anyone is charged with murder it should be the folks who truly did get that boy killed and those are his* parents. *Every American should be up in arms about this. We crucify an innocent father acting within his rights and let the negligent, lazy, irresponsible, entitled parents off the hook.* Outrageous. *The city of New York has for one hundred and fifty years operated under flagrant, wanton violation of the Constitution of the United States by denying American citizens their right to bear arms as granted them under the Second Amendment, and enough is enough, folks. Things have come to a head. They have come to a head. The time has come. Things have never been more dire for the future of our freedom, our nation. They are trampling it. This does not end well, folks. We have defeated tyranny once before and we will do it again. If Lee Fisher is prosecuted for murder, then we are all prosecuted, each and every one of us. Hear what I am telling you, folks. Listen closely. They will come for you next. They are coming. Do not for one second doubt that. You and you alone must protect yourself. Lock and load. Hold your children closely tonight. Tell them you love them. Make sure you are stocked up on ammunition and your firearms are cleaned and ready. Please, please, please, be vigilant out there tonight, patriots. Your country is depending on you.*

—Okay, he tells the driver. —You can turn it off now. He looks out the window and says, —We will do your commercial.

It is very simple, as Jenny described. They do not even have to think—she has cards written out and all they must do is read from them.

—We come from third world country, they say. —We grow up without education, suffering always. To us, America greatest country in world, to us America our only hope to one day have good life. Where we could have freedom. We go through so much to come to America. We work so hard. Only to have Clayton murdered by white man with gun. We are victims of obsolete Constitution. Constitution designed to be changed. Now is time for that change. We must repeal the Second Amendment, for it is killing us. We do not have to live this way. We must finally remove pro-gun, NRA-controlled government from office. We must pass the ammo tax in the state of New York. Vote money, not bullets. Support Repeal the Second Amendment today. This month every new membership receives free tote bag.

After the first take, Jenny comes over. —That was pretty good, she says, —but it can be better.

He says, —This isn't true. Poor? Without education? I was a doctor, she was a professor.

Jenny looks at him, smiling, but her eyes are not smiling. She leans in closer to him and says, —Have you considered the possibility that maybe I know what I'm doing? She claps her hands once and backs away, yelling, —Again!

When it is over and Jenny and her people have gone, he and she lie in Clayton's bed. —I do not feel good, she says.

—Me neither.

—Why did we do it?

—I don't know.

—I did not like it.

—No.

—What is wrong with her? Why did she act like that?

—I don't know.

It is the morning of Clayton's memorial service. They are in the car with Jenny, en route to a church they have never been to that has volunteered the use of its space for what, thanks to RSA's publicity people, is expected to be a very large turnout. Jenny says, looking at her phone, —*60 Minutes* wants an interview. I'm telling them today at two o'clock, okay?

He looks at his wife. *Take control of it or I will bite her head off,* he says to her telepathically, and she understands and says to Jenny, —We already do interview, we did not like it, no more interviews.

—No, no, honey, she says, —that was the commercial. That was for local TV and target ads online. *60 Minutes* is national, big-time. This will help the repeal effort and put big-time pressure on Congress to get serious about the ammo tax. I know you don't want to do the fucking morning show circuit, don't worry, you're not going to be chittering on the couch at *Good Morning America,* but *60 Minutes* is serious and tasteful, they are journalists. And it comes on after the NFL, so people watch it.

—Please, not today.

She sighs and says, —Fine, I'll see if they can do it tomorrow. But the window is small with these people, they lose interest very quickly, you have to strike fast. We can do it later today, can't we? What else do you have to do?

He cannot believe what he is hearing. He says, —We are finished. We are not interested in this. We want you out of our lives.

Jenny kind of laughs. —Oh, you do?

His wife touches his arm. —He does not mean it, we are very upset.

Jenny says, —It's okay, I get it. Today's not the best day. Fine. But try and see the bigger picture here. The greater good. I'm only trying to help.

—Yes, help yourself, he says. —You help yourself, just like everyone. Just like all of you.

Jenny eyes him in a new way, the air between them changes. He gets a very disturbed feeling, the way she eyes him. He wants to get very far away from her very quickly. —Maybe I was callous to bring it up on the day of his service, she says, her voice slow and quiet, —but callousness does not concern me anymore. We need this interview or Fisher will *walk and nobody will care.*

—*Please,* he nearly shouts, —just *please let us bury our son.*

—Tell me if you're with me or against me. Tell me now. Do you think Clayton's the only kid who has been shot this week? If you won't cooperate, maybe one of *their* parents will.

—*Please.*

They are pulling up to the church. People are everywhere. They are getting out. Jenny grabs his arm. —Tell me now.

He cannot speak, so his wife says, crying, —*Yes, yes, we are with you,* and Jenny lets go and they exit the car.

Inside among the crowd in pews are Raul and Kenny. Raul looks like it was somehow to be expected that someone would one day take Clayton from him. And Stacey, there she is too, with Hector. She shivers uncontrollably though it is not cold. Still looks like she has not slept or eaten. She does not know what it means yet, he thinks. No friend is someone to have fun with, or even to talk with. No sweetheart is someone to adore or even to love. A friend, a sweetheart, is an agent of change in one's life, and vice versa. *We all change each other. You can hide away and arm yourself, but you cannot avoid it. And now, because of Fisher, there are fewer friendships and less love and less change in our world of strangers. We cannot keep going like this,* he thinks, his city of friends all embracing him and his wife, kissing them, *we cannot keep taking love from girls and friendships from boys and denying them chances to change, we cannot keep going with these holes in our hearts and no one there to fill them.*

His sole task during the service is to make sure his wife is okay. She is the open vein, and he is the bone—exposed and excruciating and broken but hard and supporting the body through this amputation. An amputation with no drugs and no warning. It is not a limb that has been amputated but the whole. And only limbs are left. Everyone in here knew Clayton and loved him, many of them since he was an infant. He remembers when Clayton was a baby, grinning on park blankets, clapping his hands at passing dogs, pointing at birds and trees and people and saying, *Dere.* Many of these people here held him then. Babysat him, bathed him, changed his diaper. Look at all these people. *This is our life,* he thinks. *What a life we have made for ourselves. To be loved by a city. To be loved like this, all at once, by the friends that are your family. What if we did not have them all? What if we had been afraid to know them and give to them—they would not be here now to give to us. Look what a good young man you were, Clayton. See how you moved all these people to come here today. I will remember this feeling, I will carry it around in my own hole-ridden heart and it will never leak out. I do not want to remember you with grief or in tragedy but with pride and gratitude for the little mercy you were to me and your mother and to the city and to the country and to all of it. All of it. If a man's life is measured not by his intentions and not by his actions but by what kind of friend he was, and how unafraid he was, and how much faith he lived with, then you lived the best life of all.*

After Clayton's service the house is silent. The food rots in its Tupperwares. They do not throw it away. He keeps expecting him to come home. He will not have eaten, he will need to eat. It is too silent without him. No doors slamming. No music on too loudly. Sometimes he goes to Clayton's room and turns on his music for him, since Clayton cannot turn it on himself. He turns it up very loud the way Clayton likes it. It thumps and pops and whines. He has always hated this music, its grating, agitating alarms and shrieks and digitally altered slurred voice saying disgusting things. Try to read a book with this blasting through the house. Try to watch a film. Or have a conversation. He turns it on now, turns it up, leaves, closing the door behind himself. The walls shake. It is heinous. It is perfect.

There is no one to call him Dad anymore. No one to call her Mom. It is like there never was.

He wears Clayton's shoes around the house. He chokes on his own breath and takes them off and waits for him to come home.

Picking up more Klonopin at the Duane Reade, ignoring his friends who work there, the hell with everyone, that is how he feels today, everyone is vicious and selfish and not to be trusted. Stands in line at the pharmacy counter, prescription in hand. There is a knock on the door in the night and he opens it. They force their way inside, and he and she flee the country and they are in the basement of a homeless shelter. Everything is ready. He has the long needle in his hands. Her knees are spread. He is between them. He is reaching with the needle. She says, *Stop.* He keeps going. *Stop, stop,* she says. Ignores her. She tries to slide away, he holds her down. She kicks, but he is very strong and he keeps pushing the needle in. *Stop*, she shouts. *It is too late,* he says, *it is done.* A few weeks later the dead fetus slides out in the bathroom. She goes to get pizza. An old man sits there. He has connections with the United States. He does not notice her. Nor she him. She gets her pizza, leaves. They remain in the shelter, and there is no pain, no autopsy or Jenny Sanders or Klonopin, and no idiots with guns and no *thug* and no *hoodie* and no NYPD telling them nothing. He mops the floor of the shelter and she lies in bed and there is nothing else, and she gets pneumonia and dies of it, then the country undergoes a wave of nationalism and throws out all its undocumented immigrants and he is returned to his home country, where men snatch him right away and shoot him on the side of a highway and that is fine, that is better than this today.

After days of not seeing her, Jenny shows up at their door. He tells her, —Please leave us alone. She says she has something for them, a contact at the coroner's office, a positive result from the pressure, from the RSA ad that has begun airing.

He and his wife read the autopsy report alone, on Clayton's bed. The first shot struck Clayton in the shoulder. He was standing facing Fisher right inside Fisher's door. The bullet broke his left shoulder and severed the muscle, tendons, and nerves there but missed the major veins and arteries. The force of the bullet knocked him back against the door. It would have woken him up as well, his father thinks, reading the report. He must have been so scared. He must have screamed from fear and pain. So he was screaming when Fisher fired the next shot, which missed, the bullet hitting the door beside Clayton's head, and he was still screaming as Fisher fired a third time, striking Clayton this time in the groin. The fourth bullet was to his stomach, opening it up. The force of the bullet's entry also ruptured his liver and intestine and bowel. His abdomen would have instantly filled with blood and waste, including his mother's *fit-fit* and *fatira* he had eaten for breakfast earlier that day. This entry wound would have been intensely painful and extremely traumatic, and he would have died slowly over the course of an hour if not for the next gunshot wound. This entered him through the back, just beside the left shoulder blade, suggesting he had curled up on the floor into a fetal position to protect himself. It continued past his fourth vertebra and shattered his left clavicle, which in turn severed his left subclavian artery and, mercifully, finally killed him. It is reasonable to conclude, according to the autopsy report, that when Fisher fired the sixth and final bullet, which struck Clayton at the back of his neck and severed his brain stem, he was no longer screaming and no longer feeling pain.

—I could not have saved him, his father says. —There was nothing I could have done. He was gone. He is gone. He is never coming back.

They come out from Clayton's room. Jenny is still there. She says, —See? Now do you believe in me? Now can we be friends again? Because now that I've done something for you, I hope you will do something for me. The grand jury is expected to announce their decision any day. And any day the New York State Assembly is going to vote on the ammo tax. You are at the center of this very, *very* important time. Your responsibility to your culture is you must do *60 Minutes* and you must do it *now*.

—It is exploitation.

—Would you rather nothing at all changes in this country after what happened to Clayton?

—No, he says, —of course not.

— Because that's what's going to happen if you do not do this. I wish there was another way. I really do. I've done so much to help you. I really think it's time for you to pay me back a little and help yourself a bit.

It is remarkable how quickly *60 Minutes* can be there at the hotel suite once Jenny makes the call. A crew of four arrive in the suite, including the reporter who will be conducting the interview, a white woman named Lesley Stahl who is kind and pleasant but carries herself with the insincere remove of some of the residents of his building. He looks into the sly, fleshy angles of her face caked with makeup as she wets her throat with Fiji water and peers over her reading glasses at notes while the camera operator sets up klieg lights and white umbrellas to reflect the light, and he cannot shake the vision of Lesley Stahl reaching into a snack bowl set there for her on the side table and taking a pinch of the human flesh it is filled with and idly munching it while she prepares.

Jenny is knelt down between him and his wife as they sit on the sofa and wait. —Remember, she is saying very intensely, —we need rage. We need tears. We need *j'accuse*! Understand? Sweetie, she says, touching his wife's knee, —you are the mother who has lost your baby, your world ripped away by white male gun culture. We need you to bleed, baby, bleed! Bleed for Momma! You'll do the talking, right? The mother is more compelling than the father. But, Dad, you'll look quietly grieved, yeah? Remember, you came all this way to America to have its so-called *freedom* destroy your son. And remember, most of all: the ammo tax. Always bring it back to the ammo tax! Stress the science, the data. Here are the numbers, this sheet of paper. A little cheat sheet. Keep it down out of the camera's view. Refer to it. Ammo tax, ammo tax, ammo tax, right? Don't do the usual shit, the *one day at a time, tragedy, blah, blah, blah,* right? And whatever you do, don't fucking *forgive him.*

He is wearing a suit. He has a suit but this is not his suit. This suit is one somebody from RSA brought him. It is in his size. How did they know his size? They seemed to have it at the ready. He prefers his own suit. Jenny does not like his own suit. She saw it at the memorial service. It is not the newest suit and it is too small, he bought it fifteen years ago when he first arrived here. He needed a suit to wear to job interviews and government offices. The suit was all he could afford but it is a very good suit, it says Ralph Lauren inside it, but if it is in fact Ralph Lauren or if someone just sewed the label in something from Kmart, he does not know. But he paid zero dollars and zero cents for it. And it is good also because of how he bought it. It was a dry cleaner selling clothes out of his van parked on a curb in the Bowery. Things customers had never picked up. He took the suit off the rack, first one he tried, and it fit perfectly. He admired himself in the reflection of the storefront window there. *You're an American,* he told himself.

The dry cleaner selling it, some kind of Hispanic, was leaning against the van, watching. *Looks good on you, bro.*

How much?

For you? Hundred bucks.

The handyman laughed, started taking off the jacket. He did not have a hundred anything.

The man said, *Well, now, hold on, I might be able to do eighty.*

The handyman was supposed to be buying groceries. He pulled the money he was supposed to use from his pocket. Twenty dollars. It was all the money they had. Showed it to the man. The man stuck his tongue between his lips and made a fart noise. The handyman saw something on the tongue. Stepped toward him, scowling intently at the man's mouth. The man was scared. Backed away.

What are you doing, bro?

Show, the handyman said. The man tried to climb inside his van, but the handyman took him by the shoulder and spun him back around, pinned him to the vehicle. *Show me,* he said, prying at the man's mouth.

Leave me alone! Help!

The handyman ignored all the people stopping to look and pried the man's jaws apart, reached inside for his tongue. The man bit him but he did not care. He pinched the tongue between his thumb and finger and pulled it out so he could see it. The man was shrieking. People were hurrying by, pretending not to see.

The handyman studied the tongue and said, *How long?* He let go of the man's tongue, the man turned and spat, cowering against his van. *How long?* he said again.

Shit, I don't know, bro, it's just a normal average-sized tongue!

Not how long tongue, how long tongue look like this?

How long it look like what?

You disease. You die. You hospital.

Fuck up outta here, bro, the man said. *Gimme my goddamn suit and fuck up outta here!*

The handyman ignored him, stepped out into the street where by chance an FDNY ambulance was passing. Stopped it. Made the paramedics look at the man's tongue and they understood at once. They hurried the man into the ambulance, despite his protests, and tore off with sirens ablaze. Stayed with the dry cleaner's van and merchandise, selling clothes for whatever amount was written on the price tags.

Late into the night, a young man who looked like the dry cleaner showed up. *Bro*, he said, *you saved my dad's life.* Gave the young man all the money he had made. *Nah, keep it, bro.* The handyman removed the suit to give it back but the son stopped him. *Keep it. Take it, take anything else you want, man, on us. Dad wants your name too and where you live. He says you and him are friends for life. You ain't never paying for dry cleaning in this town again, bro.*

Manuel and his son, Julio, still do the family's dry cleaning free of charge. The two of them were over after Clayton died, that first day. Brought soup every day after from the good soup place. That is his suit. Jenny says it does not fit. Jenny says it makes him look like he just got out of prison. She says to wear this suit instead. This one, this is not his suit. He feels like a different man in this suit. He does not want to be a different man.

It is very hot under the lights. They position the cameras farther away and Lesley Stahl much closer than he expected, Lesley Stahl's knees touch his and his wife's, he can smell coffee on her breath and see red lines in the whites of her eyes. He feels cornered in a broken elevator. He feels buried in light. Rescued and attacked—it feels like both. Off camera stands Jenny, a shadow he can hardly see but he feels her. Lesley Stahl asks: —What kind of boy was Clayton? He realizes the interview has begun, the cameras are recording. —What happened that night? Do you feel race played a part? What did you teach Clayton about guns? What is it about us, why do we shoot each other at such alarming rates compared to other first world nations? What can be done about it?

His wife does the talking. —We are just taking it one day at a time, she says. A current of electricity goes through him from the feet up. He smiles. His woman. He puts his hand over his mouth to cover his smile. Behind the camera he can see Jenny putting her hands to her head in frustration. Then Lesley Stahl asks about the ammo tax vote and the New York State Legislature. His wife, his beautiful goddamn brilliant wife, says gently, —What do we care about tax?

Jenny steps out of the shadows to where they can see her and her furious, bug-eyed face.

His wife ignores her, says, —Tax have nothing to do with us. Tax doesn't stop Clayton death. Law doesn't stop Clayton death. Only thing that stop Clayton death? Faith. *Faith.* If there was faith in Fisher's heart? Clayton alive. If there was trust in Fisher's heart? Clayton alive. If there was bravery in Fisher's heart? Clayton alive.

Lesley Stahl kind of smiles and says, —But we can't pass laws putting faith into people's hearts.

His wife says, —So law cannot help us, so we do not care about law. We care about life. We have faith in life, we trust in people, this is how we live, we live armed with nothing but faith and trust, we think if more people live armed with nothing but faith and trust, and without fear, then this country we give everything to, this country we love, will stop killing its children.

Off camera Jenny is pantomiming tearing her hair out of her head, is cupping her hands around her lips and screaming silently, *What the fuck?*

He ignores her and leans forward to say to Lesley Stahl, —Law? Government? Politics? *60 Minutes*? Just part of a myth. A myth put a gun in Fisher hand and a myth put us on TV now—it is all the same myth. The same myth. Myth is no solution because myth is the problem. The only solution is life. A gun takes no courage. Political movement, political protest? It takes no courage. To live open and unarmed, always—*that* takes courage. That is the only treatment for this disease.

His wife squeezes his hand, a secret between them.

—One more thing? he says. —We forgive Mr. Fisher. We forgive hims.

After the interview, Jenny leaves without speaking to them. The mood is very tense. None of the other RSA people will even look at them except for Becky, who says only, —You shouldn't have done that. You set her back. You wasted her time.

They walk home through their city, finished with Jenny and her cause. No more. Now to move forward. They go home, put on Clayton's music, his shoes, lie in his bed, pray, not knowing what they are praying to but that it is the only thing they can pray to. They beg it for stronger faith in it, whatever it is. Then they hold their breath and wait for what will come.

The interview airs that Sunday night, following the NFL. Their friends gather in the common room on the second floor to watch, but he and she do not care about the interview, they do not watch.

Nor do they hear from Jenny. It is a relief. What peace, being alone, away from her and her followers and her meetings and her *actions*. They go through Clayton's things. —We will be able to give some of this away, he says.

She says, —I did not think it would ever be possible but now it does.

—Not now though.

—Not now, no. But soon.

There is a knock on the door. He answers it. Lucien the doorman. He is very upset. —Are you watching? he says. He comes in, goes to their television, turns it on.

Fox News. A blond woman with tanned flesh and white shiny teeth and money-green eyes shouts at them, —Breaking news just in to our studio at this hour: Department of Homeland Security officials are investigating reports that the parents of Clayton Kabede, that African American teenager shot to death in New York City last week while breaking into his neighbor's house? They have been living in the US *illegally* on *forged documentation* for over *FIF-TEEN YEARS*.

He laughs, makes a dismissive gesture at it with his hand. —It's not true. They lie.

Calls Jenny. —Welcome to the war, honey, she says in the midst of what sounds like a protest. She says to sit tight and she will be right over.

She never comes.

Later that day Howard arrives, alone. Says Jenny is busy. Howard sits in the straight-backed chair given them a few weeks ago by a tenant who was redecorating. Clayton helped bring it downstairs. *Damn*, Clayton had said, *this is a nice-ass chair. Can't imagine what it's like to have so much money you can just give away chairs like this, like it's nothing.*

The handyman felt irritated by that. *It make no difference,* he said. *A man not loser just because humble job and little money.*

I know that, Dad. Damn. What's the matter? But he did not know what the matter was. He could not say. But he did know, didn't he?

Remembers Clayton lounging in the chair sideways, his long legs draped over the arm, watching his zombie shows. He imagines Howard sitting like that now, as the middle-aged attorney puts down his cup of tea and leans forward in the chair. —It appears the opposition feels threatened enough by you, he says, —to have called DHS with an anonymous tip. Some functionary there without enough real work to do took them seriously enough to pull your papers and take a closer look.

He feels his heart shrivel. His wife looks at him. He does not look back at her because he knows it is bad and he has no solution. Nonetheless he says, —It okay, I fix it. Is it money? Maybe we can borrow it.

Howard says, —I'm afraid it's the rare problem money won't solve. It's very serious. Look, I don't know where you got those papers or who you got them from, and I don't want to know, but—

—We *earned* them. We *deserve* them. People *believed* in us, his wife interrupts.

Howard ignores her. —All I know is I have seen them and they are in fact inauthentic. You are, I'm afraid, unlawfully present in the United States of America.

—No, no, no, she whispers, looking at her husband who does not look at her, cannot.

—What does that mean? he says, though he knows what it means. It means they must leave the country. They cannot live in it.

And that is exactly what Howard says.

She stands up but does not go anywhere or say anything. She just stares down at Howard in silence.

Howard says, —We'll appeal of course, but it's a long shot, this is pretty cut and dry. Especially because, well, put it this way: it's a different story if you have a child.

He hates Howard.

—Where will we go? she says.

—You'll be returned to your home country.

She sits back down.

—God no, he whispers, —we'll be killed. He is holding her hand but it is wet and cold. Puts his arm around her.

—I cannot breathe, she says.

He is choking too. His chest constricting.

—It's not necessarily permanent, Howard says. —You will be allowed to apply for a visa from your home country.

—It not *home*, he chokes out.

—We'll put in for expedition, Howard continues, ignoring him, — and if we're approved, which I'm confident we will be, considering your high profile and all the noise Jenny will make on your behalf, there have been cases where people in dangerous countries have had residency papers in their hands in as short a time as one year. Howard stares off in a way that chills his stomach and pulls his chest even tighter. —Thing is though, and I'll have to partner up with an attorney with more immigration law experience to confirm this, but the problem is that you came here. Once someone is found to be illegally present, it triggers a bar from reentry for a mandatory minimum length of time. You should not have come here.

—How long? the handyman says, staring at the spot on the carpet where Clayton spilled something when he was ten and tried to clean it with laundry detergent, leaving a pale discoloration that made the handyman so angry because it was a new carpet—how was he angry about that? Why did he care? What is a carpet?

—For what it's worth, rest assured that Jenny is out there right now raising real hell for you, putting heavy, *heavy* pressure on officials to get them to approve a waiver.

This has the thud of dishonesty to it. —How long? Tell me the truth.

—Well, the law says ten years, but—

—Ten years? he interrupts.

She says, —I would rather die.

He corrects her. —We *will* die.

—I'm sorry, Howard says, —it's sickening. We will do what we can. But to spare the police coming here and arresting you, I've told them you'll turn yourselves in in the morning. Now having said that. Howard shifts in his chair, loosens his tie. —Jenny knows people who are willing to help. In fact, I think they represent your only option right now.

—Good, who, how?

—They can get you out of here to a safe haven. Iceland.

—But we don't want Iceland. We are Americans. America is our country.

—Well, America says otherwise, doesn't it? Look, these people Jenny knows, they can get you everything you need for a good life in Iceland. You'll have a job, a place to live. You'll have authentic papers. Full health care. Support in your retirement. This is a very good opportunity. Tomorrow morning I'll be out front in a cab to take you down to the courthouse to turn yourselves in and go before the judge, who, 99.9 percent, will have you removed back to where you came from. But there will be another car too, also waiting out front tomorrow morning. I urge you very strongly to get into that one. Do you understand me?

Iceland. After Howard leaves they look up Iceland on Clayton's computer. Last year in Iceland, another country with plenty of firearms, there were seven gun deaths. Seven. In America there were 32,179. In Iceland they do not have whatever it is inside Americans that kills. They do not have the myths about themselves. They have myths, in Iceland, but they are not American myths. America itself is a myth. Iceland is just a country. We will live in a country, not a myth. In a country there is life, in myth, death. So we will go to Iceland. Right? People like us go through what we did to get here only to find it does not exist and never has, that what does exist is a meat grinder into which they feed people like us. There is no freedom, no opportunity. Not really. For them there might be. For them. Do we not understand it yet? Haven't we learned? Can't we admit it? Won't we? The country we love and gave everything to does not exist. Myths are what they want here, even if they kill them and their children. And nobody changes because in order to change they would need to admit the truth: that it is all a myth. So they keep choosing myths over people. They choose everything over people here. Whatever it is, if they can put it before people then they put it before people. This country kills its own so it can remain the same. They would rather there be death and horror than there be change. So why would we not run for our lives? Why would we choose to be victimized again? Why don't we go, why don't we protect ourselves?

(Sheeple XII)

When she is seven years old she writes in her diary:

I love my husbin I will mary my husbin I will not mary Steven Mcdoogl he is not my husbin! Who is my husbin? I doent no! but i love him!

When she is fifteen years old she writes in her diary:

Clayton, I love you so much. You are the man for me. My soul mate, my rock, my better half. You cheer me up when I am depressed. You always know how to make me laugh. Oh and you are sexy as HELL! He he! I can't wait til end of summer. I will definitely make it worth the wait for you. Let me just say 1 word: surfboard. HA HA! When we are finally alone and joined as one on that magical night it will be soooooo beautiful. I love being your girlfriend. We are not just a silly high school relationship are we? We are for real. Baby, I cannot wait to be 16 with you. We're gonna have our licenses! You can drive out here to the boonies. And we can think of some other things to do in the car too (tee hee!). Muah muah MUAH! Next year will be AMAZING, I cannot wait. I love you, Clayton, I love you I LOVE CLAYTON. STACEY ♥ CLAYTON. SM ♥ CK.

When she is sixteen years old she writes nothing in her diary.

When she is seventeen years old she writes in her diary:

A bad day. Sucked dry & numb. Cannot sleep eat shower. Grades fucked. Mom saw my legs, she knows. Meds not working, make me fat and jittery and not sleep. New psych tmrw. Keep seeing him. Saw him at mall today. He never sees me.

When she is eighteen years old she writes nothing in her diary.

When she is nineteen years old she writes:

Finally saw the movie last week. had to turn it off. have not gotten out of bed since.

When she is twenty years old she writes:

David told me he loves me. I could only stare back at him and say nothing. He cried and said I was breaking his heart. Then he left. I felt relieved, I felt free. I could be alone again.

When she is twenty-two years old she writes in her diary:

Driving to work today I saw him walking down the street. It was him. This was the first time I had seen him in a few years. My heart turned cold, so cold. I had to pull over. It was so startling. It made me realize how much he has become a memory of a memory. I had not realized how warped and calcified he has become to me—until I saw him today. Have I made him that way? Can we do this to each other? It is like all the gray amber in my heart in which C has been locked suddenly shattered—and out he stepped, gleaming and real yet different because it is him and not the memory, it is the real him who I had forgotten in favor of whatever I have turned him into, whatever it is I remember when I remember him. It all came back today. How his voice sounded in my ear in that bed, his scent. How his lips felt. What he felt like. That was so long ago. Why am I not over it? I thought I was but I am not. I called in to work. They gave me a hard time but I don't care. I have not cared about anything, really, since C. How many times have I been fired or just left a job without saying anything to anyone? What is there to care about? I am supposed to be on the way right now to Brian's family lake house, with Brian. I called him and told him I could not go and he said why. How could I explain? I told him I had never been in love with him, that every time I had told him I was I had been lying. I could hear him dying on the other end. "How could you say that?" he whispered. "It's just the truth," I said, "it's just what people do, there is no love." He said, "I don't believe you." I said okay, whatever, and hung up.

When she is twenty-five years old she writes in her diary:

Life is being tethered to the sun & when you are young you are tethered tightly to it. But as you age you lose and you suffer and this is drifting out further from the sun, on a longer tether. And you drift further and further away & you get colder & cannot pull yourself back closer to the sun even *though you can see where you used to be, how close to it you so recently were—how warm and good it was. & you do not even know you are drifting at the time. To be alive is to feel/see/experience yourself <u>diminishing</u>. Not as it happens but shortly after. So you will know you have. This guy Ken keeps contacting me about C. This memorial thing. 10 years. Driving me crazy, wishing Ken would just let it go. And leave me alone.*

When she is thirty-two years old she writes:

I told Ken today that I love him. And I meant it. First time that has been true since C. He knew C too, he was C's best friend, I sort of remembered Ken vaguely but we did not meet really until C's 10-year memorial, 7 years ago. Since then he and I have been putting one on every year, to raise money for gun violence prevention. At the 10-year Ken told me how destroyed he was after C, that he wanted to kill himself. He had a plan and everything. After going to C's the morning after to say bye to Mr. & Mrs. K, he was going to go jump off the Manhattan bridge. But then at C's house he saw all the people there for C and Mr. K seemed to zero in on Ken, like he sensed something. He came over to Ken and put his arm around him and told him how much C loved him and how good of a friend Ken was to C & thanked him for that and told him that he has a whole lifetime ahead of such great friendships to contribute to, people to give to the way he gave to C, so keep strong and doing good because people will need you & your love. It made Ken see things differently. He thought that was heroic of Mr. K to even think of him at that moment, having just lost C. He didn't know any man could be like that. It was what C would have done. It made Ken think, the world has people in it like C and Mr. K and I don't want to leave it, I want to live in it, I want to be a part of it, there is love to be had and love to give, I will keep strong, I will do good, I will live. So he stayed alive. Ken is the only man I could ever love. If Ken were not here I would love no one. I would just spend the rest of my life the way I have been since C: getting colder and meaner and harder and sadder... God have I needed what he has brought back into me life—desperately. He brought <u>life</u> back into it. He has me going to counseling, first time since I was maybe 17, and it's helping this time. He's got me back in school, get my degree. After C I did not even apply to college, even though I'd been a straight-A student. Just didn't care. Everything felt fraudulent and hopeless and meaningless. Not anymore. Being back in school at 32 among all these 18-year-olds makes *me realize what babies we were when it happened and how sad that we had to deal with what we did so young. The way I used to deal with it, when I was a baby, was to not talk about it, but Ken makes me talk about it. He opens my heart. He pulls me back toward the sun. And I do the same for him. We anchor each other there, tightly, so we do not drift away from it. I spent 17 years after C isolated and terrified and trusting no one because love was devastating when it was ripped from me so young. I have gone along trusting nothing and no one, always afraid of everyone and thinking that made me free. I was not free. I was the opposite. With Ken only now am I free. Because I am afraid of nothing. Because I have trust. That makes me have love. He & I are the only ones who understand what the other has lost and the love we have we could have only with each other. We are one. He is my rock, my soul mate, my better half. He was my husband before we married, he was my husband before we ever even met. I write this from paradise.*

When she is thirty-three, thirty-four, thirty-five, and thirty-six years old she writes nothing in her diary.

When she is thirty-eight years old she writes in her diary:

Ken smiles and says
As he first holds our baby
"Let's name him Clayton."

SELF-PROTECTION

After the sleepless night, they leave their home and close their door behind them, most likely for good. Outside the rear freight entrance the morning air is cool. Autumn is coming, until now his favorite time of year. A black SUV idles at the curb. Behind it is a yellow cab. The back windows of the yellow cab roll down and there sits Howard, looking at them but saying nothing. The windows of the SUV are deeply tinted and they cannot see the driver. Its lights flash. He and his wife go to it. But when they get to it they keep going past and open the door of the yellow cab and get in. As Howard slides over to make room, he asks if they misunderstood him yesterday. When they tell him no, they understood him perfectly, he asks if they are out of their minds then.

—No, he tells Howard. —We're not.

—This is unbelievable, Howard says. —You have the choice of walking into a meat grinder or protecting yourself, and you're choosing the meat grinder.

He puts a hand on Howard's shoulder. —Have you learned nothing? There is only one way to protect yourself. Only one way.

His wife says, —We do not care if America disagrees, we know the truth. We are Americans.

As they ride to the courthouse, Howard sputters and calls Jenny and talks to her in a low, urgent voice. He cannot hear what

Howard says to her. He does not care. Also with them is another attorney, experienced in immigration law, who will represent them in court but has seconded Howard's opinion that there is nothing to be done for them and they should expect deportation. He does not catch this man's name, he does not care what this man says.

When they arrive and step out of the cab, they are at once lost in the morning, taken up by the other cabs and the buses and the men and women and even people who are neither men nor women all hustling with coffee and headphones toward clerk jobs and lawyer jobs and halal meat cart jobs and executive jobs and security guard jobs; the tourist families from Real America holding great big maps, born here white and Christian, heirs to the myth and still completely lost. No one notices him and her. No one recognizes them. There is nothing to indicate this is the scene where the story that consumed a large handful of the public's attention over a few days this summer will now conclude. He thinks, *They do not care for conclusions, only beginnings. Not for realities, only possibilities.* The streets and sidewalks are clear of the protestors and supporters on either side who so recently clogged them. There are no TV crews now, no helicopters, no riot police. No one yelling *USA* at them. No *60 Minutes* or Michael Bloomberg. No Wayne LaPierre, no Jenny Sanders. There are only him and her. Once again.

They stand at the base of the stairs looking up at the courthouse entrance, where cops and attorneys and scared, sad brown people hold the door for one another.

—I love you, he tells her.

—I love you, she says.

—It's not too late for Iceland.

She takes his hand, thinking about it. —No, she says at last. — Let's get on with it.

They climb the steps. His knees are trembling. There is buzzing through his chest and shoulders. His heart kicks. Off in the distance a voice calls out to them, cutting through the noise of the city, and they stop.

She is turning to try to see where it is coming from. —It's him.

Is it possible? Has Clayton found a way back? Of course it is. They will see now the stream of pedestrians parting and Clayton emerging in triumph with his arms out and stance wide, grinning devilishly at the trick he has pulled on nature and government, defying death and saving them yet again. *Ha HA! I'm back! Matter of fact, I was here the whole time! Now they gotta let you stay!*

But it is not Clayton, of course it is not, for Clayton is gone—it is his friend Elana Larson, one of the building's residents whose cats he and Clayton took care of while she was away being treated for cancer. It is Elana for whom the pedestrians part, Elana who emerges in triumph, jogging across the street toward them, calling at them and waving to get their attention. With her are his friends the Mendelsohns, who helped Clayton the last time he sleepwalked, and his friend Max, whose smoking made Clayton meet Stacey, and there are also his friends Chris and Art and the former tenants Janet and Dilbert.

—You didn't think we forgot about you, did you? Elana Larson is saying as she climbs the stairs, out of breath, still weak from her illness. As he and his wife hug her and the others and thank them for coming, another voice calls out: it is his friend Lucien, running down Centre Street, squeezing past pedestrians and dodging bumpers of short-stopping taxis, his gray pompadour wobbling like jelly. Behind him are more friends: Hector and Walter, the super from one of the other buildings on the block who is from Jamaica and lets him borrow materials and tools and vice versa and with whom he now and again on summer nights smokes a joint on the roof after hard days of work; Manuel the dry cleaner, who gave him his American suit and whose life he saved fifteen years ago; Kenny's mother, who reads and comments on every essay about international politics his wife writes and posts online, and her little girl, Gabriella; Frank the UPS guy, who referred him to his dentist, Dina, who is a very good dentist and person and now also his friend and is also here; Veronica who owns the good Italian restaurant and who is here too with her chef, Robert, and busboy Xiang; Sonny and Ben, the Hassids from the synagogue across the street, with whom he plays basketball; and there is Delilah from the flower shop, who wears a burqa and every spring saves him the first lilacs, and her little boy, Ahmed, and her husband, Al, who gives him books about art to read and whose warped floorboards he helped replace; and there is the accountant Destiny, whose office is in the building three doors down, with whom he talks cricket on rainy days at the coffee shop and whom he introduced to her now-husband, Tyler, the owner of the coffee shop, who is also here. His boss, Dave, is here too, the one who gave him the job and whom he thought was his friend, but he did not come to the memorial service and has not even sent condolences about Clayton even though Dave was the first person he showed Clayton's ultrasound image to.

—Am I fired? he asks Dave.

—What? says Dave. —No, the owner's lawyers told me not to talk to you, but know what? Fuck them. I'm here for you.

Kenny and Raul and Stacey are here too, wearing hoodies and Air Jordan sneakers just like Clayton. The kids from Clayton's church camp are here too, as are his teachers from school and what must be the entire student body. Raul is big and menacing as he barks, waving his thick arms for emphasis, —We ain't *neva* gon stop shouting his name and y'all's name, we ain't *neva* gon stop. They can get rid of y'all but they can't make y'all go away. Cuz we ain't gon *let* them. We gon be out here making sure y'all remembered. Clayton gon live forever. Forever!

His wife is in tears as she puts her arms around Clayton's friends and their friends and so is he. His heart feels like it has filled with all the heat and light there is. The fear that was coursing through his body like venom is now gone. He says to his wife, —No one can hurt us now.

She kisses him and says, —If we have to go, then this is how I want to go.

He puts his arm around her, smells her hair. They walk through the door, into the courthouse, led by friends in front and flanked by friends on the left and friends on the right and followed by friends at the rear, on all sides protected by the only thing that really works.

THE INHERITANCE
11

He is back at Rikers dreading word of the grand jury's decision. What is there to make him sit around and wait for? They will indict him on the gun. Of course they will. It is cut and dry. They will indict him, and if he does not plead guilty, then he will go to trial where he will lose and he will stay here in Rikers for years. He lies on his cot staring up at the ceiling. He tries to sleep, tries counting up to one hundred, then back down to zero. The others know the grand jury is deliberating and are making bets on the outcome. —*You nervous?* they keep asking him, enjoying his discomfort. —*You scared?* He does not answer them. He counts up to five hundred, then back down to zero, up to seven hundred, back down. His mind wanders—his son, what he is doing right now, if he is safe. He listens to his own breath go in and out. Examines his fingernails, which are very long, they were overdue for trimming before that night. How has his son been eating, how has he been sleeping? But thinking of him lying in some strange crib somewhere he does not know, confused, alone, makes Lee want to die, so instead he tries to remember every team in the National Football League. Then he does the same for Major League Baseball, then the NBA. But then he is still thinking of him, so he counts to one thousand, then back down to zero. Which does nothing, he is still thinking of him.

A gang of COs comes storming down the hall to his cell led by Hurricane, a three-hundred-pound psychopath. —Fisher! Step out!

Hurricane looks like he is going to break every bone in Lee's face. —*Oh shit!* his cellmates taunt. — *You guilty! You guilty! Bwa ha ha ha!*

Lee sits up, feeling grateful that, one way or the other, at least the wait is over. Hurricane does not look him in the eye as he steps out into the hall. Normally the man cannot stop talking, he taunts and humiliates like he's on an automatic setting. But now he is very grim, sucking his teeth. —Come here, he says. Lee stands still. — Take a step toward me. When Lee still does not move, Hurricane reaches out to Lee's collar and pulls him close, saying, —*Come here, inmate.* Then Hurricane shoves him back against the wall, Lee's head cracking against it, and pats him down, more so punching Lee's body. —Lower your drawers, says Hurricane, breathing heavily, sweat appearing on his big, wrinkled forehead. When Lee hesitates Hurricane yanks them down himself.

Lee's cellmates are all looking on, as are the prisoners in every cell up and down the hall. —*Bwa ha ha ha! He guilty, he guilty! He going away! He going to death row!*

Hurricane pulls the waistband of Lee's underwear out away from the rest of his body and looks inside, reaches in, grips Lee's testicles and squeezes. Lee cries out and tries to squirm away, but two other COs pin him against the wall with their hands. —Fifteen years old, Hurricane says into his ear. —My *son* fifteen. Hurricane squeezes harder. —You think you beat it, but it ain't over. Someone's gonna wanna put a bullet in your head and it might even be me. You might be getting out of here now but you ain't never leaving, you understand me? You gonna be locked up and you always gonna be locked up. Always.

—*Bwa ha ha ha ha!*

Hurricane lets go and tells Lee to pull up his damned drawers. When Lee has pulled them up, Hurricane twists Lee's arms behind his back and cuffs him and forces him down the hall. Icy pain is shooting all through his body from the bottom of his belly. He realizes what Hurricane said.

—Wait, did you just say—

—Shut the fuck up.

He goes with them down the hall. Inside somewhere deep he knows is profound relief and confused elation—they say, *You are getting out, soon you will see him, soon, soon*—but he does not dare trust them, he does not dare believe them yet. The COs shove him along through the TV area, where they wait for the next gate to open. Joseph is there with other prisoners watching *Judge Judy*. One of them goes, —Yo, where they taking Pills?

All the others turn to look except Joseph, who mutters, —Where you think? All he did was kill a black kid. He said he's sorry, won't do it again, they say the kid probably deserved it anyway. And now he going home.

The others are staring at Lee, believing what Joseph's saying. Resignation and rage, heartbreak and hatred—a storm behind each face. The way they look at him is worse than anything they could do to him.

One of them says, —What about me? I want to go home too. When do I get to go home?

Another says, —When you get rich.

Joseph says, —You want to get rich like he rich, you got to sell people dog meat.

—Dog meat? Like, dog food?

—Nuh-uh, I mean dogs *for* food. That's what he did.

They have been talking about it in the media. The television comedian John Oliver discovered who the ancestor was who originally made the Fisher family fortune and has been having great fun ridiculing Lee for it. Back during the Civil War, Lee's great-great-great-great-grandfather was a newly arrived, impoverished, unskilled German immigrant who fought for the North in the Second Battle of Bull Run, where he was wounded and had his leg amputated. While recovering in the hospital in Washington, he heard how the South was being decimated by the North's blockades; there were no imports, so food was very scarce. They were starving down there. Confederate soldiers retreating from battle were so desperate for food, they were eating horses, boots. Stories of cannibalism were not uncommon. Once he was able to hobble out of the hospital, he bribed and lied his way down to Mexico, where he knew from earlier travels the streets were filled with all these wild, nasty little dogs spreading disease and generally getting in everyone's way. The Mexicans did not know what to do with them or how to get rid of them, but he did. He contracted his dog removal services to the local officials there, then exported the vermin out and up into the States, building and protecting a formidable supply line, and he followed the remainder of the Civil War in a team of wagons stuffed with his livestock, setting up shop outside the battlefields on the Confederate side. When the rebels came crawling their way out of hell, starving, gaunt, desperate, he was there to feed them at whatever price he felt like demanding. And he became rich for it. Then after the war, he used that money to buy southern land and lease cotton plantations and became richer. The man was born an illiterate, simple laborer in the German countryside and died an American in Manhattan in the mansion he built up the street from Andrew Carnegie's.

Lee is processed out of Rikers Island. He insists they give him back the underwear and FUBU T-shirt he had on when they brought him in so he can get out of this jumpsuit, but the COs in processing must be confused as usual, because they hold up for him what they say are the clothes he was wearing, but it's just another, identical jumpsuit. —This what they got for you, they say, consulting some document. Hurricane loves it. *Ha ha ha.* Fucking with him. They are fucking with him. Sticking it to him one last time while they still can. One last shot at Lee Fisher. What choice does he have? He removes one jumpsuit, puts on another. And this is what he is wearing now, going home again.

A black Town Car is waiting for him outside the gate. Protestors are there. The car takes Lee to Washington Heights. Lawyers and officials facilitate the handoff. The woman seems nice enough, but then again of course she would. The first thing Lee notices is how much his son has grown. It has only been a week but he seems to be half a foot longer and ten pounds heavier. It feels very good to hold him again. Lee immediately searches the baby for bruises or scratches or any other signs of abuse.

—What's this, he says, —what's wrong with his eye?

The woman says, —His eye? Nothing.

He has her look more closely. —See? It's all red and infected. He shows it to the lawyers and officials.

The woman says, —It looks clean and white to me.

—Healthy eye, the lawyers and officials agree.

—Unbelievable, he says, —how could you let this happen?

—I let nothing happen, the woman says.

The lawyers and officials say if he has concerns he'll have to take the baby to a doctor for an official examination, and the woman keeps saying she let nothing happen, but Lee waves her off and signs what forms he needs to sign and takes his son to the Town Car, straps him in his seat.

—Hospital emergency room, he mutters to the driver.

The ride seems to take hours. Lee peers into his son's eye, everything inside him cold and sludgy. He will lose it. His beautiful eye, gone. At the hospital the doctor also says nothing is wrong with the eye, but Lee demands antibiotics anyway, and the doctor gives him a prescription, albeit for very mild ones, that Lee fills right away. He gives them to his son in the car, brushing back his hair from his forehead as they begin to heal him.

There are protestors outside his building—bullhorns, drums. Shirtless, skinny young men wander around yelling, unwashed young women wave signs and upside-down American flags. People have scarves over their faces, they wear Repeal the Second Amendment shirts, they hold banners with Clayton's face on them and chant, —Not one more! Not one more! Cops are there in riot gear, they are already making arrests: two cops drag a kid down the street. Gun rights activists scream in the faces of the repealists, cops break up fights. Reporters chase it all around; in fact most of the protestors themselves hold cameras.

But it is not spectacle or theater, at least not anymore. Lee remembers Occupy Wall Street—this is not Occupy Wall Street. Whimsy is not present here. Neither is hope. There is only desperation, fear. And whatever it began as, it is spinning out of control. And Lee sees why: there in the midst of it all like a general is Jenny Sanders, a bullhorn in her hand and a mob of media hovering tightly to her wake. Lee's windows are tinted, the protestors cannot see it is him inside, but they slap on his car anyway, yelling, and one jumps on the hood and slides off. Jenny Sanders is staring through the window, right at him. Can she see? Does she know it's him?

The driver is scared, asks what he should do. Lee doesn't know, tells him to just keep driving past the building. Then, by impulse, he tells the driver to take them out of New York, get them out of the city. They take the Holland Tunnel and emerge in New Jersey, and Lee still does not know where to go, so he has the driver find a car rental place and the driver leaves them there and they get a car, the biggest they have, a Suburban. He drives west until the concrete chips away into grass and the smog-gray sky dissipates into blue and the hordes of desperate, fearful people—all those prisoners of Manhattan—fade away and it is quiet and you can hear birds again and there is space and room for once to think and breathe.

Now what? He spends the night in a motel somewhere in Ohio, his son sleeping in the bed next to him and a chair jammed up under the doorknob. He turns on the news, is watching live coverage, when what happens to Jenny Sanders happens to Jenny Sanders. Involuntarily he cries out, —Holy shit! Clamps a hand over his mouth as the news anchors get hysterical. His son wakes up screaming and does not stop, and there is nothing Lee can do to calm him down, the bottle does not work, nor does shushing him or changing him, for hours the baby screams gutturally, agonizingly, and Lee can only look on. Late into the night the baby exhausts himself and falls asleep, and Lee drinks the motel room coffee and stays up, stunned and shocked, peeking through the blinds into the parking lot at the footsteps and whispers he keeps hearing out there.

In the morning he does not know what to do, so they keep moving, drive aimlessly south, and end up in South Carolina, where they go into a convention center in which there is a gun show. He has pulled into the parking lots of a few along the way, wrestling with getting out and going inside and getting one. But in South Carolina he goes in and they recognize him and want pictures with him. They are selling Lee Fisher action figures, they ask him to sign some. They've bought one of his paintings off eBay, it hangs on the wall of a booth. Confused, he stands there with them for pictures, but then he gets ahold of himself and declines to sign the action figures, declines to take one, and leaves without a gun, saying he's no hero, he just did what he had to do.

He continues driving. He drives in silence out of Georgia, into Alabama, then Mississippi, then Tennessee, his just another car on the interstate, no radio, unable to stomach hearing them lie about him and make her out to be some kind of hero, preferring instead to listen to his son coo in the backseat, to his son's breath as he sleeps.

They see signs for Graceland. He tells his son about Elvis Presley as he follows the signs and there it is, there is Graceland. He finds the parking lot, but the attendant recognizes him and wants to talk about what happened, and Lee changes his mind and backs out, he drives away, not watching the mansion recede in his rearview mirror.

In a Super 8 motel that night in Arkansas, his son speaks for the first time. He says, — Dada. The only person for Lee to tell is the housekeeper.

The next morning, a Sunday, he heads toward the address he has had for a long, long time but has never been to. Lee drives all day and through the night, crossing nearly the entire width of Kansas, passing Dodge City, telling his son about Wyatt Earp and the American West, all that holy lore. Late in the morning in Colorado, he arrives outside a high concrete fence on wooded property miles from anyone or anything. Lee wonders, *Is the man even alive?* Maybe he'll find him in his recliner, long dead, forgotten by everyone who once loved him. He will be decayed, half eaten by rats. The TV will still be on and turned to the news, his mummified face peeled back in eternal disgust with the state of his country. Lee pulls up to the big gate and pushes the button on the intercom. No one answers. He pushes it again. It takes a long time, revving up Lee's pulse as he keeps pressing the button, but eventually a voice answers that sounds tired, reedy but *alive.*

—It's me, Lee says.

The voice says he knows it is, he can see him on camera, and the gates slowly open. Lee drives through them. *Where the hell were you?* is what he'll say to him when he gets out of the car. He won't take the kid out, he'll leave him there. It will be a short conversation: *Where were you? Where have you been? What do you have to say for yourself?* He will be very tall, compared with the old man. He will dwarf him. His ordeal will have turned him into a hulk. His father's life will have withered him away. He will grip the man's neck, twist it like a washcloth. *Where have you been?* And his father will see what a man Lee has become, much more of one than he himself ever was. And he will weep, he will confess his wrongdoings and beg his son for forgiveness and hug his son, tell his son he loves him. Then Lee will turn away, get back in the car, and drive off, and he won't introduce him to his baby and he will never see him again.

The third wife, he remembers from when he met her at their wedding, was a small brown woman who barely spoke English and kept forgetting Lee's name even though it's the same name as his father's. She was subservient and passive and saw him through the cancer scare, but eventually he found a way to drive her off just as he drove off the second wife. The second wife was pretty, and they had two kids together who were smart and successful and everything Lee had never been. Their kids graduated from the college Lee dropped out of, got MBAs, are now high-level executives at the family corporation, and for a while they got along with his father in ways Lee never did, but now he hears they do not, they have no relationship with him anymore, he has driven them off. He drove off the second wife too, the way he drove off Lee's mother, and the way he drove off Lee himself. And now there is no wife. The man is all alone, Lee knows, and that's all he knows.

He rounds a corner past the trees into a clearing where a sprawling, lovely home sits on a little hill. A small gray man stands on the front porch, gun holstered on hip. As Lee gets out of the car, the old man is already saying something but Lee cannot make it out. He walks right up to him. The old man wears shorts and his legs are chubby and the color of ash, and he has on a gray T-shirt with a college football logo and he has little bleary eyes behind thick glasses that warp them. He blinks and blinks. His nose is bigger. When Lee gets closer his father repeats himself and this time Lee can hear it: —You should've called first. Heroically, Lee stops himself from murdering the old man right there on his doorstep.

—Where the hell have you been? Lee says.

—Santa Fe, says his father.

—Santa Fe, Lee echoes bitterly.

—Met a gal on the Internet.

—Internet. Wonderful. Congratulations.

His father does not see how angry he is or just does not care. —Anybody follow you?

—No.

—You're sure?

—Look, I just came to ask you one thing.

—Okay.

—You got anything to say for yourself?

His father thinks about it. —Like what?

—Like apologizing to your grandson. Lee points to the car. —He was in a shelter because of you, in the care of daggone crackheads.

Distress comes over the old man's face. Then something else. —He's here?

—Yeah, he's here, he's in the car.

—Well, were you planning to just let him bake to death in there?

Lee seethes, tells him to hold on, and goes and gets his son out. He carries him in the car seat back up to the porch. His father stares at him. He says to Lee, —I figured you had someone else to ask. You didn't have anyone else?

—No.

—Why not?

Lee raises his voice. —What the hell do you mean? He starts to go further but he cannot. It is one of those things where when it is inside of you it makes perfect sense, but when you take it out and say it out loud it makes absolutely none: *Because of you. I had nobody else because of you.* So instead he says, —Ain't you curious about the gun? Ain't you wondering where it is?

—Which gun's that?

—The gun.

—*Which* gun, Lee. I don't know what you're talking about.

—The one you told me I have to keep safe. The one you said was always mine and that one day I'd pass on to my boy. You don't remember?

It's obvious he does not. *Drunk himself stupid,* Lee thinks.

—Well, they're gonna destroy it, if you're interested. If they haven't done it already.

His father squints, trying to comprehend. —What do you want from me? A new gun?

—Jesus Christ, you really don't remember? That old .38, probably a hundred years old?

—You're talking about the .38 that pulls to the right?

—That's the one.

—I have it downstairs.

—No, you gave it to me before I left home.

—Oh, he says, and looks away, confused.

—The *special* gun, Lee says. —The one we Fisher men have carried for generations. Your granddaddy and his granddaddy and—

—Your granddaddy was a New York City agoraphobe and closeted homosexual who had a knack for picking stocks. I never had the knack, that's how I got in trouble. But he hardly left his office. Afraid of the world. Allergic to dust. He had less blood in him than a brand-new Ziploc bag. Carry a gun? Him? He probably never got more than ten feet of one in his life. Got his doctor to say he had bad eyes to keep him out of the war. They were all like that, until me.

This was the first Lee had heard of this. From what his father had always told him, all Fisher men were basically Teddy Roosevelt— well-off but rough, hardy.

—What? You made all the cowboy shit up? Pulled it from thin air?

His father regards him a little disdainfully. —Course not! Come on inside.

He turns and goes in and Lee follows with his son. He expects it to be foul in there—flies and empty bottles and old pizza boxes—but it is very clean and everything is new. On the walls he has pictures of his kids, including one of him and Lee, together, back on the mountain. They are working on the farm and look very happy. The fact that he has Lee's picture makes Lee feel like he will cry.

—I was the executive in charge of the four-hundred-million-dollar family trust, his father is saying. —Back then, that was a lot of money. I was in over my head and didn't know what I was doing, and I got in trouble with a stock trade. I worked out a deal, testified against some guys to get off lightly, but I still had to do a year in prison. My prison wasn't exactly your prison. This wasn't Rikers. It was a white-collar facility in Oklahoma, and we only had to be there Monday through Friday. Weekends I had me a little condo in town. I used to wander around, going to honky-tonk bars, rodeos, this and that. I liked it. They made us do landscaping at a golf course, digging sand traps and mowing grass. I liked that too. It wasn't New York City. New York City ain't real life. This, I thought, was real life. So from prison I bought some land sight unseen—mistake—and had a house built on it and moved you and your mother out from New York. And when I got out I joined you. But on my way out of town, I went into a department store and bought some dungarees and a cowboy shirt, a cowboy hat, some underwear, and that old secondhand gun. I bought it because it looked like something Clint Eastwood would have. His father whistles the first few notes of the theme from *The Good, the Bad and the Ugly*. —The guys I'd testified against were pissed. They were wannabe mafiosos. But all they ever did was send some goons out to the house to kill some of my chickens.

—It wasn't chickens, Lee says, —it was pigs.

—Couldn't have been. We didn't have pigs.

—Sure we did.

—Pigs are too much trouble. They root around, dig their way out, eat anything and anybody. We didn't have them. We had a dairy cow. Some chickens. No pigs.

As Lee tries to argue about this, his father chuckles and points to another picture, one of Lee poking his head out the door of the barn and grinning from ear to ear. —I love this one. Lee peers close at it. His face is not swollen, there is nothing oozing. His eye is completely white and healthy. Lee feels dizzy.

His father leads him farther in, saying, —I'd offer you a beer or something, but I don't have any. Pop okay?

Lee sits at the kitchen table and takes his son out of the car seat as his father comes back with sodas. He asks Lee if he may hold him. Lee lets him. He holds the baby far out from himself and stares at him silently. —Hello, he says. The TV is on in the other room, Lee can hear it. Live coverage of the latest.

Lee says, opening his soda, —No beer, huh?

—Not for me these days, no.

—Drying out after Santa Fe? Lee says with derision. The latest sure to be short-lived attempt to ease up, get a handle on it.

—More like one day at a time.

His father gets up and carries the baby to the kitchen, digs around in a drawer, returns with something in his hand. Drops them on the table. Lee doesn't know what they are.

—AA chips, his father says. —Three years' worth. As Lee examines them for evidence of forgery, his father sits back down and says, — Right now I don't miss it. But I sure did when you were calling from jail.

Lee can't believe what he's hearing.

—Look, I made mistakes with you that I learned from. I'm sorry that's the way it had to be.

—So coming to help your son, your grandson, that would have been a mistake?

—For me, yeah. Yeah, it would have.

Lee hands him the chips back, says nothing. And they sit there watching the baby, listening to the TV.

At last his father says, —Hate to say it, but she tapped into something heinous.

Lee looks at his father. For a moment, he thinks he's talking about his mother before he realizes whom he really means.

—What did she expect would happen? I don't condone it, but what did she expect? It's only going to get nastier. You need to protect yourself, if you aren't doing so already.

—A guard at Rikers said he was going to kill me.

—There you go. What are you going to do?

Lee says, —I don't know. My lawyer says I ain't out of the woods, that I should be heading somewhere they don't extradite right now.

—Are you going to?

—I don't know. Makes me sick, the thought of being run out of my country.

—An outlaw, his father says grimly. —Like Jesse James.

—Jesse James never had to leave the country, did he?

His father shrugs. —You have protection?

Lee does not answer.

—Come on.

His father takes him downstairs to the basement. Leather furniture, plush rug, and glass cases containing guns. Now this is as Lee remembers, but there are even more of them now, much more, there seems to be hundreds of them, from old one-shot muskets to fully automatic tactical weapons.

—I always buy one or two more every time she goes on TV spewing her bile across the earth. Then I send her a note telling her so. Guess now I'll have to send someone else the note. I've bought five since what happened to you. Here, take one of them.

He pulls off the wall a brand-new polymer semiautomatic pistol, hands it to Lee. It is a more powerful firearm than the old gun, it holds more rounds, it fires more accurately, it is smaller, easier to conceal. It requires less maintenance and attention, demands less skill and care. Aesthetic pleasure rushes up Lee's arm into his body. He wants this gun. He wants to hold it in his hand forever because it feels perfect there. Like an extension of himself. But he tries to hand it back. —I don't want it.

—Doesn't matter. You need it. His father says to the baby, —And when you're a bit bigger your daddy'll teach you how to use it. He'll teach you about safety and responsibility and independence. He'll pass on the traditions. The values. He looks up at Lee as though to ask, *Won't you?*

When he leaves his father's house he is very tired and his son needs to eat and sleep, so he finds a motel. He gives a fake name, pays with cash. He locks the door, jams the chair under the knob, and feeds his son, gives him a bath, sings him to sleep. And then he stays up all night, moving the bed so he can sit with his back against the wall facing the door, new gun in his hand, loaded. He starts at every noise he hears out there, feeling them coming for him, hearing his son breathe. He is ready to do whatever it takes, whatever he must to keep his son breathing, even if it means never leaving this room. The night gets darker and quieter. When it's darkest and quietest, he hears whispers outside. They are right outside the window, right outside the door. They are here in the room. Right behind him. They are all around. *Remember the trees?* they hiss. *Remember Violet? Remember a boyhood that never was? Remember? Remember?* And he does, he remembers it all. And then he remembers one last thing: what his father said today in the basement, the question he seemed to ask. *Won't you?* And he realizes it was not a question at all.

And he realizes it never was.

THE NUCLEAR OPTION

—spits in her face. He spits in her face. In an airport he walks up to a woman he does not know, who is simply doing what she believes is right for the safety of the American people, and doing it within the mechanisms of the democratic process, and he spits in her face. It is gooey, coffee-caramel color tinged with nicotine-phlegm yellow. The cholesterol and trans fat excretion of a dying species. It slides down her forehead over her closed eyelids as all her fellow travelers watch in horror, come help her, and hold him for the police—ha, yeah, no, they don't do shit, they pretend not to even see, faces buried in their phones, while the man walks off without a word, if you can call him a man.

Something in her breaks. It breaks. It is not the first time a man has spit on her—spit does not bother her, nothing does—but this time it makes her suddenly aware of how tired she is and how long she has been doing this, and how shredded she still is from Michelle a decade later. This is it, she realizes. She has taken it as far as she can. New York will be the final one.

She gets up and gropes her way blind, loogie burning her eyes, to the Auntie Anne's for a napkin, wipes it off, crying out in disgust so even if they will not see they have to hear. Then she gets on her plane, lands in New York, tries to help the Kabedes; they will not help her, they embarrass her, get in her way, would prefer to keep everything how it is, this will not do, and she can still smell the man's phlegm on her face, can still hear him call her a cunt as he walked off. If she does not act the NRA and the myth of guns will not even be dinged after Clayton, the shooting of Clayton Kabede will be forgotten and the country will keep limping along, bleeding and broken and sick and infectious, its most vital parts falling off the wind.

She has not gotten us as far as she has by being kind or even being a good person. She has tried that tactic. After Michelle, she wasted years being nice and taking the high road and appealing to the best of us. Making a difference does not take those things—it takes war. In wars they have no time for traitors—they execute them and move on. They punish those who are enlisted but refuse to fight. And those two, the parents, they were enlisted, they have been called on by their nation to fight for it but they refuse to fight for it, and so maybe it is not their nation after all. The night after *60 Minutes*, once she calms down by pounding the shit out of a treadmill in the hotel gym, she calls a late-night strategy session with Howard and Maureen, who dials in from Chicago.

—Howard, she says, wiping at her face again and again, expecting the spit to still be there because she can feel it, —look at their papers.

Howard does, says they are fine. She tells Howard to look again. He looks again. The papers are legit. Jenny tells Maureen she needs money to hire a consultant.

—For what? Maureen says.

Jenny says, —To look at their papers.

Maureen says, —Jenny, no, enough, I won't be part of this, leave them alone.

Jenny throws a fit, Maureen relents, okays the hiring of a former CIA agent to pick apart the documents. The former CIA agent is not a good man and Jenny does not know what he does to the documents, but he comes back confirming Jenny's hunch—it is not the Kabedes' nation after all. That is why they will not fight for it. She tries to have someone at RSA send in the tip to Homeland Security, making it appear like it is coming from the NRA, but no one will push the button to release the bomb, no one has the courage that she has, no one has the balls, no one has the *cunt*, apparently she will have to fight the whole damn thing herself—plan the war, fight the war, win the war.

She pulls the trigger on the bomb, the United States cruelly does the bidding of the immensely powerful, moneyed, entrenched, ruthless National Rifle Association, in whose pocket it sits, and deports those two honest, hardworking Americans even in their time of unspeakable grief following a horrific tragedy. Social media picks it up; it becomes established fact that it was the NRA, emphasizes in spectacular fashion the bottomless, dehumanizing destructiveness of the group and the urgent need for voters to eradicate its influence over society, garners more support for Repeal the Second Amendment, the ammo tax. When that man in the airport was emptying the bowels of his lungs onto her face, support in New York for the ammo tax was polling at 51–49 opposed. Today, as the parents walk into the courthouse after Jenny "crossed the line," it is now 53–47 in favor.

Victory at the Battle of New York City.

When she hears about the grand jury decision, she finds herself going to Fisher's building, bringing with her an ocean of repealists. They march down Seventh Avenue, police flanking them. NOT ONE MORE, their signs say. —Not one more, they shout. Other contingents of protestors have shut down the Manhattan Bridge, the Holland Tunnel. The mayor has declared a state of emergency. The National Guard is here, the state police, the SWAT team, counterterror platoons with armored personnel carriers with the sand of Iraq still in the tires. Jenny and the protestors overtake the block. She climbs atop a car and speaks to them through a bullhorn. They await her word to burn down the city in retribution. The system is broken, the system is guilty as hell—nothing to do now but smash and loot. She puts the bullhorn to her face. Her skin flashes red and blue from the cop cars. She thinks about Clayton's father.

—When word came, she begins, —that the grand jury reached its decision, I did not join the rest of you to watch La Cuzio's press conference, I did not need to, I knew what it would be. All the commentators and experts said of course the grand jury would indict. A gun death in New York City? Of course it would. This is not *Middle America*, for crying out loud, we are better than that here; whatever is the matter with *them* is not the matter with *us*, the grand jury will indict, no question, if not on homicide then at least on the gun. But I knew better. Geography is irrelevant. The myth does not respect state lines. The myth does not even respect whether or not you see through it. Because the myth knows you need it. You need it. New York needs the myth just like Indiana needs it, and Kentucky, and Texas. It gets us through the day so we can get through our lives. Without it we could not bear to breathe, without it, if we were to look at ourselves in the mirror, we would be unable to bear it. America is the myth. We had a choice: get rid of Fisher and the myth or keep him. I did not need to watch to know how we had decided. We decided it long ago: We keep him. We always keep him. We keep Lee Fisher and we throw away Clayton Kabede, we trade a boy for a myth, that is what we do and we do it gladly, proudly, every single time.

In the distance there is a black Hummer with an eagle painted on the side fighting its way through the crowds, as deep as it can get, and then it stops and out of it climb several men in black Kevlar with walkie-talkies and night-vision goggles dangling from their belts, scowling around with affected big-dick swagger like, she thinks, little girls imitating boys. They stare at her, flip her off. They look at each other, and one nudges another and whispers something to him, and this one's face is very pale and tight as he reaches back into the truck and comes out with something, then climbs into the truck's bed and raises the black plastic semiautomatic rifle to her, peering through the scope.

The police do not seem to see. She could say something, she could duck and move—she does not. Though he is a hundred feet away she can hear him breathing through his nose, can smell the cigarette smoke on his breath and see down inside his barrel. Michelle is in it. Michelle, curled up like a circus performer to be shot out of a cannon, her arms extended to reach out toward her, her happy, excited face: *Here I come, Mommy...* She stares at Michelle. She opens her arms. She opens them to Michelle but also to the bullet. She says to Michelle, —We choose the myth. And it's killing us. But if I can leave you all with one thing to take from this, it is that we do not have to. We do not—

He pulls the trigger.

That night, the city burns. The gunshots burst like drums across its skyline. They beat all night, in the flames and the flow of the stars and the fading skyscraper lights. In the end the fires are dead and the lights are out and all you can hear are gunshots, they never end, even when the ammo is gone.

JAMES BOICE is the author of three previous novels, *MVP, NoVA,* and *The Good and the Ghastly,* all published by Scribner. His work has appeared in *Esquire, McSweeney's, Salt Hill, Fiction Magazine,* and *Salon,* among other places. In 2006 he was selected as the New Voice in the Esquire 100. He lives in Jersey City, NJ.

@unnamedpress

facebook.com/theunnamedpress

unnamedpress.tumblr.com

www.unnamedpress.com

@unnamedpress